THE SHEIKH'S PREGNANT BRIDE

BY
JESSICA GILMORE

MILLS & BOON

First Published in Great Britain 2017
By Mills & Boon, an imprint of HarperCollins*Publishers*
1 London Bridge Street, London, SE1 9GF

© 2017 Jessica Gilmore

ISBN: 978-0-263-92336-0

23-1017

Printed and bound in Spain
by CPI, Barcelona

CHAPTER ONE

HE'D SAID HE'D be there in twelve hours, but in the end it was barely eight hours after he'd received the earth-shattering phone call when Idris Delacour strode into the cool, dark Council Chamber, his eyes still shielded against the harsh sun that had greeted him at the airport despite the still early hour. Grimly he stood by the empty seat at the end of the long table and, taking off his sunglasses, regarded the four sombre men who had stood at his entrance. They were all dressed in the customary long white robes and headdresses worn by traditionalists in Dalmaya and Idris's dark trousers and grey shirt looked both drab and shockingly modern by contrast.

He nodded at the men and waited until they took their seats before seating himself in the ornately carved wooden chair. He was aware of every curve, every bump in the ancient seat. A seat that should never have been his. A seat he was all too willing to relinquish. He cleared his throat. *'Salam.'*

They repeated the greeting back to him, the words barely uttered before he continued, 'There can be no mistake?'

'None, Your Highness.'

He flinched at the title but there was more pressing

business than his own unwanted and tenuous claim to the Dalmayan throne. 'They are both dead?'

'The King and Her Majesty, yes.'

'Terrorism?' Idris already knew the answers. He had asked the same question during the shock call that had shaken the entire chateau just eight hours before and had been extensively briefed and updated both whilst travelling to the airport and again once on the private jet that had awaited him there.

'We'll have to investigate further obviously,' the grey-faced man to his right answered. Idris recognised him as Sheikh Ibrahim Al Kouri, Dalmaya's Head of Security. 'But it doesn't seem so. It looks like it was simply a tragic accident.'

Simply? Such an odd way to describe the annihilation of an entire family. The better half of Idris's own family. 'And what? The car simply ran off the road?'

The General shook his head. 'The King and his wife were returning from a day's excursion and I believe His Majesty may have challenged the guards in the accompanying car to a race.' He paused. 'It would not have been the first time.'

Of course not. Fayaz loved to compete, always wanting to prove he was a winner in his own right, not just because of the privilege of his birth.

Sheikh Ibrahim continued in the same monotone voice, shock seemed to have flattened all his usual military pomp. 'The road was flat and empty and should have been quite safe but it would seem that either His Majesty or the other driver lost control of the wheel and crashed into the other car with a loss of all lives. We have experts on the scene and should have more information for you imminently.' He looked down at his notes. 'Four of my agents were in the crash.'

Idris pinched the top of his nose, the words spinning around in his head. He could see the scene so clearly: Fayaz laughing as the open-topped four-wheel drives wove in and out of each other's path on the wide, sand-covered road, encouraged by the screams of Maya, his wife and Queen. At what point had those screams become real—or had it all been over too fast for any of the party to be aware of how the game would end? He hoped so. He hoped they were laughing right until the end; it would be how he remembered them. Happy and so full of life it hurt.

'I'm sorry. Please pass on my condolences to your agents' families and take care of any outstanding pension and compensation arrangements.'

The General nodded and Idris turned to the man on his left, Minister of the Interior and his own great-uncle. 'What happens next?'

Sheikh Malik Al Osman pushed his tablet to one side. His eyes were heavy, his shoulders slumped as if he couldn't bear the burden that had fallen upon him. 'We've kept news of the accident under wraps while we made sure of no hostile involvement, but now you're here we'll brief state media and Parliament. The funerals will take place this evening and the official mourning period will commence then.'

Idris nodded. 'And then?'

Sheikh Ibrahim jumped in. 'Your Majesty. You know the terms of your grandfather's will. His Highness Sheikh Fayaz Al Osman and his line inherited the throne of Dalmaya, but if he died without issue then the kingdom passes to you and your line.'

Of course Idris *knew* this. Technically he had always been aware he was Fayaz's legal heir. He remembered the shock—a shock mingled with the warmth of acceptance—when his grandfather's will had been made public, cementing him firmly into the family. But the prospect of actually *becoming* King had been so far away he had never considered he would actually be called to do so. Fayaz had already been married at the time of their grandfather's death and his wife was young and healthy. There was no reason to believe they wouldn't soon have many children of their own to take precedence over Idris.

Besides, despite his grandfather's decree, Idris knew how unorthodox his claim was. 'My claim to the throne is through my mother. No King has ever inherited through the maternal line before.' Not only that but his mother's name was a byword for scandal in Dalmaya and, possibly even more unconventionally, his father was French—would the people of this proud kingdom accept the son of such a pair as their ruler?

The point was moot. His vineyard, chateau and his wine export business were all the kingdom Idris needed. He was fond of Dalmaya but he had no intention of living and ruling there. He didn't belong.

'Your grandfather's will…' the General repeated, but from the corner of his eye Idris saw a speculative look pass over his great-uncle's face and turned back to him.

'What do you think, Sheikh Malik?' Hope twisted in his chest, mingling with the fatigue and grief already consuming him. He knew how hard his grandfather had worked to keep the kingdom safe, to modernise it, to introduce universal healthcare and education. He couldn't just walk away from that legacy, not if there was no other option. But the Al Osman family was extensive. Surely there must be someone qualified and near enough the ruling branch for Idris to be able to hand over the crown with a clear conscience?

His uncle looked directly at Idris. 'His Excellency is of course correct and if Fayaz died without any issue you are by law the next King. But there *is* the baby...'

Idris blinked. He'd seen Maya just a few months ago and she hadn't mentioned any pregnancy. Besides, Fayaz would have told him straight away if he had had a child. Wouldn't he? 'The baby?' The rest of the table looked as confused as he felt. 'What baby?'

Saskia stretched and stared out at the enticing view. The sky was so bright and blue it almost hurt, the colour mirrored in the infinity pool just outside the folding glass doors and in the still sea beyond that. Another beautiful day in paradise, and if she could just drag herself off the insanely comfortable sofa and brave the intense heat for the ten seconds it took to step outside the air-conditioned villa and plunge into the pool then she would definitely have a swim. After all, the pool was the only place she was truly comfortable any more, her weight buoyed by the water, her bulk less ungainly.

Her hands strayed down to the tight bump as she caressed it. Just six weeks to go. Not that she was exactly looking forward to what awaited her at the end of that six weeks despite her daily private pregnancy yoga lessons, her doula, personal midwife and the deluxe delivery suite already pre-booked and awaiting her arrival. Nothing but the best to ease the birth of the new Crown Prince or Princess of Dalmaya.

Stretching again, Saskia winced as her back twinged. Even with the best care possible, pregnancy was the most uncomfortable experience she had ever been through. *Don't be so spoiled*, she told herself firmly, heaving herself to her feet and padding towards the doors. She was safe, ultra-healthily fed, looked after and, more importantly, so was Jack. Once the baby was safely delivered and in the loving arms of his or her parents then she and her little brother could get back to their lives. Only this time she would be able to afford to give Jack the kind of childhood he deserved. And she would finally catch a break.

Right. Saskia heaved herself off the sofa and took an unsteady step and then another, regaining her balance as she did so. *Balance.* She missed that, along with being able to see her toes and not swiping things off tables with her belly when she turned around. A swim and then she would settle down and tackle the essay she had been putting off. She might have the money to go back to university thanks to Fayaz and Maya, but if she could just get the first year completed long distance then she would have more money for a house—and for Jack.

Shucking off the loose cotton robe she wore over the frankly vast maternity swimsuit, Saskia opened the door, almost recoiling from the scalding temperature that hit her the second she stepped out. She hurried as best she could to the pool and cautiously sat herself down by the side, near the wide steps that led down into its blissfully cool depths. Sitting on the floor without needing a forklift to help her back up, that was another simple pleasure she was looking forward to.

'Sorry, little one,' she murmured, her hand slipping back to her belly. 'I do appreciate what a good baby you've been to look after for Maya but I think we're both getting a little uncomfortable here. Besides, you must be looking forward to meeting your mummy and daddy, hmm? I know they can't wait to meet you.'

That was an understatement. Fayaz and Maya were determined to be there for every step of the pregnancy. They had recorded stories for Saskia to play for the baby daily so that their voices would be instantly familiar when it was born and Maya had been as regular a visitor as she could manage. 'Not long now,' Saskia continued as she slid her aching legs into the deliciously cool water. 'Mummy comes to live with us next week so she can spend every moment with you until she can take you home. Won't that be lovely?'

Sharing this huge, luxurious villa would be very different from the old days, gossiping in the college student kitchen, but Saskia was still looking forward to some heart-to-hearts with her old friend *and* to some adult company. Fayaz and Maya hadn't wanted anyone to know that Saskia was carrying their baby and so she had been confined to the villa since her arrival in Dalmaya nearly seven months ago. No matter how luxurious it might be, a place she wasn't allowed to leave couldn't help but feel like a prison. A self-imposed prison, sure; Saskia had known every single term and condition before she'd signed the surrogacy agreement, but a prison nonetheless.

She lowered herself into the water, a shiver of delight trembling through her as the cold enveloped her uncomfortably warm skin, and kicked off. She had been warned not to overexert herself and consciously made herself swim slow, considered lengths, concentrating on her breathing and the style of each stroke. Excited as she was to start her new life, there *were* some things about her prison she would miss. There were unlikely to be any infinity pools in her future, and in London grey skies were far more probable than this never-ending blue. Saskia turned onto her back and floated, eyes shut against the bright sun.

She didn't know how long she stayed there, an ungainly mermaid basking in the sunshine, but a prickling at her neck and a sense of unease penetrated through her sun-induced haze. Saskia opened her eyes slowly, lowering her body until she was treading water upright, her hair slicked back. Whatever, whoever it was that disturbed her was behind her, at the head of the pool. Slowly she turned, awareness of her vulnerability rippling through her. She stopped. Shock hitting her hard.

'Idris?'

It couldn't be. Maya had promised her he was in France and swore she would never reveal to him that Saskia had carried her baby. No one outside Maya and Fayaz's immediate family was supposed to know the baby had been born to a surrogate at all.

But of course Idris *was* their family.

Her toes found the bottom of the pool and Saskia anchored herself as she stared at the tall man regarding her inscrutably. He looked exactly the same as he had done seven years ago. No, there were a few small changes. He was more put together, less earnest than the young man she had once been so besotted with. It wasn't just the well-cut, if slightly crumpled suit, the expensively tousled haircut or the dark shadow grazing his cheeks and chin. It was the confidence in the way he carried himself, a self-assuredness that, for all his pretence, the younger Idris hadn't yet achieved. The harsh lines around his mouth were new and looked to be forged by fatigue and grief and the dark brown eyes were dull—at first anyway.

Saskia stood tall, wishing she weren't in a tight swimsuit and stuck in a swimming pool looking up at him like a suppliant, as recognition dawned and Idris's gaze kindled, his eyebrows snapping together.

'Saskia? What on earth are you doing here?' She'd forgotten the impact his voice had always had on her, low, almost gravelly, his French accent more of a hint than a full-on reminder of his heritage.

'Taking a swim.' Thank goodness her voice didn't waver. 'The question is, Idris, what you are doing here. This is private property and I don't recall inviting you in.' Petty but the words felt good. A small revenge for the way he had treated her all those years ago.

'I'm here to see the surr…' He stopped mid-sentence, his gaze dropping to her stomach, and incredulity stole over his face. 'You? *You're* the surrogate?'

Saskia raised her chin. 'I don't see how that's any of your business. I'm not supposed to be experiencing any stress so please leave and let me get on with my swim.'

He glared. 'Gladly. Only I need to speak to you. It's important.'

'Okay. Make it brief.'

'No, not out here. You need to be sat down. Dressed.' His gaze swept down her, impersonal, as if he had never seen her body before. Never touched her. Saskia's cheeks burned but she remained upright, head held high.

'You don't give the orders round here, Idris. You ask. Nicely.'

His gaze smouldered but he bit back whatever cutting retort sprang to his lips. 'Please,' he ground out. 'Saskia, this is important. Believe me, I wouldn't be here if it wasn't.'

She held his gaze, searching for answers within its darkness, fear uncoiling down her spine. Something was very, very wrong here. Why wasn't Idris in France? Where was Maya? Saskia nodded, slowly. 'Give me fifteen minutes. Everything takes a little longer right now.'

For the last couple of months Saskia had lived either in yoga pants or sheer voluminous kaftans, which made

her look as if she were about to act as a sail in an am-
dram version of *The Tempest* but, crucially, were cool
and comfortable. Neither seemed right just now, instinct
warning her that she needed more armour than casual,
comfortable clothes would provide.

Luckily Maya had provided her with a designer pregnancy wardrobe fit for a princess. Saskia had pointed
out that, confined to the villa as she was, she wouldn't
have the opportunity to wear a tenth of the clothes but
Maya had waved off her objections. 'You can keep them
all and use them when you have your own baby, Sas,'
she'd said. Saskia hadn't had the heart to tell her that
having a baby of her own didn't figure anywhere in her
plans, sensing Maya was buying her the wardrobe she
herself wished she could have owned. So Saskia had
accepted each gift with a smile and tried not to think
about where on earth she would store several wardrobes
full of unworn maternity clothes when she finally returned home.

She selected a pair of white cropped linen trousers
and teamed them with a nude pink vest top, which gathered in a knot just below her breasts, the material flow-
ing nicely over her bump. Many redheads eschewed
pink, even as pale a shade as this, but Saskia loved the
colour. She pulled her still-wet hair back into a loose
plait and slipped her feet into a pair of flat sandals. She
was ready.

Idris was here.

The enormity of what was happening hit her anew
and Saskia reached out to the ornately carved bedpost
for support. What on earth had brought him back to her
after seven years? It was clear that he hadn't expected
to see her; he'd looked just as thrown by the recognition as she had been.

Her lips tightened. She was a different person now. Strong, independent. A survivor. Just because Idris's kisses used to make her forget who she was didn't mean he had any power over her now. She had this situation in hand. She had to.

Summoning a confidence that wasn't quite real, yet not entirely fake, Saskia left her suite and slowly descended the villa's majestic staircase. The stairway led to the large central hallway from which all the other ground-floor rooms were situated. All marble and dark polished wood, it was lined with two impossibly long, armless couches. Idris lounged on the right-hand couch, seemingly completely at ease as he scrolled impatiently through his tablet. He didn't even raise his gaze to watch her as she walked carefully down the marble stairs.

One of the many occasional tables that were scattered around the villa had been brought to his side and a jug of coffee sat there along with a half-full cup. The aroma floated tantalisingly towards Saskia. Coffee was one of the many prohibited food and drinks she had agreed not to touch until three months after the baby was born and her duties had ended. Many she barely touched anyway—she didn't have the budget for shellfish, brie or wine—but coffee was her lifeline and she missed it every day; mint tea just didn't have the same effect.

As the thought flitted across her mind Hamid, the houseboy, pulled up a second table and placed a cup of the herbal beverage upon it. Suppressing a longing sigh, Saskia smiled her thanks. She made no move to sit, nor did she have any intention of standing in front of Idris and waiting for him to notice her. Instead she picked up the cup and walked away into her favourite sitting area, the smallest of the living rooms with stunning views of the pool and the sea beyond. She curled up on the couch, picked up a book and waited for Idris to come to her.

She didn't have to wait long. A smothered exclamation was followed by short sharp footsteps. '*Tiens*, there you are. Why didn't you let me know you were ready?'

Saskia hadn't taken in a word on the page but she still made a show of finishing her sentence before half closing the book and looking up with a mild smile. 'You looked busy. Take a seat, Idris, and let me know how I can help you.' There, she had established that this was her home and she was the one in charge.

To her surprise Idris didn't react with impatience or irritation. He sat down on the chair at right angles to her and leaned forwards before jumping up and striding across the room, his face set and eyes clouded. The premonition Saskia had felt in the pool returned, fear icy on her skin.

'What is it, Idris? Why are you here?'

He turned and the grief on his face clawed at her heart. 'There was an accident. Fayaz…' He stopped and swallowed.

'What kind of accident?'

'A car accident.'

'He will always drive too fast. Such a boy racer.' If she could keep chatting, keep the conversation light and inconsequential then she wouldn't have to hear the rest. Because of course there was more. Idris wouldn't have flown over from France for a minor injury. Nor would he have come here to tell her—to tell the unknown surrogate—in person.

'Saskia.' She could only sit paralysed while he walked back towards her, each deliberate, slow step echoing around her brain. He sat next to her, so familiar and yet a stranger and, to her increasing dread, took her hand in his. Once the simple touch of his hand would leave her incoherent and unable to think about anything but him, but right now she couldn't feel anything. All she could do was wait for the words she knew were coming.

'Saskia, the accident, it was a bad one. Fayaz didn't make it. Nobody did.'

Nobody? Her free hand crept down to her belly, whether to reassure the baby or herself she didn't know. 'Maya?' Her throat was so swollen she could barely croak the word out, but she knew that he heard her when his grip on her hand intensified.

'I'm sorry, Saskia. She was with him.'

She didn't move, didn't react, couldn't react, couldn't process anything he was saying. Fayaz and Maya. Such a golden couple; beautiful, wealthy, powerful sure but also caring and loving, and they had known their share of tragedy. Years of IVF and three miscarriages had left Maya utterly bereft—which was why she had come to Saskia.

Saskia's hand stilled on her belly. She pulled her other hand out of Idris's clasp and turned to him. 'The baby? What happens to their baby?'

CHAPTER TWO

IDRIS STARED UNSEEINGLY out at the sea. He needed to get back to Jayah. The funerals would be taking place in just a few hours' time and there were a hundred and one things demanding Idris's attention, but his business at the villa wasn't done. Not nearly. Saskia's question echoed round and round his mind. What happened to the baby? Orphaned before birth. His cousin's baby and, morally, the rightful heir.

But the burning question remained unanswered: was it the legal heir? Idris had no idea; which was why he was still kicking his heels at the villa, awaiting both the lawyer who had drawn up the surrogacy agreement and his great-uncle so that he could get their advice. Advice he was praying tied in with his own plans, because *if* the baby could inherit and *if* his great-uncle was prepared to take on the Regency until it was of age then Idris could return to France as soon as the mourning period was over.

He pushed away the guilt clenching his chest. Fayaz would have understood why he couldn't stay; he knew how alone Idris always felt in Dalmaya. How out of place. Set apart by his accent, his French upbringing. Tainted by the dishonour his mother had brought on her family, not just by her elopement but by her subsequent lifestyle. Fayaz knew how duty already ruled his life, knew how hard Idris had worked to restore the chateau, the vineyards, to make the Delacour name mean something again. He wouldn't expect Idris to put all that aside for a country that had never quite acknowledged him. Would he?

The all too familiar burden of heavy expectations descended onto his shoulders. Fayaz might not have expected Idris to put everything aside, but he would have known that it was almost impossible for Idris to turn away.

Almost…

At the back of his mind another question burned white hot. What was Saskia Harper doing here? Why on earth was she acting as Maya's surrogate? The guilt pulsed harder. He'd spent the last seven years doing his best not to think about Saskia, but occasionally he would see a flash of auburn hair, hear an imperious English accent and his heart would stutter to a stop, a tiny part of him hoping it might be her.

He hadn't expected to be so numb with grief when he did finally see her again that he had barely registered the shock of her presence.

The doctor's footsteps echoed through the hallway and Idris turned to the doorway, impatient for some answers. The midwife who worked full time at the villa had taken one look at Saskia and hustled her straight to bed, insisting that she be seen immediately by a doctor. The guilt pulsed again. Fayaz would expect him to do his best for his child *and* for its mother. 'How is she?'

The doctor took off his glasses and rubbed his eyes. 'As well as can be expected, Your Highness. A severe shock at any stage of pregnancy should be avoided if possible, but she's strong, healthy and has had the best possible care throughout. However, as a precaution, I've suggested bed rest for the rest of today and that she take it as easy as possible for the next few days. It's out of the question for her to attend the funerals, of course. She shouldn't be travelling.'

The funerals. Idris clenched his jaw and refused to acknowledge the grief beating down on him. There was no time, not now. 'Of course.'

'I'm leaving Nurse Wilson in charge. She has my personal number if there are any concerns. I'll come out straight away but I don't foresee any problems. Try and keep Sayeda Saskia calm, and make sure she eats something.' The doctor paused. 'I'm very sorry for your loss, Your Highness. Your cousin was a good man and Queen Maya deserved the happiness this baby would have brought her. I'll be back in the morning.'

Idris spent the next couple of hours sending emergency emails. Just because it felt as if he were standing in the eye of a storm, unable to move while events whirled around him, didn't mean he could neglect his own concerns. He closed his eyes briefly, picturing the weathered grey stone, the chateau turrets, the acres of slowly ripening vines. He'd made his home, made his mark at Chateau Delacour, knew every inch of soil, every man, woman and child in its environs. Last night he'd gone to bed expecting to wake up to another spring day, making sure he put some time aside to join the workers in the field as they carefully hoed and weeded the precious vines. What was the point of living in the glorious French countryside if he spent all his life in an office? Instead he'd awoken to a panicked call and his life had come to an abrupt halt. The vineyard felt like a lifetime, not a continent away.

He knew his managers could take charge of the vineyard and his export business until he returned and he made sure they had all the relevant authorisation to do so, warning them that he would likely be difficult to get hold of and so they should contact him only in an emergency. He stopped as he typed a reassuring message promising them he would be back as soon as possible—he just hoped he was telling them the truth. Meanwhile a flood of panicked emails flooded in from the various ministries all needing guidance. He told each one to carry on as usual, promising an announcement on the succession imminently. He hoped he was telling them the truth as well. It was a long, testing couple of hours and he was relieved to hear the car pull up heralding the advisors he needed.

'*Assalamu alaikum*, this way, please.' Idris gestured to the stairs. On the midwife's advice he had decided to hold the meeting in Saskia's rooms—the doctor had said she was to be kept quiet but she clearly had a stake in the subject under discussion and Idris sensed it would be far more stressful for her if she was left out.

The houseboy led them up the staircase and indicated the door leading to Saskia's apartments. Idris paused, the reality of the situation hitting him anew. Fayaz was gone—and Saskia was here. Here in Dalmaya. Not quite his territory but close enough to discombobulate him with her unexpected presence.

Her bedroom was huge, the outside wall made entirely of glass, doors leading out to a large terrace filled with plants and shaded seats overlooking the sea. The room was decorated in soothing shades of blue and cream; a gigantic bed with ornately carved wooden bedposts sat on a platform at one end of the room, a seating area grouped at the other. Two doors were slightly ajar, and Idris could see they led into a dressing area and a bathroom. Refreshments had been placed onto the coffee table and Saskia was already lying on one of the three couches arranged around it. She smiled wanly at the lawyer as he greeted her and extended her hand to Idris's great-uncle.

'Please excuse me for not getting up but I have been ordered not to move.'

'No apologies needed.' The elderly man bowed over her hand. 'Sheikh Malik Al Osman. It's an honour to meet you, Sheikha Saskia.'

Idris started at the honorary title, nodding curtly at Saskia and taking the seat farthest away from her. A quick glance showed him how pale she was under her tan, the pain in her eyes reflecting the pain he saw in the mirror. He ruthlessly pressed on; there was far more at stake here than personal feelings. 'I don't have much time,' he said, opening proceedings briskly. 'So let's get going. Can somebody explain just what is going on here and why nobody knows anything about this baby?'

The lawyer nodded, setting his briefcase on the table and taking out a sheaf of papers. 'I acted for Their Majesties in this matter so maybe I should start. You have to understand, Sheikh Idris, that legally surrogacy and adoption are still grey areas here in Dalmaya. Historically if a woman couldn't conceive she would simply raise a family member's child as her own—either a sister's or cousin's or a fellow wife's child, and that child would be considered hers. Plus any child she bears during marriage is legally her husband's regardless of actual biological fatherhood; that goes for any child she raises for someone else too.'

Idris frowned. 'So all Maya had to do was call herself the baby's mother and the baby became hers and Fayaz's without any need to adopt it legally?'

'*Traditionally* that's all that they had to do. Of course, by using a surrogate they had ensured the baby was Fayaz's biological child anyway, but because Sayeda Saskia is a British citizen, and to make sure there was no confusion in the future, they were planning to adopt the baby in the British courts as well.'

'So why the secrecy? You said it yourself, raising someone else's child is culturally acceptable and the baby is Fayaz's biologically, so there should be no quibbling over inheritance.'

'Your grandfather's reforms and his subsequent decision to take just one wife, a stance followed by his son and grandson, hasn't been popular amongst traditionalists, partly because it has greatly reduced the number of potential heirs in the Al Osman senior branch. Your grandfather had just two children and his only son died while Fayaz was still a child. If it was known that the Queen couldn't conceive there would have been great pressure on Fayaz to take a second wife.'

'Maya felt like such a failure,' Saskia said, staring down at her hands. 'She put herself through hell. IVF after IVF, three terrible miscarriages. She knew how important it was that Fayaz had an heir...she knew that you didn't want...' She came to a halt, flashing one quick glance over at him. He'd forgotten just how disconcerting her green eyes were, no hint of hazel or blue diluting them.

'How many people know about this?'

'I have known from the start. Fayaz discussed it with me before they went down the surrogacy route,' Sheikh Malik said. 'As head of the junior branch of the family he wanted to make sure I had no objections, that there would be no repercussions later on. The staff here know, any lawyers involved in the adoption and surrogacy agreement and certain medical staff here and in the UK. They all signed binding non-disclosure agreements, of course. The heads of the Privy Council are now aware after this morning's meeting, but they can all be relied on to keep quiet, if it's for the good of the country. But do we want to keep it quiet? If Fayaz has a son and heir then surely we need to let people know.'

'Or a daughter,' Saskia said quietly, her hands back on her stomach. Idris could hardly drag his eyes away from her slim, long fingers as they stroked the bump; the gesture seemed automatic, maybe as much comfort for mother as for child. But Saskia was only the mother until birth… Idris watched her hands in their rhythmic pattern. No child should be born motherless. Even his own beautiful, selfish, careless mother had been around sometimes for kisses and bedtime stories. Occasionally even two nights in a row.

Of course there had been the many weeks he had barely seen her at all.

'The problem is—' The lawyer's voice recalled Idris's attention back to the matter at hand. He tore his gaze away from Saskia and concentrated on the papers spread out over the coffee table. 'A baby's paternity in this country is proven only in two ways. Either the father claims the child as his, which is what Fayaz intended…'

'What about the surrogacy agreement?' Saskia asked. 'Doesn't that prove Fayaz was going to claim the baby?'

The lawyer shook his head. 'Surrogacy isn't recognised here. The only way Fayaz could posthumously be recognised as the father would be if you had been married to him.'

Idris's heart stopped for one long, painful second

as he processed the words. There was no way out. If Fayaz couldn't legally be proven as the father, if the child wasn't legitimised, then it couldn't inherit. Which meant the Kingship fell heavily onto Idris's own shoulders. A burden he had never asked for and certainly never wanted. He glanced out of the window at the relentless blue and his chest ached as he recalled the myriad colours of the French late spring: greens and lavender and red.

'In that case who does it belong to?' Saskia's voice cut into his thoughts. 'Isn't that the most important thing we need to decide? Who is going to raise this baby? Time isn't on our side.'

Idris stared at her. 'What do you mean?'

'I *mean*,' she said, emphasising every word, 'its parents have died. It's due in six weeks and it needs a family regardless of whether it can inherit the throne or not. Could another branch of the family adopt it? Would that be what Fayaz would want? Do we know? I mean, that surrogacy agreement covered everything down to what vitamins I should take pre- and post-pregnancy. I can't believe Fayaz didn't have a contingency plan if something like this should happen.'

The lawyer nodded. 'He had named a guardian for the baby.'

'Who?' Saskia and Idris spoke together.

The lawyer's gaze shifted to Idris. 'His cousin, Sheikh Idris Delacour.'

'*Moi?*'

'Him?' Again the two of them were in unison. Idris looked over at Saskia. He'd spent the last seven years doing his best to forget about her. How could he raise a child that was half hers? A child who would remind him of its mother every second of every day?

How could he raise a child at all? His mother said all he cared about was the vineyard, about work, and for once she had a point.

'Let me see that.' He held out his hand for the sheaf of papers and scanned them quickly. Even through the dense legalese Fayaz's intentions were clear. If anything happened to Fayaz, then Idris was to be guardian to any children until their twenty-first birthday. Idris swallowed. Fayaz was just like their grandfather, intent on making sure Idris was part of the family even if he was French by birth and name. But Fayaz couldn't have meant to make him responsible for a motherless newborn; he knew nothing about children—and by the incredulous look on Saskia's face she was thinking exactly the same thing.

He turned his concentration back to the papers, flicking through them until he reached the surrogacy contract. Saskia was right, it *was* thorough, covering everything from diet to exercise to location, stating she was to travel to Dalmaya as soon as the pregnancy was confirmed and stay until three months after the birth in order to provide nutrition for the baby. It took every bit of self-possession he had not to look up at that, not to look over at her full, ripe breasts. He took a deep breath and continued to read.

All her medical bills paid, of course, accommodation, clothes and food provided throughout the timespan of the agreement, school fees paid—school fees for who? His eyebrows flew up in unspoken query, only to lower as he read the allowance made to her every week. Bound to the villa, every need catered for, she was going to be pocketing a nice profit by the end of the contract. He turned the page and stopped, rereading

the words again before tossing the contract contemptuously onto the table as he glared at Saskia.

'You're being paid for this?' It took everything he
had not to spit the words out. His cousin and his glow-
ing wife, desperate for a baby. How hard must it have
been for Maya to watch Saskia do so easily what she
couldn't, knowing that the baby was just a way for the
surrogate mother to make money?

Saskia flushed. 'That is none of your business.'

'I think you'll find it is very much my business,' he
reminded her silkily and her colour heightened. 'I don't
know why I'm surprised. You always did like to play
games. But this isn't a game, Saskia. This was Fayaz
and Maya's life!'

Her colour was still high but her eyes flashed as she
shifted. 'Maya came to me, asked me to do this. I *didn't*
play games or negotiate on payment. I took what was offered, yes, why wouldn't I? I have given this baby over
a year of my life. Restricted my diet, my liberty, taken
fertility drugs, undergone invasive procedure after invasive procedure to give this baby the best possible start
in life. So don't throw the fact I'm to be paid in my face
as if it makes me some kind of whore. Of course I was
happy to help Maya, but I was in no position to give her
a year of my life for love alone.'

'It's not a payment as such, that's illegal under British
law and the baby was conceived in the UK,' the lawyer
interjected quickly. 'It's compensation for Miss Harper's loss of income and freedom. The compensation is
to be paid at the end of the contract if every condition
has been adhered to and if Sayeda Saskia ensures that
she prioritises the baby's well-being until it reaches the
age of three months.'

Taking a deep breath to quell his anger, Idris turned

to his great-uncle. 'I know what my grandfather's will says, but surely my name, my heritage precludes me from taking the throne? Isn't there anyone more qualified in another branch of the family? Your branch?'

Sheikh Malik shook his head. 'Not without tremendous upheaval and turmoil, Idris. The kind of turmoil your grandfather spent his life trying to ensure the country would never go through again. Yes, your father is French but more importantly you're the grandson of the Great Reformer. I don't think the people will reject you. Your name doesn't matter but if it worries you it's easy enough to change it to Delacour Al Osman.' He paused, leaning forward, his gaze intent on Idris. 'I can't force you to accept the throne, but, Idris, I can and will beg you to. For your grandfather's sake, for your cousin's sake, for your country.'

A great weariness descended on Idris. His destiny was as clear as it was unwanted. He'd never appreciated his life properly before, the old chateau lovingly restored piece by piece, the vineyards, finally back in profit, and making wines he was proud to put his name to, the family coffers filling again despite his parents' best efforts. It was hard work involving long hours but it was satisfying and he was in control. Best of all it was quiet. No drama, no press, no obligations beyond those of the people who worked for him. How could he swap that for life in the spotlight, an entire country reliant on his success? For a child who wasn't his?

How could he not? His parents showed him all too well the consequences of living for nothing but self. Thanks to them he had grown up always worrying how the next bill would be paid, where they would be living next, even what they would be eating that night. Thankfully he had been able to escape to his grandfathers, to the two men who had never met but would have liked and respected each other, if their paths had ever crossed. The men who had taught him that duty and honour and responsibility weren't burdens but the measure of a man.

Sometimes he envied his mother, her carefree waltz through life, her refusal to be bound by convention. But such a path was selfish, had consequences for all those around.

A King's life wasn't his, he knew that all too well. His own needs, his own desires, his own likes always second to duty. And Idris saw his duty all too clearly. All of it.

His mind raced as he ruthlessly ousted all emotions from his mind, concentrating on the cold, hard facts, looking for the path ahead. First, it was clearly in the baby's best interests to have a mother's care right from birth. Second, he, Idris, was the *legal* heir, whether he liked it or not. But, third, at the same time the unborn baby was the *rightful* heir. Fourth, he was said baby's guardian. The pieces began to fall into place one by one.

What had the lawyer said? That if a man was married to the mother when a child was born then he was automatically that child's legal father regardless of actual paternity? He looked over at the other man. 'Let me get this straight. If I marry Sayeda Saskia then the baby will be my child, my heir, in both law and in the eyes of the world.'

The lawyer's words were drowned out by Saskia's indignant, 'There is no way I am marrying you, Idris Delacour, not if you were the last man alive!' But Idris saw the nod and he knew what he had to do. For Fayaz, for the country, for the baby. He had to marry the only woman he had ever come close to loving. The woman he had walked away from. He had to marry Saskia Harper.

CHAPTER THREE

IT WAS ALL very well being told not to allow herself to become agitated but how was Saskia supposed to stay calm when Idris dropped a bombshell more explosive than she could possibly have imagined, and then calmly wrapped up the meeting and disappeared as if she had meekly fallen into line with his insane plans? Marry Idris? The man who had ripped her heart and self-esteem to shreds and then stomped on them without mercy? The man who had let her down at the lowest point in her life?

'Sorry, baby,' Saskia told it that sleepless night. 'I know it's scary now that Maya isn't here to look after you, but marrying Idris isn't the best thing for either of us. I'm not ready to be a mother yet, and you deserve more than that. He's going to be King. He can give you everything you need.'

But he couldn't give the baby a mother who would love it unconditionally—and she knew that was the only thing Maya would ask of her. Saskia's eyes filled and she hurriedly blinked back the tears, trying to focus on her indignation instead. The only positive thing to come out of this whole mess was that her anger with Idris helped her to manage the shock of losing Maya and Fayaz. She was so busy thinking of one hundred ways to tell him that she would rather marry Jabba the Hutt than him that the grief had released some of its painful grip from her chest—although she did keep reaching for her phone ready to text Maya with a planned, clever comeback, only for the grief to descend again with all its painful intensity when she remembered she would never be able to text her again.

Not that she had had an opportunity to test even one of her scathing put-downs on Idris yet. Twenty-four hours had passed with no word from him and she had no way to contact him. Saskia stared out of the window. Of course, he had been a little busy burying his cousin and closest friend. She choked back a sob, the lump back in her throat. She wished she had had the opportunity to say goodbye too. No, that wasn't true. She wished more than anything that she could have handed her newborn baby over to Maya and seen the moment her friend fell in love with her much-wanted child.

Yes, she had agreed to be a surrogate for the money, she had never pretended her motives were anything more altruistic, but she had also wanted to be the one to make her friend's dreams come true. At least Maya had died knowing she would soon be a mother. Saskia twisted her hands together. Would Maya have wanted Saskia to raise her baby for her? She knew how much Saskia had sacrificed already raising Jack; surely she wouldn't have expected her to sacrifice more?

'His Highness Sheikh Idris Delacour Al Osman,' the houseboy announced and Saskia jumped. She hadn't even heard the car pull up, too absorbed in her thoughts. She turned, glad she had dressed ready for his return whenever it might be, in a severely cut grey linen shift dress, her hair coiled in a businesslike knot on the top of her head.

She sat upright in her chair—no more reclining, no more weakness—and folded her ankles and hands. Poised, collected and ready to do battle. But the cold words she had prepared faded as soon as Idris entered the room. He was grey with fatigue, shadows pronounced under his eyes and the grief lines cut deep. She held out her hand with no more thought than the need to comfort someone suffering as she suffered, only to drop it as he walked straight past it as if it weren't there. She leaned back and regarded him, doing her best to hide her humiliation and anger. How dared he treat her like that when he was the one who had let her down at the most vulnerable moment in her life? *She* should be the one shunning *him*.

Idris stood, back to her, staring out of the windows. Saskia regarded him for a few moments before turning to the houseboy and requesting some tea and refreshments. She sat back, displaying a composure she was a long way from feeling, and waited. Several long minutes passed before he spoke, the tea served and the houseboy dismissed, Saskia not moving or speaking, refusing to be the one to break first. Finally Idris shifted, although he still didn't face her.

'I've discussed our marriage with the heads of the Privy Council. They agree a big royal wedding is not in the country's best interests right now. We're still in the mourning period and your condition will give rise to the kind of speculation it's best to avoid. However, time is clearly not on our side so the consensus is for a quiet wedding here as soon as possible. The lawyer is drawing up the paperwork right now and we are thinking the day after tomorrow for the ceremony. In accordance with Dalmayan law it is simply the signing of a contract. Traditionally the elder of your house would negotiate the contract for you, but my grandfather decreed that women now act for themselves. As time and secrecy are of the essence the lawyer who drew up the surrogacy will advise you and I suggest you go over the contract with him before the ceremony.'

Saskia listened to every crazy word, her mind busily coming up with—and discarding—several considered responses pointing out exactly why this was such a bad idea but in the end she settled for a simple 'No.'

Idris turned slowly. 'No?'

'No. No to the wedding. No to marriage. No to spending any more time with you than I have to.'

His mouth compressed. 'Believe me, Saskia, if there was another way…'

'You don't need me. You're the baby's guardian regardless of whether I marry you or not. Marry someone else. Someone you can bear to be in the same room with.'

'This isn't about you and me. This is about what's right.'

'Oh, don't be so sanctimonious. The last thing Fayaz or Maya would want is for *us* of all people to be trapped into marriage with each other. Not for us and not for the baby.'

'And the baby's right to inherit?'

'If you adopt it…'

'You heard the lawyer. Formal adoption is still an unknown process in Dalmaya.'

'Well, then marry someone else and adopt the baby quietly, like Maya intended to.'

'You want me to woo and marry someone in less than six weeks?'

'You're about to be King. The kingdom must be full of women desperate to fall at your feet and into your arms.' Funny to think she was one of those women once—and she hadn't needed a title, just one of his rare smiles.

'There can be no ambiguity about the baby's heritage. No, Saskia, this is the best way. The only way.'

'Then you are in trouble because I am not going to marry you.' She clasped her hands to stop them shaking and waited, heart hammering.

There's nothing he can do, she told herself. *Dalmaya is a civilised country. He's not going to drag you to the altar by your hair.*

She stared straight at Idris, defiant but a little confused by the look on his face. He didn't look angry or upset, he looked amused, bordering on smug. Her throat dried.

'You signed a contract.'

'To have a baby.'

'*Non*, you agreed to a lot more than that. You agreed to do whatever is in the baby's best interests until he or she is three months old and, if required to *in extremis*, to come to its aid in later life.'

Saskia blinked. 'Yes, but that's because Fayaz and Maya wanted me to express milk for the baby for the first three months so I need to stay here for those three months and adhere to the right diet. That's all that the *in the best interests* part means.'

'That's not what it says,' he said softly, gaze still intent on hers. 'You did read the contract before signing it, didn't you?'

'Of course, and my lawyer took me through every clause…' She halted. That clause was written exactly the way Idris had phrased it. They didn't know what would happen, her lawyer had explained. What if the baby needed a blood transfusion and she, not Fayaz, was the right match? Or, later on, a kidney, unlikely as that might be? Even a donor sibling? The three months post birth she was glad to agree to; it was an opportunity to recover from pregnancy and birth in comfort and peace. The statistical chance of the *in extremis* clause being invoked had been low enough for her not to be concerned—compensation would be offered commensurate with whatever was needed and, besides, of course she would want to help if it was within her power to do so. 'It doesn't mean what you're implying.'

'Oh?' He raised an eyebrow. 'The baby doesn't need a mother for its first three months? Being orphaned before birth isn't *in extremis* enough? Tell me, Saskia, what have you been doing since the last time I saw you? Apart from dropping out from university?'

Her hands curled into tight fists. How could he be so dismissive? Act as if they hadn't once been, if not in love, so very close to falling off that cliff? Maybe it had just been her, so besotted she hadn't noticed how little he felt for her. But for all his faults, for all his arrogance, she had never known Idris Delacour be deliberately cruel. Even that last time…she hadn't actually managed to tell him about her father's death when he sent her away.

Surely Maya and Fayaz had filled him in on what had happened to her, told him about her father? She'd assumed so. But if he hadn't known she was their choice of surrogate, hadn't known she was in Dalmaya, then maybe not. Thinking about it, they had always been very careful not to discuss Idris with her beyond mentioning that he had achieved his dream of renovating the chateau and the vineyards. Her pulse began to race as she took in his politely contemptuous expression. He couldn't know, not about her father's death, not about

Jack. After all, she hadn't even known of Jack's existence when they were together.

She lifted her chin. 'This and that.' If he didn't know about Jack then she wasn't going to enlighten him. The less he knew about her life, her circumstances, the better. The less ammunition he would have.

'No husband? Fiancé? Significant other? Career? I thought not. I'm offering you it all on a plate, Saskia, a family, a home, a position that comes with all the luxuries and money a girl like you needs to get by.'

She wouldn't cry. Wouldn't give him the satisfaction of even a chin wobble. 'You know nothing about a girl like me.'

'*Non?* Well, I suppose I have the rest of my life to find out.'

'The answer is still no. You can sue me, Idris. See what people think about the King of Dalmaya suing a woman into becoming his wife. I can take that kind of humiliation, can you?'

His eyes were hard and flat. That shot had gone home. He'd always been abominably proud. 'I don't need to sue you, Saskia. If you don't marry me and legitimise the baby then the lawyer agrees you have broken the *in extremis* clause and the first three months agreement. We won't owe you a red cent. You'll leave here not a penny the richer for your year and a bit's hard work.' His eyes flicked contemptuously to the side table laden with little pastries and fruits.

The world stilled and stopped. No money? No money meant no house, no university, no way of clawing herself out of the exhausting cycle she had found herself repeating over and over for the last seven years. No money meant a return to long hours and mind-numbing work, to low wages and choosing between food and heating.

To damp flats. No money meant no security for Jack…
She couldn't breathe, the lump in her throat outsized
only by the heavy stone in her chest. She couldn't do it
all again. She couldn't…

Somehow, she had no idea how, she managed to take
in a breath, only her whitened knuckles giving away her
inner turmoil. She *could* do it. She'd done it before. She
would have no choice but to pick herself up once again.

But not without a fight. 'I'll talk to my lawyer.'

'You do that,' he said affably. 'I can afford to fight
this all the way. Can you say the same, Saskia? Daddy
must be keeping you short if you've resorted to surrogacy and you've been off the party circuit for a while.
Will any of your boyfriends pick up the tab?'

The casual, contemptuous mention of her father was
like a physical blow but she didn't waver, keeping her
voice low and cold. 'Don't you worry about me.'

'You'll be a single mother as well. That's not the kind
of accessory men look for in their dates.'

Her gaze snapped up to meet his. There was no hu-
mour in his dark eyes, just a searing contempt. 'What
do you mean?'

He shrugged. 'The lawyer was quite clear. Under
Dalmayan law there's no way of proving that the child
is Fayaz's. I don't have any obligation to take in a child
of unknown origin.'

'The agreement. His DNA…' But she remembered
the lawyer's words as clearly as Idris did.

'Inadmissible.'

'Not in the UK.'

'Saskia, we're not in the UK.'

'You'd turn your back on your cousin's child?'

'This country is going through enough right now. I
wasn't born here or brought up here. My first language

is French, my surname is French. My mother ran away surrounded by the biggest scandal of the last century. That's the legacy I inherit. I need to be seen as committed to Dalmaya. The last thing I need is a motherless baby who isn't mine muddling up the succession. Now, I'm willing to marry you, legitimise the baby and make it my heir. But it's all or nothing, Saskia. Pick wisely.'

Go to hell.

The words were so tempting but she reined them in while she desperately searched for a way out, a way to reach him. Her earlier thought ran through her brain like a track on repeat, reminding her that the Idris she had known before wasn't cruel. Single-minded, yes. Definitely ambitious. But not cruel. Not until the last time she'd seen him.

But that man, that man who had turned his back on her, he was capable of turning his back on the baby too, she was almost sure. Almost…it was a slim word to hang her hopes on to. Could she risk it?

If he was in earnest then she wouldn't just be returning to the UK penniless, she'd be returning with a baby. A baby would make finding a job, a place to live so very, very much harder…

And of course there was Jack. She'd promised him a better life. Could she drag him back to an even more difficult childhood than the one he'd left? He'd never complained before but he'd never known another way before.

'Saskia!' A voice broke through her thoughts and she looked up. Was it that time already? She'd meant to keep Jack well away from Idris but it was too late. Her brother raced through the marble hallway, dropping his bag in the middle of the room as he kicked off his shoes. His au pair followed, picking up his discarded

belongings as she went. How quickly he'd adjusted to
the heat and the space and the staff. How could she take
him back to an inadequately heated one-bedroom flat?

He skidded to a halt by her chair. Ignoring Idris's
raised brow, she held out her arms for the cuddle her
brother still greeted her with. 'Jack, how was your day,
tiger?'

'Good. I scored three goals during playtime.'

'Three goals, huh? Good to see you're learning something in that fancy school of yours. Jack, I want you to
meet someone. This is Idris. I used to...' She faltered.
'We knew each other when I was younger. He is Fayaz's
cousin.'

Jack turned, a little shyly, but stuck out his hand.
'Pleased to meet you.'

Idris threw her a startled glance as he shook Jack's
hand. 'Pleased to meet you too, Jack. Are you over visiting Saskia?' But his keen eyes were scanning Jack
and Saskia knew he had noted the school uniform, the
au pair, the houseboy standing to one side with a tray
filled with milk and cookies. All the signs that Jack was
a permanent member of the household.

'No.' Jack sounded surprised. 'I live here.'

'You live here?' His brows had snapped together and
he was looking at Jack assessingly.

'Jack is my brother and I am his guardian,' Saskia
interjected smoothly. 'Jack, go and have your milk and
cookies in the kitchen, okay? Then I think Husain has
offered to give you a swimming lesson.'

'Really? Cool!' And he was gone in a blur of elbows
and calves.

'He lives with you?'

'Yes.'

'Where's his mother?'

She shrugged. 'I'm not quite sure. She *was* in Brazil last I heard but she doesn't keep in contact.'

'Your father?'

'Dead. Look, Jack is none of your business so let's…'

If the news of her father's death surprised him he hid it well. 'If your brother lives with you then he is very much my business. When we are married…'

'You haven't listened to a word I've said, have you? I am not marrying you, Idris. Not in two days' time, not ever.' But although her words and tone were defiant despair flowed through her. There was no happy ending here. Her dreams of returning to England in just a few months ready to restart her degree and with enough money to buy a small house somewhere within commuting distance of London had turned into a nightmare. Either she returned back to the same hardship Maya had rescued her from—only this time with a baby in tow—or she stayed and married Idris. There would be no money worries if she chose the latter. But there would be no hope of escape either.

Idris reached into his pocket and pulled out a small card, which he handed to her. Numbly she took it, barely glancing at the plain black type on the crisp white background. 'My number. If you change your mind call me tomorrow. If not then I will organise a plane to take you and your brother back to London as soon as possible. The choice is yours.'

And then he was gone. Saskia put the card down, her hands trembling so much she wasn't sure she would ever be able to make them stop. She wasn't going to give in. Never.

Tucking Jack in wasn't easy; she couldn't bend over the bed any more. Instead Saskia had to perch on the side of the bed while she read to him. Saskia could forget her worries for a short while as she read the story of a boy wizard and his adventures out loud, doing all the voices as instructed.

'At least I never had to sleep under the stairs,' Jack said as she closed the book and laid it on the bedside table.

'Not up to now,' Saskia agreed.

'When we go home, will you have a bedroom too?' Jack had always thought it most unfair that he had had a room of his own while Saskia had slept on a sofa bed in the flat's all-purpose living and dining room. But it had been an impossible conundrum. The temping agency she had worked for supplied offices around London's West End. The wages were very good for a temp job but to get into work for just before nine, to pay as little as possible on transport and to ensure she could fit in with the childminder's hours, Saskia had had to live as close to central London as she could afford. Which had meant compromising on space. The exorbitantly expensive, tiny new-build flat would have been bijou for one person; for a family of two, one of whom was an active growing boy, it was oppressively small. It had, however, been home but she had given up her rental agreement when she'd left England. Who knew where the two of them would end up?

The three of them...unless Idris was bluffing. But the coldness in his eyes had given her no hope of that.

Thank goodness Maya had insisted that she be paid an allowance—and thank goodness there had never been anything to spend it on. With some careful budgeting— and she was an expert at that—she could keep herself, Jack and the baby for six months. *Where* she was going to keep them was a whole other matter. London was out

of the question financially. But London was all she knew,
except for nine months spent in Oxford a lifetime ago.

'A bedroom of my own? I hope so.'

'And will we have a garden? With a footie goal and a
basketball hoop and space for me to ride a bike?' He was
drowsy now. This was the way he always fell asleep,
talking about all the things they would have once their
stay in Dalmaya was over. He wasn't greedy, he didn't
want video games and gadgets, just space to run around
and play. Saskia brushed the hair back from his fore-
head, her heart aching. He deserved to be able to play.

'That's the plan.'

'I wish we could have a pool like we have here. Dan's
dad said he would teach us to ride and to sail, but I won't
be here much longer.' Dan was his best friend and Jack
had spent a lot of time at his house, although due to the
secrecy surrounding the surrogacy he had never invited
any of his friends to the villa. Another thing she had
promised him: a home open to anyone he wanted. 'Can
I learn to ride horses and to sail when we get home?'

'I'm not sure about that. It depends where we end up.'

'I'll miss the sun. And the sea. And the sand. I like it
here. I wish we could stay…' And he was gone. Saskia
didn't move, continuing to stroke his hair, watching his
face, mobile even in sleep.

Funny to remember how resentful she'd been when
she'd realised there was no one else to care for him,
that along with the shame and the debts and the mess
her father had bequeathed her, there was a toddler who
needed clothing and feeding and taking care of. If she
hadn't taken him in her life would have taken a very
different turn; she would probably have taken her degree, got a job. She wouldn't have lived the gilded life
she had enjoyed before her father's suicide; those circles

had closed to her as soon as his embezzlement had been discovered. But she would have found something approximating her original plans of a career in the media, a shared flat in Notting Hill, parties at the weekend, skiing in winter and beaches in summer.

Instead she had spent her days filing, answering phones, typing up reports, eating her packed lunch on a bench in a city square, shopping in sales and charity shops. No holidays anywhere, weekends spent exploring London's abundance of free museums and city parks. She knew every exhibit in the Natural History Museum, every room, every sign.

She couldn't remember when resentment had turned to acceptance and then to love. Couldn't remember the day she'd looked at Jack and seen not a burden, but a gift. The day she had started to be grateful for what she had, not what she had lost.

Hauling herself to her feet, Saskia adjusted Jack's covers. He looked so well; no longer pale and over the winter he'd escaped the hacking cough he usually caught in the damp London cold. The dry desert air agreed with him; he'd grown inches, filled out a little, and he loved the international school he now attended. He was going to find it hard to adjust going back, especially when the promised new home didn't materialise and she was preoccupied with a newborn baby.

Saskia went straight to her room, opening the sliding doors and stepping out onto her terrace. The moon was bright and round, its reflection on the sea offering her a path to who knew where. If only she could get into one of the boats moored on the wooden pier and follow its enticing, silvery road. She leant on the balcony and breathed in, enjoying the faint sea breeze that cooled the warm, desert night.

She had agreed to become a surrogate to give Jack a better life. But, damn him, Idris was right. As soon as the baby had been implanted in her womb she had taken on an obligation to put him or her first as long as they were dependent on her. She had worked so hard not to get too attached to the baby, to remember she wasn't its mother, merely its caretaker, but of course she loved it. It was half her. She felt it move, hiccup, knew when it was sleeping and when it was restless.

Didn't the baby deserve a better life too? The life it was supposed to have? It was supposed to be the Prince or Princess of Dalmaya. To grow up surrounded by the sea and the desert, to be loved and cosseted and so very much wanted. And that life was still within her power to bequeath.

Jack could learn to sail and ride, stay at the school he liked so much, keep growing stronger and healthier.

And she? She could endure…

Slowly Saskia reached into her pocket and pulled out the white card with Idris's name and number on it. She stared at it, her mouth dry and her hands numb. Married to Idris. No university, no home of her own, instead a life with a man who despised her. Who she despised.

A life that would provide for the two children in her care.

She had told herself that she had a choice but, really, she had no choice at all. Fumbling, she reached for her phone and, blinking back the tears, dialled.

CHAPTER FOUR

THE YEAR SASKIA turned eight she was a bridesmaid for her friend's elder sister. The wedding was held in the village church and afterwards the whole congregation had walked in a joyful procession along the narrow lane to Saskia's house, where her father had allowed a marquee to be erected in the old manor house's extensive gardens. It was a perfect wedding and small Saskia, starry eyed, vowed that one day she would have one just like it. Of course the manor house had been sold to pay off her father's creditors and she had given up on romantic dreams a long time ago. Still, she had never imagined that she would get married while heavily pregnant to a man who disliked her and although she had no desire for white lace or ivory organza the calf-length, long-sleeved black dress screamed funeral rather than wedding—which seemed fitting enough.

The lawyer had spent the afternoon with her, once more taking her through a contract clause by clause, although as this one was written in Arabic Saskia knew she was putting a lot of trust in him; she could be setting her name to anything. The contract went on and on, detailing expected duties, allowances, long lists she could barely take in. One thing stood out: the marriage contract pragmatically contained provisions for a divorce with generous allowances for both herself and any children resulting from the marriage. An escape clause. It didn't quite lift the suffocation from her lungs or the heaviness from her heart but at least she would be dry eyed when she signed her marriage contract.

'Sayeda Saskia, they are waiting for you.' Leena, her maid, stood at her bedroom door, her eyes bright with excitement. The staff seemed to view the whole secret wedding as wildly romantic and she didn't like to disabuse them.

'*Shokran*, Leena, I'll be down shortly.' She paused. 'Actually, could you please ask Sheikh Idris to step up here for a moment?'

'You want to see him alone? In your bedroom? Before the wedding?' Her maid's eyes widened in shock.

It was a little too late to worry about incurring bad luck or risking her reputation—after all, she was already heavily pregnant. What else could happen? 'You can leave the door open and wait in the corridor.' That should be sufficient chaperonage. She sank back onto the sofa and awaited the arrival of her soon-to-be husband.

She didn't have to wait long. The sound of his decisive tread reached her within two minutes of sending Leena for him and within seconds he stood at the door of her room, unfairly devastating in a traditional high collared cream tunic embroidered with gold thread and matching loose trousers. Saskia's heart thumped and despite herself she felt the old sweet tug of attraction low in her belly.

How could this still happen? She knew exactly who Idris Delacour was: a man who had no compunction about blackmailing a vulnerable woman, hijacking her life with no care for the consequences. But somehow her body was out of step with her mind. She noted his every detail without trying: the cut of his cheekbones, the stubble grazing his jaw, the quizzical slant of his brow, the coiled strength in his stance. His body had filled out since university, no longer a boy's rangy torso but a man's body. One used to hard work. Strong, capable.

'You didn't need to make such an effort,' she said, her mouth dry.

He cast her plain dress a contemptuous glance. 'One of us had to.'

Ignoring his cutting tone took every ounce of self-control she had. Summoning a smile from goodness knew where, she waved a hand at the chair opposite her. 'Will you sit?'

Idris didn't take the offered chair; instead he stayed leaning against the door, his arms folded. 'What can I do for you? Or have you decided you don't want to go through with it after all?' He wasn't sure whether he would be more furious or more delighted if she changed her mind about the wedding.

'Do you want me to change my mind?'

He didn't dignify her with a response. 'Saskia, my uncle, his wife and the lawyer are downstairs waiting for you. If you have cold feet…'

'I need to know what this marriage entails,' she cut in. 'What it is you expect of me. And I need to know what I can expect from you.'

'You read the contract?'

'No, it was a little tricky seeing as it is written in Arabic, but it has been read to me. Idris, I don't want to know about clauses and agreements. I want to know about you and me. About our marriage and your expectations.'

'My expectations?' He drawled the word out, allowing a cold smile to curve his mouth. 'You don't have to worry, Saskia. We may be married but I have no intention of consummating our marriage at any point. Your *honour...*' he put a faint stress on the last word and watched the flush spread across her pale cheeks '...is quite safe with me. I have no interest in rekindling our past relationship.'

Liar, his conscience whispered. Saskia Harper had been a pretty girl but she had grown into a beautiful woman. The strawberry blonde hair had darkened to a bright auburn, a colour that reminded him of the grapevines back home in France as autumn fell. She was slightly tanned, a few more freckles sprinkled across her nose, her cheeks, and her body matured and ripened. But she had changed more than physically; Saskia had always been marked by her utter confidence. No nervous freshman, she had arrived in Oxford looking as if she fully expected the world and everything in it to fall at her feet—and they had. Idris had instantly placed her in the category of privileged girls who treated Oxford not as an education but as a launch into society, a place to meet influential people and date—and marry— influential men. Her instant friendship with Maya had made it hard for him to avoid her, but, despite the naturally flirtatious way she had treated everyone, he had been immune to her enchantment.

Or so he'd thought. Looking back, he'd been a little too smug about his immunity, a little too aware of her conquests, a little too surprised to find her in the library that Saturday afternoon, struggling with her essay on Marlowe, frustrated because she'd desperately wanted to impress a notoriously difficult tutor. After he had talked it through with her, Marlowe's immortal words had made sense in a way they never had before.

> *O, thou art fairer than the evening air*
> *Clad in the beauty of a thousand stars*

A woman like Saskia could launch one thousand ships, her beauty and intelligence and the depths he spied under that confident exterior utterly beguiling. Utterly dangerous. But in the end, just like Faustus's creation, the woman he'd thought he'd seen was just an illusion.

This new, older Saskia was no pushover either, but she didn't look as if she expected life to roll over at her feet any more. There was a hardness in the green eyes that hinted at past hurts.

'No, Idris. I'm not even remotely concerned with your sleeping arrangements.' That voice though! Still clear and cold, each word spoken with precision in her most English of accents, like a lady dowager in a breeches and bonnets film. 'I want to know how this works day to day.'

'How this works? You're going to be the Queen, Saskia.' And he the King. The words still sounded absurd, the whole situation unreal. He, Idris Delacour, a King, with all the pomp and circumstance and responsibility and lack of privacy it entailed. His chest tightened. He wasn't ready. He didn't think he would ever be ready.

Idris glanced at Saskia, noting the tension in her shoulders and tell-tale shimmer in her eyes and a bolt of sympathy shot through him. He instantly clamped down on it. Like him she was a victim of circumstance.

Like him she had no choice but to see this through. Pity wouldn't help either of them.

'Queen, yes. But, what does that entail? Can I drive Jack to school, go shopping in the bazaar, have some kind of job?' Idris understood the subtext all too well— she wanted to know if she'd have any freedom. The sooner she understood—the sooner he accepted—that freedom as they knew it was over for both of them, the easier the rest of their lives would be.

'Saskia, you are about to become a very privileged woman. A woman with a driver, an expense account, a bodyguard. There's a gym and spa in the rooms at the palace being prepared for you, the palace stables are world renowned, you'll want for nothing. Sure, take your brother to school, shop to your heart's content but always have at least two guards and your driver with you. Try the bazaar every now and then by all means, it will make good PR, but there are some very exclusive malls, some with Dalmayan designers, who would love your patronage.'

Her lips tightened, frustration clear on her face. 'Malls. Right. That's one day a month at the most sorted. Working out, an hour a day or so. What about the rest of the time? Maya was on the Council, wasn't she? And Patron of several projects. Will I do that?'

'Maya had a degree in economics from Oxford. You dropped out of your English degree before you even took your first-year exams,' he reminded her.

'And I've been working ever since,' she retorted. 'I'm used to being busy.'

'You'll be busy,' he said silkily. 'Schools to open, dinners to attend, dignitaries to entertain, that kind of thing. You are going to need more than a day a month at the mall because you will be photographed and judged and God help you if you are found lacking. You will need to research every guest, every function, dress appropriately and make the right kind of small talk. And you will need to look like you want to be there and like you want to be with me. That's your role. That's what I expect from you as a wife. What Dalmaya needs from you as Queen. A hostess. A well-paid, professional hostess. Is that within your capabilities?'

If he hadn't been studying her so intently he would have missed the wobble of her chin, the flash of hurt in her eyes. 'A hostess. Thank you for clarifying. That's what I needed to know. If you will give me five minutes I will meet you downstairs.'

Returning to the downstairs study, Idris tried to pull his mind back to the documents in front of him, but all he could see was the look on Saskia's face as he had spoken. She had tried to look impassive, he could tell, her hands twisted and her chin tilted high. But those green eyes were as impressive as ever and they had been burning with emotion; with anger, with humiliation.

'Dammit,' he swore. He had promised himself he would never let Saskia Harper get under his skin again but in one conversation she had brought out the very worst in him, just as she had all those years ago.

She was about to become his wife and he owed her his loyalty and courtesy at the very least. If he continued to forget himself around her then this marriage was going to be a long, bleak affair. He had to do better. For the baby's sake if not his own.

The ceremony took so little time Saskia couldn't believe she was actually married. Sheikh Malik, Idris's uncle, made a speech in Arabic and then she and Idris signed the documents. That was all. Usually, Sheikh

Malik informed her, this was just the precursor to the marriage celebration, but in their case there was to be no party, no celebration. No family and friends gathered round to mark the occasion. That was fine. She didn't feel much like celebrating anyway. A speech she didn't understand, a contract she couldn't read and no ring. The stuff of daydreams. It was a good thing she didn't believe in romance.

Short as the ceremony was her head throbbed by the end of it, her feet aching in the unaccustomed heels. All Saskia wanted was to be left alone by everyone including—especially—her new husband and go straight to bed. The beaming smiles on her staff's faces and the delicious smells emanating from the kitchen suggested she was unlikely to get her way. She glanced over at Idris. The last thing she could cope with was a cosy evening *à deux* and she had sent Jack to his friend's house for the night, not wanting him to witness the short, loveless ceremony. Her mind raced with possible excuses, reasons to put the meal off and then inspiration struck; she turned to Sheikh Malik and his sweet-faced wife with her most welcoming smile.

'I know we are all still in mourning.' The words were a guilty jolt at her conscience. So few days since her friends had died, but she was so caught up in her own tragedy the bigger tragedy seemed distant somehow. 'But my kitchen staff wanted to mark the wedding and have been cooking up such a feast there is no way Idris and I will be able to manage it all. Would you join us for dinner? And you are very welcome as well,' she added to the lawyer. Idris's narrowed eyes made it clear that he understood exactly why she had extended the invitation. But he didn't gainsay her; he probably looked forward to a romantic meal as little as she did.

A white-covered table and chairs had been set up on the terrace, overlooking the sea. Jewel-coloured lanterns were strewn through the trees and plants creating a magical effect straight out of *The Arabian Nights*. Saskia stepped out onto the mosaic-tiled floor, her throat swelling as she took every carefully constructed detail in: the candles on the tables, the cushions scattered over the benches, the beautiful table decorations, the soft music floating out of hidden speakers. Her staff had gone to such an effort and if this really were her wedding night, if she had married someone she loved, then this would be the most charming, romantic dinner possible. Blinking back sudden, hot tears, she stepped over to the terrace rail and looked out at the floodlit beach below, the sea a dark shadow beyond.

'The city is that way.' She jumped as Idris spoke, unaware he had followed her. 'The mouth of the river is just there, you see? Where those lights are, that's the ships heading up to the port. Ships have been sailing up the river Kizaj for thousands of years to unload their cargoes at the harbour here and to take spices and silks back to Europe and further afield.'

Saskia turned and shivered when she realised just how close he was standing, almost within touching distance. The lanterns cast a soft jewelled glow on him, his face a mosaic of reds and greens and blues. The light made him seem younger, like the boy she had once known. The young man she had been so desperately in love with. Her heart ached, the locked-away memories flooding back as she looked into his dark eyes.

She had been so young, just eighteen. New to university, new to Oxford, she hadn't taken long to fall in with a crowd as self-assured, as gilded as she had been then; it hadn't taken long to realise she and Maya were kindred spirits. Young, beautiful, rich, indulged, confident. Looking back, she barely recognised that Saskia Harper. Did she envy her that innocence? Maybe.

Maya had already been engaged to Fayaz. Saskia, fresh from school and ripe for adventure, had been shocked that the poised girl with laughing eyes was ready to make such a commitment, but as soon as she had seen her with Fayaz she had understood; they had fitted together in a way she had never imagined fitting with anyone, fitted in a way she found herself envying. The revelation that Fayaz was Crown Prince she had taken in her stride; her exclusive boarding school had been full of royal offspring, many without a throne, the children of oligarchs and old aristocratic families.

But she hadn't been able to take Idris in her stride. He had already graduated from the Sorbonne and was doing a postgraduate year at Oxford. Older, serious, disapproving; she hadn't understood why she was so attracted to him then, naive for all her sophistication, but somehow he had got under her skin, into her very blood, with that first unsmiling nod. It hadn't been his looks—he was handsome but she had known many good-looking boys—nor his conversation—he barely spoke to her—but she had craved his approval more than anything she had ever known.

And when she had finally got it, when he had finally looked at her, into her, as if he knew her very soul, she had fallen. Hard.

It hadn't been easy. He had been so disciplined, so focussed on his future, and she had known he thought she was too flighty, too flirty, too frivolous. She had been all of the above, unapologetically so, refusing to change for anyone, wanting Idris to love her despite her flaws. She'd thought he did love her.

She'd been wrong.

It would be so easy to fall into that trap again. To believe that she could win him round. To think that behind that cool, sardonic mask there was a boy who needed saving. A boy only she could save. But if the last seven years had taught her anything it was that there were no happy endings and, in the end, the only person she could rely on was herself.

And yet she didn't step back. His eyes were so dark, like the bitterest chocolate, his skin a warm olive, his profile proud and aloof. She knew every millimetre of his face by heart. It was imprinted on hers. Trembling, Saskia raised her gaze to meet his, preparing herself to meet the old disdain, only for a fiery jolt to blaze through her whole body when, instead, she saw the old flicker of desire, a hunger she hadn't seen or felt for such a long time.

'Idris,' she whispered, raising her hand to his cheek, the rasp of his roughened skin setting every nerve in her fingertips on fire, a flame that licked its way right down to her toes with an almost painful intensity. He had always been able to ignite her with just one touch. Slowly his hand travelled up to cover hers and she closed her eyes, all her senses concentrating on his touch, only for them to fly open as his hand dropped hers and he stepped back, beyond her reach, shutters slamming down over his gaze, the desire extinguished as if it had never been.

'Sheikh Malik, Sheikha Salma,' he said, walking past her as if she weren't there, hands open, a smile on his face as he greeted his aunt and uncle as they stepped onto the terrace. Saskia took a deep trembling breath and turned, her own smile firmly in place. She could do this. What other choice did she have?

It was like being in a play, remembering her lines and her cues, ensuring she had the correct expression at all times and that her audience believed her confidence and interest to be real, even when her thoughts strayed to those brief seconds she and Idris had stood looking out over the sea. Luckily Idris's uncle and aunt were all too aware of the reasons for the hurried ceremony and worked hard to put Saskia at her ease. Sheikha Salma was a charming woman in her mid-fifties and she spent much of the meal asking Saskia about her pregnancy and plans for the baby and suggesting shops and places to visit that Saskia might like.

The conversation moved naturally on to the Sheikha's own children, all now grown up and living away from home. 'They are all so independent, not like when I was young,' she confided in Saskia. 'Adil is right here, in the army, but Aida works for a bank in London. Very clever girl. But clever won't bring me grandchildren.' She cast a longing look at Saskia's stomach. 'Farah is a teacher in Jayah but she lives in an apartment with other girls. In my day such a thing would have been completely scandalous but she just laughs and tells me I am old-fashioned.' She shook her head. 'There we are with our big house, room for sons- and daughters-in-law, for grandchildren, and it is just us rattling around.' She laughed but there was a sadness behind the laughter. 'Progress is not always such a wonderful thing.'

'I've looked after my brother, Jack, since he was two. The hardest thing to adjust to was the lack of privacy or time to myself—he wanted to talk to me even when I was in the shower! But now I can't imagine life without him. The thought of him growing up and moving on is unbearable. I hope you get some grandchildren soon but, please, you must visit the baby whenever you like.' As if on cue the baby kicked and Saskia automatically ran her hand over her bump, offering unspoken reassurance, an unspoken promise. The decisions she had made were hers alone; she would never burden the baby with guilt, never let it know that raising it, loving it were thrust upon her.

'And what about you, Sheikha Saskia? What did you do when you lived in London?'

'I was a temp,' she said. Idris and his uncle were both listening in and she forced a smile. 'Not the most high-powered career but it had variety.'

Sheikh Malik smiled back at her in response. 'There is always a need for good temps in the world.'

'That's true. I always had work.'

His wife patted Saskia's hand. 'But now motherhood will keep you busy. For the next few years at least.'

Saskia stilled. She needed to prove that she was more than just a brood mare. Prove to herself—and to Idris—that she had worth beyond that which her body gave her. 'I'm sure that's true and I know the first few months will be hard, but I would like to work as well. I have just completed the first year of a law degree, long distance, and, even though I know I won't be able to practise, I would still like to finish it and maybe find a way to use it.'

Sheikh Malik raised his eyebrows. 'You were planning to be a lawyer? You should have drawn up the contract today. Is that what you always wanted to do?'

'Not for a long time. Originally I assumed I would head into PR or something. I did a lot of temping for law firms, mainly big city firms, and it was fascinating. I would take minutes, or type up letters and think, well, I could do this.'

'I see, you wanted to work for one of the big city firms. That shows a lot of ambition.'

'They certainly pay well.' Idris leaned back in his chair, his eyes full of scorn. 'Money's a great motivator, isn't it, Saskia?'

'No. Not corporate law, although obviously that has its place, it isn't completely full of big business types thinking about a big wage packet.' Her fingers tightened on her glass as she met Idris's gaze as evenly as she possibly could. She knew full well that he had rebuilt his family fortunes back in France, restored the vineyards to produce wine that sold for more than her weekly rent. He didn't live on some kind of moral high ground—every shirt he possessed was handmade. 'I wanted to do family law. Advocate for those who can't speak for themselves. I'd still like to do that in some capacity. One day.' She raised her water glass to Idris, allowing the defiance to gleam in her eyes. She would achieve her dreams, Queen or not. She would just have to redefine what those dreams were and not let anyone, no matter how igniting his touch, stand in her way.

CHAPTER FIVE

'SASKIA? A MOMENT, PLEASE.' It was couched as a request but Idris knew that she was fully aware of what he really meant.

It was a command.

Saskia stilled, half turned away, her full body angling towards the door leading back into the villa, poised for flight. 'It's late and I am very tired. It's been a long day.' His uncle and aunt had only just left after what had been a curiously lighthearted evening in the end.

'This won't take more than a few minutes.'

She hesitated for another long moment and he tensed, relaxing as she let out a small, indignant huff. 'If it really can't wait.'

Idris nodded at the servants, still clearing the table, and at his signal they melted away, leaving the two of them alone. 'Please sit.'

'I'd rather stand.'

He gave her stomach a pointed look, but he didn't press the matter. If she chose to be uncomfortable who was he to stop her? '*Bien*. Stand.' He picked up his brandy glass and studied the liquid just covering the bottom before setting it down and transferring the same keen study to his new wife. 'Is it true what you said just now? You're studying law?'

'Yes.' Her eyes flashed as she tilted her chin defiantly. 'I'm not in the habit of lying, Idris. I just completed the first year online—and passed with honours, with the intention of transferring to a bricks and mortar university for the next two years and for my qualifying year. But plans change.'

'Yes.' He knew that all too well. It was common ground between them; enough of a common ground to build a marriage on? It was a start. 'That's why you agreed to become Maya's surrogate? To pay for your degree?'

Her face reddened. 'And to buy a house. Jack needed a proper home. *We* needed a proper home.'

It still made no sense. 'But what about your father's money?'

Saskia stared at him, incredulity sharpening her gaze. 'Come on, Idris, you know what happened to my father. Don't tell me there's not a nice little dossier on your desk right now.'

He nodded his head in acknowledgement. Of course the Dalmayan Secret Service had torn her life inside out the second the marriage had been agreed and he had spent last night reading the slender file, disbelief increasing with every word. Where was the trust fund? The parties, the boyfriends, the socialite existence? Instead all they could find on Saskia was a tiny rented flat in Wood Green, temping jobs, menial at first, better paid once she had taken some courses to improve her administrative skills. The only scandal was seven years old and lay at her father's door.

He hadn't been able to sleep last night, trying to reconcile the entitled girl he had known, the girl he had tried not to fall in love with, with this backstreet Cinderella, toiling her twenties away. 'I'm sorry to hear about your father. I know how much you loved him.'

'Sorry? Because he was a thief? Because he committed suicide? Because in the end I adored a liar and a sham. Save it. I don't need your pity, Idris.' The words and tone were dismissive but she leaned against the chair as if for support, her knuckles whitening as she clutched the chair back.

Idris's lips tightened. The coward had shot himself the second he was discovered, leaving Saskia to deal with the mess. 'He was a clever man. He *must* have left you something. I understand you have to be careful not to flaunt it but surely there's enough money for you to live...' He couldn't believe a man like Ted Harper hadn't hidden money away in offshore accounts ready for this kind of eventuality. That he would have abandoned his beloved only daughter to poverty.

But Saskia shook her head vehemently. 'He left me nothing. Nothing except shame and debts.'

'Your mother couldn't help you?'

'She was never really part of my life. They divorced when I was small. Idris, why are you dredging this up? You knew about my mother back then. Why would anything have changed?'

'I know you weren't close but surely she didn't just abandon you?'

Saskia put her hand in the small of her back and straightened, her face contorted with effort. Idris glared pointedly at her unused chair but she ignored him, leaning against the table instead. He almost admired her stubbornness. Almost. 'She didn't want any publicity that might connect her with my father. She had remarried and her celebrity yoga business relies on good press and good karma, which I apparently was very short of.'

She blew a frustrated breath. 'I mean, I don't know if I had turned up that she would actually have sent me from her gates but there was Jack...'

Yes. There was Jack. For some reason the boy was Saskia's responsibility—which now made him Idris's. Three days ago he'd had no responsibilities beyond the vineyard and his business apart from his mother's occasional dramas and bailing out his father on occasion. Now he had a kingdom, a wife, a dependent child and another on the way. It was as if he had pressed fast forward on the game of life and been catapulted five years on with no real idea how he got there.

'Where is his mother?'

'I don't know and I don't care. That woman. God, Idris, she didn't want to be a mother at all. She was my father's mistress, I didn't even know of her existence— or of Jack's—until a week after my father...a week after he died. I was still at the house then, gradually realising just what a mess he had bequeathed me, and she turned up at the door demanding her maintenance. Apparently she had only agreed to keep Jack in return for a lavish allowance. No allowance, no Jack. She just walked away and left this tiny boy behind in the hallway, as if he was an unwanted cat...'

Idris pictured the bright-faced boy running into the villa, disgust twisting his stomach at the thought of someone just abandoning their child. 'There was no one else who could help?'

'No. It was all down to me,' she snapped. 'I was—I am—the only person I can rely on. I found that out the night my father died...'

Idris stilled, an unwelcome realisation creeping over him as he added two and two together and came up with a sickeningly certain four. Her father had died seven years ago. She'd dropped out of Oxford seven years ago. He had ended their relationship seven years ago...

Ended it because she was a distraction, because he knew all too well where following your heart not your head led. The final straw had been the evening she'd shown up drunk and hysterical. He'd turned her away—and that was the last he had seen of Saskia Harper until three days ago.

But looking back he recognised that neither drunk or hysterical were typical of her. She was carefree, sure. Insouciant. Thought rules were for other people, but she wasn't the dramatic type. He swallowed, casting his mind back to the press cuttings, trying to recall the date of her father's suicide. 'The night your father died?'

Saskia whirled around, her aches evidently forgotten as she faced him, tall and defiant. 'It's such a cliché, isn't it? The worst day of your life? And you know, until that day, every day had been pretty damn good. Since then?' She shrugged, an angry, brittle movement. 'There was the day I was fired when I didn't let my boss feel me up in the photocopier room, the day I literally couldn't afford baked beans. The day I realised Jack had been going to school with holes in his shoes. The day I dragged myself to work with flu because there's no sick pay if you're a temp. The day Maya died. Yeah, there's been some competition for the worst day of my life but the day my father died still holds the crown.'

Every word dropped heavily straight into his heart. How had he not known? Not known that her gilded life had tarnished, not known that she had willingly accepted a burden far too heavy for her? Guilt flooded through him, guilt edged with anger. Anger at every person who had let her down, himself possibly included in that tally. Idris curled his hands into fists as he vowed to hunt down that particular boss and make him regret he had ever set foot in the photocopier room.

'That day,' she continued, her eyes harder than the emeralds they resembled, 'the police turned up at college to take me home. They told me that the man I idolised had shot himself. That they suspected fraud. That there was a possibility that everything I had, everything he'd lavished on me, had been bought with stolen money. I identified the body, answered questions until I couldn't speak, saw enough papers to realise that their accusations had merit and all I wanted was you to help me make sense of it all. Somehow I got myself back to Oxford, I don't remember how. But you weren't there, not at your flat, at your college, nowhere. You weren't answering your phone or texts. I bumped into Tatiana and, although her all-day party-girl shtick usually bored me, that day her offer of a drink seemed like a good one, and so did the next and the next and the one after that because I needed to somehow be numb. I got to numb, stupidly I kept drinking past numb, and somewhere along the way I hit hysterical. That's when it seemed like a good idea to try and find you again. To find comfort.' She held his gaze, proud and true like the Queen she would so shortly become. 'And you sent me away.'

There it was. Two and two did make four, after all. He held a degree in maths and business—how could he doubt it? He'd ended their relationship on the day she had lost her father, lost her entire life. Ignorance did not seem much of an excuse. If he had known why she had turned up so late, so drunk, so incoherent, then of course he would have acted differently. Been gentler. But he hadn't asked, hadn't given her the chance to tell him. She had just had her world destroyed and he had put in the final boot, stomping down on what was left of her. Shame twisted in his gut, hot and fierce.

But the truth was he would still probably have finished their relationship, not that night but soon after. She had been the ultimate distraction and his work had started to pay the price. Idris had known his path—it was straight and clear and sensible and there had been no room on it for a red-headed siren no matter how seductive her song.

He knew all too well what happened when people threw duty away for love: it tore families apart. Duty came first, always.

For once the certainty didn't feel quite as comforting as it usually did. It didn't matter; the undeniable truth was that Idris had made a success of his life thanks to his one hundred per cent dedication and commitment. He'd restored the vineyards, restored the chateau, built up a business. The Delacour name was no longer a fading star, relegated to gossip pages, but a force to be reckoned with. He had inherited the crown as a worthy heir. As a man who achieved. A man who built and restored. It was enough. It had to be enough. It was what he had.

'Why did you?' She no longer sounded angry, she sounded exhausted, and Idris glanced over at her, concerned. The baby wasn't due for six weeks and so far he'd done a terrible job of helping her to keep her stress levels down. 'I thought you loved me. You never said it, but I could have sworn I used to see it in your eyes, in your smile. Feel it in the way you touched me.'

The air around them grew thick with memories, the scent of the night-blooming jasmine permeating the terrace. Idris's grip tightened on his glass as her words sank in, as he remembered the softness of her skin, the feel of her hand in his, the way she'd shivered when he'd traced a finger along her cheek, along the curve of her waist, the swell of her breast. 'Maybe I did,' he said hoarsely. 'Maybe I was close, at least as much as I was—as I am—capable of loving anyone.'

Her eyelids fluttered at his words. 'I'm glad it wasn't all in my head.'

'Sit down, Saskia. Please,' he added and, after a quick glance at him, she slid carefully into the chair, accepting the glass of iced water he pushed over to her with a wan smile. 'You know that Fayaz was my cousin?'

If she was surprised at the change in topic she didn't show it, nodding slowly. 'Of course, your mother was his aunt.' She looked up. 'Shouldn't your mother be Queen then, instead? Or is that not allowed here?'

'It's not been done, nor has any King inherited through his mother as I am doing, but my grandfather, the Great Reformer, didn't allow little things like thousands of years of tradition to stop him.' He stopped, visions of the proud, straight-backed man flooding his thoughts. Would he be proud of the man Idris had become? Of the sacrifices he had made? 'If things had been different maybe my mother would be in Dalmaya preparing to take the throne right now, but she hasn't set foot in the country since she was nineteen. She's not welcome here.'

'She's been exiled? In this day and age?'

'Not officially, but as good as.'

'What on earth did she do?'

What hadn't she done? His mouth twisted. 'She ran away with her ski instructor when she was nineteen.'

'Okay. That doesn't sound too awful.'

She didn't understand; how could she? 'Saskia, in this country arranged marriages are still common, and education for girls over eleven still relatively new. My mother was a royal princess, a role model, and she not only lived with a man she wasn't married to but she was pictured—extensively—smoking, drinking, flirting. She modelled, did some acting. There were nude shots. She left the ski instructor for a racing driver and then, after some public scenes, she left him for my father. My father is a well-known *provocateur*, an artist, and there's no controversy he hasn't courted…their parties, their affairs, their arguments have been photographed and written about for the entirety of their marriage.' Neither cared. His father thought even noticing such things beneath him; his mother just laughed.

'Compared to an embezzling fraud they don't sound too bad to me, but I'm the first to admit my standards are pretty low. An actual parent would be nice to have.'

He barely heard her, trying to find the right words to explain. 'That night. That night you came to me, my mother had called me. My job, Saskia, my role, was to be the sensible one, to be the grown-up. It still is. There was no room for three juveniles in my family and neither of my parents had any intention of growing up.'

'What did your mother want, that night?'

He cast his mind back to that day. His mother hadn't been able to speak at first; it had taken hours to calm her down. 'There was some transgression of my father's. It wasn't uncommon, for her to call and cry at me, but this was worse than usual. It took three hours to calm her—she was hysterical, threatening to leave him, to kill herself. To do something crazy. She is quite capable of anything when she is in that mood. I couldn't ignore her, no matter how much I wanted to.'

He poured himself a little more brandy, trying to remember the emotions of that night. It was all so long ago; he had been a different person then, still a boy in so many ways. 'For the first time, academically, things were slipping. I wasn't in control and that scared me. My essay was late, my tutor concerned, my final proposal flawed, work in general not up to scratch and I knew it was because I was spending too much time with you. *Non*,' he said as she looked ready to retort. 'The fault was all mine, but I knew I had to remedy it. My future, the family expectations demanded it.

'And then you turned up and it was like watching my parents' marriage mirrored in our still fledgling relationship, seeing our possible future in their present. My mother crying, my father frustrated because he couldn't work, I could smell the alcohol on you, you made no sense…'

'I see.'

'I couldn't allow myself to be dragged into any more drama. I couldn't allow my feelings for you to develop any further, to distract me any more. I didn't know how serious things were for you, and I am truly sorry I didn't find out and help…'

'I didn't need your help. I just wanted your support.'

He couldn't, didn't answer. What was there to say? He couldn't lie and tell her that of course he would have supported her, shouldered her troubles, carried her needs and expectations along with all the others that had been thrust upon him. They'd only been dating for a few months. His mother might throw caution to the wind for the very idea of love but Idris had spent his life living with the consequences.

'I know,' he said finally. 'But it wasn't the first time, Saskia. Not the first time you turned up and demanded attention no matter what I had planned, no matter what I was doing. No, you had never been drunk before, never hysterical—but you were impulsive and wanted me to be impulsive too.' Spontaneous, she had called it when she cajoled him to miss a tutorial, take the weekend off, jump on a train and head off who knew where. He hated spontaneity, had grown up with it. What was wrong with order and a planned existence?

Saskia twisted her water glass around and around. 'Did you ever wonder where I was? Why I dropped out? Did you ever ask Maya about me?'

The honest truth was he'd been relieved. Relieved she wasn't there to distract him any more. Relieved he would no longer be tempted and could bury himself in his work. Relieved that, in the end, he hadn't allowed emotion to weaken him. 'Saskia, you knew so many people, had so many invitations—to parties, to ski resorts, to country houses. There were so many men waiting in line for you to notice them. You talked of studying abroad, of travelling. It didn't seem like you needed Oxford the way others did. I just assumed you'd flitted on to another university, another place. Maya didn't mention you to me once. I didn't ask.'

His assumptions had strengthened his resolve. If she could drop out that easily then at heart she was the party girl he had first met, not the scholar agonising over her Marlowe essay. If she could just flit away from one life then she was a butterfly like his mother, never settling. His assumptions had made it clear he had done the right thing. His assumptions had been wrong.

'She didn't know where I was. I bumped into her on Bond Street a couple of years ago but that was the first time I had seen her since I left Oxford. I didn't mean to cut ties so completely. I went home to try and salvage what I could with every intention of returning, but one week later there was Jack. And, honestly, I couldn't face people's pity—your pity—I couldn't bear the shame, for people to know how far I had fallen. From then on it was a battle. A battle to keep Jack fed and clothed and warm. Oxford was a lifetime ago.'

'You were never tempted to walk away from him?'

'We're all allowed to be weak for a moment, Idris. We're all allowed to be tempted. It's how we proceed from there that counts. But yes, there were times.' Her voice dropped and she stared into her water glass as if it held the answers. 'Times when we were hungry, times when Jack was ill. Times when it was all so bleak and so hard that I didn't know how I was going to get up the next day and start again when I wished for someone to rescue me.' Had she hoped that he would find her and make it all better—or did she know he was no knight in shining armour for all his inherited military titles?

'So when Maya found you and asked you to have the baby you said yes.' He'd judged her with such contempt when he'd seen the contract, but in the end what choice had she had? None, just as he had given her no choice over this marriage.

'Not at first. Her terms were very, very generous but they drove a hard bargain. Three months of a special diet and exercise to make sure I was healthy. Fertility drugs, which are not pleasant, believe me. Then as soon as it was confirmed I was pregnant I was flown here, to live in seclusion. Yes, it's beautiful here and I have everything I could need but I wasn't allowed to leave. No deviating from the prescribed exercise or diet. No seeing Jack's school or meeting his friends. No sight-seeing. And you know the rest. I was locked in for life. If the baby needed anything I could give then I would be legally bound to. I would never be truly free of my responsibilities. I had to weigh all that up against the benefits.'

'And it was worth it?'

She turned her hand, staring at her glossily painted nails. 'I thought so then. I can't wish the baby away but I can wish we could turn the clock back three days and avert that accident.' She sighed. 'I didn't just jump at the money. I thought about it long and hard. But Jack and I needed a real home. And he deserved to have things other kids his age had, to be able to go to clubs and swimming and on holiday. To have the adult in his life around before school and in the evenings, not spend his time in a jigsaw of breakfast clubs and childminders' and friends' houses until I got back from work. And I deserved the chance to take my degree. To try and be something more than a glossy smile and a bright manner. But it wasn't an easy choice. And if I'd known the outcome…' Her voice trailed off but he understood.

She would have chosen to remain in poverty rather than be trapped into marrying him. He couldn't blame her.

'Would you really have done it?'

He looked over at her. 'Done what?'

'Turned your back on Fayaz's baby?'

He paused, lifting up his brandy glass and examining the amber depths. 'I told myself yes, but in reality?' He shrugged. 'I hoped I would not have to make a decision either way.' He glanced at her curiously. 'How about you? What if I'd simply cancelled the contract and told you that you could leave the baby here, take Jack and go home?' Would the woman who had given up her whole life for her small brother have turned her back on her baby?

She was silent for a long time. 'I don't know either. My pride wants me to say that of course I would have gone, head held high. But in reality?' She shrugged. 'Maybe I would still be here. Probably I would still be here.' Her hand stole to her stomach. 'He or she is my responsibility. Not because a contract says so but because it's half me. I've nurtured it and loved it and looked after it. I could have handed it over to Maya gladly because I knew she wanted it so much. But how could I have walked away and left it with you when you had so much else thrust upon you?'

Idris pushed his chair back and hauled himself to his feet, suddenly exhausted mind, body and soul. He held a hand out to Saskia. She stared at it for a long moment before laying her cool hand on his, allowing him to help her up. She made to pull away once she was on her feet but he kept her hand imprisoned in his. 'Truce?'

'Truce? In what way?'

'You're right. We are married now. We have a child to raise. Two children,' he amended and her eyebrows shot up in surprise. 'Neither of us chose this but here we are. We both have things to regret from back then, but that shouldn't stop us from doing the best we can now with the cards we've been dealt. Let's make a pact.'

'A pact?'

'To respect each other. Honesty.' Idris closed his eyes and thought of his parents' marriage. About the profligacy, the constant drama. Of the extravagance. Respect and honesty seemed a good antidote to that. So it was best not to dwell on how soft her hand was under his. Or to remember the way she was back then. Fearless and so full of passion it shone out of her. Better not to remember the way she'd made him feel. Because down that path lay a madness he had no intention of ever returning to.

Respect and honesty. They were worthy goals. They were all they could possibly ever have.

CHAPTER SIX

THE MOURNING PERIOD was over at last—officially at least. Idris wasn't sure when he'd actually stop grieving although, with a sharp stab of guilt, he knew he was grieving for his lost life as much as for his lost cousin.

With the end of the mourning period came a lightening of mood throughout both the palace and the country and Idris's advisors were beginning to discuss an official Coronation date. He'd attended Fayaz's Coronation and knew what the day entailed: ceremonies, speeches, inspections of the guard, feasts; an interminably long, unbearably hot day under scrutiny for every single second. Thankfully Saskia would need to be by his side for the whole time, which meant an imminent date was impossible.

She had elected not to return to the royal palace with him after their wedding, preferring the cooler sea air to the stultifying city heat—and the truth was adjusting to his new life, to his new role was easier for him without her. The distance gave them both the opportunity to ease into this marriage, into this truce, slowly. Time to adjust to the truths unearthed on their wedding night.

Idris headed over to the villa twice a week, but there were no more confidences, no more heart-to-hearts. No moments when memories swirled around them thick with regrets, with remembered intimacies. It was best that way. Nothing had really changed; he still had a path to follow, a duty to fulfil. It was best he walked that path alone. Besides, he was still coming to terms with the knowledge that he had wronged her all those years ago. He had been so sure of himself back then. But he had lacked compassion. Lacked honour. The truth burned into him. No wonder she could barely meet his eye, ensured they were never alone.

His PR department had waited until the wedding ceremony was completed before sending out a brief press release introducing His Highness Sheikh Idris Delacour to the world as the prospective King Idris Delacour Al Osman. The press release had dwelled on his loving relationship with his grandfather and Fayaz, and his successful business empire before briefly mentioning that he was recently married and his first child would be born imminently. It wasn't a lie even if the intention was to mislead the public into thinking the marriage of greater duration than it really was.

Luckily the docile and reverential Dalmayan press didn't look for any more details. As expected the European—and especially the British, frothing with excitement at the new Queen's nationality—press were a lot more interested in the newly royal couple and had published several exposés of their student affair, digging up Saskia's father's suicide and subsequent disgrace in gleeful detail and reliving every one of his mother's scandals. But they didn't seem to suspect that the baby wasn't Idris's nor that the marriage wasn't real. As long as it stayed that way let them dig.

He pushed his laptop to one side and swivelled his chair to look out of the office window. The palace gardens were internationally renowned, an oasis in the desert interior of his coastal country. Long terraces, each planted to a different theme, led down to the extensive lawns, palms fluttering overhead, and the garden was famous for its many fountains providing a cool comfort for those who worked inside the palace walls. Further out, beyond the lawns and just out of view, were the stables, home to over one hundred thoroughbreds, many past or present racing champions. The stables had been one of his favourite places to visit during his long holidays in Dalmaya. A place where Idris and his grandfather had bonded, where he had felt as if he belonged. He hadn't had time to visit once in the month he had been back in the country.

Saskia used to ride, he remembered. She'd said all the horses were sold after her father's death and she hadn't ridden since. Maybe he should give her a horse, as a wedding gift. It would make for some nice PR photos after all...

A buzz from his personal mobile phone interrupted his thoughts and he turned back to the paperwork-laden desk to look for it, apprehension hammering through him. Not many people had that number. His chest tightened when he saw the name on the screen. Saskia. Usually she preferred to contact him through their assistants, just as he contacted her in the same distant way.

He pressed answer. 'Yes?'

'Idris?' She sounded breathless. Frightened. He pushed his chair back, jumping to his feet.

'What's happened?'

'The baby. Idris. I think it's on its way. Come quickly. I can't do this alone. Please, please come now.'

Idris didn't think he had ever moved so fast, not even thirty-two days ago when he had received the phone call from Dalmaya telling him of his cousin's death. He wasn't sure what compelled him most—the fear in Saskia's voice or the knowledge she had called him, begged him to help. Of course, there *was* no one else. First Maya and Fayaz, then Idris himself had made sure of that. Saskia had no friends, no family. She was as alone as he was. More so. He still had his parents, little though he saw them.

It usually took an hour to drive from Jayah, the capital city, to the villa but today Idris made the journey in less than forty-five minutes, his security detail barely able to keep up with his bike. He knew that his guards disliked his motorcycle, thinking it a risk, hard to guard and dangerous to ride. Idris had given up too much when he took on the throne. There was no way he was relinquishing his beloved, carefully restored vintage Triumph as well.

He got to the villa to see Saskia, her midwife and the doula, a woman trained to be her birth partner, walking towards a waiting car. He pulled the bike up to a stop and swung off it, removing his helmet as he intercepted the small group. Saskia was pale, her freckles standing out in stark relief, leaning on the two women as they escorted her to the car. Idris tucked his helmet under his arm as he reached her side. 'Are you all right?'

She nodded. 'Yes. Only when people said it hurts I didn't realise it hurts this much. Oh, no…here we go again,' and Idris could only stand there helpless while she gripped the hands holding her up, her face contorted with pain as she was reminded to '*Breathe*, Saskia, breathe.'

'Her contractions are quicker and longer than I would expect at this stage,' the midwife told him as Saskia sagged against her. 'It's imperative we get her to hospital as quickly as possible. Are you coming with us? Are you planning to attend the birth?'

Idris froze. Maya had intended to be with Saskia, he knew. Now, although she had two paid personal attendants with her and a whole team waiting for her at the hospital, she didn't have anyone on her side, anyone who chose to be there, for whom it wasn't a job. They had called a truce. Had many years of marriage ahead. But did that mean he should attend the birth? It would be one thing if Saskia and he had married for love and if the baby were really his; this felt as if he would be intruding into a world he was not meant to see.

'No,' Saskia gasped. 'Jack. He's scared. He needs…' She bit her lip as another tremor ran through her body and the midwife and doula exchanged concerned glances.

Idris jumped at the opportunity to be helpful in a way that didn't involve witnessing childbirth. '*D'accord.* Don't worry, you just get yourself to hospital. Jack and I will be absolutely fine.'

They were brave words, but as Idris watched the car pull out of the gates he realised he had barely exchanged a word with his small brother-in-law beyond asking how school was. He didn't know any children, didn't know how to interact with them. That was going to have to change with not one but two children in the royal nurseries.

There was no sign of Jack as he entered the villa. The whole house was unusually quiet and still; the airy villa had a family air, all the staff on first-name terms with Saskia and her brother. It was usually a welcome release from the formality of the palace; today it just felt empty.

Idris wandered fruitlessly through room after room before thinking to check the terrace, where he found

Jack slumped on a lounge chair, a huge umbrella providing shade from the late-morning sun. A handheld games console lay on his knee but it was switched off and his thin face had the kind of determined set to it Idris recognised as a way to hold back threatened tears. Idris perched on the lounge chair next to him. 'Hey.'

Jack barely looked over. 'Hello.'

'How's it going?'

A shrug.

Idris blew out a breath. Was there a book he could buy—*How To Communicate with Pre-teens for Dummies* maybe? He'd met Jack maybe eight times now but struggled to think what to say to the boy—especially as it was clear Jack was confused by Idris's new status in his life and more than a little wary of him. 'Saskia is on her way to the hospital now. I'm sure we'll hear as soon as there is any news.' He wasn't sure who he was trying to comfort most: Jack or himself.

'Will she die?'

Idris stared over at the small boy. 'What?'

'Saskia. Will she die? She sounded like she might. She was crying and saying it hurt.'

'That's how it is, Jack. Having a baby hurts and there's nothing you and I can do but wait. But *non*,' he said, hoping fervently that he wasn't lying to the tense child. 'She isn't going to die. She has the best doctors and midwives in the country helping her.'

'Maya died.'

'Yes, yes, she did. But that was an accident, not because she had a baby.'

'She was *supposed* to have the baby. Saskia was growing the baby for Maya. That's a secret and no one but you, me and Saskia must ever know.'

It was a big secret for the boy to keep. 'No. Do you know why it's so important?'

'Because you are the King and the baby will be the next King if it's a boy.'

'That's right. I know it seems odd but if you have any questions or worries then just come to me, any time.'

Jack nodded. 'Saskia says we are staying in Dalmaya, that we won't be going back to London.'

'Once the baby is born you'll be living in the palace at Jayah. But you'll go to the same school you're at now. Does that sound okay?'

'Will my friends be able to visit? Will there be room for me to ride my bike?'

Idris suppressed a smile as he thought of the hundreds of rooms and hundreds of acres in the palace grounds. 'Plenty of room for friends and bikes.'

'That's good. I didn't have a bike in London and the flat was too small for friends to come over. And will…?' He hesitated. 'Saskia said once the baby was born and we went home we would have our own bedrooms.'

Idris blinked. 'You didn't before?'

Jack shook his head. 'Saskia slept on the sofa only it turned into a bed and we had to share the wardrobe and things.'

For the last seven years Idris had been the only occupant of a chateau with enough bedrooms for him to choose a new one every night of the week if he chose while Saskia bunked down in the living room. His chest tightened. 'You'll definitely have your own room with plenty of space for all your things. No sharing required.'

'And will Saskia stop crying?'

Idris stilled. 'What do you mean?'

'In London she used to cry when she thought I was asleep. When things broke or there was a school trip or when my shoes got holes. When we moved here she stopped crying until Maya died. Now she cries every night. She thinks I don't hear her but I do. I don't want her to cry any more.'

'Nor do I,' Idris said softly, the weight of his responsibilities bearing down on him. It had been too easy to forget about Jack, but the boy wasn't just Saskia's charge, he was Idris's too. And, like his big sister, he had been carrying burdens that were far too heavy for him. Idris knew what it was like to be young and helpless and yet feel that the weight of the whole family rested on your shoulders. He could at least relieve Jack of his load. 'Let me worry about Saskia, okay? You worry about school and homework. Deal?'

Jack didn't move but some of the tension left his body. 'Then I guess I don't mind staying. Dan's dad is going to teach us to ride and to sail and that will be cool.'

Idris made a mental note to get Dan and his family checked out. 'We have horses and boats at the palace.'

'You do?'

'*We* do,' he corrected the boy. 'I married Saskia and that makes us family.'

'The baby too? Saskia has to be its mum now Maya isn't here to take care of it.' The big brown eyes turned their disconcertingly direct gaze on Idris. 'And you are going to be its dad.'

A *dad*. Idris stared back at the small boy as the word echoed round and round in his head. He'd known he would be the baby's father and that was fine; father was a more formal word, a more formal role. It called to mind school reports and admonishments. Guiding and helping. But a dad? A dad was a whole other being. A dad loved and played. A dad stood on the sidelines at a match and cheered. A dad held hands during first footsteps and carried small people on broad shoulders. A dad read stories and checked under the bed for monsters. He could be a father but could he be a dad? A good dad?

He was aware that Jack was waiting for a response and tried a smile. 'I suppose I am.'

'Saskia says it makes no difference, that I'm still her boy. She says that's the amazing thing about love, that it just keeps expanding to fit all the people you need it to fit. She says I'll love the baby too but I don't know. My friend Dan has a baby sister and he says she does nothing but cry and get messy and he can't play with her. I don't think that sounds like a lot of fun.'

'Babies aren't that much fun at first,' Idris agreed. 'But I think they grow on you. I don't have much experience of them myself.' He suppressed the urge to look at his phone. He'd hear if there was a call and he didn't want to worry Jack any further. 'What do you want to do? We could sit around here and worry or we could do something.'

'Like what?'

'What do you like to do?'

'Well,' Jack confided. 'In London we mostly went to museums and parks because they're free but it's a bit hot for parks and I don't know where the museums are.'

Idris's mind flew to the stables. To how he and his grandfather seemed to strengthen their bond every time they went there. 'Come on,' he said. 'Let's go to the palace and you can check out your rooms—and then we can see about your first riding lesson.'

'Saskia!'

All she wanted to do was sink into the firm, cool

pillows and float away, but Saskia forced herself to sit up and smile as Jack ran into the room. 'Hey there, my boy. Are you okay?'

'I've been to the palace and I have not one, not two, but three rooms all to myself. And a bathroom! And there's a staircase which takes me to your courtyard so I'm not far away. And Idris gave me a riding lesson and says I have a very good seat.'

Saskia blinked at the torrent of words. 'Goodness. Sounds like you've been busy.'

'Idris says I can have a horse all of my own when I show I'm ready to take care of him, if you say it's okay. It is okay, isn't it?'

She looked over Jack's head and met Idris's eyes. He was lounging against the far wall of her hospital room—a room much more luxurious than many five-star hotels could boast. He didn't look bored or strained; he looked amused. A quiver of hope ran through her. Jack needed a father figure; she was well aware of that. If Idris took a liking to him it would make such a difference to the boy's life. He'd never complained about not having the time and money to do the things his school friends took for granted but she knew their straitened, cramped existence wasn't much fun for a growing and active boy. At least money and space were no longer issues, although myriad other problems had cropped up in their place like some kind of hydra; she sorted one obstacle only to find another three in its place.

'I'm sure it is. A horse is a big responsibility though so make sure it's what you really want. Now, are you ready to meet…?' She paused. 'Well, technically he's your nephew. Do you want to be Uncle Jack or shall we go with brothers? Up to you.'

'I'm the oldest either way but I don't feel ready to

be an uncle yet,' her brother confided and Saskia suppressed a smile at the solemn note in his voice.

'How about you, Idris?' She swallowed. The marriage was about to begin in earnest; there would be no going back once Idris acknowledged the baby as his. 'Do you want to meet your son?'

He nodded, those dark eyes still fixed on her, and Saskia smiled an instruction at the nurse. 'They put him in another room so I could get some sleep,' she said. It had physically hurt her when they took him away, even though she knew he was warm and safe and looked after. She could have sat and looked at him for an eternity and never got bored. For the first time she wondered what she would have done if Maya had still been alive. Was this instant rush of utter love because she knew he was hers to love and care for or would she have felt like this anyway? Would giving him up have torn her in two? She would never have to find out but, for the first time, Saskia was easier about the choices she had made and the life that lay ahead. It might not be what she had dreamed of but her brother and son would be with her and safe. She wasn't trapped, she was lucky.

She straightened as the nurse brought the baby, bundled up in a white blanket, into the room, shaking her head when the nurse made to hand him to her, even though every fibre in her wanted to reach out and take him and never let him go. 'It's time he meets his father,' she said, her gaze fixed on Idris.

Uncertainty played over Idris's face but he pushed off the wall and allowed the nurse to settle the baby in his arms. He pushed the cloth off the baby's head and stared down at the small, wrinkled face. Saskia held her breath.

Please let him love him.

He looked up, finally, his eyes suspiciously wet. 'He looks like an Al Osman,' he said gruffly and she knew exactly what he was trying to say: *The baby looks like Fayaz*. He did; from the silky black hair to the dark eyes, the coffee-coloured skin such a contrast to her own, he was Fayaz's son through and through. She swallowed, fighting back her own tears, grief rising once again for the young parents who would never meet their perfect son. 'Yes,' she said.

'There's a look of you too.'

She almost snorted. 'Me? There's nothing of me in there, which after all I went through feels a little wrong.'

'Oh, there is, a certain expression, a tilt of the chin. He might not have inherited your red hair but I am pretty sure he's inherited your stubbornness.' He looked across, his expression soft. 'Was it very bad?'

She shot a quick glance at Jack but he didn't seem to be listening, standing close to Idris and engrossed in pulling faces at the baby. 'I've never been torn apart by wild horses but I imagine it was close.'

He grimaced. 'Lovely.'

'No. It wasn't. Maya was keen I try and do it all naturally although, believe me, nothing about that felt natural, but in the end I had no choice. It all happened very quickly, too quickly they said. I couldn't have had drugs if I had wanted.' She blew a breath out, trying to wipe away the memories of those shocking, agonising hours; she'd felt so alone despite the team of doctors, despite her personal midwife and doula. She'd needed a friend, someone she trusted to tell her it was all going to be okay. She had even wished that she hadn't sent Idris to Jack, had asked him to come with her. He might not be friendly but he was familiar. 'So, what shall we call him?'

He glanced up, surprised. 'I get a say?'

'You *are* the dad.'

Surprise and something she couldn't read flared in the dark eyes. He didn't answer for a while; when he did his voice was hoarse. 'Something that works for all of us. Something Dalmayan, French and English for a baby with all those cultures in him.'

Saskia's heart clenched at his words. By including France in there Idris had claimed the baby as his in the most natural way possible. 'That makes it easy. It's going to narrow down the choices anyway! What do you think, Jack? Any favourite names?'

Her brother frowned. 'Harry after Harry Potter?'

She nodded. That would work. 'Maybe. Idris? What do you think?'

He was looking deep into the baby's eyes. A private communion. At her words he glanced up. 'Did Maya and Fayaz have any preferences, do you know?'

'I think they mentioned Sami. It means…'

'It means *exalted*,' Idris said softly, staring down at the baby. 'A big meaning for a little person. Do you like it?'

'Yes. I really do. Do you?'

'Yes. Come along, Prince Sami Harper Delacour Al Osman, I think your mother wants you.' Carefully holding the baby, he walked slowly across the room, bending as he handed Saskia her son. Their hands met and for the first time in weeks Saskia didn't flinch away, holding his gaze, answering his smile with one of hers. He had claimed her son, accepted her brother and by doing so he had bound her to him irrevocably. For the first time that didn't feel quite so much like a prison sentence. For the first time Saskia hoped they could really be a family.

CHAPTER SEVEN

'THAT WILL BE ALL, thank you.' Saskia smiled at her assistant, breathing a sigh of relief when the diminutive brunette left the courtyard Saskia tended to use as a living-room-cum-office. It wasn't that Saskia didn't want to be busy, to be useful, but she was hoping for something more interesting than learning how to address an ambassador and the exact depth of curtsey needed when she met another Queen.

She had come to the palace straight from the hospital. A huge, sprawling, ancient monument in marble, the Al Osman seat of power felt more like some kind of gigantic temple combined with a government building than a home. High walls kept the city at bay but the palace complex was as busy as any thriving metropolis: armed guards, civil servants, advisors, gardeners, drivers, maids and cooks working and in many cases living inside the gates.

Saskia and the boys were housed at one end of the building, their rooms at the back away from the hustle and bustle of the formal governing offices and chambers. Saskia's own suite was on the first floor: a bedroom, sitting room, small but well equipped gym, study, bathroom and dressing room arranged around an internal courtyard. Her rooms were traditionally decorated with jewel-coloured mosaics and cool, marble floors, bright throws, rugs and cushions softening the effect. The bedroom and sitting room both had doors leading onto the terrace, which boasted a small infinity pool as well as shaded hammocks and seats overlooking the vast, lush gardens. Not that she could reach the gardens, not without travelling through what felt like acres of corridors and down staircases, flanked at all times by her guards and maids. It was easier to stay on her terrace and look out.

Sami had his own suite next to hers: a bedroom, nursery, bathroom and en suite accommodation for his three attendants, and Jack's rooms were on the floor above, a secret staircase connecting his playroom directly to Saskia's courtyard. She didn't know where Idris's rooms were; she hadn't been invited to see them.

Living in the palace was like being a guest in a sumptuous hotel: lovely at first but cloying after a while. For the first six weeks, still adjusting to the demands of a tiny baby and healing from the birth, it had been wonderful to have no demands made on her at all. No laundry, no meals to even plan let alone cook, no need to lift a finger or use her brain in any way. It had been the same at the villa but there the staff had been much, much smaller, the villa her domain. If she wanted to cook or bake the kitchen was hers to use or not. Here she had no idea where the kitchens were. She relayed her instructions to one of her maids, or phoned or even ordered online. Just like a hotel.

Odd how appealing her old staple of beans on toast seemed now, eaten at the kitchen counter, book in one hand, cup of tea right by the other.

'What's so funny?'

Startled, Saskia looked up. She hadn't even heard

Idris come in—but then her rooms were about as private as Piccadilly Circus, an ever-rotating crew of cleaners, florists, stylists, masseuses and aides wandering in and out seemingly at will. 'Funny?'

'You were smiling.'

Were her smiles that rare? She realised with a shock they probably were, especially when he was around. Grateful as she was for the way he seemed to have taken to the boys—and they to him—the past was still too present, too raw, especially after its exhumation on the night of the wedding. She wanted to find a way to be friends, partners, but she couldn't help being wary. She had to protect her bruised heart somehow.

'I was just thinking that only a year ago I would have been happy never to eat beans on toast ever again—and now it sounds like the most delicious meal imaginable.'

'Order it, then. There are plenty of British supermarkets around if the kitchens don't have any in stock. Which they probably don't have,' he added with a superior sneer, which was all French.

'I can't order it, Idris. That's not the point of beans on toast.'

He didn't reply, just raised a sardonic eyebrow and she shut her mouth with a snap, achingly aware of how entitled she sounded before trying again. 'It's not the beans exactly.'

'It's not? That's a relief. The palace chef has earned Michelin stars at three different establishments. If he knew you were yearning for baked beans he would walk out on me.'

'The truth is…' Saskia looked around her, at the gorgeous courtyard in which she sat. Trees shaded the shallow long pool filled with fish, plants growing with an abandon not allowed in the extensively manicured gardens, at the carved wooden benches laden with cushions, the coloured lights that came on with a tap of an app. There was even a large TV screen hidden behind a mosaic if she wanted her own secret cinema experience. 'I'm bored.'

That eyebrow again. One day she would shave it off. That would teach him. 'Bored? You've just had a baby. I thought being a new mother was meant to be tiring and hard. I didn't know there was time to be bored.'

Stay calm, Saskia.

'Most new parents don't have night nannies, day nannies and nursery maids,' she pointed out. 'They are trying to fit in never-ending piles of laundry, buying nappies and snatching sleep. My laundry is done for me, the nursery is equipped with everything Sami needs before I know he needs it, I get more sleep than I ever have before.' She blew out a frustrated breath. 'Listen to me. It's not that I'm not grateful. I got six weeks to rest up and recover and thanks to all the amazing people who have been helping me and taking care of me I actually feel fitter than before I got pregnant. I know how incredibly privileged I am.' She paused, trying to find the right words to express her frustrations.

'For the last seven years I've worked and taken care of Jack and started studying for my degree but now I'm not needed to take Jack to school or make his snack or supervise his homework or make sure he has everything he needs. And I know that I should be relieved to be freed of some of that work but I'm not made to do nothing. I can't even get on with my degree; I didn't register to study online this year because I expected to be back in London by now. And part of me wonders what the point of studying even is if I'm never going to be able to practise anyway.'

Now she had started venting she realised she couldn't stem the words if she wanted to. 'I spend my days working out, letting the stylist tell me what to order and learning about etiquette. The highlight of my day is when Jack gets back from school and I'm not alone any more. Truth is I thought I was hemmed in in that tiny flat of ours but at least I was free to walk out the door whenever I wanted…'

'You're free here.'

'If I take my maid and the guards.'

He didn't deny it. 'It's safer that way.'

'In the palace? In my home? These apartments are gorgeous but I have barely set foot outside them in three months. I need a purpose, Idris.'

'There's time.' To her surprise he walked purposefully across the room and sat on the bench by her side. It was a long, wide bench, made for reclining, it should have been plenty big enough for two, but his proximity made the bench shrink or maybe she, like Alice, had grown bigger. He was dressed in Western clothes, light linen trousers and a short white shirt. Saskia stared at his forearms, at the light smattering of dark hair on olive skin, trying not to remember how it felt when she used to slide her hands along his arms, the strength in every muscle, the way his hands would capture hers. 'We haven't even planned the Coronation yet.'

'The Coronation?' Her stomach contracted at the thought of the pomp and circumstance surrounding such a huge event. At the thought of the publicity. She'd had a tiny taste of notoriety after her father's death; there was nothing like a former society girl brought low to get the paparazzi salivating, and she had no desire to ever be in the spotlight again.

'Normally they hold the official Coronation for the

new monarch directly after the mourning period has finished for the old; it's meant to be a sign of hope after the darkness of grief, but, for several reasons, it was decided to wait for six months this time.'

'What reasons?'

'To give you time to recover from the birth. To give me time to get my business affairs in order. To give Dalmaya time to adjust to me and for me to adjust to living as a King. So if I decided to step aside and let one of my cousins take over—or if they wished to ask me to step aside—then it could be done with as little scandal as possible.'

Of course, this was as big an adjustment for him as it was for her. She forgot that sometimes. Not that he showed it in any way. 'I didn't know you were considering not staying on as King.'

She looked up at him but his gaze was hooded, his eyes giving nothing away. It was frustrating how hard he was to read. 'I hadn't intended to. I always loved being here, thanks to Grandfather, but Dalmaya isn't my home. I'm too Western, too French. He held up his hand, turning it from palm to back as he stared at it. She followed his gaze, her own lingering on the strong, well-shaped hand, the long, elegant fingers, her pulse speeding up. 'Of course in France I was always too dark, too Eastern. Growing up I didn't really fit in anywhere. But I made myself as French as I could be. I restored the chateau, restored the vineyards. Made myself a success. Now I have to start again. Remake myself again.'

'So why don't you go back?' She wanted to add, *Why force me into this marriage?* but managed to stop the words escaping. She didn't want him to revert behind the polite screen again.

'If it was just me then maybe. But Fayaz trusted me to do what was right for his son…'

Despite herself, despite every promise she'd made to herself not to allow herself to feel anything but mild amiability towards Idris, Saskia's heart ached at the desolate tone in his voice.

'So the Coronation is in two months? What does it entail?'

'A day of ceremonies, parades, photos and feasts. I would like you to be involved in helping plan it, especially where the children are concerned. I would like them both, Jack too, to wear traditional dress. After all, he is your family and that makes him mine.'

'Jack? Why does he have to be involved?' Panic rose in her, inexhaustible and painful.

Idris's brow crinkled in puzzlement. 'I thought he would like to be included.'

'But it's public, right? The ceremony. He'll be the focus of attention. People will want to know who he is and why he's there.' Saskia jumped to her feet and began to pace, agitation twisting inside. 'His mother left him because she was no longer being paid to care for him, Idris. And every day for a month, two months, many weeks after that day, I prayed that she would be sorry and she would return for him. And then every day since I've prayed she wouldn't. Because she just *left* him with me, Idris. I have no actual legal guardianship. It didn't occur to me at first that I might need to, and then I couldn't afford it.' She swallowed. 'And I was afraid that if I tried to make him mine, if the authorities realised, then they might think a one-bedroom flat and a sister who worked forty hours a week wasn't a fit environment and take him away from me. But if his mother sees me on TV or in a magazine and realises

Jack is still with me and I have money, or access to it, then she'll be back, I know it.'

'You love him?'

'Of course I love him! I've raised him. He's mine.'

She was a lioness, fierce in her defence of her cub, and Idris couldn't help being a little envious of Jack, that the boy had someone who would always fight for him, always put him first.

He pulled out his phone and punched in a quick message then sat back and watched her pace. Saskia hadn't lied when she said she was in great shape; she might have railed against her recent seclusion but her skin glowed, her hair shone and she looked fit and toned with new, enticing curves. Curves he couldn't drag his eyes away from despite himself. 'It's usual for the King to take a tour of the country after the Coronation, an opportunity to meet all the different types of people who live here from the fishermen to the nomads, and for them to meet him,' he said as if she weren't still stalking up and down, despair flaring in her green eyes.

She halted and swivelled. 'What?'

'A grand tour. I know, it sounds a little medieval and obsolete when even the nomads have smartphones but it's the custom. Only we're going to go on our tour before the Coronation. The Council think it will help ease any fears about my dual nationality—and to be honest I barely know Dalmaya at all, only this palace and the city and the coastline where you were staying. My grandfather always vacationed there. It's important I understand the land a little more before I am formally crowned. We leave on the first leg in a week. My aide has sent yours a list of what you'll need. Your stylist is already working on your wardrobe and your assistant will make sure you're fully briefed.'

'You want me to embark on a grand tour? Are you insane?'

'Not that I know of. I thought,' he added silkily, 'that you were bored. You needed a purpose. Here's your chance. Time to practise being a Queen, Sheikha Saskia.'

'But…but…the boys need me. The last couple of months have been a huge adjustment for Jack and Sami can't even sit up yet. How can I just take off for weeks at a time?'

'No taking off needed. At least not much,' he amended. 'Unlike my ancestors we have access to cars and planes and helicopters. We may need to be away for a night or two here and there but mostly we can fit each visit in in a day. It will mean early starts and late nights but you said yourself you're well rested and raring to go.'

'A few nights? Will we have our own rooms during those nights?'

He stilled. Nobody at the palace thought it odd that Saskia was housed so far away from his own quarters. Fayaz and Maya had shared a suite but his grandfather had always had separate rooms from his grandmother and *his* father had had several wives, each with their own distinct quarters.

On the tour Saskia and he would be visiting and staying in places far more humble than the palace and in this day, this age, people would expect their French King-to-be and his English wife to sleep in the same room.

His throat tightened. He had told her that her honour was safe with him and the implication had been clear—

separate rooms, separate beds. He hadn't fully realised the implications for either of them.

The thought of housing a discreet mistress somewhere chilled him. As for Saskia, did he really expect her to opt for a life of chastity? As Queen, the standards expected of her rightly or wrongly were higher, harder, the judgements harsher. The people would turn a blind eye to any extracurricular activity Idris might choose to indulge in. Saskia would be disgraced for ever.

A sudden pain in his palms surprised him and he glanced at his hands; he hadn't realised that his hands had curled into fists until his fingernails dug into his palms. He didn't want her turning elsewhere, to somebody else. 'I don't know any of the details yet.'

'But…' She paused, lips compressed, as his aide bustled in, two folders in his arms. He passed them to Idris with a bow, then bowed towards Saskia before backing away. Saskia eyed the folders. 'What're they?'

'Answers. To some of your questions at least.' He put the blue folder down on the bench beside him and held out the green one. 'Here.'

Cautiously she took it, flicking it open. 'What's this? I don't understand.'

'The palace needs to be aware of any possible problems, Saskia. They've been monitoring my mother from the day she eloped. They've probably monitored me as well, although no one will give me a straight answer about that. And now you bring a new family into the mix and it's a complicated one. Your father left a trail of headlines. Well, we can counter that with the fact you've spent the last seven years living quietly and working hard. But your mother? Jack's mother? Jack's existence? They're more problematic.'

'So you tracked them down? I could have told you

where my mother was.' She dropped the green folder contemptuously onto his knee but her eyes flickered to the blue folder and he knew she wanted—needed—to see the contents. 'She runs a yoga retreat in New Mexico, along with her third husband. She says she has achieved inner peace. That was why she didn't want me to come over when it all happened. Too much negative energy surrounded me apparently.' She was going for scathing, pretending she didn't care, but the hurt in her eyes was unmistakable.

'She's no worry to us at all. Your stepfather…'

'I've never met him. He's no father to me in any way.'

Idris paused. 'Her husband,' he amended, 'has some wild ideas. He's written several books about UFO sightings and aliens amongst us but seems harmless. We won't be inviting them to the Coronation.' He looked at Saskia to see how she would take the news but she didn't as much as nod.

'Of course not. She walked out of my life when I was three and never walked back in again. She doesn't even send me a birthday card most years.'

'This is what we compiled on Jack's mother.'

Her composure crumpled, her hand shaking as she took the folder from him. 'I used to wonder what kind of woman had a child for money. Until I became that woman.'

His own words echoed back at him. He knew better now. 'The situations don't compare. Besides, you didn't raise Jack for money.'

'No,' she said hollowly. 'You know, Rosa was with my father for four years yet I didn't even know she existed. He bought her a house, made her an allowance but she didn't accompany him to functions or meet his friends. What kind of person is happy in that kind of second-rate relationship? She said she didn't mean to get pregnant but Daddy was delighted when she did. Persuaded her to have the baby, promised her he would look after her if she did. But he still didn't marry her. Didn't live with Jack, help raise him, not properly. Just visited. I didn't even know I had a brother until after my father died. I think that hurt more than anything else.'

He nodded at the file. 'Go on. Open it.'

Her hands shook as she flipped the folder open and then she hissed a long breath. He knew what she saw. The portrait. A family portrait. Rosa with her much older husband, a baby in her arms, a toddler by her side. 'She has more children?'

'She married well. Very well. That's Chuck Weissberger, multimillionaire retail King. They live in Connecticut in a riverside mansion.'

'She got her rich husband after all,' Saskia said tonelessly, still staring at the contents of the folder.

'She did. And he has no idea about Jack. He's very family orientated. If he knew she had abandoned a child that marriage would be over quicker than she could beg for forgiveness. She's not coming anywhere near Jack, Saskia. He's safe. My lawyers are petitioning for us to legally adopt him right now. Rosa signed the papers last week. I was going to get you a horse as a wedding present but I thought you might appreciate this more.'

The folder fell out of her hands, the contents spilling onto the mosaic floor. 'I...you...what did you say?'

'The adoption proceedings are going through. It does mean I will legally be Jack's father. As we are married it would have been too complicated to apply in just your name.' From a single, child-free businessman and winemaker to a married father of two and King in one step. From simple Monsieur Delacour to Sheikh Idris Delacour Al Osman, ruler of all he surveyed. The thought wasn't as terrifying as it had been several months ago.

'But how? I don't understand.'

'Rosa has signed a deposition to say you had been Jack's primary caregiver for seven years and giving up her parental rights and we have statements from Jack's old school in London, his childminder and your neighbours. The lawyers don't anticipate any problems. They obviously need to interview you—and me as well. We'll all fly back to the UK in a month for the final interviews.'

It had all seemed so simple when he'd put this in motion. The first day he had spent with Jack, the day of Sami's birth, it had been painfully apparent that mixed in with the boy's worry about Saskia, excitement about the baby and the thrill of discovering the palace and his first riding lesson, Jack had also been harbouring deep fears that a baby of her own might alter his own special relationship with the only mother he had ever really known. For seven years it had been just the two of them—now Jack found himself in a family of four. And something in the boy had struck a chord. Idris knew what it was like to be a child and unsure of your place in the world, in your family, that fear that everything and everyone could just disappear.

If there was anything Idris excelled in it was solving problems and the solution here seemed so simple. They were already a made-up family. All they needed to do was cement Jack's place. But now, looking at Saskia's white face, he couldn't help but wonder if he had overstepped. He wasn't really Saskia's husband, Jack wasn't his brother and they weren't a family. They were a glossy PR exercise.

'I thought,' he said carefully, 'that this was the right

thing to do.' Legitimising Jack's presence in her life made things easier for him, for the crown, but it was also his way of making amends for forcing her into a life she had never asked for.

Her face crumpled. 'I… Oh, Idris, thank you.' She threw her arms around his neck, his shirt clinging damply as her tears began to flow. All he could do was put his arms around her and hold her while she wept. Hold her and try not to notice how good she smelt, like night-flowering jasmine, how her body melded into his as if it belonged there, the silkiness of her hair on his cheek. Try not to remember that this was the closest he had physically been to another human being for longer than he cared to remember. Tried not to remember how she used to feel in his arms, how he had once made her gasp. How she had made him feel invincible, an intoxication he had fought and lost against over and over. All he had to do was hold on.

CHAPTER EIGHT

TEARS WERE A PRIVATE, shameful indulgence. They had been ever since her father's death, since the moment she left Idris's apartment with nowhere else to turn.

But now she'd allowed that first tear to fall. Now someone else was holding her up. Now arms were around her, a strong shoulder supporting her. Now for the first time in many, many years someone else had taken part of her burden and it undid her.

Saskia shuddered as great, racking sobs forced their way out: grief for Maya and Fayaz, wistfulness for the life she had planned and would never now live, guilt at how much, how very much she loved Sami, a love she knew Maya would be grateful for and yet that somehow felt like a betrayal.

Fear for the long years ahead, Queen of a country she didn't know. Worry at being married to a man she barely knew and yet knew all too well. And now gratitude. This man she'd thought didn't know her at all had realised the dearest wish of all. Jack was hers, always. Rosa didn't want him, wouldn't take him away. And the rest of his childhood would be safe and happy and filled with security.

She was barely aware of Idris's hand on her back, moving in slow, comforting circles, of his mouth pressed into her hair telling her softly that it was okay, that it was all going to be okay. She was barely aware of the solid strength of him, of the way she fitted right into him, of his subtle sandalwood scent. Barely aware until, with a gulp, the sobs began to subside and then, then she was all too aware. Each circular caress burning hotter and hotter, the touch of his mouth branding her, every nerve firing up at the feel of his fingers. She tensed, regretting it immediately as his hand stopped its torturous caress, as he lifted his head away from hers, stepped away. The absence of his touch a physical ache.

'Feeling better?' His voice was low, hoarse. Had he felt it too? That connection? Or was he just being kind, desperate to grab his folders and escape his hysterical wife?

'No.' She wasn't sure what she was doing—although she was aware she was probably making a terrible mistake. But she also knew that she was desperately lonely. Had been for a long, long time and here in this palace, surrounded by people, in almost unimaginable luxury, with two beautiful, healthy children, she was lonelier than she had ever been before. She knew that she felt safer than she had for a long time while in his embrace. She knew that she craved human contact. Touch. Idris's touch.

She'd sworn she would never be vulnerable again. Not in front of Idris, not in front of any other human. Sworn she would never let him reject her again. But looking at the suppressed need in his dark eyes, she was certain that he wouldn't reject her. Certain that he craved her touch as much as she craved his.

'No? I'll call your maid. Maybe a massage and a nap will help.' He took a step away but Saskia caught his hand as he turned, her fingers sliding into his so easily it was as if they were meant to be there.

'I don't want a massage. Or at least,' she amended, 'not from my maid.'

'You don't…' With primal satisfaction she noted his eyes flare as he took in her meaning. 'What *do* you want, then?'

'We're married, Idris. We have two children. You want me to accompany you on this grand tour, stand beside you at your Coronation.'

'Our Coronation,' he said huskily, his eyes fixed on hers.

She moved a little closer. 'Yes.'

'You didn't answer, Saskia. What do you want?'

'I want to remember what it's like being me. Who Saskia is. Not a mother, not a consort. I want to feel like a woman again.' She lifted her gaze to his, emboldened by the passion smouldering in his dark gaze. 'It's been a long time, Idris. Help me remember.'

He didn't answer straight away and Saskia held her breath. If he rejected her again…she kept her eyes fixed on his and saw the moment the flames burst into life, a bare second before his fingers tightened around hers. 'Are you sure?'

'Stop asking me stupid questions and kiss me already,' she retorted with a smile, but he didn't return the smile, just stared at her consideringly, an intense look in which she felt as if the clothes had already been stripped from her body and that she were laid bare before him.

'*Non*, not yet.'

Rejection slammed into her, hard and painful and all-consuming, but before she could turn away he had pulled her in close. 'I thought you wanted a massage.'

She froze, need pulling at her. Devouring from the inside out. 'I...'

Now he smiled, slow and triumphant. 'I asked you if you wanted a massage, Saskia, and you said—correct me if I get the words wrong—you said *not from my maid*. From which I deduce that you do want a massage. Am I right?'

Her mouth was so dry she could barely speak, her insides a quivering mass of want. She summoned every vestige of sass remaining. 'Are you offering?'

'Think you can handle it?'

'I'm sure I can handle a massage, Idris.' The gauntlet was well and truly thrown down and she quivered with anticipation as Idris drew a finger slowly down her cheek.

'Are you sure about that?' But he didn't give her time to answer; still holding her hand, he turned, leading her out of the courtyard and into her pretty bedroom, not hurrying, every step utterly precise. Saskia caught her breath as she caught sight of her bed, huge, perfectly made and suddenly looming larger than life. But Idris ignored the bed, leading her into her dressing room, a space bigger than the kitchen/diner/living space in her old apartment. Half the room was taken up with her dressing table and walk-in wardrobes, the other with a professional hairdresser's sink and chair—and the massage couch. She swallowed as she looked at the innocuous-looking platform, half covered with a white sheet.

Idris took one of the fresh, folded towels from the pile next to the table and carelessly laid it out over the sheet before turning back to her. 'Okay,' he said. 'Strip.'

Saskia folded her arms. 'Turn your back.'

His eyes gleamed. 'I don't think so.'

She hoped he didn't see her hands shaking as she

raised them to the first button on her dress. Slowly she undid it then stilled as she reached the second. She couldn't do this, couldn't undress in front of him, not while he stood waiting, watching.

'Changed your mind?' he asked softly.

Tilting her chin, she undid the second button. 'No.' Then the third, then the fourth. She wore a yellow silk maxi dress, which buttoned up the front from the waist to her throat, and as she reached the fifth button and the fabric fell away to reveal the silk of her bra, the flesh spilling out over the cups, desire washed over his face, Idris's eyes flaring. And then she understood, then she knew. She had all the control here. She kept her gaze on his as she slowly, deliberately unfastened the last buttons then shrugged the straps off her shoulders and let the dress crumple, falling in folds at her feet.

She stepped out of it, reaching behind her, not allowing her gaze to falter as she unhooked her bra and, clad only in her bikini pants, strolled slowly over to the table. She knew his gaze was fastened on her, knew his breath was coming faster as she straddled the table, slowly lowering onto it, her head cushioned on her arms, her back and legs bare to him, just the wisp of peach silk barely covering the curve of her bottom.

She had no idea how she managed to lie so still, so nonchalant, eyes closed. She heard footsteps as he crossed over to the shelf where her oils were kept, then the fragrance of her favourite jasmine, bergamot and rose blend wafted through the room. She swallowed, her insides quivering as his steps slowly but surely neared the table, the silence as he reached her side almost too much to bear. She waited for four or five excruciating, timeless seconds before he touched her, a light line drawn from her neck to the base of her spine and, de-

spite her best endeavours to stay cool, she shivered at
his touch, His laugh was low and triumphant as she
reacted. Another line tracing back along the first before his hands moved to her shoulders and he began
to knead.

A massage was supposed to relax and unknot, but
every inch he touched tensed up with need, her skin
burning under his clever fingers. Saskia buried her head
deeper in her arm to try and stifle the moans his touch
elicited. He touched nowhere her masseuse wouldn't
touch, his movements precise and measured; all her
senses were concentrated on his every move until she
knew she couldn't play this game any longer. She turned
and sat up, winding her arms around his neck, pulling
him in, pulling him close, hungry for his kiss, hungry
for his touch, hungry for him. And with a guttural moan
he obliged, picking her up, his mouth on hers and carrying her through to the bedroom. Saskia knew there
were one hundred reasons why this was a bad idea, one
hundred reasons why she needed to safeguard her heart;
recklessly she pushed them all to one side because right
here, right now, this was all that mattered. She needed
to feel, she needed to not be alone, she needed to be
wanted, to be noticed, and under his mouth and hands
she finally came alive.

Idris disembarked from the helicopter, scanning the
desert until he saw Saskia standing under a canvas shelter on one side of the palm-tree-fringed, sandy landing
strip. It was as if they were in the middle of nowhere.

It was noticeably hotter out here. Although Jayah
was twenty miles inland it was built on either side of
the wide tidal River Kizaj and so, although it didn't
benefit from the sea breezes that kept much of the coast

at a bearable temperature, it was usually manageable except during the very height of summer. The heat in the desert was more oppressive, a visible shimmering wall, and Idris was glad he had opted for the coolness of traditional robes, a headdress protecting his head and eyes from the sun's glare. Saskia was also traditionally dressed in long, loose gold trousers in a light fabric, over which she wore a long-sleeved cream and gold tunic, a matching scarf wrapped around her head. Her maid stood by, a bag filled with water, moist towels and suncream at her feet. While preparing for the trip there had been some concern over Saskia's fitness to cope in the desert, her red hair and pale skin designed for the cold, sun-starved, northern European climate, not the relentless sun. But she would have to endure if she was to be accepted.

She didn't ask for this, his conscience whispered, but he pushed it to one side. Neither of them had asked for it but here they were. They had to deal as best they could.

He moved to her side and their guards and attendants fell in behind them as, on cue, a group of people on horseback emerged from behind the trees and dismounted. A middle-aged man in bright robes strode towards them and bowed his head. The nomads were a proud people who traditionally recognised neither borders nor rulers, although pragmatically accepted the Dalmaya's sovereign rule. Idris and Saskia nodded in response, a polite acceptance of his role as leader of his tribe.

'*Mahajan*, Your Highness Sheikh Idris Delacour Al Osman, Princess Saskia,' he said.

Idris knew the tribal leader had studied in France and England and spoke both languages perfectly. '*Salam*,

Badr Al Bedi. Thank you and your people for offering us your hospitality,' he replied.

'Come, we have horses for you. Let us ride and talk as we go. We have much to discuss.'

'It is an honour to be asked to ride your fine horses. The mounts of the Al Bedis are coveted across the world,' Saskia said, and by the beaming smile she received in response Idris knew she couldn't have said anything better.

Two hours later he was even more impressed. Saskia had obviously read all the briefing documents and managed to keep up in the general conversation. Old topics such as grazing rights, territorial disputes and minority rights were touched on and Saskia showed that she was aware of the history and disputes, with a knack of acknowledging the issues and then deftly turning the conversation to something less contentious. She would have made a good lawyer.

The Al Bedi weren't continuously on the move, often making camp for weeks or even months at a time while smaller trading parties journeyed to the bigger cities and coasts, especially during the hotter summer months. Badr Al Bedi explained that they would spend the first day riding to the large summer camp, where his own family had sheltered during the summer. Now they had reached the last days of September the camp would soon be dispersing, the feast tonight the last in that particular spot.

Tomorrow Idris and Saskia would accompany a trading party who were taking a group of horses to the nearest town. The town was two days' ride away from the camp and Idris, Saskia and their entourage would be picked up from there. The first stage of their Royal Tour would be completed.

'It's a good thing,' Idris said quietly to Saskia, 'that you're not vegetarian. We're being honoured with lamb tonight. It's a dish always served to honoured guests.'

They were just arriving at an oasis for a rest stop and water. Saskia and Idris were slightly ahead of the group, their host falling behind to check on some detail, their entourage and most of their personal guard trailing behind, although Idris knew several guards had ridden ahead and to the side of the main group. He might not be able to see them but they would have a very clear idea of where he was while keeping an eye out for any possible threat.

Saskia laughed at his words. 'Actually I did eat a mainly vegetarian diet for most of the last few years, though that was mainly for financial reasons, but that very thorough surrogate agreement was very clear that I needed to be a carnivore until Sami was weaned. I don't miss meat when I don't eat it, but I'm not going to turn down a feast cooked in my honour either.'

'I hope you feel the same way when they present you with the yogurt. It's very much an acquired taste. Of course, you can sweeten it with honey but a true warrior takes his—or her—yogurt straight.'

'I'm sure I can…oh!' Saskia broke off in alarm as her horse danced backwards. Luckily her grip hadn't been too loose on the reins and she managed, somehow, to keep her seat as the beast neighed and then reared, its front legs kicking out. 'Whoa, come on, boy.'

But Idris's own horse had also taken a step backwards and he could see quite clearly what had spooked Saskia's mount. A viper of some type must have been dozing in the shadow of the tree and been disturbed by the horse's footsteps. It was half coiled, half upright, swaying from side to side, fangs clearly exposed. Idris couldn't tell who was more scared, the snake or the horse—or who was likely to do most damage.

'Whoa!' The horse reared again and Saskia fought to stay on. Idris's heart thumped, adrenaline running through his veins as he assessed the risks. If the viper bit the horse Saskia might fall; if she managed to dismount safely then she would be directly in front of the angry snake. Could he manoeuvre his horse over and take the reins safely or would he just spook his own horse and make matters worse? He looked behind. They were further ahead than he had realised and although several horses were galloping towards them there was a real possibility they wouldn't reach the group in time.

Saskia was still hanging on, her lips white and her face pale but determined as she battled the terrified horse, the snake hissing louder, pulling itself up further, weaving closer and closer. Idris pulled his own pistol from its holster; the pistol he had baulked at wearing when it had been issued to him, and pointed it at the snake, his hand steady despite his thundering pulse. If he missed the even more terrified snake would strike. If he killed the snake then possibly both his mount and Saskia's would bolt. He checked again. It would be at least thirty seconds before the head horseman reached them and the snake was swaying in...

'Idris. Do it. I have this.' Her voice was low and tense, her grip hardening on the already panicked horse's reins.

He inhaled, concentrated—and shot. Time slowed down to an unbearable lassitude, the sound of the pistol reverberating around and around and all he could do was take his own mount in a firm hand and wait and hope and pray... The snake buckled then collapsed and

Saskia's horse, maddened beyond any control, took off, Saskia clinging grimly on.

He swore and dug his heels in, urging his own horse after her, Badr Al Bedi and several of the palace guards close behind him as they chased the terrified mount across the sands. Saskia was hunkered down low, obviously concentrating on staying on rather than trying to check her horse. 'Just hold on,' Idris muttered as he urged his horse on. 'Hold tight.'

What if something happened to her? How would he tell Jack? How would he raise Sami, made motherless twice before he was even able to speak? How would he be able to raise two boys and govern this harsh, beautiful country on his own? He might not have chosen Saskia but she was his partner now—in every way— and he didn't want to take this journey alone.

His blood thundered as her horse increased his pace. She'd only just come back into his life. He wasn't ready to lose her again. Not yet.

She was close, so close, any moment now he might be able to grab the reins and help slow her horse. But at that moment her horse tripped, twisted and, with a sickening yell that froze his blood, Saskia fell, rolled and lay crumpled in the sand.

CHAPTER NINE

'I FEEL LIKE a prize idiot.' Saskia stared down at her strapped ankle and winced. If pride came before a fall then humility was the result of one—humility along with a sprained ankle and many bruises. 'And I've ruined the whole visit. Badr is embarrassed and I can't go to the feast and...'

Idris held up a hand and Saskia stuttered to a stop, both surprised by his high-handed manner and more than a little indignant.

'You have ruined nothing. In fact, right now, several ballads are being composed about the flame-haired Queen who rides like a warrior...'

'...and who falls like a fool.' Now the adrenaline had faded away the realisation of how close she had been to something much worse than a sprained ankle and bruises shivered at the edge of her consciousness. Much better to concentrate on embarrassment than near death.

Luckily she hadn't been unconscious for long. She'd come to blearily to find herself cradled in a pair of strong arms. Cradled by Idris. Had blinked to see the fear on his face, fear that had quickly drained away, replaced by the same calm, shuttered look he habitually wore—unless he was with the boys. Or unless they were in bed.

'I didn't think self-pity was one of the signs of concussion.' Idris held up his phone so she could see the medical website he was referring to. 'But if it is we need a helicopter out here immediately. You are obviously in a bad way. I think we should get one anyway,' he said for the tenth time in the last hour.

'I'm fine. Honestly. My shoulder and leg got most of the impact. Thank goodness I remembered all my pony club training and insisted on wearing a riding hat. I know you thought I was in more danger of heat stroke than I was of falling off but this way I got to suffer two in one.' The hat had been almost suffocating and only pride—and a childhood in which the importance of wearing a riding helmet had been drilled into her—had kept it on her head. Thank goodness she had; although there was a definite tender spot on her scalp she was sure that she had got away without any serious injury. 'Idris. It's bad enough I had to ride to the camp behind you on your horse like a child. Bad enough that I've been told to eat soup and have an early night and miss everything that was organised in our honour. If I get helicoptered out of here, two days early, then people are going to think I can't hack the desert life here. That I'm not fit for this role.'

'No one who saw you handle that horse would ever say you weren't fit. The Al Badi would love to claim you as one of them. The first thing we need to do when we get back is get you a mount of your own. You are far too good a horsewoman to go without.'

Well, they did always say to get right back on a horse. As a girl she'd been fearless, the higher the jump, the wider the ditch, the better, never thinking anything of heading straight into the stable no matter the horse's temperament. Today she realised just how mortal she

really was. The thought of getting back into the saddle—
of allowing Jack to have another riding lesson—made
her chest swell with panic and her stomach drop, fear
breaking out like perspiration. But horse racing and
horse breeding were national passions—and a significant part of the Dalmayan economy—and if she was to
have a role and a life here then one fall couldn't stop her.

She stretched out and winced again. Idris and she
had been housed in a beautiful white canvas tent, held
up by two poles, the inside draped in gorgeous orange
and red silk matched by the intricately woven rugs that
covered the floor and the cushions heaped on the low
couches and the wide bed. Intricately carved tables
housed lanterns; jugs of chilled water and bowls of fruit
were dotted around the interior. It was all very inviting and usually she would have been utterly charmed.
As they had ridden in she had noticed that the tents
all ringed a large central square, covered over with a
huge canopy, a fire pit prepared in the middle and surrounded by seats. All set up for the feast and festivi-
ties. The spicy smells emanating from the cooking tents
made her mouth water and her stomach rumble and the
thought of bland soup failed to lift her spirits.

'Idris, I don't need you here keeping an eye on me.
Go out and enjoy the lamb and the songs and the fire.
It's not like I'm far away. It seems a shame that they
went to such an effort and for one of us not to attend.
And you said yourself that things have been tense between the crown and the Al Bedi for many years, since
your grandfather's reforms. This is a good chance for
you to start off in a more positive way. I'll be fine. I have
soup coming, after all.' She tried to smile and, after a
searching look at her, Idris nodded.

'You're right. I know Badr takes this whole accident

personally. It would be good to show him that we are not holding him to blame.'

'It's not like he planted the snake there.' She managed not to shudder when she said the word. Saskia hadn't ever had any phobias before but she was pretty sure she was going to see that particular snake in her nightmares.

'No, but the horse should have been better trained.' Idris sounded grim and she looked up.

'That was pure instinct, Idris. He was a perfect gent up to that part. In fact...' She swallowed. Along with snakes she would be quite happy never to see that particular grey stallion again. But this wasn't about her. It was about diplomacy, about a proud man, about a country. 'I would like him. As my own.'

Idris stared at her incredulously. 'Are you insane?'

Possibly. 'He was on his way to market so let's buy him. Just think how proud Badr, how proud the whole tribe will be if they see him on TV or in a magazine. Knowing he's in the royal stables. My first real contact with Dalmaya.'

'They'll never let you buy him. They'll insist he's a present.'

'If they do, then we'll accept.'

Idris stood, obviously torn between accepting that she made sense and an understandable desire not to allow any of the family near the horse again before agreeing with a curt nod. 'I'll talk to Badr. But tomorrow you ride pillion behind me again. No arguing or I will definitely call a helicopter.' And with that he was gone.

The evening passed slowly. Saskia's head throbbed, her ankle ached and every bruise was making its presence felt in its own unique way. The soup had been delicious although she really hadn't been hungry at all once she started to eat but, under the solicitous gaze of the local healer, she managed to finish the bowl and eat some of the flatbread as well. The sounds of laughter and music drifted into the tent and, lulled by the sound, she drifted into sleep.

The sound of the tent unfastening woke her and she looked up to see Idris undressing by the light of the lantern. The shadows played on his back, highlighting his slim muscles, the dips and hollows in his back, and she swallowed. He was so ridiculously attractive. How could she keep her heart safe when his nearness made her tremble, her name on his lips made her ache? When just the sight of him half naked and unaware made her forget every bruise?

She shifted and he turned, his eyes black pools in the darkness. '*Pardon*, Saskia. I didn't mean to wake you.'

'You didn't. I wake every time I turn over.'

'I think it's best that I sleep over here.' He gestured to one of the low couches and Saskia felt that old ache of rejection spread out from her chest, chilling her bones. He was willing to have sex with her but sleeping together was an intimacy too far. In the palace it kind of made sense for him to return to his own room. Maybe. But out here?

'It's very narrow,' she pointed out, trying to sound non-committal, as if she really didn't care one way or the other. Of course she shouldn't care… 'If you fall off and hurt yourself we'll both be riding pillion. It's not going to be very kingly when you show up at the trading post tucked up behind Badr, is it?'

He scowled. 'I don't want to hurt you.'

'Idris, this bed is big enough for four. But we can put a pillow down the middle if you would feel safer,' she added sweetly, and the scowl intensified as he stalked towards the bed and climbed in. Saskia held her breath. She often shared a bed with Jack, at least she had done before getting pregnant, but she hadn't slept beside another adult—beside a man—since Idris all those years ago. Here they were again.

'You're sure I'm not hurting you?'

'There's at least a metre of space between us,' she said. 'You may be overestimating your masculine powers.'

To her surprise he chuckled, low and deep. 'It's a good thing you're injured or I'd make you regret that.'

Could it be her husband was actually flirting with her? Flirting knowing that there was no way they would be having sex as a result? *Probably* no way they would be having sex. She flexed her ankle and only just managed not to yelp as a jolt of agony ran through her. No, make that definitely no way. 'Promises, promises.'

Saskia turned on her side and faced away from Idris but the drowsiness had ebbed. She was all too achingly aware of him despite the space between them; the slope in the mattress, the sound of his even breath, the scent of him. She swallowed, want racing through her hot and sudden, the throbbing of her bruises replaced by the steady thrum of her heart, the ache in her breasts, the pull deep at the base of her stomach. It was just good old lust, a biological imperative, she knew that. She'd been without a mate too long and now she had started sleeping with Idris her body was urging her on. Evolutionary science at its most basic. But thinking scientific thoughts wasn't calming her hormones; they were continuing to jump around like excited cheerleaders urging her to cuddle in closer, urging her to 'go on, reach out and touch him…' She turned over, lifting a hand then dropping it. It was late. She was supposed to be staying quiet and getting some rest.

With a huff she turned back over, wincing as she landed on a bruise, and grabbed the thin pillow, punching it to try and get some more support.

'Trouble sleeping?' Idris drawled, sounding like a man who had never suffered a restless night in his life.

'No,' she lied. 'I'm fine. It's just…' She paused. She didn't want to sound like a whiny girl and admit every bruise was making itself felt and her ankle was tight and seemed to be three times its usual size. 'I'm a soft European who needs something more than a thin bolster for a pillow,' she said instead. 'It's hard to get comfortable.'

There was a long pause and all she could hear was the frantic thump of her heart until: 'Come here, then,' and she heard the unmistakable sounds of Idris shifting across to the middle of the bed. She scooted back a few inches until she collided with the solid wall of his body, heat instantly enveloping her, a heady mixture of body warmth and those pesky hormones brightening even more at the realisation he was bare-chested. A strong, bare arm slipped around her neck, another across her stomach. 'Better?'

'Uh-huh,' she said unconvincingly even to herself.

That laugh again, low and rumbling right through her until every atom quivered. 'Still not comfortable?'

'Well…' But whatever she was about to say was lost as Idris swept aside the fall of her hair and pressed one kiss to the back of her neck.

'Does this help?'

'Maybe a little…'

'Then maybe this…' another kiss, just below her ear '…will help a little more.'

'Mmm, just a little bit.'

'And here?' This time the hollow between her neck and shoulder. She shivered and felt his amusement reverberating through her. Amusement tinged with something more dangerous. 'Of course, you are an invalid. Tell me if it gets too much.'

'I think I can cope with a little more.' Saskia arched against him as his mouth found the delicate skin behind her ear, his breath sweet and warm and, oh, so tantalising. 'In fact this is definitely making me feel better…'

'In that case…' his hand slid up her waist to graze the tender swell of her breast '…I think it's best that I carry on, don't you?'

Saskia was awake again and, judging by the jerkiness of her movements, in some discomfort. Should he have overridden her wishes and called a helicopter to whisk her back to Jayah? The moment Idris had seen her crumpled and still in the sand, that damn horse racing away from her… His pulse escalated at the too-recent memory, at the fear that had taken over as he had raced towards her. Understandable fear: he had just lost his cousin; he was responsible for Saskia's presence in the desert, for her safety; she had two children dependent on her…but there had been something else behind that mad dash, a thought he hadn't been able to banish.

I've just found you again.

Which was ridiculous. He had never lost her in the first place; he had chosen to exclude her from his life.

He sighed. It didn't matter how much he justified his actions back then. It didn't matter that he had made the right decision at the wrong time and in the wrong way, he was still shamed whenever he thought about that last night in Oxford. It said a lot, a hell of a lot, about Saskia that she didn't hold it against him, that she was willing to be not just a trophy wife in a loveless marriage but a partner, that she didn't want to spend her life shopping and living a privileged expat dream but wanted to find a role that stretched her and gave back to the country she now lived in.

She shifted again, this time letting out a small, hastily smothered cry and Idris was out of the bed in one stride, heading over to the water jug to bring a glass over to her. He moved back to the bed, sitting by her side, helping her sit up. The tent was dim in the predawn grey but he could see that her sweat-soaked hair was pressed to her scalp, that her eyes were huge and fatigued with pain.

'Here.' He passed her the glass and she accepted it with a wan smile of thanks. Idris touched a hand to her cheek and was relieved to find it cool. At least she had no fever.

'I really think…'

'No, no helicopter.' She drank again and passed the glass back to him, lowering herself against the thin bolster with a grunt. 'I just don't want to slow the caravan down too much.'

'Don't worry about that. Can I get you anything else?'

'That glass, next to the fruit bowl. It's got some kind of natural painkiller in.'

He reached out and scooped it up, nose wrinkling as he sniffed the cloudy liquid. 'Are you sure this is safe?'

'Alya, the healer here, is a qualified nurse as well as a traditional healer. It's fine. Disgusting but works miracles. Not that I enquired too closely what was in it.' She downed the contents of the glass and pulled a face. 'Ugh. Anything that tastes that nasty has to be good for me, surely.'

He half smiled, watching her as she drank. 'As predicted Badr insists on gifting you the horse, although I want it put through its paces by the best trainers at the stables before you go anywhere near it again. We can't run the risk of it throwing you again.'

'There's always a risk, Idris. Horses, cars—we know that more than anyone.' She was silent for a moment and he thought she was falling back asleep but then she turned to face him, eyes still too wide, too shadowed but her face more relaxed, the drawn expression of pain softened. 'You know, the nearest clinic is a day's ride away. Alya works between there, here and another clinic three days' ride in the other direction.'

'Hmm?'

'That's where the schools are too. She says the children do a lot of learning remotely when they're between schools and she diagnoses a lot through video calling. It's odd, isn't it? No cars and living in tents but everyone has a smartphone.'

'It's the way of the world.' Where was she going with this? It didn't sound like idle conversation. There was a spark in Saskia's eyes he hadn't seen for a long time.

'She's the only qualified midwife as well. She says most of the women give birth in special tents, attended by traditionally taught women. Mortality rates are higher than in the cities because there's no way to get them to hospital when things go wrong. Alya lost her own baby just a year ago, a miscarriage that might have been prevented if she'd got to a hospital in time...'

'It's a tragedy, I admit, but this is a nomadic tribe. Clinging onto tradition means tragedies happen. It's the price they choose to pay. Dalmaya is a big country and there are huge swathes where there is very little approaching civilisation—or at least the trappings of it.'

'That was pretty much Alya's answer. That these things happen. But if I had concussion or had broken my leg then we wouldn't have left that to fate, would we? You wanted to call a helicopter in for a sprained ankle and a few bruises!'

'I still want to call a helicopter to make sure that's all that it is.'

'If there's a helicopter for me then why not for Alya and her patients? To get people to clinic in minutes, not days, to hospital if the clinic can't manage, to transport her and the one other nurse out to patients?'

Idris couldn't answer. Money? Dalmaya was a rich country. 'Tradition, I suppose.'

'Tradition stated that girls stayed at home and didn't go to school, let alone university—and your grandfather's edicts may have worked in the cities but not out here in the desert. Luckily Alya's father indulged her and allowed her to study and now, thanks to the Internet, all Al Bedi girls are educated and any that wish to study further have the freedom to go on to college. True, most prefer to stay at home but at least they have that choice. Technology helps girls get to school. Why can't it help with medical emergencies? Beyond a videocall diagnosis, I mean. The Al Bedis contribute a lot to Dalmayan culture—the horses, the tourist camps. We should give something back. Something of value. Lifesaving medical help shouldn't be restricted to princesses by marriage.'

Slowly Idris got to his feet, looking around at the tent, now illuminated in the pinks and reds of a desert sunrise. It all looked so traditional but the bed easily pulled apart for transportation. The glasses were made in China and bought from a Swedish furniture store. The Al Bedi might seem unchanging but they knew how to incorporate what they needed from the modern world to keep their traditional life viable. Allow their girls to study and bring their expertise back to the tribe, welcome tourists and by doing so safeguard their freedoms and their lands.

His grandfather, educated at Oxford and the Sorbonne, had been full of reformist zeal. He had taken the oil money and invested it, not into a lavish lifestyle for a few, but into a new Dalmaya. Invested it into schools and hospitals and opportunities for all who wanted to take advantage of it. But like all reformists he had been iron-willed and impatient of those who didn't see his vision—and the Al Bedi had not been the only ones who had rejected his Western influences to modernise at a slower pace. Fayaz had been King for too short a time to break the coldness between the throne and the nomads. Could this idea, a flying medical service, be the thing to bring them properly onside? Badr too was new to leadership and far more conciliatory than his father had been…

And Saskia had complained of being bored. This idea of hers could solve two problems before they were even formally crowned.

He turned and looked at her, still obviously sore but lit up with enthusiasm. 'How do you know all this? About the healer…'

'Alya.'

'She was with you for what, an hour? Working for most of that. And yet you seem to know her life history!' It would usually take Idris months if not years to work up to that level of personal detail. 'And it isn't just Alya. You were incredibly well prepared when you were introduced to Badr, not just about the right way to be introduced, but you asked all the right questions, had him charmed within an hour.'

'I read the briefing documents,' she said then smiled. 'Look, I admit that when you knew me before I may have come across as a little self-absorbed.' He raised an eyebrow and she coloured but carried on. 'Of course I was. I was an only child, doted upon by a dad who gave me everything I wanted before I knew I wanted it, raised to think I was the most fascinating, desirable, interesting person in the world.'

It should have made her unbearable, yet that confidence, that utter sureness in herself had been self-fulfilling. Everyone had wanted to know her, the girls had wanted to be her friend, the boys had all wanted to sleep with her.

'It was a shock when I started temping. No one cares about a temp. They want you to be up to speed straight away and to blend in. That's it. I blundered around my first few jobs acting—thinking—like photocopying was below me—even though I had no idea how to use the machine—that I was too good to make coffee and people should be falling over themselves to help me. A few bruising encounters showed me how wrong I was. And I soon realised that to get the good jobs, I had to be the best. Be prepared, do my homework, cause as few problems as possible and solve as many as possible. Be so indispensable they want you back.'

'So that's what you did.' It wasn't a question.

'It wasn't easy but yes, I learned what the most important things were: security codes, how to work the printer, where the kettle was, how the switchboard worked. How to retain that information. How to ask the right questions. How to fit in. Turns out temp skills are very transferrable for being Crown Princess, for being

Queen.' She laughed a little self-consciously but she was right. She'd walked into this hostile tribe a stranger and a foreigner and would ride out a valued friend and ally because she'd taken the time to ask the right questions, and, more importantly, to care about the answer. Something he should have learned in all his business dealing. Maybe he had where stock and figures were concerned but not with people.

'But you wanted to change careers?'

'Well, yes. Temping was fun but turns out it was temporary.' Her smile made it clear the pun was purposeful. 'I wanted a new challenge, to be able to put down some roots. But I liked problem solving, helping. I thought I could do that as a lawyer.'

'You can do that here,' he said, aware how brusque he sounded. 'Look into an air ambulance. Look into costings and potential problems as well as benefits and write me a report—or commission one. Then we'll talk and, if it adds up the way you want it to, then I'll talk to the Council. Or you can...'

The somewhat self-deprecating smile broadened until it shone from her eyes. 'Really? I can do that? Thank you. That's amazing. Thank you, Idris.' She made to rise but fell back with an 'Oof!' as her ankle hit the floor and he stepped back, shy of her thanks.

'I'll get your maid.' He grabbed his robe and hastily threw it on, backing out of the tent before she could say another word. He didn't want or need her gratitude, not for merely giving her a purpose and not when his plan suited him just as well as it suited her. Nor did he want to dwell on how it had felt to sleep with her nestled in close, her hair soft on his chin, her body warm and yielding against his. And he definitely didn't want to think about the day ahead, Saskia sitting before him on a horse all day long, every jolt pushing their bodies together. It was going to be a very long, very hot journey and he was going to need every bit of self-control he could muster.

CHAPTER TEN

'HAPPY BIRTHDAY!'

Saskia blearily opened one eye to see a card and present practically touching her nose and, right behind the garishly wrapped gift, Jack beaming down at her.

'Morning, tiger,' she croaked, a quick glance at her watch confirming that, yes, it wasn't yet six a.m. 'Is that for me?'

'Let Saskia have her coffee first,' Idris interjected. Saskia refocussed to see him standing behind Jack, Sami in his arms. She smiled a weary thanks at him; she had only started drinking coffee again a few weeks ago but was already as addicted to her favourite wake-me-up as she had ever been.

As she struggled to a sitting position her maid put a tray on the bedside table; figs and freshly cut oranges, little cinnamon-dusted pastries and a pot of steaming coffee making an aromatic and visually appealing feast. Saskia took a fresh-smelling Sami from Idris as he poured her coffee, adding exactly the right amount of milk to it. He was already dressed, but this was the first time she had seen him upon awakening since their night in the desert. Even on the occasions when they shared a room on one of their tours he awoke, dressed and left before she stirred and although he now came to her most nights in the palace he was gone before she awoke.

She understood it, his need to separate the intimacy of sex from the intimacy of sharing a bed, but her heart still ached when she woke in an empty bed—or when she tried to fall asleep, all too aware of the empty space beside her, his scent still permeating the pillows.

'Open it, open it.' Jack thrust his present at her and, laughing at his eager face, she accepted it.

'Okay, okay.' Slowly, more to tease Jack than out of patience, she slid her finger underneath the sticky tape, her mouth opening as the paper unfolded to reveal a slim A4 book, the front cover a posed portrait of Jack and Sami. She took a deep breath as she opened it, discovering pages full of photos of both boys, some posed, many candid shots—including plenty of Jack as a toddler and small boy, several of her posing for selfies with him. 'What? How did you get these?' She glanced at Idris in shock. Most of the photos existed only on her laptop or on her email account.

'Jack knows your password. We only looked for the albums with him in there,' Idris added hurriedly.

'There are no other albums.' She mock glared at Jack. 'A hacker eh? I need to change my password. But this is lovely, so thoughtful. Thank you.' She swallowed, aware of the lump in her throat, the burning at the backs of her eyes as she flicked through page after page, memories unfurling as she looked back at the last seven years of the life she had shared with her brother. She glanced towards Idris, trying to convey her thanks. He must have thought of this gesture, noticed she only had one framed picture of Jack on her bedside table and that was years old.

'This is from Sami.' Jack held another gift towards her. 'I helped him choose it.'

'It looks intriguing.' Saskia took the bulky, heavy present with raised eyebrows, squealing as she opened it to see her favourite chocolates, wrapped cheese, oatcakes, a packet of scones with a pot of jam and her usual brand of tea. The food in Dalmaya was fantastic but occasionally she yearned for a Wensleydale and pickle sandwich, a chocolate bar or a cup of Earl Grey tea. 'Amazing. What a clever baby.' She kissed Sami and then Jack. 'And isn't he lucky to have such a helpful big brother?'

She reached a hand out towards Idris, who had awkwardly curled his tall frame into the small nursing chair next to her bed. He had to have organised these presents, had heard her occasional wish for a 'plain cup of English tea' or her laughing promise to Jack that when they next visited London she was going to eat scones until she burst. Their eyes connected and Saskia ached with wishing that this was real, that they really were a family bound by love and the bonds of affection, not by duty and an attraction born from nostalgia.

Her eyes roamed over the familiar face, pausing at the hollows in the lean cheeks, the early-morning stubble grazing his chin, the curve of his proud mouth, the fall of the dark hair, her mouth drying out as she drank him in. Her commitment to Jack had made it near impossible to date but the truth was that although, thanks to her temping jobs, she had met plenty of men, had had plenty of invitations, she had never been tempted to accept. Idris was nothing but temptation and like Eve she fell, night after night.

'This is from me.' His voice was gruff as he handed

over a small box and Saskia's eyebrows rose in surprise
as she took it.

'You didn't have to.'

'I believe…' a teasing note entered his voice '…that
the correct response is thank you.'

'Thank you.' She repeated it as she bent her head
to examine the small box, her heart thumping harder
than ever. Her fingers felt too big, refusing to work
as she carefully opened the present, folding the paper
neatly and putting it to one side, aware she was delay-
ing opening the box.

It was probably a duty gift. She had been given plenty
of jewellery over the last few months, Dalmayan custom
dictating that a woman's worth, a family's wealth should
be reflected in the jewels she wore. Glittering ropes of
emeralds and sapphires and amethysts, jingling ban-
gles of gem-studded platinum and rose gold, elaborate
headdresses and tiaras, heavy rings—she wore them
on formal occasions, for feasts and celebrations and
some meetings. They helped transform her from plain
Saskia Harper, hard-working temp, to Sheikha Saskia
DelacourAl Osman, soon to be crowned Queen of Dalmaya. She fumbled with the catch; finally opening the
box. 'Oh!' A slender charm bracelet sat inside, two tiny
charms already attached. Jack leaned over, pointing
to one. 'That's my hand print, all shrunken down and
made into gold, and that's Sami's. Do you like it?'

'Like it? I love it.' She could hardly get the words
out for the lump in her throat. A year and a bit ago she
would never have believed this possible. That she could
be lying in such luxurious surroundings, a warm, contented baby in her arms, a healthy thriving Jack by her
side and married to a man who surely must care about

her even if he didn't love her. She should be happy. It was greedy to wish for more.

Saskia lifted out the bracelet and studied each tiny charm, knowledge racing through her. She didn't just wish for more, she craved it, just as she had long ago. She had craved Idris Delacour's love then and she craved it now, and, despite everything, part of her had never stopped loving him.

'Jack tells me you have a long-standing birthday tradition.' Idris's elegantly French-accented rumble broke into her thoughts and she started, sure her wishes must be written all over her face.

'Tradition? Yes.' She smiled at her small brother. 'We always spend the morning at the V&A because it's my favourite museum and then we have a picnic in Kensington Gardens, right by the fountain.'

'With bought food not a pack up,' Jack added. 'And lots of cake.'

For the first couple of years after she took Jack in Saskia hadn't celebrated her birthday. It was too much of a reminder of what she had lost. Before every birthday had been an event, a celebration orchestrated by her father. But as Jack got older he insisted they do something special and so the tradition had been born. Her favourite museum and then a little celebratory autumn picnic.

Later, as they put down tiny roots in their neighbourhood, there had been other celebrations, a glass of wine with their neighbours, dinner at Jack's friend's house, but the birthday picnic remained a staple and Saskia loved it, never wishing that she could replace it with the lavish parties her father had always thrown for her.

'I can't manage the V&A but how do you fancy a night at the villa and a picnic on the beach instead?'

Idris suggested and Saskia almost sagged against her pillows with relief at the idea. The autumn was a particularly hot one this year and even the well-ventilated marble halls of the palace felt oppressive at times. The very thought of being back by the sea, in a place where the staff were more like friends, where she felt at home, not like a pampered guest, was the most perfect gift of all.

'Don't we have a Council meeting today?'

'I'm sure you can be excused under the circumstances. I'll make your apologies.'

'Oh. Right, thank you.' Disappointment flooded through her at his calm, almost dismissive words. Of course she didn't need to be at the meeting; of course he didn't want to come to the picnic. He was making all the right gestures but that was all they were, right? And she was a fool for wanting more, for hoping for more.

'You're not coming?' Jack looked up, the disappointment on his face a mirror to that which Saskia was trying so hard not to show. 'But, Idris, you promised me a horse-riding lesson on the beach. And you said we'd play cricket. Please come, it won't be the same without you.'

The sun had begun to redden when the nanny retrieved the two tired, sandy boys to take them back to the villa for baths and bed, Jack well and truly exhausted by a day of horse riding, cricket and swimming. Saskia turned and watched the small group climb the steps to the villa, her face soft with love. 'What a fantastic day he's had. Thank you, Idris.'

'You don't need to thank me. Besides, it's your birthday. Have you had a good day?' Idris hadn't intended to accompany the family to the villa. He had so much work to do, so many meetings to attend, a day and a night off seemed unachievable. Turned out he couldn't say no to a pair of beseeching brown eyes and a small boy's flattery—nor had he escaped the flitting wistfulness on Saskia's face when he said he'd stay behind. They didn't want anything more from him than his company. It was a refreshing change in a world where his grace and favour was sought at every turn.

'A lovely day, thanks. I would have liked to have ridden but my ankle is still a little weak. Blissful to swim in the sea though. I stuck to the safety of the pool when I was pregnant but there's nothing like the wildness of salt water.' Saskia looked a little like a wild water creature herself, the red hair still damp, pinned back off her face, a turquoise sarong knotted around her waist.

'As good as the V&A?'

'Well, I do hate to miss out on my annual pretend-I'm-in-a-costume-drama trip. I only just made it last year—we moved out here just a couple of weeks later. I was a few weeks pregnant at the time, already feeling tired and queasy, so the picnic wasn't quite the treat it usually was and even the regency costumes couldn't distract me!'

Idris led her over to the picnic area, just below the villa. A gazebo had been erected to protect Saskia and Sami from the sun, colourful woven blankets and cushions laid out on the fine white sand and several of the villa's loungers brought down to the beach. Now the light was beginning to fade torches were lit and the fairy lights strewn around the gazebo's edge sprang into life. The housekeeper and houseboy were busy setting dishes out on the long low wooden table and aromatic aromas filled the evening air.

'*Shokran.*' Idris nodded at the beaming pair. 'We'll serve ourselves.'

'I didn't expect you to stay for dinner.' Saskia seated herself on a lounger, peering over as Idris lifted the heavy silver lids to reveal a slow-cooked lamb stew, couscous, bursting with vegetables and plump raisins and spices, flatbreads, round falafel and a platter filled with figs, peaches, grapes and melon. 'Goodness, the kitchen have done us proud. I hope they don't expect us to eat it all. I've only just digested lunch! Do you have time to help eat enough so the cook isn't offended before you head back?'

'I thought I might spend the evening here. It doesn't seem worth going back to the palace when I promised Jack more cricket tomorrow.'

Saskia stilled, her eyes fixed on him. Idris didn't meet her steady gaze, busying himself with filling her plate. She knew as well as he did that it would take him only an hour to return to the palace, that he could be back before Jack had even noticed his absence.

Idris had never stayed at the villa before. It was Saskia's territory. He had no rooms here, nowhere to run, nowhere to hide. His pulse began to beat hard and fast as he handed her the plate and poured a glass of the rich red wine, imported from his own estates. 'If that's okay,' he added, setting the wine down beside her.

'Of course, we're married, you don't need to ask my permission.' She picked up the wine, lying back against the padded back of her lounger with a contented sigh. 'When I first came here I couldn't believe it, that this view, this beauty, was to be mine for a whole year. I'm glad you kept it on. The palace is beautiful, but it doesn't feel like home, not like this place does.'

Idris poured himself a glass. 'I'm glad that you have a place in Dalmaya where you feel like home.'

'Do you have somewhere too?' Her gaze was far too penetrating. 'In the shock of all these changes it's easy to forget that this life is almost as new to you as it is for me. Do you feel at home?'

'Sometimes.' He paused, weighing his words carefully. 'Not in a place, not yet. When I take Jack riding or sailing or Sami for a walk. When we're in Council and the leaders stop bickering and listen to my suggestions. When I see the solution to a problem.' When he was holding Saskia, his mouth on hers, her body wound round his. Then he felt at home—and yet also like a trespasser, on ground he had no right to occupy.

'You miss France?'

'Not so much France as the vineyard, the chateau.' He stopped, trying to find the right words. 'I knew what was expected of me there, who I was. I'm still working that out here. My grandfather, my Dalmayan grandfather, would tell me that his blood ran in my veins, that I was an Al Osman in all but name, but I knew that to everyone else I was the French son of an immoral woman. I had to be better behaved than Fayaz, stronger, cleverer, nicer. It made no difference. They all loved him anyway. Everyone loved him. He had that gift.'

'Did you come here a lot when you were a boy?'

Idris shifted, uncomfortable with the personal turn the conversation had taken—and yet relieved to share. Now he was living in Dalmaya full time, the memories and what-might-have-beens haunted him around every corner. '*Non.* My mother, she and my grandfather didn't speak at all. But when I was eight he invited me over. Acknowledged me as one of the family. Usually I spent all the summer holidays with my *grandpère* at the chateau so I began to spend the winter and spring holidays here. Just four weeks a year.' Weeks he had both loved and loathed. Loved for the bond with the proud old man—and because this desert kingdom was in his blood, just as his grandfather claimed.

Loathed because he was always an outsider, always other. 'There was some resistance when Grandfather named me as his second heir. This is why we must always be above reproach, you and I. There is no room for error, for scandal, for gossip. I must be my grandfather's heir, not my mother's son, and you have to be the perfect Queen. It won't be easy but it's the only way.'

Saskia nodded, her face pensive. 'Does your mother miss Dalmaya? I know when the Manor was sold, it felt like part of me had been ripped away. I was raised in that house, and suddenly I was homeless. To lose a whole country must be worse.'

'She knew what she was doing,' he said, his mouth compressing into a thin line. 'Knew that if she crossed that line she could never go back and yet she jumped right across it with no thought for how it would affect me or her father.'

Saskia put her glass down. 'I am angry with my father every day. Angry because every moment of my childhood was a lie, because he abandoned me, abandoned Jack. I don't see any reason, any excuse for what he did. But, Idris, your mother is still here, still in your life. That has to count for something.'

'Oh, I know she loves me. I know she's proud of me. She is very free, very open with her affection—everyone she meets adores her.' His mouth softened as he thought about his beautiful, whimsical mother.

'It's just in her way she's as much a child as Jack and because *mon père* thinks of nothing but his art, if he decided we needed to be in Switzerland then off we went to Switzerland, no matter that we had nowhere to live, I had no school to go to. It would work out, my mother always said, details were for other people— for me—to worry about. As I grew up I realised other children didn't spend some months with money to burn and other months without a centime, that they didn't flit from town to town, country to country. That they didn't worry about paying the rent because their mother had bought a new dress or get home from school and cook dinner not knowing where their parents were. My time with my two grandfathers, here in Dalmaya, at the chateau, they were the times when time slowed, when I knew who I was.'

'They must have been two exceptional men.'

'Yes, they were.' He paused again, recoiling from the disloyalty of his thoughts. 'Yes, but they always expected so much from me. They never met but they were similar in many ways, both needing me to right the wrongs of the past, to be everything my parents weren't, to be the legacy they needed. They made sure I knew where my duty lay and how to achieve it.'

He hadn't noticed her leave her lounger, noticed her walk around to sit by his side until a cool hand covered his. 'No wonder you got so irritated when I suggested you skip a lecture to jump on a train and see where we ended up!'

Memories flooded back. 'But somehow you persuaded me and we found ourselves up in that little town, with all the thatched roofs and the castle.'

'The sun was out, so even though it was freezing we sat in the pub beer garden and shivered as we had our pints.'

'Then we walked along the road and quarrelled over

which house we would buy. You wanted all the tiny, impractical cottages…'

'And you wanted all the boring, sensible houses with no character.'

'You would love the chateau,' he told her, sliding his fingers through her hair. 'It has all the balconies and turrets and hidden rooms you could desire. My grandfather lived in a suite on the ground floor while the house crumbled. Restoring it has taken me five years—and now it's done I won't get the opportunity to enjoy it.'

'You could.' She placed a hand on his cheek, turning his face to hers. 'You chose not to. You chose to take on Dalmaya and Sami and me even though we were the last things you wanted.'

Had it been a choice? It had felt like an inescapable destiny. 'I didn't…'

'You did have a choice. No one would have blamed you for walking away. No one but you. You don't choose the easy path, Idris Delacour, and you don't make it easy for those of us who are journeying with you, but you choose the right path.'

'Even back then?' Her breath was soft on his cheek, her eyes full of a compassion that struck him to his core.

'Not the way it happened, but you're right. I didn't respect your need for privacy or your boundaries. I just jumped straight in wanting everything my own way. It's funny.' A soft, nostalgic smile curved her mouth. 'I don't recognise that Saskia but I do envy her. Her utter self-belief and confidence in her right to be heard and loved and her knowledge that she mattered. She was a little selfish and a little foolish but she wasn't all bad.'

'She took in a small child while she was reeling from her father's death. That doesn't make her selfish and foolish. That makes her someone with a huge heart.'

Saskia's eyelids fluttered shut, red staining her cheeks. 'You make it sound far more heroic than it was. I did what I had to do.'

'Maybe we're more alike than we realise.' Idris slid his hand to the back of her neck, her still-damp hair heavy on his skin. 'Maybe it's a good thing we ended up here together.'

'Maybe.' The word was a breath as she leaned in towards him. Idris lowered his head to capture her mouth with his. They had mutual goals, they had compatibility and they had this chemistry. Was it enough? Once he had thought he might be on the verge of falling in love with her and had recoiled from the idea, recoiled from the extra sacrifices love demanded. Now she was here, their lives irretrievably intertwined. And right now, right here, he wouldn't have it any other way.

CHAPTER ELEVEN

'GOOD, YOU'RE READY.' Idris strode by Saskia and paused at the door, clearly impatient to be off. 'Is there a problem? There's time to run through the briefing notes in the car.'

Tapping one expensively shod foot, Saskia remained standing by the first of five pillars that ran the length of the aptly named Gold Salon. 'No problem, but when it's taken over an hour of three people's time to get me ready I would appreciate a comment to let me know I pass muster.'

Despite the secular nature of the country many Dalmayans were still deeply religious and old traditions ran deep. Most women still covered their legs and arms as a matter of course, and in rural areas it was common to cover hair as well, although the veil was rarely seen. Saskia had adopted these traditions out of respect for her new country. It made sense to fit in with her compatriots when she was working and mixing with Dalmayans. However, tonight's reception was at the British Embassy and she knew her outfit would be under intense scrutiny. Her decision to wear silk trousers with a matching, long, close-fitting tunic instead of an evening dress would mark her as different, apart from her own compatriots, and she wasn't sure she was ready for that, to give up her old identity so completely.

At least she wasn't expected to cover her hair in the city. Her maid had styled it into a loose, gleaming chignon, the bright red locks set off by the green and gold silk of her *salwar kameez*. But the long diamond drops in her ears, the emerald and diamond headband holding her hair off her face, the matching collar covering her throat in tiny glittering gems and the heavy emerald and gold spheres ringing her wrists and fingers went far beyond any Western tastes in jewellery. Saskia wasn't sure she would ever feel comfortable wearing the value of a house in Mayfair on her body.

'Is it too much?'

Idris's eyes gleamed as he looked her over, head to toe, her body tingling in response to his deliberate scrutiny. 'You look stunning—and I am looking forward to unwrapping every inch of you later.'

Her stomach clenched at his words and the wolfish smile that accompanied them. 'Promises, promises,' she said, walking forward and taking the arm he proffered, allowing him to lead her out of the palace and to the waiting car.

He came to her every night now and although he still usually slipped away to sleep in his own rooms, occasionally, worn out by the demands of the day, he would fall asleep in her bed. Saskia loved those nights, loved curling up next to him. She had to keep reminding herself not to be too happy. Not to take any of his affection for granted. Not to consider their intimacy as anything more than two people thrust together and making the most out of a difficult situation. As anything more than lust. To remind herself that they were getting close to a real friendship and that was more than she had ever thought possible four months ago. Remind herself that there could be nothing more.

Idris had warned her, back on their wedding night. Told her that he didn't know if he was capable of love, confirmed that he had walked away from what they had shared then without a backwards glance. Only a fool would be ensnared twice.

But no matter how much she reminded herself she still would find herself sneaking looks at him during formal occasions, find herself shivering at the touch of his hand, find herself basking in his approval when he bestowed one of his rare smiles on her, find herself needing him every night.

She told herself that this was perfectly normal— after all, he was still her only confidant in the whole country, the adult she spent most of her time with—but deep down inside, she knew. She was falling in love with him again. Not with all the fire and drama of first love: a crush mixed with lust mixed with the hedonistic optimism of youth. But with a deeper, steadier, more realistic love. This wasn't just passion or a need to be liked. It wasn't about winning, about craving, about impressing. She was falling in love with the way he made time to listen to everyone at Council meetings even when they seemed interminable. She was falling in love with the man who had a framed picture of his vineyards and chateau on his desk but had walked away from his beloved business to do the right thing. She was falling in love with a shrewd negotiator and a patient diplomat. She was falling in love with the man teaching her brother to ride. The man who spent an entire hour playing peekaboo with Sami. The man who had safeguarded Jack's future. The man who made her feel that she had something to offer. The man who made her feel that she was worthwhile.

Dangerous, forbidden feelings. But try as she might she couldn't push them aside.

Idris seemed preoccupied as their car drove smoothly along the great driveway leading from the palace to the gates, barely speaking for the first few minutes. Saskia smoothed her tunic, trying to calm her nerves with deep breaths. She had been to several formal receptions over the last few weeks, she had done her research on to-night's hosts and guests but still her stomach tumbled with nerves.

'Thank you for wearing traditional dress,' Idris said abruptly and Saskia turned from her perusal of the narrow city streets.

'Of course. I probably would have even if you hadn't requested it. It seems appropriate somehow.'

'There is still an inordinate amount of interest in us, especially in the UK press. They print stories every day, all inaccurate, print photos every time we're in public...'

The air swirled and stilled. Whenever she closed her eyes it was easy to conjure up those claustrophobic few weeks after her father's death, cameras everywhere, her face on the front pages as every detail of her extravagantly funded life was laid out for people to moralise over. 'They photograph us?'

He waved an impatient hand. 'That's to be expected but what wasn't expected is the amount of interest after several months, several quiet months at that. They report that we argue about your spending, that my mother hates you and wants to be crowned Queen...'

'I've never met your mother!'

'It doesn't matter.' His eyes were weary. 'My parents were tabloid staples in their day. Your father dominated the headlines. You're the spoiled socialite brought down to earth, I'm the wine king. To them we're a match made in heaven and truth has no place in the fictions they spin. Tonight, we will be on British soil for the first time since we married. This is a good chance to make the right impression. There will be members of the press there, influential people. Let's start putting these lies and rumours to bed. I don't want Jack or Sami reading about us the way I grew up reading about my parents. I want this intrusiveness to stop. Show them you have changed, Saskia, that you are the dignified, compassionate Queen Dalmaya needs.'

Saskia's hands began to tremble and she folded them together so Idris wouldn't notice. How had she not known that these stories were circulating—and why hadn't Idris warned her before? 'I'll do my best.'

'Do better. These parties aren't fun, not for you and I, they're work. You mustn't let your guard down just because every accent is English and the people seem like friends. They're not.'

He leaned back, every inch the unapproachable King. Saskia swallowed, trying to quell the nausea swelling inside at the thought of the ordeal that awaited her. Usually she felt a little as if she was playing a part, the traditional dress and elaborate jewellery her costume, her briefing document, her lines, and it was getting easier to step into each situation and perform. Idris was right— tonight would be different. Everyone there would be watching her, scrutinising her, would think they knew all about her and suddenly she felt more like a child playing dress up than a Queen.

The British Embassy was housed in a walled palace in the old town. Armed guards manned the outer walls but the royal car was waved straight through to the inner courtyard. The building was an odd contrast of traditional Dalmayan architecture, all mosaics, courtyards and pillars, and bureaucratic efficiency. As Saskia was escorted through the courtyard and double-height hallway, with its domed ceiling and pillars standing to attention on either side of the walkway, she caught glimpses of glass-walled offices, of laptops and printers and all the other accoutrements of modern-day work life. The hallway opened into a huge receiving room, which was all luxurious charm from the fountain in the middle to the sparkling chandeliers hanging from the high ceiling, each ray of light rebounding off the diamonds she was so liberally bedecked in so she felt as if she were in a spotlight as she moved into the room.

It was already full. Men and women in evening dress stood in intimidatingly glamorous and confident groups, every single eye turned to her, assessing her. Wait staff circulated with canapés and drinks and, with a jolt, Saskia realised that nearly everyone was drinking champagne. Dalmaya wasn't a dry country but most Dalmayans didn't touch alcohol and the export duties on wine and spirits were so high that even those that did rarely partook. Idris drank wine most evenings— his own brought straight to the palace from the Delacour vineyard's cellars—but not one of the dinners she had been to had served it.

The tray was presented to her and she hesitated, glancing at Idris for guidance, but he was talking to the British Ambassador and didn't notice her dilemma. Then he reached out and took a glass without breaking off the conversation. Saskia exhaled. *In that case...* With a smile of thanks she took a glass and took a sip. The champagne was tart and refreshing, as unlike the cheap cava she had occasionally treated herself to as the diamonds on her wrists and at her throat were unlike her mass-produced high-street jewellery.

'Welcome, Your Highness, it's an honour to have you here. It's been quite a few months, motherhood, a new country and such a prominent role,' the Ambassador's wife said as she escorted Saskia away from the group. 'It must be a lot to adjust to.'

Some of Saskia's tension ebbed away at the friendly tone. It was nice to be able to speak her own language without feeling like an ignorant foreigner. She had been so busy letting Dalmaya adjust to her, get used to her, that she hadn't put any thought into her own life here. She had her boys and, now, work of sorts, looking out for communities and people who needed help and finding ways to alleviate that need, but she still had no friends. Maybe Idris was being pessimistic; this could be her chance to meet some women she clicked with. Potential friends.

She smiled. 'It is. I have a lot of help, of course, so I haven't had to do any of it on my own.'

'And His Highness Sheikh Idris must be of great help as well. After all, he's had to straddle two cultures for many years. Have you known him long?' The Ambassador's wife's eyes were bright with curiosity and, with a sinking heart, Saskia knew she would need to tread carefully. Everything she said would be remembered and repeated.

'Many years,' she answered with a polite smile. 'We met at university. I was at Oxford with his cousin's then fiancée.' They had discussed whether to keep her friendship with Maya quiet, another layer of protection for their secret, but although Saskia's stay at Oxford had been cut short she'd been well known there and there must be many pictures of Maya and her floating around.

As they toured the room Saskia's optimism ebbed even further as she conceded that Idris's caution hadn't been misplaced. Everyone wanted to meet her, but all they seemed to be interested in was finding out any gossip about her marriage or trying to get a contact at the palace. In the first, long, hot hour she didn't meet one person she could imagine having a relaxed coffee with, let alone an actual friendship, and the lonely reality of her new life hit her anew. Her feet ached, her head ached, the jewels weighing her down as she smiled and made small talk feeling more like a robot fulfilling a role than a real person.

'Rob, can I introduce you to Her Highness Princess Saskia Delacour Al Osman. Your Highness, Robert McBride runs a well-known adventure travel company specialising in Middle Eastern excursions.'

Saskia held out her hand, an automatic greeting on her lips when she caught the twinkling blue eyes of the man she was being introduced to and stopped, her first real smile of the night curving her mouth. 'Robbie? What are you doing here? I thought you were destined for accountancy! It's so good to see you. Robbie and I were at the same college at Oxford,' she explained to her hostess. 'It feels like a million years ago since we were karaoke duet champions in the union bar!'

'Saskia Harper! I mean...' he took her hand and executed a perfect sweeping bow over it '...Your Highness—or as I always remembered you, the Sandy to my Danny. I was always hopelessly devoted to you but you only had eyes for one man—and...' his gaze cut across to where Idris stood in a sea of suits '...I see you still have. You look beautiful as always, like a vision from *The Thousand and One Nights*. So what have you been up to since disappearing from Oxford? If Royal

Highnesses are allowed to make small talk with lowly subjects like myself?'

'I think I can make an exception.' Saskia took the champagne he handed to her and allowed him to usher her to a place near the spectacular fountain. 'Never mind me. I want to hear all about you and why you are organising desert adventures not spreadsheets. What on earth are you doing here?'

These events were always the same. A lot of hot air and people trying to get his approval ahead of more formal meetings. Not that Idris could blame them. He had once been on the other side, the exporter looking for good deals and favourable tariffs, the producer knowing if potential customers would just try it then they would instantly be converted to his wine, his brandy, his brand.

It would be nice though not to have to spend an entire evening never committing himself, on guard at all times. Fayaz had known what was in store for him and, from an early age, had built a small but trusted circle of friends including Maya so he could have time away from responsibilities, commitments and those attempting to take advantage of his position. Idris had always been slower to make friends and to trust people and now he had no one. Nobody except Saskia.

Had they ever really talked during those long ago lust-fuelled nights? He didn't remember much conversation. But now they talked. Now he listened to her thoughts and ideas, ran his ideas past her, trusted her advice. It was as if they had been set adrift from the rest of humanity and they might never have chosen to spend their lives cooped up in a small boat together but somehow they had made peace with their situation, realised that by cooperating they would somehow make it even if that destination was unknown and not where either of them had set out to go. Or something, his mouth twisted wryly. Overblown metaphors had never been his style.

The noise was almost overpowering. Although most people were speaking in English there were enough other languages audible enough to make the room resemble a flatter Tower of Babel. Idris himself had conducted conversations in Arabic, French and his faltering Italian as well as English. The most relaxed group seemed to be by the fountain; a younger, more fashionable group had congregated there and judging by the peals of laughter they weren't discussing trade tariffs. For one self-indulgent second he wished he were free to head over and see what was so amusing—but the truth was he had never been one of the cool crowd. Always working, always aloof. What had Saskia seen in him all those years ago? What did she see in him now? Or was she just making the best of a bad deal? She was pragmatic, especially where providing for the boys was concerned.

The laughter intensified and he looked back over at the lively group, freezing as he saw the sea-green silk, the red hair, the flashing of precious jewels identifying his wife. She stood in the middle of the group, a half-empty glass of champagne in her hand, smiling up at a tall, fair man. Recognition flared as the man turned—hadn't he been one of Saskia's acolytes in Oxford? Richard? No, Rob. Robert McBride. They used to sing together, he remembered, perform elaborate karaoke duets, which always brought the bar to a standstill, arms wrapped around each other, exchanging kisses as if they were compliments. Jealousy shot through him, cold and sharp as a shard of ice. His eyes narrowed. How much had she had to drink? Did she know everyone was watching her, judging her? Or did she simply not care? She had always loved being the centre of attention…

As he watched Rob put a hand on her arm—*on his wife's arm*, jealousy whispered—and leant in to whisper something in her ear. Idris watched her eyes widen before she blushed and laughed. Another sip of champagne.

People were watching her—of course they were. Even without the title, the jewels, the traditional dress, she lit up the room. But the soon-to-be Queen of Dalmaya shouldn't be the centre of attention in this way, shouldn't shine so brightly or so freely. It wasn't decorous.

She put her hand back on Robert McBride's arm, laughing, and Idris's chest tightened. A soon-to-be Queen certainly shouldn't be flirting, especially not in public. Had she lost her mind? His gaze dropped to her glass of champagne. How many had she had? Was she tipsy? Her eyes glittered too brightly, her smile was too wide.

A remark was addressed to him and Idris nodded and smiled, adding automatic replies when it seemed appropriate, but he couldn't drag his focus from the group. He tried to catch her eye but she didn't look in his direction once. And then Rob handed her his glass, Idris wasn't sure why, but he was rolling up his sleeves and the group was widening around him, giving him space. Saskia stepped back too, both glasses high as she backed up and then time seemed to slow down to a trickle as she seemed to trip, turning that weak ankle, and she fell backwards, still laughing, still holding those damn champagne glasses, as the liquid cascaded down her front, turning the delicate silk translucent, the dampness moulding the material to her breasts as she fell into one of the giant urns serving as plant pots. The room came to a standstill everyone turning to look, phones pulled out in a flash as one of the bracelets fell from Saskia's wrist and fell to the floor scattering precious stones like confetti.

CHAPTER TWELVE

'PLEASE COME WITH US, just for a little while.' Jack's eyes pleaded for her to say yes and Saskia's heart ached as she shook her head with as big a smile as she could muster.

'Best not. You'll enjoy the park more if there are no cameras around, you know that. Be a good boy, listen to Faye and look after Sami.' She kissed him on his unresponsive cheek, hating the disappointment on his face, then kissed the baby, deliciously wrapped up in a padded all-in-one. 'Are you sure you're okay with them both, Faye?' Lucy, the day nanny, had the day off but the nursery nurse, Faye, had been trained at one of the UK's most exclusive childcare colleges and Saskia knew the two boys would be in safe hands. Besides, two bodyguards would be trailing them at a discreet distance the whole time. 'Say hi to Peter Pan for me, Jack, okay?'

He nodded, the sullen look receding from his face. The two of them had made many trips to see the famous statue over the years and he was thrilled that they were staying within walking distance of Kensington Park.

Saskia turned to the window, uneasy until she saw them turn into the park free of any press interest. London was a cold contrast to Dalmaya, the autumn the grey, windy, drizzly variant. Grey like her mood. It was her fault she couldn't take the boys out herself, her fault they had to exit the embassy by a side door, on a constant lookout for the press. She had messed up.

It didn't matter that the fall had been an accident, that despite appearances to the contrary she hadn't been drunk. No matter that the clasp had been weak on her bracelet. What mattered was the photo. The photo that was on every gossip website and in most papers. A drunk-looking princess, laughing as she sat in a giant, priceless plant pot, a glass of champagne held aloft in both hands, their contents dripping down her so her outfit was see-through, her breasts, her underwear clearly visible, diamonds and emeralds showering from her wrists. She looked as if she were participating in some kind of drunken orgy, not tripping over her own shoes. And to Idris, appearances seemed to be everything.

Not that she had realised that at first. He had appeared at her side like a superhero, helping her get up, shrugging his jacket off so that she could slip it on, joking that it was a good idea he had worn Western clothes, taking the glasses out of her hands and putting them on a tray and then escorting her from the room, all before she had really grasped what had happened. But when she had turned to thank him in the car he had frozen her out. 'We'll talk about this later,' he had said, as if she were an errant teen, not his wife. But there had been no later. He hadn't come to her and she hadn't been invited to any Council meetings. Instead she had been left alone in her rooms—to think about what she had done?—until it was time to travel to London. She had assumed Idris would be accompanying them but he wasn't in the car nor on the private jet and there was no sight of him here in the embassy nor any indication that he was planning to join her there.

He had warned her, it was true. She had to be dignified, make sure there were no errors, and she had ignored his advice, giddy at seeing a friendly face. But
the punishment outweighed the crime. Was this how it
would be? Would she spend her entire marriage fitting
in, treading carefully, alone? Idris had walked away
before—and by his own admission he hadn't looked
back even once.

She wouldn't, couldn't live like that. Couldn't set that
kind of example to her boys. Couldn't undo those painful seven years of self-discovery and growth.

But Idris and she were married and tomorrow she
would be talking to a social worker, proving that she
was the right person to look after Jack, that Idris was
the right person to father him. And he wasn't here. Even
if he turned up would they be able to put on a united
front? Could she spend the rest of her life pretending?

Even worse the paparazzi were everywhere. The social worker would have to be escorted through them,
which was going to be an excellent start to the interview. The photo had stirred the already feverish press
into a feeding frenzy and her father's suicide, Idris's
mother's elopement, their own affair at Oxford were
dissected, written about and discussed as if they held
the answer to world peace, climate change and space
travel in their sordid details. She hadn't been able to
take Jack to the theatre or the museums or anything she
had promised him; instead she had been stuck inside
the Georgian town house that housed the embassy, just
as she had been stuck inside the palace, inside the villa.

Saskia curled her hands into fists, blinking fiercely.
No more tears. She was done with them. She was an
adult now, not a teen forced to grow up too soon. She
had two boys to care for and she needed to decide how

she wanted to live the rest of her life. Was she any happier now for all her designer clothes and the diamond watch on her wrist?

If she wasn't prepared to live like this, then what were her options? She swallowed. Divorce, she supposed. Divorce wouldn't affect Sami's chance to inherit the throne. He was legitimate now, after all. And if the adoption was finalised first then Jack would be safe. And for all Idris's threats nearly six months ago she knew now he wouldn't leave the children penniless. Nor did she think he would try and take them from her.

She looked around her at the warm colours and comfortable, elegant furniture. Once she had walked the streets of Kensington, playing the *Where would I like to live?* game. She had always chosen either a mews house or a town house, complete with basement and attic like the houses in the old-fashioned children's stories she loved so much. Nothing ostentatious. No basement cinemas. Instead she had yearned for a large kitchen diner, for cosy furniture you could sit on, warm furnishings, not acres of marble covered in spindly chairs. No gilt.

Here she was in exactly that house, in a large Georgian terrace with black iron railings in the front and a garden out back. The royal apartments were situated on the first and second floors and the décor was testament to Maya's good taste, showcasing the best of Dalmayan décor while still accommodating itself to the vagaries of British weather with stoves, throws and huge rugs giving the large rooms a much-needed cosy feel. Saskia had made it, was living in her dream home. And yet her victory was completely hollow.

Despite the warmth Saskia shivered. It was time to take control of her life, not allow circumstances to buffet her from disaster to makeshift solution. Taking care of Jack, getting pregnant, marrying Idris, these had all been thrust upon her and just because two out of the three were the best things that could have happened didn't make her lack of agency any less real.

As for that third...marrying Idris had brought her security, true, financially and personally. The clothes she wore cost more than her previous entire wardrobe had, the watch on her wrist would have paid for a year's rent. Sami was hers in every way and soon Jack would be. Hopefully. But she couldn't spend her life with someone who didn't like her. The knowledge she was in love with him just made her isolation worse.

Accidents happened and there was every chance Saskia would mess up again unless she spent her life hidden in the confines of the palace walls. If Idris couldn't understand that then what chance did she have? Maya had often spoken about the future pressures awaiting her as Fayaz's wife and Queen. Society held women to a higher, more unachievable standard, she had said one night, and it was doubly, triply true in Middle Eastern countries, even ones as theoretically progressive as Dalmaya. She loved Fayaz, but she knew marrying him meant surrendering many of the freedoms she took for granted. That she would be watched, judged every moment. But, she said, with Fayaz by her side, supporting her, needing her, it would be worth it.

A dull ache pulsed in Saskia's chest, in her heart. That, right there, was the crux of the matter. Maya didn't just love Fayaz, she had known that she could depend on him too, no matter what. Could Saskia say the same of Idris? If he truly supported her, needed her, then they could laugh off any subsequent embarrassments. But if he was just going to freeze her out...

She deserved better. She was no longer a spoiled

teenager. She was a hard-working mother of two with so much love to give and if that wasn't enough for Idris...

Staring blindly out of the window at the Georgian square, at the private garden in the middle of the square, at the photographers still loitering with intent, Saskia acknowledged the truth: she couldn't live this way, loving Idris, destined to disappoint him. She couldn't raise the boys with that kind of marriage as a role model. She turned and picked up her phone, finding Idris's details, and fired off a quick text.

We need to talk. In person.

Idris's phone buzzed and he glanced at the screen to see Saskia's name flash up followed by a short text. Just four words but they shot straight to his heart. The words *We need to talk* never boded well but, he conceded, he didn't deserve anything more. He had left Saskia to travel to England alone, left her to face the fallout from the photo alone. If he had stayed next to her, laughed the picture off, then the story would have died by now but his absence was raising speculative headlines.

He got stiffly to his feet and headed over to the window, looking out over the old courtyard, at the stone barns and the grey walls. He should have followed Saskia to London; instead he had come home, to Chateau Delacour. Oh, he still needed to sign some papers, to delegate some more of the responsibilities, but he knew he could have done that from the palace or the London Embassy. The vineyard was running smoothly in his absence thanks to his more than capable manager but the chateau was his home in a way the palace could never be. Generations of Delacours had lived here and tended the fields just as generations of Al Osmans had lived in the palace and tended Dalmaya.

Maybe he could step down when Sami was old enough and return here, to vineyards and fields. To the old grey chateau, weathered and crumbling in parts. To the deep green of the French countryside and the peace and tranquillity. To a life where a mistake meant ruining a year's vintage, not ruining a country, a life, a marriage. To a place that used to feel like home.

He should have gone to London. He just didn't know how to speak to Saskia, what to say. Where to begin. He'd spent his life avoiding drama in every permutation. He didn't have the weapons to deal with it now. Or the armour.

He needed a walk, wanted to examine the bare vines. The grapes had all been picked in his absence, a few trodden in the traditional way at the harvest festival, the rest pressed. He'd missed both. Hadn't tasted the grapes, hadn't stood in the traditional wooden tub, barefooted, the grapes squelching under his cleansed feet. Despite a childhood being dragged around France, around Europe, despite the darker skin and name that marked him out as foreign in a countryside that still regarded outsiders with suspicion, he had always felt at home here. Here and in the stables at the palace. These were the places his two grandfathers, proud men who had never met, had passed down their wisdom and their traditions and their family pride. He didn't think either would be proud of him just now.

Nor should they be.

He reached the front door as a car drew up, a sleek silver convertible he didn't recognise. His chest tightened as a chic, petite figure sprang from the driver's side, her dark hair barely touched with grey swept up in a loose bun, huge sunglasses obscuring half her famously beautiful face.

'*Yaa bunaaya,*' she said, hands outstretched towards him.

'*Maman.*' It took a second for him to recover from the shock of her arrival and step forward to take her hands and kiss her on both cheeks. 'This is a surprise.'

'But a welcome one, I hope?' She reverted to the English they usually spoke at home. His father had no Arabic and, despite living most of her adult life in France, Princess Zara still spoke barely passable tourist French.

'Of course. Come on in. Would you like coffee?'

'But you were just leaving.'

'Only for a walk.'

'Then I shall accompany you and we shall dine together later. You are sure I am not interrupting you, Idris? You aren't on your way to London perhaps?'

'Tomorrow.' He couldn't miss the social worker's visit and Saskia was right. They did need to talk. 'You seem very well informed about my whereabouts.'

'A mother has her ways, even a mother who missed her son's wedding and has yet to meet her grandson?' She raised an eyebrow and shame shot through him. Shame mingled with uncertainty. Lying about Sami's heritage seemed like the right thing to do in the abstract but lying to his own parents was another thing completely. And would they tell Sami the truth one day? After all, Jack knew some version of it. The marriage, the deception had all made such sense in those first grief-laden days but now nothing seemed to make any sense at all.

He took her arm and, after shooting an incredulous glance at her delicately heeled suede boots, which seemed totally unsuited for walking through the vine-yards, set off away from the house. He let her chatter on for some minutes; about his father's latest project, their plan to move to the Alps for the winter, some gossip about mutual friends before he said jerkily: 'Sami is your great-nephew, not your grandson, although I consider him my son and I hope you will think of him as a grandchild.'

'I see.' She didn't, he noted, sound surprised.

'Maya had trouble conceiving and so she asked Saskia, my wife…' if his mother noticed him stumble over the words she made no sign '…to have a child for her. As a surrogate. Fayaz was the biological father and Saskia the mother. But they died before the baby was born and before they could acknowledge him as theirs. So I…'

'So you married the mother, told the world the baby is yours so he can inherit. Of course you did. It is exactly what I would expect you to do.' Her voice was oddly neutral, neither approving or disapproving.

'What else could I do?'

His mother patted his hand. 'You could have walked away, Idris. No one would have blamed you. But you were always one to shoulder all the responsibility whether it was yours to shoulder or not. So, I have a daughter-in-law and a grandson. When will I meet them and why are you not with them?'

Her words reverberated around his head. She made it sound as if he had choices. As if he could just walk away from his duties and responsibilities—as she and his father had. Didn't she realise that someone had to pick up behind them? 'You've seen the photo, I expect. The headlines. The speculation. Is that why you're here?'

Her hand tightened on his arm. 'I need a reason to

see my son? It's not easy when you have made it clear you don't want me in Dalmaya, never mind that it was my home once. But yes, I saw the photo. Not that it matters. Photos are never the whole story, not even half the story. The press are never kind to the young and the privileged once they transgress and she, I think, is being punished more for her father's sins, for my supposed sins, than for one moment's lapse in concentration. Is she managing?'

'As far as I am aware.'

'As far as you…' Her lips compressed and she didn't speak for a long moment. They reached the edge of the vineyards, stretching out over undulating low hills, the sky a clear blue, the air crisp with the hint of an autumnal chill. The Princess tugged him towards a bench, set in the side of the vineyard, placed there for the tourists who came to watch the grapes grow, the wine made, to sample and to buy, and, after gingerly inspecting it for dirt, sat down and looked at her son.

'I blame myself, Idris. Your father, he likes me full of *joie-de-vivre* and so I am. Not thinking about tomorrow or worrying about what-ifs. He didn't want to be weighed down by responsibility, by all this…' She waved her hand, encompassing the vineyards and the chateau. 'By his name and expectations. That was a breath of fresh air to me, as someone for whom family expectations had been so all demanding.'

'So you both just turned your backs on everything and everyone.' Leaving him to fulfil both families' expectations.

'No, no. I was already disgraced, remember? Your grandfather. He had plans and we all had our place in those plans. Me? I was to be the example of perfect modern womanhood: educated and career-minded, chaste and sensible. I was to study and then come back to Dalmaya and spearhead women's education. Marry wisely and raise my children to carry on his dreams. I hated to study, Idris, and knowing I had years and years ahead of me... Running off with Pierre wasn't a moment of madness, it was calculated. A Dalmayan Princess who eloped with her ski instructor? Worse, who left him within a year? I knew I would be free. I didn't realise...' here her voice faltered '...that my freedom would be so absolute. That your grandfather, your uncle would cut me off so completely. But if I had known I would still have done exactly the same.'

Idris sat and stared over the fields as his mother's words sank in. He had always thought of her as impulsive and thoughtless. Not someone weighed down by expectations who sought her own path to freedom.

'I met your father soon afterwards. He was so talented and his ideas, his rejection of his birthright and all that went along with it called to me. It's not easy being married to a genius, especially one who thinks commercial is a dirty word. Neither he nor I were brought up to budget and I know it wasn't easy living from boom to bust over and over. Travelling around all the time. And I know that we are both so volatile, it wasn't the most peaceful of childhoods. Too much smashed crockery. That's why I made sure you spent so much time here, or in Dalmaya. I was happy that my father wanted *you* there, if not me. But maybe those two old men put too much on you. Wanted you to make up for the sins of your parents. I was so angry when my father went against convention and named you in the succession, when your *grandpère* left you this place with its debts and obligations. But you like responsibility. You have made the vineyard a success. I know you will be a great King, my son.'

'Thank you.' It was hard to get the words out.

'But you can be…' she hesitated, choosing her words carefully, it seemed '…rigid. You make your mind up and that's that. I am feckless and court scandal. Well.' She shrugged. 'I see why you think that. I don't always think first and the papers will never allow me to forget my transgressions. But I love you—I always have. I love your father. I would never do anything to endanger our family. Even when your father had that infatuation with that model of his, you remember?'

'I remember.' His mother had phoned him, hysterical. That was the day Saskia had come to him for help and, angry at already losing his day to one woman's drama, he had turned her away, turned his back on her for good. Shame lay, heavy and painful on his heart.

'I was so angry. So humiliated, Idris. I could have walked away. But he is my husband and you are my son and so I swallowed my pride and I stayed—although he knows there must be no more *affaires*. He may be French and an artist but I cannot abide anything as boring as a cliché. I know you don't see it, think it, but I love you, *yaa bunaaya*. I am so proud of you. But I just want you to be happy.'

'You don't think I am happy?'

'I know you're not. I think you're scared to be, Idris. I think you see your worth in work and solving problems and taking on the world. You were embarrassed by me, I know that. And I think that photo has embarrassed you too. Love is about forgiving, Idris. About looking beyond the obvious to what is real and true. About never being too proud to say sorry. And true happiness is loving and being loved, no matter how inconvenient, and I think you are too scared. And that must be on me. And I am so sorry.' Her large eyes shimmered with tears. Idris sat rigid and then sighed, leaning against her for the first time in a long, long time as her words sank in, each one painful in its truth.

'Thank you, *Maman*. I need to get back to London. Do you want to come with me and meet your grandson and your daughter-in-law? If she still wants to stay married to me, that is.'

CHAPTER THIRTEEN

NEITHER IDRIS NOR his mother spoke much on the walk back to the chateau, his mother's words spinning round and round in his head. She had never been the kind of mother to dish out advice or talk about feelings; he loved her, but, he acknowledged, maybe he'd allowed his view of her to be shaped by his disapproving grandparents, by the persona she adopted. He'd never wondered what it must be like being exiled from your home, cut off from your family, married to someone whose work always came before anyone and everything.

Shame flushed through him, scalding in its intensity. His mother had been badly hurt by his father's affair, so hurt she had turned to her only son for advice and help—and all Idris had wanted was to end the phone call and get back to work. Just as he had wanted to put Saskia in a taxi and close the door on her. He had thought his work, his peace more important than two people who had so desperately needed him. What kind of man did that make him?

And here he was doing the same again. Saskia had worked incredibly hard to fit in at the palace, to be the Queen Dalmaya needed her to be. She sat up late revising customs and history and language. She knew the names of the wives and children of everyone they met, when to speak and when to stand back. She had a gift of summing up a situation with one glance and defusing it or working out a solution, whether it was an air ambulance for the Al Bedi or a new community centre in the poverty-stricken town they had visited last. The only thing she complained about was not having enough to do.

How had he thanked her? By treating one mishap as a catastrophe. By freezing her out. Just as he'd frozen out his own mother. His fear of drama and confrontation when it came to anything personal meant he would rather walk away than sort out a difficult situation. Rather leave Saskia to face the press alone.

He loved both his grandfathers and was grateful for everything they had given him, but from them he had inherited a sense of shame. Shame every time his mother was on the front page of a gossip magazine, shame when his father's latest, controversial exhibition hit the headlines, shame when their relationship was the subject of speculation. From them he had learned the value of hard work, a good lesson it was true, but not of compassion. Of pride but not of humility.

Saskia knew all about humility and hard work. She was filled with more compassion than anyone he had ever known. She was straight and true, always putting her own needs last—which was why she needed him. Needed him to put her first. But he had let her down again.

There would be no third time. That he swore.

'I've messed everything up, *Maman.*' Idris felt her falter as he said the words, then she slipped an arm through his and squeezed it.

'Idris, you of all people know that there is nothing that can't be fixed. Just look at this place. Your grandfather left a tumbling-down building, cellars full of antique equipment and a work ethos steeped in traditions that were out of date before he was even born. In just a few years you have restored the chateau and made Delacour wine one of the most sought-after brands.'

'Places and things and figures I can fix, but neither Oxford nor the Sorbonne offered me a course in human emotions,' he said. 'Even if they had I probably wouldn't have taken it.'

'Do you love her? This Saskia?'

He winced at the directness in his mother's gaze. 'That's a complicated question.'

'No, no, *yaa bunaaya*. It's the easiest question of all. If the answer is no then you must decide whether you can live with a lifetime of duty with no chance of love. If the answer is yes then you must win her back.' She patted his arm. 'Don't worry. I'll help you.'

Idris touched his mother's hand in thanks while her question repeated over and over in his mind, in his heart. Did he love Saskia? He'd told her once that he'd been as close to loving her as a man like him could ever be. Was that true or was it a way of hiding from anything as messy and real as love?

He desired her, that was true enough. He respected her intelligence and compassion. He liked the soft expression that stole over her face when she was rocking Sami, as if he was the most precious thing in the world. He admired the way she had raised Jack, the comradeship between them, her determination to give him the best childhood she could. She frustrated him, her obstinacy out in the desert when she wouldn't allow him to call the helicopter—but it had paid off. The Al Bedi had been impressed by her courage and her insistence on owning the horse that had thrown her.

She was beautiful, that went without saying. But hers was a beauty that went beyond the physical, a sweetness in her soul that hadn't been soured by the hardships she'd endured.

And he desired her. No matter he had already listed it. It was important enough to list twice. He couldn't imagine holding another woman, kissing another woman. Loving another woman…

His hands curled into fists. Of course he loved her. How could he not? Deserve her? That was a different matter. He had to prove he deserved her, prove he was worthy, show her how much he loved her—everything that she was. He stepped up his pace, heading towards the chateau.

How did a man prove his love? Especially a man who had screwed up so royally. His brain began to tick, pulling in ideas and thoughts and images, discarding others. He'd always been a good problem solver, now was the time to prove it. 'Don't worry, *Maman*, I have a plan.' He fished his phone out of his pocket and searched for a number. 'Faye? Is Jack there? Great, pass him to me. I need to check something with him.' For his plan to work he needed to enlist some help and Jack was his go-to guy.

Saskia didn't know whether she was more grateful that Idris made it to London in the nick of time or furious that he had waited until barely a half hour before the social worker was due before sauntering in, a glamorous, petite woman at his side. It took her one glance to identify the woman as Zara Al Osman Delacour, the famous Runaway Princess herself. She didn't look scandalous in her neat little black suit, her coiled dark hair only lightly streaked with grey and an emotional smile on her face; she looked happy.

'Saskia, I am so excited to meet you at last. And you, Jack. I am to be your *grandmère*, I understand.' She pronounced the French word with a distinctly Anglo-Dalmayan accent. 'I have many, many plans for the two of us. I do hope you like trips out to exciting places. And this? This must be Sami.' Her face softened.

Saskia glanced over at Idris, uncomfortable with misleading his mother about Sami's parentage, but his expression was inscrutable and she couldn't catch his eye.

'Ah, he does look like Fayaz. That makes me so happy. A fragment of happiness from such a tragedy. Yes, Idris told me,' she said quietly as Saskia looked at her in surprise. 'You are a very brave young woman.'

'Thank you.' Saskia swallowed, the lump in her throat almost more than she could bear as Sami's great-aunt kissed him, sadness mingling with love on her vivid face.

'Fayaz came to visit me when he started Oxford,' Princess Zara said. 'He and Maya, he wanted to meet the fun side of his family, he told me. He was a lovely boy. I cherished my friendship with them. Thank you for giving them this hope, Saskia. And thank you for doing what needed to be done. It can't have been easy.'

'Nothing worth doing usually is,' Saskia replied, taking her son back, conscious of the older woman's scrutiny as she did so. She caught Idris's eye and for a moment she thought he was going to say something to her, but at that moment the social worker was announced and everything around her, every other emotion and problem, disappeared, her entire focus and will centred on convincing this stranger that she was a fit mother for the small boy.

Thankfully a scandal involving two reality-show stars, a fight and an arrest had lured the press away late last night so they could welcome the adoption official through the front door of the Embassy. She didn't mention the photo at all; the only hint that Saskia and Idris weren't like any normal couple looking to adopt came in a few questions about living with security and how Jack was adjusting to palace life. Luckily Jack was so enthusiastic about his life in Dalmaya the subject was quickly dropped.

'That's a lovely wee boy you have there,' the social worker said with a smile as Saskia saw her out at the end of the two-hour session. 'You've done a good job, Your Highness.'

'I've been very lucky,' Saskia answered, more than a little choked. 'What happens next?'

'Next?' The social worker looked surprised at the question. 'We'll notify your lawyers of the court date. I don't think you will be waiting long, not in a case as straightforward as this.'

Saskia waited until she had left before sagging against the wall. Straightforward? That had to be good, right? She glanced up the stairs to where the family were waiting for her. Idris had been wonderful throughout the interview, calm and measured, even when the questioning had felt intrusive, no hint of the coldness that had characterised the last week. And he had brought his mother to the Embassy—officially Dalmayan soil. The first time the Princess had been anywhere near her home country in over thirty years. Saskia didn't know what to think. All she knew was that it was time she and Idris had a good, long talk and this time she was going to be the one calling the shots.

Intentions were all very well, but try as she might

Saskia didn't manage to get Idris alone at any point for the rest of the morning. He disappeared several times for long periods, once or twice with Jack. If the idea didn't seem ridiculous, she would have said he was avoiding her on purpose. He didn't seem cold or angry—at times his expression rested on her with a heat that made her quiver. But every time she made a move to draw him away he slipped away so seamlessly she couldn't see how he had managed it.

'We need to talk,' she managed to quietly say as they finished a celebratory lunch in honour of Jack's interview and Idris paused, his gaze serious.

'I know. Later. I promise.'

Frustrated, she made to turn away and he caught her arm gently, pulling her around to face his scrutiny. 'You look tired.'

'I've not been sleeping, worrying about this interview I suppose. My head is pounding,' she admitted, softened by his concern.

'Why don't you lie down for a couple of hours? I'm sure two nannies, one man and one doting grandmother can take care of two boys for an afternoon.'

Excuses sprang to her lips. She didn't want to show weakness to anyone, especially not Idris, but the words wouldn't come. Truth was she was exhausted, physically and emotionally, and although an afternoon nap wouldn't cure either it could only help. 'Okay. I will. Thank you.'

The short sleep refreshed her more than she thought possible; a quick shower and a change of clothes and she felt like a new woman, ready to talk to Idris, ready to make sure her feelings were not just heard but that some kind of consensus about the future would be made. She put a hand to her stomach, trying to press away the nerves, the fear she might get this wrong. The boys deserved a loving family, that wasn't in doubt, she just needed to ensure there was a place for her in Idris's life. A place where she would be happy and respected if not loved.

The spacious living area seemed strangely quiet. Saskia wandered through the snug, the living room and the less formal sitting room used primarily by the boys, but there was no sign of anyone. She sat by the window and looked out at Kensington Gardens, feeling a little ridiculous at how forlorn she was. Of course there was a reasonable explanation for their absence; they were probably in the park. She was overtired and a little overwrought, that was all.

She blinked back a tear. 'I don't even know why I'm crying,' she said aloud. Maybe it was the relief that the adoption seemed to be going well. Maybe the anticlimax that after gearing herself up to tell Idris how she felt, she hadn't managed to say more than a few words to him. He couldn't just waltz in here and expect everything to be okay...

She should head out to the park and see if she could find them. Now the press had gone she'd be able to walk out of the front door and straight over the road like any normal tourist. Mind made up, Saskia headed back to the pretty master bedroom she had chosen to occupy, only to come to an abrupt halt. A small bag she had never seen before sat on her bed, a note on the top. Her heart sped up to a panicked thrum. That hadn't been there a few minutes ago. Who had put it there? Was Idris sending her away? She stared at the note for a long moment then slowly walked towards it, picking it up gingerly as if it might come to life under her fingertips.

> *There's a car downstairs.*
> *You're expected at the London Palatial Hotel spa.*
> *There may be scones.*
> *Enjoy.*
> *I*

Saskia read the note through and then through again, her heart slowing as she took in the words. An afternoon to herself in a spa was an unusually thoughtful gesture—or not that unusual, she thought, fingering the charm bracelet she rarely took off. She took a deep, steadying breath. Maybe it would be a good thing to have some time out before she tackled Idris.

The famous spa was as imposingly luxurious as Saskia had heard, although as Princess Saskia of Dalmaya she was accorded the kind of reverential welcome plain Saskia Harper with her maxed-out credit card and second-hand clothes would never have enjoyed. She pushed that thought away, determined to wring the most out of the hot stone massage, facial and manicure that had been booked for her.

By the time she was escorted to the personal hot tub with rose petals sprinkled in the water and candles lit on every conceivable surface she felt like a new woman and ready for the difficult conversation that lay ahead. It wasn't that she didn't appreciate this thoughtful gesture, but she recognised that through her entire childhood she'd been bought off with lavish gifts. Her questions had never been answered. She had never found out why she didn't meet her father's dates, why her mother had left her, where her father's money had come from. Not until it all came crashing down.

She needed knowledge and agency, not just gestures.

Before she knew it her time was up and a smiling assistant helped her into one of the luxurious silk robes, guiding her to a small dressing room. Saskia stopped at the threshold and stared. A beautiful, full-length dress in her favourite pale pink hung on the wall, its cap sleeves embellished with a silver thread, the same thread accenting the waist and the hem, tiny delicate crystals shimmering in the chiffon overskirt. Silver sandals and a matching clutch bag were carefully placed on a stool and a make-up artist stood by the dressing table, the tools of her trade spread out in front of her. 'Please take a seat, Your Highness,' she said. 'Would you like your hair up or down?'

'I...' Saskia looked over at the dress again. 'I don't actually know where I'm going.' What on earth was going on? Her pulse sped up; surely she wasn't heading straight to an official event? Not when she was still living down the last one?

'Half and half, I think, if we're going to use this tiara.' The stylist held up a delicate silver chain punctuated with crystals in every twist.

'Fine. Thanks.' Every item in this room was perfect, exactly what she would have picked for herself, from the rose-pink bra and knickers draped over the chair behind her to the tiara dangling from the stylist's fingers. Only she had no idea who had chosen them for her and where she would be going in them.

Saskia took a deep breath, willing her panicked pulse to calm. She'd spent the last seven years micromanaging every second. It was the only way she had managed to survive. She didn't know what Idris expected from this gesture but as far as she was concerned their talk had just moved from important to urgent, and once they had had that talk she'd know whether she could stay with him, or if the marriage he offered was too painful for her to bear.

CHAPTER FOURTEEN

IDRIS PACED UP and down the famous domed foyer, reflecting that with all the marble and archways it was a little like being back in his own palace. He should feel at home, but, despite the coolness of the autumn evening, his suit felt too warm, too constricted. He pulled at his bow tie, wishing he'd opted for Dalmayan formal dress rather than the restrictions of a tuxedo. He glanced at his watch. Saskia should be here by now. Had he done the right thing, springing this on her? What if she hated it? What if he had got it all wrong? Relying on the judgement of a nine-year-old boy and of his impulsive mother could be the biggest mistake of all.

No, not the biggest mistake. That had happened seven years ago. It was time to atone.

His heart thumped as the great doors finally swung open. Saskia stood poised at the entrance, eyes wide as she looked in at the well-lit hall. 'What on earth are we doing at the V&A?' She stepped inside but made no move to come any closer to him.

'It's your favourite place.'

'Yes. But…' She shook her head, the soft waves of her hair rippling as she did so. 'I don't understand.'

'I wanted you to know that I notice things, that I'm not quite as cold, as unfeeling as I appear. I wanted you to know that I know your favourite colour is pink even though fashion tells you not to wear it.'

She tilted her chin at that, one hand touching the ends of her vibrant hair. 'It's a stupid rule.'

'You look beautiful in pink,' he said softly. His mother had picked out her dress with her unerring eye for style. Saskia was like a goddess of light, the silk and chiffon draping every curve and falling in folds to the floor. Marlowe's immortal words came back to him, just as they had that day at the library all those years before. She could launch one thousand ships, ten thousand and he would be at the very lead, doing whatever it took to win his wife back.

'I know afternoon tea is your favourite meal. How were the scones at the spa, by the way?'

'Delicious.' Her face was still suspicious. 'Everyone else was on watercress soup. I thought I might be lynched, especially when I spread the butter on extra thick.'

'I know that you prefer white gold to rose gold and your jewellery less ostentatious than Dalmayan fashion.' The delicate tiara flashed, wound through her fiery hair, and the charm bracelet glinted on her wrist. 'And I know I owe you an explanation.'

She held up one elegant hand. 'Idris, why did you put those clauses in the wedding contract?'

He stilled. This wasn't what he had expected her to say. 'Clauses?'

'Yes. I asked one of the embassy staff to translate it for me. There were clauses in there that weren't in the version my lawyer read to me. Handwritten clauses, which were evidently added after I'd approved the draft.' She watched him carefully. 'In the version I read I was to have appropriate alimony for the boys if we divorced. Generous alimony, life-changing alimony but appropriate. In the version I read this week I have been given the villa outright, I am allowed to divorce you at any time with no contest, keep full custody of the boys, as long as I bring Sami to Dalmaya every summer, and I'm entitled to the kind of alimony people tear each other apart in divorce courts for. That's not just generous, Idris.' She swallowed. 'That's an invitation. An invitation to divorce.'

He had added those clauses the night after they slept together, knowing they had crossed a line they might not be able to retreat back to. Idris held her gaze. 'I forced you into marrying me. I wanted to make sure you had options, a genuine choice.'

'I didn't go into this marriage intending to end it as soon as it got hard. I'm not saying I thought we'd grow old together but neither was I planning to cash my chips in and waltz out as quickly as I entered. My word means something, Idris.'

'I know.'

'Was it about giving me a choice or about giving me a push? I know I embarrassed you, embarrassed the palace...'

'No, Saskia. You didn't.' Here it was. The moment he had been both anxious for and dreading. The moment he told her who he was and what he was and allowed her to judge him. To walk away if he was unworthy. The moment Idris Delacour stopped hiding from life, from love, from the agony of feeling. 'The truth was I was jealous.'

'Jealous?'

'Jealous. You were having so much fun, and not with me. That's understandable.' He huffed out a laugh. 'I sent you into that room with a list of strictures and rules and didn't think for a moment that a woman in her twenties, a woman who's done nothing but be responsible for the last seven years, might need to unwind sometimes. Just because I never allow myself to unwind. When you fell I could have, should have laughed it off. It was nothing, but all I could see was headlines, judgements.'

He paused, searching for the right words to confess. 'The truth is I was still reeling from seeing how happy you had looked just before you fell, how happy you were away from the palace and the responsibilities I had forced on you. Those aren't escape clauses, Saskia, they are a promise that you can walk away any time. That I was wrong to bully you into this world. God knows, it's hard enough for me, and I at least had some training, some awareness of what it entails.'

Saskia's eyes were fixed on him, her gaze almost painful in its intensity. 'It was just so nice to see Robbie I forgot why I was there. What I should have done was arrange to see him later, at the palace, when you were there and we could have caught up away from prying eyes and cameras. I know that now. I was just so tired of everyone watching me, of being on display all the time, I relaxed too much. The fall was an accident but it wouldn't have happened if I'd been more careful.'

She took a deep breath. 'The thing is I can't guarantee I won't mess up again, Idris. In fact I can guarantee I will. I'm not trained for this, any of it, and I'm not naturally dignified like you and Maya. And that would be okay, if I thought you were on my side. But if you are going to freeze me out every time I mess up...' She shook her head. 'I don't need obscene alimony or want it. But if you're not on my side then I can't stay with you. Not even for the boys because they shouldn't have to grow up seeing that...'

His heart swelling, Idris walked over to his wife, to the woman he knew he loved so much he would let her walk away if that was what she needed—the woman he would then spend every moment winning back, proving he could love her the way she needed to be loved, valued for everything she was. He took her hands. 'Look at me, Saskia.'

She raised her eyes to his, the vulnerability in their depths striking him harder than anger or hatred ever could have.

'I am on your side,' he said. 'Always. It took me a while to realise that, but I am. I let you down, back when we were younger, and I let you down last week. I let you down because I put my pride first, because I didn't want to admit I was jealous. Because I didn't want to admit I loved you.'

The words echoed round and round the great hallway. 'You…you what?' Saskia was trembling, with hope, with the first glimmers of happiness, with fear that this was all a dream.

Idris's grip tightened on hers and she returned the pressure, holding on as if he were all that was holding her up. 'I love you, Saskia Harper. You have grown into an extraordinary, intelligent, compassionate woman and Dalmaya is lucky to have you as its Queen. Saskia, I am so proud to be able to call you my wife and I'm so sorry that I haven't made that clear, that, rather than show the world how much I love you, our wedding was behind closed doors.' He looked down at her, the dark eyes simmering. 'I said I wanted to give you choices, Saskia, and I am. Here, today.' His mouth quirked into a half-smile. 'If that's what you want, that is.'

'Choices?' All she could do was parrot the words back to him.

'Choices. And this time the choice is genuinely yours. Either we stay as we are, a marriage of convenience. Joint monarchs, parents, hopefully friends. I know it won't be easy, not after the events of the last few weeks, but I promise to work harder, to make it easier.'

Saskia could feel the beat of her heart, each one just that little bit faster than the one before, the rush of her blood around her shaking body. Could she go back to the marriage of convenience she had agreed to? Knowing that she loved him and that he loved her?

'Or,' he continued, 'you take advantage of the clauses in that contract and walk away, no hard feelings.'

Just like that she could have her life back. The house, the degree, the career. They didn't hold the allure they once had. She was beginning to love Dalmaya, the people and the desert and the all-encompassing heat. She could see a role there, a way to make her mark on the evolving country. 'They're my choices?' The hope had fizzled out, flat like left-out lemonade. He'd said he loved her but there was no love in this sterile pair of choices. She tried to tug her hands away but he still held them firmly in his grasp.

'No. There's one more.' The tenderness in his eyes was new and as Saskia stared into their dark depths she knew she had no defences against it. All she could do was stand there, holding onto him. 'Through there, in one of the galleries and the gardens, are your friends. Work colleagues who miss you, fellow students who can't wait to discuss essays with you, neighbours hoping you're coming back. Some of our old Oxford friends— including Rob—who mourn Maya and Fayaz as much as we do. Jack's old school friends and their parents.

You told me you had no one, Saskia, but when my mother, Faye, Lucy and I rang around the names Jack gave us I realised you made an impact on every person you knew. The mother whose sons you took to the park with Jack when her baby was colicky. The neighbour you made stews for when she was ill. The students you coached online. The other temps you supported through job after job. They all love you and they are all here.'

The litany of names was a revelation. Saskia felt the truth of Idris's words as each one sank in, warming her from within. She'd been too scared to let anyone in, to confide in them, to admit how hard it was but she hadn't been a lone wolf, not all the time.

'They're here?'

'Officially they've been invited to celebrate our new family, a party for Sami and Jack. But there's an official standing by ready to marry us, if that's what you want. If you want more than signing a contract in a language you don't understand. If you want to make vows, a commitment. Because that's what I want, Saskia, to tell the world how much I love and cherish you. To make you my wife in more than name, to make you the wife of my heart.'

It took several moments for his words to register. To realise just what he was saying. 'I…I…' She pulled her hands away and placed them on her hips. 'You call that a proposal, Your Highness Sheikh Idris Delacour Al Osman?'

The anxiety vanished from his eyes as Idris's mouth tilted into his rare and, oh, so sweet smile. 'Sheikha Saskia Harper, Princess, mother, wife, Queen. Will you do me the very great honour of becoming my wife in reality as well as in name?' He reached into his pocket and pulled out a box, opening it up as he sank onto one knee before her. 'Rubies, Saskia. Red like your hair, like the desert sunset, like the fire in my soul. A fire I didn't even know existed until I met you.'

At his words her heart swelled, all the love she had been keeping banked up, hidden away, finally rushing free, filling every nerve, every atom, every cell with the knowledge she was his as he was hers. Saskia stared at the antique ring, her heart swelling, then back at Idris, allowing herself to soak in the tenderness, the hope and passion in his eyes.

'Yes. Of course I will. I thought I loved you when I was nineteen, and in some ways I did, but I was just a child. I didn't really understand what love was. But I do love you now, with all my heart, and I want to marry you, properly, with vows and meaning and love. Yes, I do.'

Idris slid the delicate ring carefully onto her finger before getting up, joy writ all over his usually impassive face. 'You won't regret it,' he vowed as he held her close. 'I love you, Saskia.'

Looking up at him, she saw the truth of it and knew that although their road would never be an easy one if they could walk it together they could face anything.

* * * * *

*If you enjoyed this story, check out
these other great reads from
Jessica Gilmore:*

*A PROPOSAL FROM THE CROWN PRINCE
HER NEW YEAR BABY SECRET
UNVEILING THE BRIDESMAID
IN THE BOSS'S CASTLE*

All available now!

"Already?" She frowned faintly. "Here or the motel, huh?"

"Well, I have a guest room if you'd rather. No problem for me."

The offer was out before he knew it was coming, and then Matthew seconded it. The idea of having someone new in the house seemed to appeal to him.

Vanessa's hesitation seemed obvious. Matthew was already running on about how they could read his library book together, but she had drawn away. He could feel it. Pulled back into herself.

"Look," he said finally. "I'll guide you to the motel if you want, but like I said, mostly truckers and transients stay there. This house is okay if you want to stock it up. I was only thinking about you being here alone if the blizzard gets bad. You'd be stuck, and the phones aren't working."

He could swear she felt torn in a bunch of different directions. But then she surprised him.

"If you're sure I won't put you out…"

That settled it, he decided. A night or two. As soon as she'd made her decisions about the house, she'd drive away.

Matthew was ecstatic. Tim watched him with a faint smile, but once again reflected on how much that boy must miss having a mother. He hoped a couple of days wasn't long enough for him to fit Vanessa into that role.

* * *

Conard County:
The Next Generation

A CONARD
COUNTY
COURTSHIP

BY
RACHEL LEE

First Published in Great Britain 2017
By Mills & Boon, an imprint of HarperCollins*Publishers*
1 London Bridge Street, London, SE1 9GF

© 2017 Susan Civil Brown

ISBN: 978-0-263-92336-0

23-1017

Our policy is to use papers that are natural, renewable and recyclable products and made from wood grown in sustainable forests. The logging and manufacturing processes conform to the legal environmental regulations of the country of origin.

Printed and bound in Spain
by CPI, Barcelona

Rachel Lee was hooked on writing by the age of twelve and practiced her craft as she moved from place to place all over the United States. This *New York Times* best-selling author now resides in Florida and has the joy of writing full-time.

Chapter One

She never expected to find a man in the house. Vanessa Welling stood on the wet sidewalk between two low banks of melting snow and looked at the house she owned but didn't want. The hatred and pain that rose in her had been planted nearly twenty years ago by the man who had lived in that house, the man who had destroyed her family, and she'd like to set a match to the whole place.

She'd tried to get out of it, had argued with the lawyer who had called her to tell her it belonged to her. Unfortunately, Bob Higgins had deeded it over to her before he died in prison, and the really odd thing—to her, at least—was that he was free to do that even if she didn't want it. She couldn't refuse it. She couldn't give it back, and right now she was responsible for the taxes on the place. She would remain responsible for them and any code violations or fines until she managed to dump it.

Her stomach burned, her eyes felt hot in her head and everything she had tried to bury was rising sickeningly inside her.

Had that man thought this was some kind of atonement? Because it wasn't. No house could give her back her father or the years lost to his alcoholism. No house could give her back everything else that had been ripped from her at a tender age, wounding her in ways that remained with her.

She had never wanted to see this town again. She remembered how her father felt the people here must be judging him, thinking him a fool for having lost his ranch and every bit of savings to Bob Higgins. His bitterness had branded itself in Vanessa's heart, and her mother hadn't done much to erase it. Belinda Welling had been quieter in her response, but despair had filled her days. Her husband's alcoholism had overwhelmed her, and Vanessa felt that in many ways she had had to raise herself.

Now here she was, owner of the house that had belonged to the beast who had destroyed everything, and she had to at least see to fixing it up enough that she could sell it. Get rid of it. Remove any demand that she ever return here.

The street was quiet, but it was early on a Monday afternoon. Kids in school, parents at work and weather less than hospitable.

The key in her hand felt acidic, hot, as if it would eat a hole in her palm. She wanted to fling it into the snow.

Just get it done, she told herself. Just walk in there, face the memories that lurked and would probably pounce to remind her that this had once been a favorite place of hers to visit. She'd arrange whatever needed to be done, then get the hell out of this town before the whispers started, before people began to ask each other if that was Milt Welling's daughter and hadn't he been a fool to trust that Higgins guy with everything he owned?

As she walked up toward the porch, freshly laid salt crunching beneath her feet, she felt a sharp gust of icy wind. After twenty years she had no intuitive understanding of the weather around her, but to her that gust spoke of an approaching snowstorm, as did the clattering of leafless branches on the trees that lined the street.

Or maybe she was imagining it. Why not? She was walking toward the door of a house that had populated her nightmares. All that was missing was some spooky, threatening music.

How over the top could she go, she wondered as she leveled the key at the lock and felt a small burst of self-amusement puncture her anger and apprehension. Bob, the man who had ruined her family, was dead. He couldn't hurt her anymore. And leaving her his house? Probably his final laugh at someone else's expense, not an attempt to atone at all. That would fit.

It wasn't as if he hadn't stolen money from anyone else. He'd just stolen more from her father. As in everything.

Just as she turned the key in the lock, the door opened and she stood face-to-face with a tall man wearing a khaki work shirt, dusty jeans, work boots and a loaded tool belt slung around narrow hips. His eyes were the same gray as the leaden sky above, his face perfectly chiseled and showing some faint smile lines around his mouth and crinkles at the corners of his eyes. His dark brown hair was tousled and dusty. *Um, wow?*

"Hi," he said, his voice deep and pleasant. "Something I can help you with?"

Well, this was totally unexpected. This was *her* house, yet there was a stranger in it. Could he help her? But then her memory kicked in. Hadn't the lawyer said something about sending someone to look over the condition of the house?

She found her voice at last. "I'm Vanessa Welling. Who are you?"

His dark eyebrows lifted, then he smiled. "Ah. I guess Earl didn't tell you he'd hired me to check out the place, and he told me he didn't expect you before the weekend. I'm Tim Dawson. I'm a building contractor—Earl sent me. If you want, I can wait outside while you look around. Or just come back another day."

Why should he do that? But then she realized he must think that she might be uncomfortable about entering an empty house occupied by a man she'd never met before. She ought to be, but strangely she wasn't. Anyway, if anyone should leave, it ought to be her. She didn't want to be here at all.

The door still wide-open, both of them poised to leave, Vanessa shook her head a little and thought that her life had turned into a series of vignettes written by someone else from the minute Earl had told her she'd inherited this house. Nothing had run in its usual course since then.

"No," she said. "You're working. Frankly, I'd be happy never to see the inside of this place."

"I heard from Earl you didn't want it. That stinks."
He stepped back, giving her space to enter if she chose.
"It always bothered me that someone could just deed
a property to someone else even if they don't want it.
Never understood that one."

"I'm still trying to wrap my brain around it." Hesi-
tantly, she stepped through the door into the wide foyer.
It had once been an elegant house, but it had been a long
time since anyone had lived here. Some of the wallpaper was peeling. "How bad is it?"

"The place got winterized before the previous
owner…left, so there's surprisingly little damage to
important stuff. Plumbing still works, in other words.
No broken pipes. Right now I'm finishing up work on
the heater to see if I can get it operating again. It's an
old model, but I don't imagine you even want to consider a new one."

"Not if I can help it. I don't want to live here, I just want
to get to the point where I can get rid of it without having tax liens and code violations follow me through life."

"I can see that. Well, I was just going out to my truck
to get a valve, so take a look around. I'll be happy to
answer any questions I can."

She watched him walk out the door, thinking that it
was criminal that a man that good-looking had walked
into her life in the last place on earth she wanted to be.

She watched him cross the street to a white truck
with small lettering on the side. That explained why
she'd never guessed someone would be in here.

Then she forced herself to turn and face the inside
of the house. To face memories that should have been
good but had turned to ash.

* * *

Vanessa Welling was a pretty woman, Tim thought as he crossed the wet street and opened a compartment on the side of his pickup. Maybe more than pretty, but since she was clearly unhappy at the moment he couldn't be really sure. Right now, she was simply a catalog of externalities: auburn hair, mossy-green eyes, a bit on the tiny side.

Earl Carter, father of the local judge, was a font of history when it came to this county, especially the ugly legal parts. The story of how Bob Higgins had managed to rob the Welling family blind was the stuff of novels or movies…except according to Earl, this kind of thing happened all the time. Con men, con jobs—and the Wellings hadn't been the only ones robbed. Apparently, a number of others had fallen for Higgins's financial planning business, to their detriment, but only the Wellings had lost more than a retirement fund.

Sad story. Vanessa would have been a kid when it all happened, but from what Earl had said, she remembered enough to be filled with loathing. Imagine inheriting the house of the man who had ruined your family. Tim couldn't make up his mind if Higgins had been diabolical or regretful.

Anyway, Vanessa had a problem to deal with, and he'd bet she wanted to make her decisions and get the hell out of Conard County as fast as she could.

Shame, because he'd like to get a chance to know the woman behind that haunted, heart-shaped face. Not that it mattered, really. Just a reaction to a new face. He had his hands full enough raising a seven-year-old

boy whose mother had died. A change of pace might
be nice, but it would be transitory.

He was just crossing the street again with the valve
he wanted in hand when a black Cadillac pulled up. It
was an older car, kept in scrupulously good shape by its
owner, Earl Carter. Earl pulled up against the curb on
the far side of the street and rolled his window down.
"She's here?"

"Oh, yeah."

"I just got her message." Earl, a pleasantly plump
man who was awfully popular around town for a lawyer, shook his head faintly. "Sorry, I didn't think she
would be here so soon."

"It's not a problem. But she's clearly not happy to
be here."

"No kidding. I'm sorry I couldn't find her a way out.
Is she inside?"

"Yeah. I just came out to get a valve for a gas line."

"I'll go in with you. Two strange men in one day
might be too much."

Tim almost laughed. They would still be two strange
men in the otherwise empty house with her. Hardly
likely to make her feel easier, except that Earl slightly
resembled a teddy bear. The years and some beer had
given him a bit of a belly and softened his face. He
looked kindly by nature.

"Well, come on, but she was looking as if she wanted
to burn the place down."

"Probably does," Earl said, climbing out. He might
be the last man in town who wore a business suit rou-
tinely. Even his own son, the judge, often wore jeans
under his judicial robes.

"Let me call inside first," Tim suggested. "Let her know we're both here. This can't be easy for her."

"It's not," Earl said. "Not at all. Bet she hits the road just as quick as she can."

"Maybe." He wasn't about to predict what anyone else would do. Dangerous game, that.

"She didn't want this place," Earl mused, pausing on the walk before heading for the porch. "She may change her mind, though. With a little work, this house will become prime real estate. Great location, good size. She should make a pretty penny if she shapes it up."

"Sure, we sell so much prime real estate around here." Tim's tone was dry. Given the kind of work he did, he knew how sluggish the market was locally. Nothing new for this town. Boom or bust. Right now, it was more bust.

"Cut it out, boy," Earl said. "We'll get that ski resort and this house would make a good bed-and-breakfast."

"Now that's prime optimism," Tim answered. "That ski resort has been a pipe dream forever. I'd bet the landslide finished the idea, even if Luke is back to checking the geology for a developer."

"Someone's paying him," was Earl's answer. "So someone is interested in doing it."

Someone had been interested in the possibility of a resort on the mountainside Tim's entire adult life. So far nothing had been done beyond clearing a few ski trails, a small investment in downtown improvement with brick sidewalks and Victorian lampposts, and a survey of the hotel site. Then the landslide. Tim just shook his head and wondered if being an eternal optimist was part of how people survived around here. He tended to lean toward optimism himself, despite everything. He had a kid to think about.

"Let's get going," he said. "I need to finish work on the heater in time to go pick my son up."

Earl glanced at him. "He doesn't walk home?"

"Not when a blizzard is in the forecast." Tim nodded toward the sky. "Rapid temperature drop this afternoon. Whiteout conditions."

"You don't say. I should pay more attention, I guess."

Tim smiled as they climbed the porch steps and he opened the door. Earl was a gadabout when he wasn't being a damn good lawyer. Why would he pay attention to the weather report? He could get to his son's house or Mahoney's to have beer with friends. Unless court dates had to be postponed, the effects of bad weather on Earl would be minimal.

Opening the door and leaning in, Tim called out, "Ms. Welling? It's me, Tim, and I've brought your lawyer with me. Earl Carter."

As he and Earl crossed the threshold, he heard hurried footsteps from the back of the house. Still wearing her jacket, with her hands stuffed in her pockets, Vanessa managed a smile.

"So you're Earl Carter."

"One and the same." Earl smiled. "Lots of time on the phone, but nothing like face-to-face." He stuck out his hand, and Vanessa freed hers to shake it. "Well, what do you think?"

"About the house? Besides the fact I don't want it? It needs work, Earl. I supposed Mr. Dawson knows how sound it is generally, but paint is sagging on some of the walls. Sagging! I don't think I've ever seen that before."

"Bad paint job," Tim remarked. "Old paint. Lack of care. Nothing that can't be fixed."

"This place looks like a headache," she said frankly. "I wish you could have stopped Bob Higgins from doing this to me."

Earl shook his head. "He did this all on his own. I never knew about it until he died. Then everything landed on my desk."

"It landed on me like a ton of bricks," she said. "I never wanted to come back here. Never."

Tim decided it might be a good time to step out of the conversation. "I need to go put this valve on the heater so I can get it up and running again. It's getting cold in here. There's a pot of coffee in the kitchen. Why don't you two help yourselves?"

He headed down to the basement, acutely aware that without heat, given the coming cold, this place could suffer a lot of damage now that he'd turned on the plumbing again. Eventually that heater should be replaced, but he had a feeling Vanessa Welling wouldn't be the one to do it.

In the chilly kitchen with Earl Carter, Vanessa pulled out a chair and sat at a table she remembered all too well.

"Bet you remember this house," Earl remarked.

"I don't want to talk about it." She really didn't. Good memories had been turned into a nightmare by the man who had inflicted this house on her, and she had little desire to look back.

"You used to play with the Higgins kids, didn't you?"

She looked at him. "I think I said I didn't want to talk about it."

"You did," he acknowledged. "But I don't want to talk about your memories. That was a lead-in to how you're sitting here. After Bob Higgins was arrested, his wife took their two kids and left. I got to wondering why she didn't sell the house at some point, then I learned why. She never owned it. It was his, lock, stock and barrel."

"That fits," Vanessa said tautly. The guy didn't even take care of his family. He'd made sure everything was his, even their house.

"So, anyway, I only looked into it to find out how it had come to you. When you said you didn't want it, I hunted his ex-wife up and suggested that you might be willing to give it to her. She was as interested as you were. Didn't want to even think about it. So here we are."

"So he ruined everyone's lives."

"That's how it looks. She's remarried. Even changed the last name of the children."

Vanessa nodded slightly and looked down as Earl put a mug of coffee in front of her. That looked better than anything she'd seen since arriving here. Well, except for Tim Dawson. "I hate this, Earl," she said, reaching out to grip the mug in both hands for its warmth.

"No better man than Tim Dawson to take care of it for you. He'll be quick, he won't overcharge and he won't do more than you want and need him to do."

She raised her gaze to his. "But what about selling it?"

"We'll get that done somehow, too. We haven't got the busiest real estate market, but a house like this, reasonably priced, should sell. And you can afford to price it reasonably, because your only sunk costs are going to be for basic repairs and taxes."

She hadn't thought about that, and it made her feel slightly better. She could sell it for a song, then it wouldn't be her problem anymore. Or maybe she could even find a place to donate it, once she was sure it was safe. A house left basically abandoned for twenty years might have all kinds of safety problems. No termites, though, according to Earl. That had been the first thing he had checked out.

So…it would be okay, she told herself yet again. Lately that had become a mantra.

Earl let her have some silence, for which she was grateful. She was still trying to deal with the mess of emotions coming back here had awakened in her. She had a lot to be angry about, a lot to be sad about, and feelings she had put away long ago had all surfaced with her return, with having to deal with this house.

The past had become present, through no choice of her own, and for the first time she considered just how much she hadn't been able to get over. No, it seemed more like she had plastered over all the cracks and the plaster was giving way. She'd even started having bad dreams again.

Some things were better left buried, and she wished all of this had remained in its grave. What the hell had Bob Higgins been thinking? He'd had no conscience about robbing her family into abject poverty. Why would he have gotten one at such a late stage in his life?

Chilly air stirred suddenly, and she heard a distant *whoompf* that probably indicated Tim had started the heater. Considering that he had the water running now, that was an excellent thing.

A minute later he appeared, wiping his hands on a

rag that he jammed into the back pocket of his jeans. "All set. They make much more efficient models now, but this will do. It shouldn't break down, anyway. And when you're ready to go, I'll winterize the house again."

He grabbed some coffee of his own and joined her at the table.

"I was just getting ready to leave," Earl announced. "I have a three o'clock meeting. If you need anything, call me." He handed her a business card along with a warm smile, then walked out.

When Vanessa remained silent, Tim spoke. "I guess this hit you like a ton of bricks."

"To put it mildly."

He just shook his head, unsure what he could say. "I've got to run soon as well. I need to pick up my son from school. I'll bring him back here so we can have some time to discuss what has to be done and whether you want to do any more than that."

She nodded. "How old is your son?"

"Seven. Anyway, we're going to be getting a sharp temperature drop anytime now, and I don't want him out there walking in subzero temps."

"I'd forgotten." If she'd ever really known. "It can change fast, can't it?"

"Very fast. And we're just sliding into winter, so nobody's really ready. Blizzard tonight, maybe. If you can stand it, you might want to stay here rather than at the motel. We can get you some food in so you don't have to hoof it or drive to get a meal. The thing about the motel is that it's used mainly by truckers and transients. You might feel safer here, much as you hate it."

"I'll think about it."

He stood. "I'll be back in fifteen or twenty minutes...
unless you'd rather I didn't come back."

For once since getting here she didn't feel like hesitating. "No, come back. I'd like to meet your son."

He nodded once with a smile, then left the kitchen.
She listened to his boots cross the foyer, then the front
door opened and closed.

Earl had done his best, Tim was a nice guy and
maybe she could survive this trip after all.

But the thought of being snowed in here? She shuddered. There'd be no way to avoid the memories then.

From what Earl had told him, Tim guessed this visit
had to be a painful one for Vanessa. Although she'd
been a child his own son's age when her family's life
had fallen apart, she probably remembered enough
to find it uncomfortable to return. While it was old
news, when Bob Higgins had died in prison, people
had recalled his life and crimes, and inevitably Tim
had learned something about the man.

He'd apparently set himself up as an investment adviser and had a few impressive pieces of paper framed
on his office wall. He'd even been licensed by the state.
Everyone knew him, most people liked him and it hadn't
taken him long to get his business rolling.

It must have rolled well for ten or twelve years before
it caught up with him. Tim didn't understand exactly
how the scheme had worked, but Bob had persuaded
people to entrust him with their money to invest, and
most had only given him amounts they never needed
back, or if they needed to pull something out, they'd
been able to.

But Vanessa's parents had been different. They'd thought their investments were growing so well that Bob Higgins had managed to persuade them to give him even more, promising them a fortune. They'd mortgaged their ranch and had learned the bleak truth when they needed money from their investments to pay that mortgage.

Tim didn't pretend to understand how it all had worked or why Higgins had persuaded the Wellings to mortgage their ranch. Maybe because he was getting to the point where he needed money to pay clients a return?

Regardless of it all, the Wellings had left town, and Bob Higgins had been exposed and sent to jail.

But he could see no earthly reason why the man would have deeded his house to Vanessa. No *good* reason.

He joined the line of parents waiting in their vehicles at the elementary school. The temperature had begun to drop, and the teachers were blowing clouds of fog when they spoke and hurried the children along. Cheeks quickly brightened to red, and there was little of the usual horseplay. The cold had shocked the kids, too.

Tim started to smile as he watched his son, Matthew, race toward the truck. The boy reminded him of his mother, Claire, with his round face, a splatter of freckles across his nose, and a dark blond hair. Every time Tim saw him, he felt an ache for Claire.

Leaning over, he unlatched the door and threw it open for the boy. Matt scrambled in then used both hands to close the door. As usual, Matt did everything at top speed.

The door was open long enough, however, for Tim

to feel the dangerous cold deepening outside. If the forecast held, they might need to close school tomorrow. Occasionally it grew too cold to expect children to walk to school or to bus stops.

"How was your day, kiddo?"

"Okay," Matthew answered. He grinned as he struggled to buckle himself in, showing off the two new front teeth that were emerging. He'd just outgrown the child seat, but was still having trouble with the regular seat belt.

"Just okay?" Tim asked.

"Well, Orson turned green around his neck and got all ruffed up." Orson was an exotic lizard who lived in a large aquarium. "Ms. Macy said something must have scared him. That was probably Tommy. He kept banging a penny against the tank."

"Why did Tommy do that?"

Matthew shrugged. "I guess it was fun. Everybody was pretty mad about Orson, though. He doesn't bother anybody."

"I don't imagine he does. Lots of homework?"

"Not much. Two work sheets."

At last able to pull out of the line, Tim drove back toward the Higgins house—although he supposed it was the Welling house now—and listened to Matthew's cheerful recounting of the day and his pride in bringing home his very first library book from the school.

It wasn't as if Tim hadn't been taking him to the public library all along, but the school library was something special.

"Where are we going, Daddy?"

"Back to the house I'm working on. There's a lady there now—she owns the house. So…"

"Company manners," Matthew said with a sharp nod of his head. "Is she a nice lady?"

"I think so, but I just met her before I came to get you."

"She's not a witch?" Matt asked, scrunching up his face and making his small hands into claws.

"What *have* you been reading?" Tim asked, eliciting a giggle.

"Fun stuff. Ms. Macy says I'm too young for Harry Potter, though."

"Oh. Did you want to read it?" He suspected Ms. Macy's objection arose more from what some parents around here thought of children reading about wizards and magic.

"Joey's brother did. He loves it."

"Well, I'll see what I can do about getting a copy from the library. You can try it and see."

For that he received an ear-to-ear grin.

Occasionally when he talked with his son, Tim felt a nostalgia for his own childhood, when everything had been simple and magical. Other times, though, when Matt was having a problem of some kind, Tim was more than glad to be so much older. He suspected that feeling would grow when Matthew hit his teens.

This time he pulled up right in front of the house. Vanessa had parked in the narrow driveway, so there didn't seem to be any reason to leave curb space. Especially with the temperature dropping so rapidly.

Matthew started to pull his backpack out with him, and Tim stopped him. "You won't need that until we get home."

"But I want to show the new lady my library book!"

Tim let him go but wondered if Vanessa would be pleasant, bored or annoyed. Matthew wasn't her child, after all, and for all he knew she had little patience for youngsters. Still, how annoyed could she be over a library book?

"Company manners," he reminded Matthew as they walked toward the front door.

"I know, Dad." The boy's tone was a touch exasperated, making Tim smile faintly. How fast they tried to grow up.

Vanessa was still sitting in the kitchen with her coffee. Apparently she'd felt no urge to explore the house. Sooner or later, she would have to do a walk-through with him. He could understand her being angry with Higgins, but the house? No, she hadn't wanted it, but surely she didn't have anything against the house. It was an inanimate object.

"Ms. Welling, this is my son, Matthew."

She had lifted her head at the approach of their footsteps, and now she managed a faint smile. "Hello, Matthew. If you want, you can call me Vannie."

"Vannie?" he repeated as if memorizing it. "I got a new library book. Wanna see?"

Kids, thought Tim. They got through the rough spots as if they weren't there, skipped over the awkwardness of first meetings and just accepted everyone as a friend.

"I'd love to see," she answered. Her expression remained pleasant and her tone neutral. Okay, she'd be polite.

"We can't take too long, Matthew. Vannie's going to need to get some groceries before the snow starts."

He looked at Vanessa. "The cold out there will snatch your breath."

"Already?" She frowned faintly. "Here or the motel, huh?"

"Well, I have a guest room, if you'd rather. No problem for me."

The offer was out before he knew it was coming, and then Matthew seconded it. The idea of having someone new in the house seemed to appeal to him.

Vanessa's hesitation appeared obvious. Matthew was already running on about how they could read his library book together, but she had drawn away. He could feel it. Pulled back into herself.

"Look," he said finally. "I'll guide you to the motel if you want, but like I said, mostly truckers and transients stay there. This house is okay if you want to stock it up. I was only thinking about you being here alone if the blizzard gets bad. You'd be stuck, and the phones here aren't working. Cell phones can become unreliable when the air's full of blowing snow."

He could have sworn she felt torn in a bunch of different directions. But then she surprised him.

"If you're sure I won't put you out…"

That settled it, he decided. A night or two. As soon as she'd made her decisions about the house, she'd drive away.

Matthew was ecstatic. Tim watched him with a faint smile, but once again reflected on how much that boy must miss having a mother. He hoped a couple of days wasn't long enough for him to fit Vanessa into that role.

Chapter Two

Vanessa hoped she hadn't made a mistake. Tim Dawson seemed like a laid-back sort of guy, however attractive, and his son was a trip. It ought to be okay for a few days.

But honestly, the thought of being stuck alone in Bob Higgins's house because of a blizzard had been more than she could face. As she'd sat there, waiting for Tim to return with his son, memories had clamored, and maybe the worst part was that they were so confused.

So much for thinking she'd dealt with the past and put it away. The house had dug it all up again. It would have been okay if the memories had been bad, but the thing was, they were good memories, which made Bob Higgins's betrayal all that more difficult to deal with.

When she stepped outside to follow Tim to his house,

the icy air astonished her. The temperature had fallen that fast? She wore what she'd thought would be an adequate wool coat, but it wasn't enough.

She hurried to get into her car and out of the wind. Matthew had told his father he wanted to ride with her, but before she could say anything Tim had squashed that. Good. She liked the kid as much as she could, having only just met him, but she was far from being ready to drive him around. Also, she knew next to nothing about children.

Maybe she should have gone to the motel. The town had only one, it seemed, and the reviews hadn't been exciting. Truckers and transients? And what if she got snowed in there?

She shook her head at herself. She wasn't usually a ditherer, but then she'd never faced a situation quite like this before. Not as an adult making her own decisions.

A town she had nearly forgotten that held secrets about her family that might cause people to judge her. Her dad had certainly thought so. A house from the man who'd destroyed her family. She couldn't imagine staying there by herself to deal with the good memories that refused to jibe with later reality. Worse, the bad memories from later were more sharply engraved on her mind. She didn't want to relive her dad's deterioration and death. All that bitterness. Her mother's despair.

She hoped Bob Higgins had gone to hell, then caught herself. She didn't wish that on anyone. But that was the problem with being back here. Having thoughts like that. She was going to face a very ugly part of herself until she was able to walk away.

Tim lived right around the corner. He pulled into a

paved driveway that left enough room for her to pull in beside him. She was relieved she wouldn't be blocking him in or leaving her car on the street to interfere with snowplows.

From the outside, the two-story house appeared tidy—freshly painted white, black shutters all in good condition. A side door led into a mudroom, and from there into a warmly decorated kitchen, painted yellow with sunflower decals along the soffits. A woman's touch.

"Your wife won't mind?" she asked, a belated concern. It almost embarrassed her that she hadn't asked earlier.

"I'm widowed," Tim said as he bent to give Matthew a friendly pat on his behind and sent him to put his backpack away. "Homework before dinner."

"Okay, Dad, but I still haven't showed Vannie my book."

"After the work sheets are done, okay? She'd probably like to put her suitcase in the spare room and settle a bit."

Matthew looked at Vanessa and grinned. "I don't have much homework."

"Then I'll have to hurry my settling in."

Matthew dashed off, leaving Tim and Vanessa alone for a moment.

"He's cute," Vanessa offered.

"He's also endlessly energetic. Don't let him bug you too much. Come on, I'll show you your room."

Miserable as she had been by herself at the Higgins house, now she felt a desperate need for a few minutes alone. With her emotions all topsy-turvy, she needed just a little time to let them settle.

Closing the door behind her in the guest room seemed like a sure way to get that done. Tim brought in her suitcase, told her where to find the facilities, then left her alone in a lovely room.

She suspected he cherished the memory of his wife, because little enough had been done to erase a woman's touch. No man had chosen those white ruffled curtains or thought to put an embroidered oval doily on the top of the mirrored dresser. A comforter decorated with forget-me-nots covered the queen-size bed, and matching rugs scattered the polished wood floor.

Definitely his wife's choices, she thought, along with the pale lavender paint on the walls.

So he hadn't changed a thing. That told her something about his grief. Then she thought of his son, the boy without a mother, and reluctantly her heart went out to them both. The fact that she didn't make relationships didn't mean she didn't care.

It was the relationships that could frighten her. But for Tim and Matthew...that wasn't enough to unnerve her. She didn't intend to be here that long.

She enjoyed a few minutes by herself, changing out of her traveling clothes into more comfortable green fleece, pants and thick socks. Then she decided it was time to go out and face the world of Tim and Matthew. Hanging around in her room might seem rude to Tim after he'd been awfully nice to invite her to stay here.

As she passed the dining room, she saw Matthew hunkered over some papers, chewing on a pencil. He flashed her a grin and went back to work.

She found Tim in the kitchen, washing and patting

down a whole chicken. "Can I help?" she offered automatically.

"No need. Just have a seat at the kitchen table. Coffee?"

"No, thank you. Maybe some water?"

"There are bottles in the fridge, and glasses in the cabinet beside it if you want one. I'm a bottle drinker, I'm afraid. Anyway, apologies for not getting it for you, but my hands are covered with chicken."

"I don't expect to be waited on," she assured him. "It's kind of you to give me shelter from the storm. Honestly, I didn't want to stay alone at the house, and Earl's and your description of the motel made me uneasy."

Tim nodded as he placed the chicken in the roasting pan beside the sink. "You'd probably be okay there, but you aren't going to want to have to cross the highway in a blizzard this cold just to get to the truck stop to eat something. Anyway, with this weather moving in, they'll be packed...and so will the truck stop diner." He flashed her a smile. "My house is so much nicer."

"It is," she agreed readily. "Your spare room is beautiful. Your wife?"

"Yeah."

She watched him oil the chicken then wash his hands again, wondering if mention of his wife was off-limits.

When he was done prepping the chicken, he washed his hands again then leaned back against the counter as he dried them with a towel. "My wife passed six years ago. Pulmonary embolism, if you can believe it. Out of nowhere. Matthew has absolutely no memory of her. I can't decide if that's good or bad."

"I wouldn't know," she said carefully. "I am very sorry for your loss."

He tossed the towel to one side. "You get used to the most incredible things. Anyway, yeah, she decorated most of the house. Your room was her pride, though. It wasn't often she could find everything she wanted that would match." He rested his palms on the counter behind him. "What about you?"

"Me?"

"People you're in a hurry to get back to?"

"I work at a natural history museum, and they told me to take whatever time I needed." Indeed, they'd been very kind. But she was also acutely aware that she hadn't answered his questions. He'd been straightforward with her, and she felt she needed to give him something in kind.

"My parents are both dead, and there's no one else." And never would be. No risks of that nature. She'd seen the price up close and personal, as they said.

He didn't press the issue but instead turned to pop the chicken in the oven when something beeped. "We eat early around here. Better for Matthew. Tonight we'll have broccoli with cheese and boxed stuffing to go with this. I hope that sounds good."

"It sounds great."

He got himself a bottle of water from the fridge. She still hadn't gotten one for herself, so he placed one in front of her with a glass.

"So what do you do at the museum?" he asked.

"I help connect dinosaur bones. Unfortunately, they're rarely discovered as a complete kit. Weather, erosion, what have you, have scattered and mixed the bones. So my job is to figure out what they are and which ones belong where."

"Do you assemble them?"

She shook her head. "Not unless there's an extraordinary find. No, mostly we catalog and put them away for safekeeping and later study. It's not like we know everything."

"Matt would probably love a trip to see dinosaur bones."

She smiled. "I'm sure he would. And this summer there'll probably be several digs going on around this state. Wyoming is a great place for fossil beds. He could see someone pulling them out of the ground...if he has the patience."

"I've read about that. Just never thought about taking the time. Guess I should."

A silence fell, and she felt awkward about it. With people she knew, silences could be allowed, but she didn't know this man that well. "You don't have to entertain me," she nearly blurted.

He lifted one corner of his mouth in a half smile. "That goes both ways. Besides, once he finishes his homework, Matthew will take over the entertaining. You'll probably be begging to go to your room for some solitude."

A laugh trickled out of her. "I've hardly met him, but he seems high energy."

"I've often wished we could tap some of that energy for ourselves as we get older. It's amazing. He can wear me out sometimes."

"All kids are like that, right?"

"I would worry if one weren't." He glanced at his

watch. "Want to move into the living room? I've got an hour before I need to start the rest of dinner. We could check in on how bad the storm will be."

She was agreeable and followed him into another tasteful room. His wife was a living presence here, she realized. In a good way. She had created a comfortable, lovely home.

He flipped on the wide-screen TV to the weather station. Whatever else had been in the programming had given way to a nearly breathless description of the storm that bore down on them, complete with advice not to travel and to stay inside if possible.

"These are going to be killer temperatures," the woman reciting the weather said. "Not a time to decide to make snowballs, kids, or a snowman. You could leave your fingers behind."

"Or worse," Tim said. "Do you remember when you were a kid living on a ranch?"

She looked at him. "Earl's been talking?"

"Earl knows darn near everything. Like the sheriff. I'm fairly certain he doesn't share things that are personal. Is it some kind of secret that you lived on a ranch?"

She shook her head but felt the memories jar her again, just as she thought she'd managed to put them away once more. "I just don't remember very much of it. I was seven when we moved away, so all I have left are snatches. Why?"

"I just wondered how many cold mornings you stood at the end of your road waiting for the bus. Do you remember those?"

"One or two," she admitted. "It was just me, of course,

but when it got really cold my dad would drive me to the stop and we'd wait together. Once the snow was so deep he couldn't drive me, so he forged ahead of me so I could walk." She smiled faintly, enjoying the good memory of her father. "I remember how the snow was practically up to his waist. Behind him I was walking through a tunnel."

Tim smiled. "We don't often get snow that deep right here. It tends to fall farther east because of the mountains."

She nodded, not really caring. Her only agenda was to get this house out of her hair and go home. Then she remembered Matthew. "He's taking a while with his homework. I thought he said it was just a little bit."

"Compared to what he usually has, it probably is. But he knows I'm going to check it, and he doesn't want to be sent back to fix his mistakes."

That drew another smile from her. "He's a cute kid." And he was. He could have been included in a Norman Rockwell painting.

"I think so. Of course." He looked toward the windows, as it sounded as if someone had thrown sand against them. "Ice pellets. It's begun. I need to go pull the curtains to keep this place warmer."

He closed the ones in the living room first, a deep burgundy that complimented the dark blues in the furniture and was picked up in the area rug centered on the floor. She sat by herself with the TV weather running at a quiet volume, the forecaster clearly happy to have something interesting to report.

The journey that had brought her here was certainly an odd one. She'd never expected, nor had she ever intended, to see this town or this county again. Not because anything so bad had happened to her, but because of the aftermath of what had happened to her family.

All she remembered of that time was having to move, leaving most things behind, but also leaving her friends behind. She remembered having friends back then. Not the kind of reserved friendships that came later in her life, but she'd known other people, other kids. Whisk— they were gone.

Changing schools, changing lives and listening to her father's endless bitterness. He'd turned some of that bitterness on this town and county, on the people he had known here, people he was sure were making fun of him or looking down on him.

After that move, and several others that followed, Vanessa had begun to feel like a visitor in her own life, ready to move on at a moment's notice.

But she didn't want to think about that now. Anyway, she'd been round and round about it all for years before she decided to put it away. The past couldn't be changed, and concentrating on it seemed like a waste of time.

So coming back here? That seemed like a step backward, a step in a direction she didn't want to go. Being here would resolve nothing, but it had sure stirred up a lot of unpleasant feelings and memories.

Whatever had Bob Higgins been thinking? Once upon a time she'd called him "Uncle Bob" and played with his children in that very house. Then her father had told her endlessly and repeatedly what an awful man Uncle Bob was, how he'd stolen everything from her family. She'd learned to hate him.

Now that house. It didn't make sense, and she

guessed she would never understand. She just had to find a way to dump it as quickly as possible. Get back to her normal life.

All of a sudden, Matthew came bouncing into the room. "All done! Daddy says it's okay so I can come talk to you."

She shook herself out of her reverie and summoned a smile. "You were going to show me your book."

"Later," he said decisively. "Daddy says you work with dinosaur bones. Are they really big?"

She liked his enthusiasm. "Some are huge. As long as this room. The ones I like best are the small ones, though."

"Why?" He scooted onto the other end of the couch.

Why? How to explain that to him. "Everyone loves the big bones," she said slowly. "And they're easier to find most of the time. But the little ones are like a secret."

That made his eyes shine. "Do you find out the secret?"

"Sometimes. Has anyone ever showed you a picture of the bones in your foot?"

He shook his head.

"Well, there are lots of tiny bones in your foot. Your foot wouldn't move very well without them. But someone looking at them if they were scattered around might put them together and finally figure out how your foot works."

He nodded, looking very intent. "So it's like a puzzle?"

"Exactly. Sometimes I make mistakes and put pieces from different puzzles together, and I have to figure out what's wrong. But when I find enough of the pieces of the same foot puzzle, I know how the dinosaur's foot worked."

"Do you do that all the time?"

"Once in a while."

"I'd like the small pieces, too," he decided. "More fun. But the big pieces?"

"More exciting for everyone," she agreed. "Youngsters like you are always coming to the museum to see the big dinosaurs we've managed to put together. It can be wild to stand on the floor and look up, up, up to see the head of the dinosaur. It makes me feel very small and very glad there aren't any more dinosaurs around."

He clapped his hands with delight. "I wanna do that sometime."

"I'm sure you can," Tim remarked, entering the room. "We'll take a trip and do that."

"Goody!" Matthew was satisfied. "Now can I show you my book?"

"Of course," Vanessa answered.

Matthew skipped from the room, and Tim said, "If he's imposing, let me know."

"He's not." She had to smile. "His excitement is refreshing. Too bad it's winter. There's an escarpment about a hundred miles from here where they've been making some incredible finds. Closed until spring, of course."

"I feel almost ashamed for not knowing about that dig."

She laughed, warming to him. "It's not making the news like the weather is. Most paleontologists work in obscurity unless something really big or new is discovered, and even then it rarely catches the eye of the mainstream media. You'd need to keep up with journals."

"Well, I don't have a lot of time for that, between work and child. Does a dinosaur fascination last long?"

She blinked, surprised. "In what way?"

"I mean, do kids stay interested long enough that summer can get here and I can take him to the dig?"

She laughed, shrugging. "Some kids stay fascinated for years. Others are in and out of it in a short time. The dig won't necessarily be all that interesting for him at his age, though. They might have a few things laid out on a table, but unless they're working on pulling a big piece out of the ground, it might seem dull to him." She hesitated, then said, "Listen, if it's okay with you, I can send him some materials from the museum. One of them is a wooden puzzle, where you have to put the pieces of bone together and made a 3-D model. It's really popular."

"Thank you." His smile grew wide. "I'm sure he'd love that."

"Consider it done."

How easy it was to talk about her work. But it had always been an easy topic for her. Working in a museum suited her in more ways than one. It certainly helped keep her largely by herself. Yes, she had a few girlfriends, but it wasn't the kind of closeness that would cause her to grieve if she had to move on.

Casual relationships. That was all she had, and she was content that way. Sometimes she wondered if she were just an oddity, or if she were broken in some way.

But at nearly thirty, it hardly seemed to matter. Not when she was content with her life.

Until that damn house.

Matthew bounced back in with his library book. Tim was curious to see what he'd chosen, so he sat on the far end of the sofa from Vanessa and let the boy sit between them.

It turned out to be a book of jokes, some of them well beyond the youngster's comprehension, but he seemed fascinated by all the knock-knock jokes. Tim could have groaned. He knew Matthew's memory for things that interested him, and he suspected he was going to be treated to knock-knock jokes for months. Or at least until Matthew found a new interest.

"Maybe it's time to get Harry Potter," he said.

Matthew immediately forgot his joke book. "Really?"

"Really," Tim said. He'd vastly prefer listening to summaries of the day's reading of Harry Potter than a slew of bad jokes.

"I've read Harry Potter," Vanessa volunteered. "You're going to love it."

Matthew beamed. "I think so. Ms. Macy thought I was too young." He frowned suddenly. "I don't think it's in the school library."

"Maybe not," Tim said. "It'll be in the public library, and if not, we'll go to the bookstore and get it."

"Why wouldn't it be in the public library?" Vanessa asked.

"Some people can't tell the difference between fiction and reality," he said. "Surely you remember the uproar back when about kids reading about witches and warlocks?"

"I didn't pay much attention. I was too busy reading."

He laughed. "Surely the best way to handle it."

They endured a few more bad jokes. Tim didn't mind Matthew reading them. He was, after all, reading. What he dreaded was the possibility that the boy might still find them funny and worth repeating a long time after he'd returned the book.

"Time to get the rest of dinner going," he announced. "Matthew, can you set the table?"

"The good table?"

"Of course. We have company."

Once again, Matthew dashed off to carry out his assigned task.

"You shouldn't go to any trouble for me," Vanessa protested quietly.

He shook his head a little. "This is a learning experience for Matthew. Plus, he likes being able to help. So, wanna come supervise me while I make boxed stuffing and frozen veggies? I might mess up otherwise."

The way he said it made her laugh, and she gladly followed him back into the kitchen. The rattle of ice against the windows was audible in there, and Tim felt a snaking draft.

"That cold air is the heat coming on again. It'll get warm soon. Boy, it sounds miserable out there."

"It certainly does," she agreed. "And thank you for your invitation to stay here. I'd have been miserable in the Higgins house."

"The Welling house now," he reminded her. "And you're more than welcome."

It *was* her house now, but as she watched him finish the dinner preparations, she felt an urge to share something with him, maybe so he could better understand her reactions. "Did Earl tell you what Bob Higgins did to my family? And to others around town?"

"Something about an investment scam?"

"Yeah. I don't get exactly how he did it, but he got people to give him money to invest. Periodically he'd pay out to them, especially if they had a need, but somewhere along the way he must have spent too much money to keep up the pretense that he was actually investing it. That's when he talked my father into mortgaging the ranch, promising him that his so-called investment fund would not only pay him enough to meet the mortgage payments, but would give him extra. Bob was my dad's lifelong friend. I don't think it ever entered his head that Bob was conning him."

"God, that's awful. I don't understand people who steal from others, especially when there's a trusting relationship involved."

"I don't get it, either." And it was a primary reason she found it so hard to trust. "It was especially hard on my father. He'd lost everything, we moved away and gradually he became an alcoholic. We moved again several times when he lost jobs and then…well, the alcohol killed him."

"My God! I'm so sorry, Vanessa." He'd stopped mixing the stuffing, and the vegetables were still waiting beside a microwave container. After a moment, he visibly caught himself and returned to his tasks. "I can't imagine how awful that had to have been for you."

"Eventually you don't feel it anymore. Anyway, I think the stress killed my mother. She was awfully young for a heart attack." She sighed, watching him move with the grace of a man in great shape doing the minor little things of mixing the stuffing, starting the microwave, putting a pat of butter on the bowl of frozen broccoli.

A man who could handle everything, she thought. Construction, fatherhood, cooking…he had a full plate, all right. Much fuller than hers, which seemed to be mostly filled with her own melancholy memories right now.

She missed her dinosaur bones. They spoke to her, too, but in ways that excited her. People didn't have that effect on her. She couldn't trust them to tell a true story, unlike the bones, which couldn't lie.

And that probably made her neurotic, she thought with an unexpected tickle of amusement as Matthew erupted into the kitchen. That boy was like a human power plant. "I think I did it right."

"I'll check in a moment," Tim answered. "Did you get yourself a glass of milk? And did you ask Vannie what she'd like to drink?"

Vanessa suspected this was a new stage for the boy. He looked a little surprised, then said, "I get to do the drinks?"

"You can carry a glass of milk into the dining room, can't you?"

That big, engaging grin. "Sure." He turned to Vanessa. "You want milk, too?"

"I'd very much like a glass of water, thank you."

She was charmed, enchanted, and so very glad not to be riding out this storm all alone at the Higgins house.

Matthew was just tall enough to reach the bottom shelf of the upper cupboard by stretching, and he pulled out two glasses. He stuck his tongue out and bit it while pouring one glass half-full of milk, clearly taking great care. The other was more easily handled at the sink.

Then, carefully, he picked up both glasses and carried them away.

"You must be very proud of Matthew," she remarked. Tim had pulled the stuffing from the microwave and replaced it with the frozen broccoli. The machine hummed quietly.

"I am," he agreed. He fluffed the stuffing with a fork, the recovered it with a glass lid and faced her, an easy posture leaning back against the sink. "I keep hoping Claire would feel the same."

"Your wife? I'm sure she would."

"Well, he's not perfect. He has his moments." He straightened. "I promised to check the table setting. Be right back."

Then she was alone in the kitchen, and alone with her own thoughts. Inevitably she wondered if there hadn't been something she could do about that house that wouldn't have involved her. Odd, when her memories of being there were so sketchy, that it should have such a strong impact on her.

Uncle Bob. Aunt Freda. She never heard what happened to Freda and the girls, other than that they'd left Bob behind when his misdeeds came to light. And Earl had said that Freda had changed the girls' last names. Like her family, they'd fled from destruction wrought by one man without a conscience.

Because he couldn't have had a conscience. He'd used every one of his friends in a horrible way. Her dad had just suffered the biggest losses.

Then Tim reappeared as the microwave dinged to announce the broccoli was ready.

Time for dinner.

* * *

By the time Tim decreed bedtime for Matthew, they were able to pull back the living room curtains and see a world turned into a white whirlwind that reflected the interior light.

"Not a good night to be out," Tim remarked. "I hope everyone heeded the warnings."

Matthew, Vanessa had noticed, had grown very quiet since helping to clear the table and load the dishwasher. He hadn't spoken at all.

"Are you feeling okay?" she asked him.

"He's feeling just fine," Tim said drily. "He's hoping I didn't notice that he failed to go upstairs when I said it was bedtime."

"There's no school tomorrow!" Matthew protested.

"Maybe, maybe not. We don't know for sure yet. Either way, it's bedtime for buckaroos, and yes, you can read."

Matthew tried slumping his shoulders and dragging his feet, but when that didn't get a response, he perked up and ran up the stairs.

Tim just shook his head and smiled. "There's some decent coffee in the pot if you want some. Sorry I can't offer dessert."

"I'm not used to it. It was a great dinner, though."

"Thanks. Just the basics. Anyway, I need to go up and tuck him in, make sure he doesn't skip important things like brushing his teeth. Make yourself at home."

She did just that, curling up sock-footed on the end of the couch with a scientific journal she'd pulled out of her carry-on bag.

The house had central heating, so it must have been

her imagination that it was getting colder. The coffee she'd brought in here with her helped only a little.

So she tried to bury herself in the most recent paleobiology publication. She didn't have an advanced degree, but she possessed an unquenchable curiosity about vertebrates of the past. She'd lucked into a great career field, because one of her professors in a class she'd taken just to round out her core requirements had noticed something about her and encouraged her.

She'd be forever grateful to him for that gift. And with time, she'd grown knowledgeable enough that her lack of advanced education had mattered less and less, although she picked up a course from time to time.

Tonight, though, concentrating on a morphology study didn't hold her attention. Well, of course not. She'd been going through quite an emotional earthquake since Earl Carter had called her with the news.

Lowering her head, she tried to force herself to pay attention, but the words on the page just seemed to swim in front of her. Maybe she should try reading it on her laptop, where she could magnify the print.

But there was something she'd always loved about holding a journal, the way it felt, the way it smelled, the brand-new unread pages. She viewed each one with a fresh excitement that she didn't at all feel when she read online.

So she kept trying, wondering how long it took to put a little boy to bed—and wondering why she should care. She was in a cozy place with nothing to worry her, at least until sometime tomorrow.

Between one breath and the next, she drifted off with the journal in her hand and her head on the overstuffed arm of the sofa.

* * *

Tim had one of those revelations that only a parent could have. When he helped Matthew get into his pajamas, he discovered the boy was wearing four pairs of briefs.

"What's this?" he asked, genuinely curious. "Why so many?"

"You told me to put on new ones every day."

Apparently, he'd left out an important part of the instructions, Tim thought as laughter rose in him. He quelled it, funny though this was, because another thought occurred to him: the boy couldn't have been bathing. He wouldn't have worn all those underpants if they were wet.

"Okay," he said slowly. "And how do you handle your socks?"

"New ones every day. I was going to tell you my shoes are getting tight, too."

Tim could easily imagine that they were, even though they were almost new. "So how many socks do you have on each foot?"

"Four."

"What started all this?" he asked, genuinely curious.

"When you were doing the laundry and said I hadn't worn enough underpants or socks for a week. Fresh ones every day."

Tim remembered that conversation clearly. Oh, man. "I left out part of the instructions, kiddo. The part about taking off the dirty ones before you put on fresh ones. Come on, let's get rid of all these in the hamper and put you in the shower."

Tim wondered if he'd ever learn how literal a child

could be. Probably not. He'd keep making these simple mistakes until Matthew grew up enough to fill in
the blanks.

With his son showered, dried and in fresh pajamas,
Tim scooped him up and carried him to bed. God, it
felt so good to have this boy in his arms. He smelled
sweet and just so right. Not much more of this, though.
One way or another, Matthew was going to get too big,
and from what he'd seen of slightly older kids, he'd be
lucky to snag a hug.

But for now he took pleasure in the moment and just
wished Claire could share it, too.

Sometimes he felt his wife around, as if she peeked
in on them, as if her love still existed. Maybe it did. And
maybe, like an angel, she kept watch over Matthew. He
certainly hoped so.

Though it had been six years since Claire's unexpected passing, he still missed her. Missed all the little
things they had shared, which in retrospect seemed a
whole lot more important than the big things.

Glances over breakfast that seemed to warm the air.
Shared looks of understanding that needed no words.
Being able to reach out and just hold her hand. Those
little things had turned into a huge gap in his life.

He wanted no replacement for Claire. He didn't think
it was possible, and he wasn't looking. Most especially
he didn't want to upset Matthew's life. His son seemed
to have adapted quite well to the fact that he didn't have
a mother, unlike his friends.

Whenever someone pressed Tim on the subject—and
yes, he knew they did out of some kind of concern—
he simply said that was for later. After Matthew was

grown. Safely down the road and something he didn't need to think about now. Not when he had his son to concern him, and not when he was still aching with loss.

He was learning that you never stopped grieving. It just softened with time. Or became like a comfortable old friend, always there, never gone. At least it didn't cripple him the way it once had. He could pause, absorb and acknowledge the pain, then keep going.

Matthew made that essential.

Downstairs, he found Vanessa curled up on the couch and sound asleep. He thought about moving her to her room then decided against disturbing her. If she woke up on her own, she could go to her room then. In the meantime, she looked comfortable, and it wouldn't be the first time that sofa had been a bed.

Out in the kitchen, he opened his laptop and logged in while he brewed fresh coffee. He had more jobs than the Higgins house. There were a couple of remodel and repair jobs he'd promised to email estimates on by Saturday, and he needed to finish them.

He paused a moment, thinking of the woman sleeping in his living room. What a cutie, he decided. A lovely woman, and she'd handled Matthew's sometimes overwhelming energy well.

Then he returned to work. Two things in his life, mainly. His son and his work. Everything else paled beside them.

Chapter Three

Vanessa awoke in the dark. All the lights in the room were off, and in a faint spill of light coming from elsewhere, she needed a couple of seconds to orient herself. Tim Dawson's house. Conard County. *Oh, God.*

She sat up, rotating her shoulders and neck to ease the stiffness, and put her slightly crumpled journal to one side. How rude of her. The man had given her shelter, served her a fine meal, and she'd responded by falling asleep on his sofa while he put his son to bed?

Well, maybe he wasn't terribly offended. She guessed she'd have to wait until morning to find out. She could hear the blizzard now, howling outside as if it were alive. She was *so* glad she wasn't alone in that ruin of a house she'd inherited, or at the motel where she'd be stuck in one room alone, probably listening to the more regular patrons celebrate the weather with whiskey.

In fact, though she didn't drink often, a whiskey didn't sound too bad to her, either.

She rose, grateful she'd changed into comfy fleece earlier, and stretched every muscle in her body. There was nothing quite like a good stretch. Feeling better, she headed toward the light, which was coming from the kitchen, and was surprised to see Tim at the kitchen table, computer in front of him and stacks of paper surrounding him.

He looked up at once and smiled. "Good nap?"

"I was so out of it," she admitted. "I'm sorry I fell asleep on you."

"I don't remember inviting you here to be entertaining. You obviously needed the sleep."

"And I really could use some water. My mouth feels so parched. Oh, God," she added as the thought struck her, "was I snoring?"

"If you were, I didn't notice. Do you want the chilled bottled water? Or would you rather have something else? I finished the coffee, but I have soft drinks— all the diet variety, I'm afraid—or I could make hot chocolate."

"Right now just water would be great." Moving by instinct, she found the glasses in the upper cupboard beside the sink. "You want any?"

"I'm fine."

She chose to get water from the tap and drained a whole glass before she left the sink, then filled it again halfway and ventured to join him at the table. "Working?"

"Yup. Almost done."

"Don't let me disturb you."

Sipping her water, she closed her eyes, listening to

the sounds of the storm outside, and the sounds the house made in response. A gust of wind could cause the slight creaking from somewhere upstairs. If snow was falling, it was mixed with ice that rattled against the window glass. Without even looking she was grateful not to be out in it.

Or, frankly, by herself.

For some reason, being in this town had made her feel isolated. Maybe because she'd left behind the friendly faces of her coworkers and her immediate neighbors in her apartment building.

Maybe because since she'd arrived, she'd met three strangers and knew very little about any of them. Matthew probably couldn't be included in that, though. There was little doubt as to what he thought about anything.

But Earl, even though she'd talked to him a number of times on the phone, was still a stranger. And for all she was sharing Tim's house tonight, she knew very little about him except he was a contractor, he had a son and he'd lost his wife.

Just an outline. But what did he know about her? That she worked with dinosaur bones in a museum, that her family had lost everything to Bob Higgins and that she didn't want this house that had fallen into her lap.

He probably wondered why that was. Not everyone would look at a free house as a problem, even if it did need work.

She had to admit she wasn't sure herself why she was reacting so strongly. Yeah, the man had cost her family everything and turned them into wanderers. Yes, her father had drunk himself to death, but that had been his choice, not Bob's. She'd suffered because of what had happened nearly twenty years ago, but this seemed to go beyond bad memories.

Maybe it had bored a hole in her soul, somehow.

With a snap that startled her eyes open, she heard Tim close his computer case. "Done," he said. "For now, anyway. When the numbers start to look like fish swimming through a tank, it's usually a good time to stop."

She liked his ready sense of humor. She envied that it seemed to come so easily to him. She wasn't a very humorous person herself. In fact, if asked, she'd probably classify herself as...too reserved, she decided finally. Not sour, but reserved.

"So, about your house," he said. "It's structurally sound. A couple of roof rafters could use replacing because they got wet at some point, but there's no dampness up there now. You could probably let those skate."

She nodded, feeling unready to discuss this, but knowing she couldn't evade it indefinitely. After all, she'd come back to take care of it, and an inheritance from Bob that she hadn't turned down was the last of his savings. She figured since he'd dumped his white elephant on her, she needed the money to fix it up and pay the taxes. She just hoped it was enough. Lowly museum assistants didn't make huge salaries.

"To make the house interesting to a buyer, there are some basic things we need to do. Caulking. The weatherizing in the windows and doors is cracked, unattended for too long. The attic fan is dead. The floors sag and are weak in a few places." He stopped. "I don't want to overwhelm you. The question is, do you want to pull it together just enough to hopefully attract someone by marketing it as a major fixer-upper? That'll cost you a pretty penny in terms of what you can make off it, and frankly, with the amount of cosmetics it needs, that might not even work. You saw the paint sagging on the wall. I don't like that."

"It's ugly," she agreed.

"It's more than ugly. It might be lead based."

Her heart lurched. "I thought that was illegal!"

"It is now. But it was only in 1978 that it was banned in housing. Now how many walls do you think got painted over with latex or oil-based paints and never stripped?"

Her mind was dancing around as if she had hot coals inside it. She didn't want to hear this. Want to or not, she was stuck with it. "We should knock it down and clear the lot."

"Maybe. I'm going to have an inspector check the place out first." He popped open his computer. "I reckon if there's lead, knocking it down and clearing out the remains will cost as much as a basic fixup and getting rid of as much lead paint as we might find. And—here's the important thing—unless you can sell that empty lot, you'll still owe taxes as if the house was on it."

She was flummoxed. "Really? *Really?*"

"Best and highest use."

That did it. Vanessa put her head in her hands and muttered, "I want my dinosaur bones."

"Earl mentioned that you wanted to donate the house, but ask yourself if it would be ethical to give it to a church or preschool before we deal with any health threats."

Her head snapped up. "Of course not!"

He smiled. "Good."

Then his question struck her. "You certainly didn't imagine that I'd pass that lead paint along, especially to children."

"In this world," he said slowly, "you never know. I've had people come to me who wanted to cover a multitude of sins with fresh paint or linoleum."

"So Bob Higgins wasn't the only con artist around here."

"I wish I could say he was." He rose and stretched his arms, making her acutely aware of his flat belly. "Let's go back to your bedroom. No, I'm not sending you to bed, but I want to be sure you know where everything is and feel free to use it."

This time, having escaped her self-absorption, she knew instantly that this room had once been the master bedroom. Those forget-me-nots and the colors were his wife's choices, she had realized earlier, but now they took on meaning that almost made her squirm.

"Private shower, too," he remarked, pointing to a closed door.

She wanted to ask outright but caught herself. No point in prodding this man's wounds. She ought to understand that herself. "Where do you sleep?"

"Upstairs, just down the hall from Matthew. He used to have nightmares and be scared there was something under his bed."

She suspected that was only part of the reason, but it was good enough. "I hope he's outgrown that."

"Mostly. It still happens occasionally. So, when we can get out into the world, do you want to go over your house with me? I can make a list of the absolute essentials, but I still need your input."

She nodded slowly. "I'm still trying to figure out why I hate that house. I know why I didn't want to come back to this town. My dad spent his last years vilifying this place. But the house? I vaguely remember having fun there as a child."

He tilted his head to one side. "Why was your dad so down on the town? They didn't rip him off."

"I think he believed people around here thought he was an absolute fool. He felt they were judging him."

He nodded slowly. "Higgins was your dad's friend, right?"

"Lifelong."

"Well, I reckon I'd get a bit paranoid, too, if my best friend stole everything from me and my family. I'd feel like an idiot for having trusted him, I'd feel wounded beyond words and, yeah, maybe I'd feel like I was in the public stocks, when in truth a lot of people were probably thinking, *there but for the grace of God*."

She sighed. "You might be right. I just know what my dad believed. Anyway, I never wanted to come back here, and Earl probably told you how badly I wanted to get out from under that house."

He pursed one side of his mouth, then said, "Well, judging by what Higgins did, you could always just deed it over to someone else. Just quitclaim it to some wealthy guy half a continent away. Won't he get a shock?"

She laughed. She couldn't help it—the idea was so funny. "That wouldn't be a nice thing to do."

"It wasn't nice that Higgins bombed you this way, either."

She looked away suddenly, realizing that he might have just touched on the core of her problem with this whole mess. Not the past at all, but the present. A house she hadn't wanted, a headache, an expense. Like Bob Higgins was reaching out from the grave for one last swipe. "You think he was bombing me?" Her voice had tightened, and tension arose within her again. Mainly because Tim seemed to be confirming her own suspicions, suspicions she'd been trying to ignore.

"Truthfully? I don't know." He led her down the short hall back to the kitchen. There he asked her if she wanted some cocoa or warm milk. She opted for the cocoa. "Thank you."

"I don't know about you," he remarked, "but when it's howling and cold like that outside, I feel an urge to get cozy inside. It's not like that cold out there is reaching me. Some atavistic response, I guess."

Interesting choice of words from a guy who made his living as a building contractor. For the first time, it crossed her mind that she might have become a bit of a snob over the years. An intellectual snob. Why wouldn't the man be smart and have a great command of the language? Because he worked with his hands? That didn't mean he didn't have a brain.

Man, this whole trip was shaking her up in so many ways. Facing a childhood she couldn't remember, facing once again the years of her dad's deterioration, facing an anger that had been planted in her by chaos and one man's bitterness.

She wasn't ready for any of this, yet here it was. And she sure as hell didn't want to deal with it right now. "If you owned the house," she said slowly, "what would you want to do with it?"

"Now that's an interesting question." He made the

cocoa from packets and only needed to add boiling water. Soon he was sitting at the kitchen table with her again.

She waited, watching him slowly stir his mug with a spoon as he thought about it. He wasn't going to treat the question lightly.

"The house-flipping business isn't exactly booming around here," he remarked. "Real estate sales are sluggish. Not dead, but not fast, either."

Oh, great, she thought. She'd probably be stuck with that damn house forever.

"Anyway, if I were going to own two houses here, I'd fix up the Higgins place, stem to stern, and sell this house."

His answer truly surprised her. "But why? This is a beautiful house!"

"Also a size that would be easier to sell," he said with a shrug. "Already beautifully decorated. By my wife."

She bit her lip, feeling uncomfortable. She usually kept a safe distance from others, riding the surface of emotions without getting caught in the deep waves. But Tim's simple statement pierced her armor a bit, and she felt sorrow for him. "That must be...difficult for you."

"Not exactly the word I'd use. It does remind me of her and that I miss her. It may be time for me to move on. As for Matthew, he doesn't remember her at all. She's photos in an album. Moving around the corner would probably be an exciting adventure for him."

"But why take on a house you couldn't sell?" she pressed.

"Because I wouldn't want to sell it. Fixing it up bit

by bit would probably take most of the rest of my life. A major project."

That sounded so darn lonely to her. Here he was living in a beautiful house he probably felt he couldn't change, a kind of memorial. Changing it would be like erasing his late wife. A new house…a clean slate. And he'd be busy with it.

For the first time, she considered that the Higgins house wasn't just a pain for her. Something she had never wanted, something she didn't want to deal with. Maybe she needed an attitude adjustment. Tim obviously thought the house had potential and promise. Maybe she should try a different perspective, if she could manage it. However this fell out, she wasn't going to be here long, and she should stop resenting it and just deal with it. Maybe even enjoy it a bit. Somehow.

"What happened to your wife?" she asked, hoping she wasn't being intrusive. Somewhere in the fog of the upheaval that had been dominating her mind, she had the feeling he had already told her. Had he? If so, forgetting about something so important to him should embarrass her.

"Pulmonary embolism," he answered matter-of-factly. Maybe he hadn't told her before. "Blood clot in the lung. They were never able to pin down the cause, but I guess that doesn't matter. What matters is that it was fast for her."

"That's so sad."

He nodded. "Goes without saying. So, yeah, I'd take that house and make it over, and when I got done it would be a jewel. And I'd enjoy every minute of making it into one."

"I could quitclaim it to you," she remarked.

He laughed. "I wouldn't feel right about that. Don't even consider it. I'm sure we can get you something out of that property. And whatever we get would be rightfully yours, if you ask me."

The storm continued to rage throughout the night. Tim didn't sleep well, but he seldom did when the weather turned bad. Claire had called him the night watchman, laughing as she did so, but bad weather made him restless. He wasn't expecting anything terrible tomorrow, except a lot of shoveling. But he still got restless.

After Vanessa went to bed, he walked in socks around the house, up the stairs and back down again. He'd warned her he might pace, so she wouldn't worry if she heard anything, but he tried to keep his step light and silent anyway.

Moving away from this house? He hadn't been kidding when he told Vanessa it might be time for him to move on. There were a lot of ways he could do that, though. The first one was simple: redecorate.

The problem with that was equally simple. Claire's taste and identity were stamped all over this house. It was odd how easy it was for him to remember each new find of hers and how excited she had been about them. The way the structure of this house had taken on a whole personality because of her. Simply wiping away the beauty she'd created here felt like a betrayal of sorts. As if he were erasing her from his life.

She could never be erased.

So moving on might literally require moving. He

couldn't, not with his own two hands, remove her from this house. So, yeah, if he owned the Higgins place, he'd let someone else make the changes here as they wanted and he'd start a whole new project.

But he didn't own the Higgins house, and he hoped Vanessa had just been joking about turning it over to him. He didn't want that, would never want that. He hoped he'd made that clear enough.

Then his thoughts turned to Vanessa. Quite a pretty young woman, especially those mossy-green eyes of hers. He didn't think he'd ever seen quite that color before. It reminded him of a creek bank in the summertime shade. Peaceful.

But he felt little peace in her. She had relaxed when talking about her work, but then he felt invisible walls rising, putting space between her and everything else. It wasn't just the reserve one might feel with a stranger. It felt to him like something much more, something much deeper.

So maybe he ought to stop thinking about how pretty she was, or the way her sweater earlier in the day had cuddled her breasts and revealed a surprisingly tiny waist.

She had the kind of figure a man could dream about, from what he could guess through her clothes, even the loose fleece she had put on after arriving here.

Another kind of complication he didn't need in his life. He had a son to think about and was scrupulous in his behavior as a result. If he went out on a date, which was rare, he was always home at an early hour. Setting an example, he hoped. Making Matthew feel secure, he hoped.

Not that Matthew seemed to have any major insecurities. If he did, he hid them well for a child his age.

But being a solo parent had made him acutely aware of his responsibilities. He didn't have a backup crew to step in and pick up any slack or correct any of his mistakes. Matthew wasn't by any measure a difficult child, and his heart seemed to be in the right place. But Tim was acutely aware that if he made mistakes they might affect the boy for life.

The school counselor had told him to relax a bit. There was no evidence he was doing anything wrong. But he could never quite believe it. He was flying on a wing and a prayer.

The wind blew another blast of ice at the windows. As cold as it was, the snow shouldn't be icy. At least that's what he thought, but he could be wrong. He could be wrong about so many things.

Finally pulling out his laptop, he looked up digs for dinosaur fossils in Wyoming. If Matthew was still interested come early summer, they ought to take that trip that Vanessa had suggested. There was one museum, a little on the expensive side, that would take the two of them out to participate in a dig. For his own part, he was more interested in something less commercial.

He was sure he could find an opportunity, especially with Vanessa's help. He had no trouble imagining Matthew's excitement, even if all they did was watch from the sidelines or see some bones emerging from the ground.

Then he remembered Vanessa putting her head in her hands and saying she wanted her bones back. It had been cute, and funny, and so terribly truthful all at once.

Bones would certainly be more peaceful. But life seldom left anyone alone.

He closed his computer after checking the weather report, then shut his eyes for a few minutes, just listening. The storm wasn't easing yet. Time to take another swing by Matthew's room, make sure he was still sleeping.

As for himself, he really ought to try to get some shut-eye. Thing was, he knew all he'd do was try. All his life, storms at night had made him restless. He could never explain why.

In her own room, the former master bedroom, Vanessa listened to Tim's quiet movements through the house and tried to get some sleep herself. After all that had happened today—the long drive from the airport, her viewing of a house that had somehow become part of her nightmares and her evening with Tim and Matthew— she ought to be ready to crash.

Instead she remained wakeful, listening to a restless man walk the hours of the night. She wondered if it was really that storms made him edgy or if it had other roots. But why should she wonder? If he'd been dealing with it for a long time, he probably understood it better than she ever could with a few guesses.

Though the bed was comfortable and the room cozy, she couldn't help wishing she were home in her own bed, facing another day in the bowels of the museum sorting through bones, making sure they were properly identified and preserved. So much that came out of fossil beds had been protected by nature for ages, but once exposed, all the elements of decay could resume their work. Especially since they had found that in many dinosaur bones the marrow still contained living tissue. Which had, amusingly enough, explained the slightly unpleasant smell paleontologists had been associating with those bones for a long time.

But she was comfortable in that environment, sure in her knowledge, excited by possibilities, and enjoying the scientific conversation and discussion. Definitely in her element.

Now she had been yanked away, however briefly, to face an environment she didn't know how to handle as well, leaving her comfort zone so far behind she almost felt like she was in free fall. What was going to happen from all of this? Would she be able to deal with those old demons, many of which traced directly back to her father, some of which were due to being uprooted so many times?

Did she *have* to deal with anything?

Oddly, she realized she was envying Matthew. Stable home, great father, an unshadowed childhood. Which assumed a lot, she admitted to herself. She didn't really know him yet—or Tim, for that matter.

But Tim was thinking he might move on. Her idea of moving on wasn't a good one. She hoped that it wouldn't adversely affect Matthew.

Then, with the quiet footsteps becoming a background to the storm, she drifted into dreams.

Matthew's piping voice awoke her in the morning. Half dozing, she listened to Tim trying to make him speak more quietly, but that amount of energy couldn't be easily contained.

It was still dark outside, and for some reason that made her think of Christmases when she was really young and couldn't wait for her parents to come tell her that Santa had been there.

Those days had been much better, much happier, and to be fair, until the mess with Higgins had blown up, she'd had a happy childhood. Probably much like Matthew's, except Matthew didn't have a mother.

She wondered how much that saddened him, or if he just felt it was the normal way of things. According to Tim, he couldn't remember her at all. But other kids had mothers. Maybe that had an impact. To judge by the sound of Matthew's voice right now, however, the boy was perfectly happy to be facing a snow day.

The sounds made her smile.

A little later, after a nice warm shower, she dressed in her warmest fleece and socks, and made her way to the happy sounds in the kitchen. Just as she opened the bedroom door, she heard Tim say, "She's not here yet. Hold your horses. You're not going to starve before I find out if she wants any."

Her smile grew wider as she walked down the polished hall, around the dining room into the kitchen. Before she had a chance to say good morning, Matthew was hopping up in front of her.

"You want pancakes, don't you? With *real* maple syrup?"

"Let the lady open her eyes," Tim scolded mildly.

"I'd love pancakes," she assured Matthew, then took Tim's gesture to sit at the kitchen table.

"With *real* maple syrup," Matthew reminded her.

"I haven't had any real maple syrup in years." She smiled her thanks as Tim put coffee in front of her.

"It's a treat," Matthew informed her. "Daddy says it's expensive, so we only have it once in a while."

"Like once a year," Tim interjected. "You want anything in your coffee?"

"Black is great," she answered.

"Settle, son," Tim said to the boy, "or I won't dare let you help with the pancakes."

Matthew immediately embarked on a valiant effort to contain his excitement. Vanessa decided pancakes weren't a regular item in this household. Still, even though he grew quiet, the boy's energy was palpable.

He climbed on a step stool beside the counter, while Tim measured the mix and milk into a large bowl, and listened intently as Tim told him they didn't want to mix it too much. Beside them was an electric griddle, and Tim showed how to test when it was ready by flicking a little water on it.

"See the droplets dance? That says the griddle is really hot and ready. Now remember, pancakes don't take long. You're going to start with a small one, okay?"

Vanessa enjoyed the entire show, start to finish. Matthew managed to make himself a stack of small pancakes, and Tim brought a plate of larger ones to the table. Vanessa offered to set the table, but Tim rightly pointed out she didn't know her way around the kitchen and it would only take Matthew a moment. He proved it. Almost instantly she had a plate, fork and knife in front of her. A butter dish was added, and soon they were all eating.

Vanessa savored the maple syrup and commented on it.

"I told you it was good," Matthew said immediately.

"Special treat," she agreed. "A very special one."

Tim spoke. "Hardly worth making pancakes without it."

Matthew giggled. "You make them with blueberry jam, and sometimes with cinnamon and sugar."

"And not very often."

Matthew screwed up his face. "I know. Not healthy."

Tim chuckled. "Anyway, Vanessa, we're going to be shoveling snow as soon as the storm lets up some more, and Matthew wants to make a snowman. Care to join us?"

"That sounds like fun." She meant it, and realized that her discomfort with coming back to this town was rapidly evaporating. She didn't feel as if she were wearing the mark of Cain, and now that she was here, she thought how silly her concerns had been. Why should anyone care what had happened over twenty years ago? And even if they did, she'd been a child like Matthew back then, not responsible for any of it.

Of course, there was still the house, but as she got her feet under her, she was beginning to think she'd be able to handle that. She'd face it and deal. She could do that.

A smile remained on her face as she helped load dishes into the dishwasher after Matthew and Tim emptied the previous load. While they put them away, she watched so she could learn. If she was invited to stay over again tonight, she wanted to be able to help more.

It was still snowing rather heavily, a fact that Vanessa had utterly missed because all the curtains were drawn against the cold. But when Tim peeled back the curtain over the sink, she saw white flakes whirling everywhere.

"This is so cool!" Matthew pronounced.

"You think so?" Tim answered. "Wait till I hand you that shovel." He dropped the curtain and eyed Vanessa. "You may not remember, but heavy snow didn't used to be common. Now we're seeing more of it. Back when, most of the snow dropped before the storm crossed the mountains, and then dropped the rest farther east. These days we're getting snowed in almost as much as anybody else."

"That's cool," Matthew insisted. "Maybe no school again tomorrow."

"Don't count on it, kiddo. These roads will be clean before the day is over."

Not even that dampened Matthew, however. He skated off to the living room, announcing he was going to pick a DVD to watch.

"The creeks and ponds will be full this spring," Tim said as he joined her at the table with some coffee for himself. She declined his offer of more. "Happy ranchers. Water can often be a problem around here. As for your house…" He shook his head. "A lot of shoveling and plowing is going to have to happen before we can get over there."

"I'm not exactly on the edge of my seat," she admitted.

"What is it about that house?" he asked. "It's just a building, but it seems to mean a whole lot more to you."

She looked down, running her fingertip slowly across the tabletop as if she were doodling invisibly. "It's hard to explain," she admitted. "It's more feelings that any specific thing. Mixed feelings."

"I'm interested," he said.

She could have felt pushed. This was some pretty

personal territory. But for some reason, she felt the question was friendly, not prying.

She hesitated for another few seconds, seeking words that wouldn't sound totally crazy. "I had a lot of fun there when I was little. Bob had two kids, just a little older than me, and we'd go over to visit the family on weekends. The girls and I played a lot, and Bob often had some little gift for me. My parents and Bob and his wife seemed to be really good friends. I always looked forward to those visits."

"I see. But then it changed."

"Radically. At first I didn't even grasp that something bad was going on. We stopped going over there, but I knew my dad still went. Then there were angry phone calls. Any time I asked when we were going over there again, I was told that they weren't our friends anymore. I didn't get it. I didn't even really get it when we moved across the country, except that I lost everything and everyone I knew except my parents. It was years before I began to find out what had happened."

"And when you did, you knew where to focus a whole lot of confusion and hurt."

"Oh, yeah," she said. "Oh, yeah." She sighed. "I know it was long ago, but it changed me, changed my life. Things were never the same again. Never. I remember that we'd been a happy family up until then. Afterward...no happiness left."

"I'm really sorry. That's a sad story. And all because of one man's greed."

"My dad trusted him," she said, finally raising her gaze, but not to look at Tim. Instead she looked toward the sink, finding it easier than seeing an expression on another's face. After all these years. All these years and those old pains could rise up and strike her in the face. Shouldn't she have outgrown all that by now?

She certainly thought she had, but this trip, this entire series of events, was teaching her that it wasn't true, that all she'd done was bury things that, zombie-like, could rise up with the right stimulus.

Tim spoke. "Your dad's trust being abused that way…that's the hard part to swallow, I'd think."

She nodded slightly, unsure if she agreed.

"For me, at least," he continued, "I think I could deal with the loss of everything I own better than I could deal with someone abusing my trust and friendship so egregiously. But it's never happened to me, so I don't know what I'm talking about."

"You may be right," she said after a few seconds. "Like I said, it's all mixed up. My dad never recovered, whether it was from being treated that way by a friend, or from losing everything he and his family had worked for, or from both. And I got it all secondhand. All I know is he drank himself to death over the next fifteen years, we had to keep moving because he'd lose his job and have to find another, and every move stressed my mother and required *her* to find a new job. She didn't survive him for very long."

He shook his head, frowning sadly. "That's bad. I'm not surprised you don't want that house. Didn't want any reminders like that."

"I can't imagine what Higgins was thinking," she admitted, her voice taking on an edge. "My dear old uncle Bob, as I used to call him. Destroyed my family then dumps this on me? Earl keeps trying to make it sound like Bob regretted what he'd done and wanted to make up for it. I don't think he was capable of any such thing, Tim."

"Maybe not." He paused. "Probably not. A guy who could do what he did—if he didn't have a conscience back then, I doubt he grew one in prison."

"Me, too. You know, part of what made it so hard on my dad, I think, was that his trust for Bob's financial management abilities helped draw in other people. I don't think he felt ashamed just because he got robbed, but because he unwittingly helped others get robbed. I think that's the reason he always felt that he'd be judged harshly if he came back here."

"That could be." Tim paused thoughtfully. "Did he make you feel that way, too, that folks here would judge you?"

Stupid as it sounded, she admitted it. "Yes."

"Now I'm really sorry. I'm sure we have some rotten apples here—what place doesn't?—but you were only seven. How could anyone hold you responsible?"

"I know it sounds silly." She shrugged one shoulder. "It seems I have some leftover hang-ups."

"Coming back here would certainly wake them up. Want some fresh coffee or something else?"

She'd only downed half the cup he'd given her before breakfast, and she realized that the taste of maple remained on her tongue, growing a bit cloying. "Coffee, please."

He rose, emptied her cup in the sink and poured fresh for both of them before returning to sit across from her. From the living room, she could hear the noises of what sounded like a fast-paced cartoon. It wasn't a far reach to remember her own snowy mornings and weekends in the Before Days, as she thought of them. When it had been too bitterly cold to run around outside, only then had she been allowed to watch TV in the daytime.

Her spirits began to rise again, and she decided to push off the entire matter of Higgins and her family for another time. It was beginning to seem that she'd be dealing with this mess for the rest of her life. That didn't mean she couldn't have fun in between.

"Matthew is adorable," she said, pointedly changing the topic.

"I agree, of course." He smiled. "I think shoveling will slow him down a bit. Then a snowman. When was the last time you made one?"

"A snowman? When I was Matthew's age. It used to drive me crazy, though, because I could never get them to look like a drawing or photo, perfectly rounded. Mine looked kinda clunky."

"Well, we'll work on that skill today," he joked.

She grinned. "I could always find rocks for the nose and eyes, but Mom would never part with a carrot. Anyway, I was never really happy with ones I made."

"Did you have any help?"

"I was a singleton, and no one else on the ranch was interested. Too busy."

"Well, nobody's too busy today."

She decided that sounded really good.

Chapter Four

Many hands made for swift work in clearing the snow, and for the first time Vanessa helped build a snowman that looked as if it had stepped from the pages of a storybook. Matthew and Tim showed her how to smooth it out, and Tim wasn't stingy with the carrot. He even broke off some small limbs from his shrubbery to make arms.

"Want a photo of that?" he asked with a wide smile.

The shoveling and building of the snowman had kept them warm, but finally they started to chill and headed inside. Tim served up a big pot of hot chocolate along with some chicken soup.

"Not the best flavor combination," he remarked, "but I think it's going to go down well."

Vanessa admired the easy way he handled everything. He could repair things, build things, clear a side-walk, make a snowman and cook very well. A man of many talents.

A very handsome man of many talents.

But then she reminded herself not to pay attention to her unexpected attraction to him. She was just passing through, the way she had for most of her life. Senseless to invest herself in people she wouldn't know for long. As a self-protective posture, it had become part of her personality, and it worked. Even at the museum, where she would probably continue working for a great many years, she kept a certain reserve, a space between her-self and her coworkers.

"So what's it like working at the museum?" Tim asked as they ate. "Lots of interesting people, I bet."

"Dinosaurs," said Matthew, almost as if he were cor-recting his father.

"Well, yes, dinosaurs," she agreed. "And knowledge-able people. I learn something every day." She turned to Matthew. "But I don't only work with dinosaur bones."

His eyes widened a shade. "Really? Is there other good stuff, too?"

She had to laugh. "Lots of good stuff. Bones don't have to be big to tell a story."

Matthew thought about that while he drank cocoa then looked at her while wearing a chocolate mustache. "How can bones talk?"

That was one of her favorite subjects. "They don't talk like you and I do. But they definitely have stories to tell. When I study them, I can learn when they lived and how they lived, and maybe even how they died. I can tell if they were babies, or grown-ups, and did they live alone or have families. Now, not every bone is going to give me all that information, but with time and more bones, it's like putting a puzzle together into a picture."

He nodded, evidently grasping what she was saying. "So they don't tell a story but they make a puzzle picture."

"That's one way of looking at it," she agreed. "But over time I get more than just one puzzle picture. That's when I start to get a story."

"Okay. But dinosaur bones are the best."

She and Tim laughed. "You come visit my museum sometime, and I'll show you."

"Uh-oh," said Tim just before Matthew turned to him.

"Can we, Dad? Can we?"

"Albuquerque is a bit of a drive," he answered.

Vanessa hesitated, realizing she had put him on the spot without intending to. "Sorry," she said to Tim.

His smile turned crooked. "Frankly, I was expecting this from the moment you mentioned dinosaurs. We'll see, Matthew. We couldn't go before next summer, regardless. And maybe by then you'll want to go to a truck museum."

Vanessa stifled a laugh, pressing her lips tightly together.

"I don't like trucks that much," Matthew said decisively. "Anyway, they don't have museums."

"I wouldn't be so sure of that," Tim replied. "There seem to be museums for just about anything."

But Matthew was already moving on. "Do you dig up the bones?" he asked Vanessa.

"Sometimes," she answered.

"I wanna do that."

"Maybe you'll get the chance. It's fun—for a little while, anyway. Then it gets hot, you get tired, and it takes a long, long time to get some little bone out of the ground. Longer for a big bone."

Tim spoke. "I take it you prefer working in the museum."

"Mostly. But I get into the field once in a while. When I'm there I don't do much of the digging, but I do a lot of preservation work. Some of those bones come out of the stone ready to crumble. They haven't been exposed the elements for maybe millions of years, and they start deteriorating the minute they hit the air and humidity."

"I never thought about that."

She was grateful to him for keeping the subject in a safe area—safe for her. Because tomorrow they were going to have to make their way back to the Higgins house, and she was going to have to face some very old demons. She'd rather pull bones out of limestone. "We try to preserve right at the site if we can."

Easier to talk about than that damn house. She'd been able to forget it most of the day, but now it was looming again. It seemed ridiculous to give it so much power over her. She'd survived that period of her life, after all, even though it had eventually cost her so much.

But the simple fact was that over the years she'd learned to hate it. Or fear it. She couldn't decide which. Everything about that period had gotten tangled in her mind as a child, and it seemed that growing up hadn't untwisted the knot.

Later that evening, after Matthew had gone to bed

for the night, she and Tim relaxed in the living room. She sat on one end of the dark blue couch while he sat on the other. On the coffee table was a small plate of bakery cookies.

The wind had picked up again, rattling the windows just a bit, and Tim remarked that he hoped they didn't need to shovel again tomorrow.

"When the snow gets dry enough, and the wind blows hard enough, I can shovel the same dang snow six or seven times. It's annoying. One blizzard with reruns."

She smiled at his description. "We don't see much snow in Albuquerque, although we get some. Usually light, rarely more than an inch or two. I mean, you have to spread eleven inches of snow over the whole winter, on average. We might get a powder this month, like confectioner's sugar, but the most of it will come after Christmas. I consider that a plus, I guess."

"Right now, I would, too. But I like living here, for the most part." He hesitated then said, "Thinking about the house is still bothering you, isn't it?"

"Yes," she admitted, her lips growing tight. "It's not just the reality of what happened."

"No?"

Then, on impulse, she told him something she'd never shared with anyone else. "I have nightmares about that house. Which is weird, because I always had fun when I was there. But the nightmares have come from time to time over the years."

"Nightmares how?"

"It starts off feeling normal, but then everything

changes. I'm all alone, and it gets darker. You know how the upstairs has that hallway?"

He nodded. "L-shaped with three bedrooms coming off it, and the bath."

"Exactly. Except in my dream when I climb the stairs, it straightens out and seems to go on forever. A long, long hallway lined with closed doors. The closest thing I've ever seen to it is a hotel. Anyway, I know it's Uncle Bob's house, but I'm afraid of all those doors. Afraid of what's behind them. And all I know is that I *have* to walk past all of them to the other end. I don't have a choice."

"That's creepy," he said quietly.

"It sure feels that way when I'm dreaming it. But it sounds almost absurd when I say it out loud."

"I don't think so. I can imagine it, actually. Everything distorted, so you know where you are, but it looks different, and all those closed doors that could conceal anything? Creepy. Nightmares are more about feelings than images anyway, don't you think?"

"Depends," she said after a few seconds' thought. "But mostly I agree with you. There haven't been too many horrific images in my nightmares, but there's always been plenty of fear or terror. Urgency."

He nodded and draped his arm along the back of the couch while crossing his legs loosely. He looked so relaxed that she envied him. Her entire body ought to be relaxing, too, with all that time spent shoveling and building a snowman. But instead of feeling weary, she felt herself winding up. Anxiety about tomorrow?

"I could quitclaim the house to you," she blurted. "You said you'd love to make it over, to move on."

At that she felt tension run through him, although he didn't seem to move a muscle. "No."

"No?"

"Come on, Vanessa. You deserve to get *something* out of this mess, miserable though it's making you. Secondly, I wouldn't accept it, because it feels wrong. Unethical."

"But I want to get rid of it. I told you."

He looked straight at her. "Yeah, you did. But what you really need is to deal with it."

His blunt statement deprived her of breath. He was telling her what she needed to do? He hardly knew her. How dare he? "What are you saying?"

"You mean I shouldn't poke my nose into your affairs. Maybe you're right. But you make it my affair when you talk about giving me that house. Could I do a lot with it? Sure. But that's not the point here. The question is whether you're going to run from a problem."

Oh, that scalded. It scalded even more because it reminded her of her childhood, of her father, who had run from everything right into the bottom of a bottle.

She wasn't like that.

Was she?

She wanted to glare at him, almost hating him in that moment, because he had left her feeling emotionally naked. Why had he done that? It felt cruel.

When he spoke again, his voice was quiet. "Guess I was out of line. And probably wrong."

But he wasn't wrong, she admitted. As knotted up as her feelings were over all of this, she recognized that kernel of truth. She wanted to run from all of this, from facing her past, from dealing with that house and all the memories it evoked. Except for the threat of taxes pursuing her down the years, or fines for code violations, she'd have ignored the entire situation.

This man, who had known her for such a very short time, had somehow looked all the way to her soul, to one of the most private places inside her. It was unnerving.

It was also embarrassing. She thought of herself as reasonably strong, having survived so much in previous years, including the death of both her parents. Now she was staring a huge weakness in the face and wondering if *that* had been the reason she had believed herself to be a sturdy survivor. Because she fled from all the difficult things?

Gah. Hiding in the museum with ancient bones and colleagues for company was a nice little hermitage, she admitted. Yes, she loved her work wholeheartedly, but she allowed little time for anything else…like a life.

Maybe some reevaluation was in order—but not right now. First she had to deal with the Higgins house, whether she wanted to or not. Tim was right. She couldn't run from this one.

It'd be nice, though, if she could. Just head back to Albuquerque and work and forget all about the house and the town she had been raised to think of as judgmental.

But whose judgment? It was beginning to seem as if that were her dad's. She had absolutely no reason to think poorly of this town. She hadn't met anyone but Tim and Earl yet, but both seemed nice. Particularly since Earl appeared to know the whole sordid story. He'd been anything but judgmental. From his first phone call to tell her Higgins had left her the house, he'd been totally sympathetic about her concerns, her resentment and her anger. He'd also been totally honest about the position her uncle Bob had placed her in.

But whether she was being fair to the town or not, it remained that she had her own issues—issues that were coming starkly into light because of that damn house. And Tim's insight.

She leaned forward for a cookie, realizing that she was beginning to get hungry again. She wasn't used to being so physically active most days. Not shoveling-snow active, anyway. It had kicked up her appetite.

"Want me to make you a grilled cheese sandwich or something?" Tim asked. "Or will cookies be enough?"

She glanced over her shoulder at him, still leaning forward. "Reaching for a cookie means I'm starving?"

He laughed. "Not necessarily. Just trying to be a good host."

She turned then, still sitting on the edge of the couch, and gave him a smile. "You're being a wonderful host. You took in a stranger, and you make me feel like I belong here, just like you and Matthew. That's a gift."

"Is it?" He shrugged slightly. "Honestly, I couldn't imagine you staying in the Higgins house all by yourself especially during the storm. Big, empty place. You'd have had heat and water, but I can't testify to much else yet. It's been unoccupied for a long time. I'm concerned about the air in there. I'm going to have it tested. Once I got the heat going, I don't know what might get into the air with time, and while I've been leaving windows open while I work, you wouldn't be able to do that during this storm. Anyway, there I am, looking at a house that's barely getting back into livable state, and you, not knowing a soul here…how was I going to leave you there? What if the power went out? The heat wouldn't shut down but you wouldn't have a single light."

"That would have been spooky," she admitted.

"Spookier than your dream, probably. And once the storm really set it, you'd have nowhere to go to escape. Then there's the motel." He grimaced. "I don't know for sure, but I suspect the some of the truck drivers who got stuck there might think it was a great time to booze it up and have a party. A different kind of creepy for you."

"I'm sure. That even crossed my mind earlier. But you still didn't have to make me so welcome in your home. I'm grateful to you."

"You're welcome. I'm enjoying your company, and Matthew certainly is, too. I think he's got a thousand times more questions than he knows how to ask about dinosaurs."

And that reminded her. "I'm sorry I brought up a trip to the museum. That put you on the spot."

He shook his head a little. "He may forget all about it and move onto a new fascination. If he doesn't…well, he needs to go to places like that. It might have been easier to take him to the place here in Wyoming, but if he wants to go to your museum, maybe over spring break. My busiest time of the year is summer, so it's hard to get away. But in the spring? We could fly down and spend a few days."

"He'd love it," she assured him. "We've got more than dinosaurs to look at. All kinds of sciency things and habitats he can walk through. He might like being able to travel back sixty-five million years in time and feel as if he's really there."

"I'm sure he'd like it."

"We have interactive displays, too, where he could try things out." Then she caught herself. "I sound like a travel brochure."

"That's okay. I was enjoying it." His dark gray eyes seemed to dance. "You're making me want to visit, too. However, with a boy that age...for all I know, next year he'll be begging to go to Cooperstown."

She leaned back, nibbling on her cookie. "It's true, I guess. I've seen kids go on and off dinosaurs pretty fast. We have summer programs and after-school programs, and I hear from the leaders that kids are always changing which program they want to be in. They kind of flea-hop around, thirsty for new things all the time."

His smile changed subtly, and something about the shift made her heart skip and a drizzle of purely sexual hunger run through her. What was different?

But it was as if the very air had changed. From talking about the museum to this? She must be imagining it. After all, she'd been fighting her attraction to him since they'd met—a whole day and a half ago. Too soon, too fast.

And maybe that very thing would make it safe, said a portion of her traitorous mind. How much threat could there be in something that would be over almost before it started?

"So..." He drew the word out. "You know I'm widowed. But what about you? Husband? Boyfriend? Girlfriend?"

"None of the above," she answered, trying to sound flip but instead hearing her own voice come out on the husky side, revealing entirely too much.

Then, almost as quickly as the air had started to turn

smoky with desire, he swept it away. "I always thought it was good to be happy on your own before getting involved with someone. Less neediness."

Well, he was probably right about that, but where was this coming from? "What are you trying to say, Tim?"

He shook his head a little as his expression grew almost rueful. "I think I'm trying to avoid taking this moment to places it shouldn't go. We only met yesterday, and I don't want you—or me, for that matter—to regret you accepting my hospitality. You should be safe here."

"What if I feel safe?" she asked impulsively. Her cheeks heated almost instantly with embarrassment.

"Then tell me that again in a few days. Now about tomorrow... I want to give you a really good tour of the house. We can talk about how much you want to do before you have to get back home. How much is essential and how much might help with selling it."

All business again. Somehow she felt as if she'd just lost an important opportunity. Surprisingly, the loss made her ache.

In the morning, there was no escaping the return to reality. She rode along with Tim when he took Matthew to school, but then they headed to the Higgins house.

"Matthew's a real pistol," she remarked.

"A constant joy," he agreed.

Then silence fell, mainly because she felt tension winding around her, stretching her nerves. No matter how hard she tried to tell herself it was just a house, that it was not some kind of living beast that could attack her, she was afraid of the memories it might evoke, so it might as well have been alive. Or haunted.

Usually she could look back over her past with a reasonable amount of objectivity. Time had passed, and she had grown up, the loss of her parents no longer as fresh. Yes, she still grieved for them, but the grief had grown quieter. And in the case of her father, the anger had gradually worn away. He'd been a crushed man, and while drowning himself in alcohol had been stupid and cruel to those he loved, he'd been a mortal and had succumbed. People made mistakes. It wasn't easy to recover from some of them.

So the man had made two huge mistakes in his life. He'd completely trusted a lifelong friend, and then he'd tried to wash away that mistake in alcohol. Even his few attempts at AA had failed.

He couldn't live with himself.

And that's what the Higgins house signified to her now. Adulthood had helped her to gain some understanding of the mechanisms that had affected her life, but it hadn't quite relieved her of all the fallout.

Even now she would unexpectedly turn a corner in life and be drawn up short as she realized she was facing a scar from the past. She hadn't walked through all of that untouched. She'd have to be insensate not to respond to the difficulties and wounds.

But the important thing was that she deal with it, get this job done and return to her life. While she tended to be solitary outside work, she had a great time at work and with her colleagues. Relating on a professional level was comfortable—comfortable enough that sometimes she went out to lunch or after work with a couple of people. But it didn't extend beyond that.

The house loomed before them as Tim turned into

the driveway. Memories couldn't hurt her, she reminded herself. So why was she so unnerved? Because the place would remind her of a brief time when her life had been full and happy, and how that had been so suddenly ripped from her.

Ludicrous. She'd dealt with that. She was beginning to feel like a whiny child.

The house smelled different from when she'd first entered it two days ago. Evidently the heat had warmed it through and through, and maybe had pulled old odors out of the walls. It was definitely musty, but she thought she could detect the aroma of Bob's cigars.

"Oh, man," she murmured as she stood inside.

"What?"

"Can you smell the cigars? Bob had one going all the time. I guess the smell is in the walls."

"Probably in the furniture, too. I presume you're going to get rid of it. After twenty years in an unregulated environment, I'm not sure it's any good anymore."

"I certainly don't want any of it." Most assuredly. The couch in the living room—she remembered jumping on it with Bob's daughter Millie, until they'd both been scolded. The rug had provided an area where they built towns and drove toy cars or set up tea parties for their dolls.

The kitchen was no better. She'd eaten a lot of home-made cookies in there. And upstairs were bedrooms where she'd played or sometimes spent the night. Even the backyard was haunted with memories of barbecues when Bob would invite a lot of his clients. Or his marks, if she were honest about it.

"Let's gut it," she said abruptly.

Tim looked askance at her. "Do you mean that? Really?"

"Gut it," she said again. "This whole town will be better for losing every possible memory of Bob Higgins. I mean, even his wife left him and changed her last name. The kids, too, I think I heard." She stepped farther inside. "If we can do it, I want to erase every mark in here that Higgins left behind."

He gave a low whistle. "That could get expensive."

"He left me some money. Earl advised me to keep it until I caught up with expenses. I just wanted to give it away, but maybe he was right. If I possess some of his ill-gotten gains, how much better if I use it to erase his existence?"

At that, a laugh escaped Tim. "Check. Erase Bob Higgins. Maybe we can do it without bankrupting you if you want to help."

"I've got a couple of weeks of vacation. I was planning to use most of it for a skiing trip in the mountains back home, but I could use it for this." She felt a smile spring to her lips. "You know, I think it would give me a great deal of satisfaction."

He shook his head a little, but his smile remained. "And to think I was trying to budget for minimal repairs to make the place pass an inspection for sale. Now you want to go whole hog?"

"As much as I can. I'll be thrilled, for example, if I never have to smell that cigar again."

He chuckled. "All right. We'll go room by room and make a list. If you really want to gut this place, though, the first thing we need to do is get the furnishings out. It'll make the rest of the work easier. But still, we need to spend a few hours checking it all out to see what's worth donating and what just needs a one-way trip to the county dump."

"Fair enough." Mentally she rolled up her sleeves. "I should have brought a way to mark things or list them."

"I've got stuff I left in the kitchen." He paused. "Or we can hold a sale on Saturday, let folks come by and browse and buy anything they want for a dollar or two. That might get you a little money to add to the kitty for cleaning this place out."

"You think anyone would want this stuff?"

He shrugged. "The mattresses wouldn't attract any interest. But a bed frame? Maybe that dining room table? The wood still appears to be in good shape. Anyway, some of it might appeal to people. Then we go through what's left and decide what might make a good donation. It could save you moving and haulage costs, if nothing else."

That sounded good to her. "But won't it hold up progress if we leave the furnishings until the weekend?"

"I suggest we move most of it into one or two rooms. Then we can work on the rest." He pulled a cell phone out of his pocket. "Let me see if I can get a couple of my buddies over to help out."

As she stood looking at the big, heavy sofa that was probably almost a hundred years old, she thought that was a great idea.

Vanessa was amazed by how fast things happened. Four of Tim's friends showed up, one of them with a big box truck, and soon furniture was moving. Some of the items went right into the box truck for a trip to the dump. The rest wound up gathered in the living and dining rooms, with a bit of spillover into the hallway.

When Bob's wife had left, she must have taken every item of real value from the house, while leaving the furniture behind. A move on the cheap. They did, however, run across a closet and dresser full of a man's clothes.

"Donate," argued Tim. "Plenty of people truly need clothes in decent condition. They won't know it's Bob's stuff."

"Probably not," she agreed. The clothes were fairly nondescript and could have been owned by anyone. "They need to be washed, though. The cigar smell is strong."

"There's a washer in the basement. I think it still works. Shall we find out?"

With the moving done, they were once again alone in the house together, and the afternoon had begun to fade into the season's early twilight.

"Your friends really helped a lot," she remarked as she and Tim put the clothes in plastic trash bags to carry downstairs. "They should send me a bill."

"They won't. It's the kind of thing friends do."

She'd never tested her friendships that far. If the thought had ever crossed her mind, she'd have been sure no one would have time or want to. Interesting. Maybe she needed to think about what that meant about her, not her friends.

Tim sensed that Vanessa was experiencing some kind of inner turmoil beyond being expected to deal with a house she'd never wanted to see again. Since she didn't bring it up, however, he let it rest. How could he ask, anyway? He hardly knew her and didn't have the right.

Since it was time for Matthew to be coming home from school, he suggested they leave the laundry for morning. She was agreeable and appeared eager to see Matthew again.

Ha, he thought with silent laughter. His son had a better way with the ladies than he did.

The circle in front of the school was filled up with parents' cars, while the bus circle at the side was beginning to move out. Matthew came running toward them as they eased into the circle, but he was not alone. Tim recognized Ashley McLaren, the fourth-grade teacher, and right behind her Julie Archer, the kindergarten teacher. Since Matthew was quite definitely in the second grade, Tim waited to see what they had to say. "I wonder if Matthew got into something he shouldn't have. Why else would two teachers from other grades be coming with him?"

"I..." Vanessa's tentative answer broke off as Matthew opened the front door on her side and said, "Ms. Archer and Ms. McLaren know you, Vannie."

Tim's gaze leaped to Vanessa's face, and he saw huge uncertainty there. Also a passing urge to flee.

"Vannie!" exclaimed Julie. "My gosh, it's been years. You remember us? Julie Ardlow and Ashley Granger? We used to hang together a whole lot at school."

For a few seconds Vanessa appeared totally at a loss, then she summoned a smile. "I remember you," she said. "Sort of. It's been so long."

"It's been way too long. So when we found out you were in town from Matthew..."

The boy was already climbing behind her into the crew seat.

"We decided," Ashley interrupted Julie, "that we've got to get together. Just for coffee if you don't have time for more. Or maybe lunch. And I've got an additional request. Matthew says you work with dinosaur bones at a museum. If I beg nicely, will you come talk to my class? I'm sure they'd love it."

Tim almost smiled, but smothered the expression. He could sense both Vanessa's shock and her reluctance, but there were two bright-faced women from her past making friendly overtures. She was going to get reeled in by simple courtesy, and he couldn't help but think that would be good for her.

Then he started wondering what else Matthew had been talking about. It might be time to teach the boy that what happened at home stayed at home. He'd never felt the need before, but Vanessa's privacy had been pierced without her permission. For all he knew, she might be furious about this by the time they drove away.

But for now she was smiling, assuring Julie and Ashley that she'd love to meet for coffee, but she'd have to figure out when she could. "I'm clearing out the old Higgins house," she offered by way of explanation.

"I heard that man deeded his house to you," Ashley said. "I didn't know whether to be indignant. I thought for sure you'd just sell it without even looking at it."

"Earl Carter said I had some things to do first."

"I guess he'd know." Julie shrugged. "Anyway, give me a call when you can find an hour or so. Or if you want help dealing with the house, I'm sure we could find some time."

"We're freezing these folks," Ashley said. "The inside of that truck must feel like a meat locker. We'll let you go, but we're not hard to find. And let me know about talking to my class, okay?"

Tim felt the silence almost acutely as they at last eased from the circle and headed toward his home. "Sorry about that," he said after a few seconds.

"Did I do something wrong?" Matthew asked, apparently rediscovering his ability to chatter. "I was just talking about Vannie and how she works with dinosaur bones. Everyone was jealous that I get to talk to her. That was all."

"From little seeds big things grow," remarked Tim. "Did you ask Vanessa if it was okay to talk about her?"

Matthew grew uncharacteristically silent. Then, "Wasn't it? Is it some kind of secret?"

Oh, man, Tim thought. How was he going to explain the difference between secrets and confidentiality? About not talking about people without their permission? Especially when the person in question had a job that fascinated him.

"It's okay," Vanessa said. "It's okay. He didn't do anything wrong."

But maybe he had, Tim thought, shooting her another glance as he cornered into his driveway. Vanessa had lost her peppy look and appeared to have begun brooding. Well, when he could get Matt off to bed, he was going to ask her about her reaction.

But something else happened first. Vanessa climbed out into ankle-deep snow. Matthew tumbled out after her. All of a sudden she gasped.

"What?" Tim hurried out from behind the wheel and around the front of his truck.

Vanessa had bent over and was scooping snow into her bare hands. "You little brat. I didn't bring gloves."

But just as his heart froze with shock, he realized she had begun to laugh. A round circle of snow powdered her jeans, and a second later she had hurled a snowball back at Matt. Shrieking with laughter, the boy ducked and ran.

Tim leaned against the side of his truck to watch and see how far this went. It couldn't last long, given Vanessa was making snowballs with her bare hands, but it lasted for a few minutes, anyway. Snowballs flew back and forth, with Matthew giggling like mad and Vanessa laughing.

But at last Vanessa held up both her hands. "You win, Matthew. My hands are frozen now."

He came hurrying over, still grinning. "I'm sorry. That was fun. Maybe you should get some gloves."

"I have some, but not on me. Warn me beforehand next time."

Tim walked with the two of them into the house and immediately turned on the hot water tap. "Try to thaw your hands," he suggested to Vanessa as she pulled off her jacket. "Man, your fingers are red."

"My own fault," she said cheerfully. "I could have called quits sooner. But that was fun. Thanks, Matthew."

Tim began boiling water for hot chocolate and sent Matt to change into play clothes and to get ready to do his homework.

"I'm sorry," he remarked.

"For what?"

"Matt inadvertently put you on the spot. Maybe you didn't mind running into Ashley and Julie, but to be asked to give a presentation on dinosaurs?"

"He didn't put me on that spot. Ashley did." She turned off the hot water and dried her hands on the nearby kitchen towel. "That feels better."

"I'm sure Ashley would understand if you tell her you can't give a presentation."

She sat at the table and put her chin in her hand. "It's weird."

"What is?" He waited, hoping he was about to learn more about this complex woman. Behind him, he heard the quiet vibration as the pot began to simmer.

"I didn't want to see anyone when I came back to this town. I was afraid of the judgment. I think I told you. Anyway, I just ran into two of my oldest friends. They were friendly. I survived. But I can barely remember them."

He nodded. It wasn't surprising, considering she'd left at the age of seven. If he hadn't lived here his entire life, there were loads of people he'd probably have trouble remembering. For that matter, except for Matthew, he doubted Ashley and Julie would have recognized Vanessa. "I think you could walk these streets in almost perfect anonymity if you want. As long as Matthew zips his lip."

She shook her head a bit. "He really didn't do anything wrong. He was excited about dinosaurs or he probably wouldn't have said much. I get it."

"But where does that leave you?" he asked. Damn, this felt awkward. His son had blurted something totally innocent, but in the process had exposed this woman to something she'd been trying to avoid. The fact that it had gone well didn't mean it was okay. Vanessa hadn't planned to stay more than a couple of days, now she was talking about giving up her vacation to erase every sign of Bob Higgins from that house, then into her life had walked two people when she'd been trying to avoid facing anyone in this county.

Because of a fear she really didn't need to feel. How could anyone blame a little girl for any of what had happened? But her father had turned the area into a bugaboo for her, making her expect horrible reactions.

He poured hot water into cocoa mix in three mugs. One he placed in front of her before taking a second into the dining room, where Matt was pulling papers and a workbook out of his backpack.

"Did I do something wrong, Daddy?" he asked as he slid onto the chair in front of his homework. The mug of hot chocolate went onto a corner of the place mat.

"Not a thing," Tim said after a moment. Really, was this the kind of issue he wanted to use to demonstrate that families had to have some privacy? In this town, unless you kept your mouth shut, it wasn't long before everyone knew everything that was going on in your life. Since little of it needed to be secret, that was okay. But there were always things people wanted to keep private, from personal disagreements to the size of their bank accounts. Matthew would have to learn, but maybe not today.

Vanessa had been shocked, but she didn't seem overly disturbed that two old friends had found her. Maybe, when she got used to the idea, it would even make her feel more comfortable here.

He wanted that. He was surprised how much he wanted that. Mentally it put him back on his heels. There was no way she would stay here, he wasn't in a position to move to another state and try to find construction work, and he didn't want to uproot Matthew anyway. So of all possible women he could get truly interested in after all these years, he might be picking exactly the wrong one.

If he was. He smothered a sigh as he went back to the kitchen to start dinner. He didn't want Vanessa to hear it and ask if something was wrong. He was drawn to her. Sexually, of course, but it was more than that. In the short time he had known her, he'd sensed a kernel of true sorrow inside her, hidden behind the walls she seemed to erect against the rest of the world. But he didn't know her well enough to judge even that.

He just knew that she was fascinatingly complex, like a puzzle he wanted to solve, and that he sensed she was withdrawn in some truly important ways. Why?

And why did he care? She was just passing through.

At least today might have taught her she had nothing to dread in this town.

Chapter Five

When he reached the kitchen, Vanessa was still sitting there, cradling her cup of hot chocolate with both hands. Her face revealed nothing at all, smooth as an unused canvas although a pretty heart shape, until she noticed he was there. Then a smile sprang to her lips. "Woolgathering," she said.

"Sometimes a productive thing to do. Anything useful?"

"Maybe." She paused, and he didn't question her while he sat with his own cocoa. He waited silently, giving her any time or space she needed, room to follow a different line of thought if she chose.

A few minutes later, however, she surprised him. "I'm beginning to wonder how bent I still am because of my upbringing."

"I'm sorry? What do you mean?"

"Oh, I don't know. My dad filling me with anger, for one thing. I thought I'd left that behind. His alcoholism. But I don't think that's even the worst of it. We moved constantly because he drank. He lost one job after another, and I wound up always being the new girl wherever we went. I never made real friends, first because I didn't have time, and second because I figured I'd be gone in a few months. I'm beginning to wonder if I'm still living that way."

There was no answer for that, of course. At least not from him. Impulsively, he reached across the table and rested his fingertips on the back of her hand. She didn't pull away, much to his relief, but the almost physical jolt of electricity he felt when he touched her warned him that his desire for her was growing rapidly. Dangerous ground, he reminded himself. She'd showed no interest in him, maybe because she didn't feel the attraction, or maybe because of what she had just been talking about.

She'd made herself sound as if she were living behind high emotional walls because of the way she had grown up. Maybe so. He doubted she was sure herself, merely questioning if something in her had been irrevocably changed by her past.

But wasn't everyone affected by their past? He knew he was. The loss of his wife had seared grief deep into his soul, had left him with a loneliness that nothing could erase. His life was full—he had his son, whom he dearly loved—but he no longer had Claire. She'd been a bright and shining spot, and her death had left a blackened crater in her place.

He dated rarely; he pursued no relationship with any woman. Why? Because he was afraid? Or because he felt it would be some kind of betrayal of Claire? Or maybe both. If he couldn't sort that out, how could Vanessa sort out all the things her childhood had done to her?

Did it have to be sorted out? As the thought occurred to him, he spoke it. "Why are you wondering? Does it matter if you're content?"

"I'm wondering if I'm content." She surprised him by turning her hand over and clasping his fingers. "Let me ask you. You were terribly wounded by the loss of your wife, I'm sure. Are you content with the way things are?"

What a devil of a question, he thought, staring at their clasped hands. Content? In a way he supposed he was. But that was a long way from what he'd had before. He and Claire hadn't been deliriously happy all the time, or even much of the time. Life didn't allow that. But he'd been happier than he was now. More content. "It's not the same," he said finally.

"I'm sure it isn't," she admitted. She squeezed his hand almost gently, then withdrew hers. "I'm just wondering how it is that I manage to avoid feeling deeply for anyone. I've been at the museum for a few years now. I ought to be settled. I ought to have a crowd. But there's a part of me that never connects beyond the surface. As if I'm guarded all the time. Is that normal? I somehow doubt it."

He frowned. "Not everyone's the same. Some people are introverts. Maybe that's all it is for you. Are you thinking you're not normal?"

"I'm thinking that maybe I don't know what normal is."

He shook his head. "I'm not sure there is one." He

was beginning to ache for her again, sensing some kind of sorrow in her that she was struggling to come to grips with. He hadn't the faintest idea how to help. No words of wisdom. Life for him was a constant round of just getting by and being grateful for what he did have. If it wasn't enough, then too bad. The feeling would pass.

She spoke after a couple of minute. "Meeting Julie and Ashley today—like I said, I barely remember them. It was such a long time ago, and I was so young. But… what if I'd stayed here? Grown up with them? They're obviously so comfortable together, and they seem to still be friends. Would I have been like that? On the inside rather than always on the outside?"

Oh, man. "You're talking to a building contractor here," he reminded her. "Good with the hands, but not so much with the brains."

"Oh, cut it out," she said almost irritably. "Admittedly, I haven't known you long, but you don't strike me as stupid. Not even a little."

"Well, then, you're walking into territory I'm not competent to deal with."

Her mouth curved in one corner. "You think I need therapy?"

"Not for me to say. Just thinking that you're talking about something I can understand, but I don't have any way of responding that might be useful."

"But you understand?"

She looked almost eager, he realized. She needed something, and he just wished he knew what it was and how to provide it. Seven-year-olds were easy for the most part. Adults not so much. "I miss my wife," he said. "I'm not looking for a replacement. In fact, that would be impossible. And I guess I've kinda been avoiding getting involved again. Maybe I'm afraid because losing Claire was so painful."

She nodded. "I can understand that. I don't blame you for being afraid, either. I'm just wondering if I'm experiencing the same thing in a different way. So many losses over the years until finally I gave up. But maybe not. Maybe this is who I would have been if I'd always lived here and grown up with my friends."

He couldn't answer that, obviously, and she didn't seem to expect him to. She might be right, though. Examining the detritus his loss had left in its wake, he could only wonder about experiencing the same thing repeatedly. He'd probably become some kind of hermit. Well, except for Matthew. Matthew had kept him going through the darkest days. From what she'd so far said, Vanessa had nothing. Both her parents had evidently failed her, leaving her insecure and lost as a child.

She'd been avoiding looking at him directly, except for brief glances, as if she was afraid of even that much connection. But then, surprising him, her gaze fixed on his. In her mossy-green eyes, he read hunger. But hunger for what? The kind of connection she'd evidently been missing her whole life? Or something else? Passion? He sure felt a strong need for sex with her himself, but he was old enough to know such things passed and could easily make a mess. He was sure she didn't want that. No more messes, no more losses. After all, he was avoiding that himself.

But something about Vanessa was special. He just wished he could put his finger on what drew him, apart from her beauty. Her loneliness? That wasn't a great place to start. Two lonely souls wouldn't necessarily be good for each other.

Why was he even thinking like this, anyway? She'd be going home soon enough. Did he want another hole in his life? Absolutely not.

He heard someone knocking on the door. A glance at the clock told him it was only a few minutes past nine. Late for a neighborly call, maybe, but not too late. Or it could be one of his customers. Occasionally one would get a bug about something in the evening after looking over progress on the job or thinking over a proposal for work and call or drop by. Although in this weather, dropping by seemed like the least preferable choice.

He rose, excusing himself, and went to find out who was there. A young man he knew mostly by sight was standing there. Larry Crowley, he believed.

"Hey, Tim," the young man said. "I heard Vanessa Welling is here. We were in school together when we were kids. I spent some time at her dad's ranch. Is she around?"

Tim eyed him, seeing a pleasant-looking young man with a smile. Average height and build. "Kinda late for a social call," he remarked. Not that he had any right to prevent Vanessa from seeing anyone.

"Yeah, sorry. You probably don't know because I'm not around town a lot, but I'm a long-haul trucker. Gotta leave again at dawn."

Instead of letting the frigid night swallow all the heat from his house, Tim invited Larry inside. "I'll see if she has a minute," he said, leaving Larry in the small foyer.

"Thanks. If not, just tell her I said hi."

"Okay." He walked back to the kitchen. Vanessa was sitting upright in her chair. She must have been listening.

"Larry Crowley, old friend?" he questioned. "Just wants to say hi before he leaves again."

She blinked, evincing surprise. "Larry?"

He watched her search her memory, then she nodded. "Amazing. Julie and Ashley surprised me, but someone else? I *do* vaguely remember him, though. He liked playing with cars in the dirt."

Tim could have laughed. That sounded like a kid. "Did you play with him?"

"Sometimes." She rose, put on a smile and walked out to the foyer.

He hesitated near the kitchen door, letting her have her moment with an old friend. Listening. Why he felt edgy he couldn't have said.

"Larry," she said. "It's been ages."

"Yeah. You're looking good."

"So are you."

Tim relaxed. Then the bomb dropped.

Vanessa had only the vaguest memory of Larry Crowley, a very young boy covered in dust with a passion for tiny metal cars. She had one or two images of him at her parents' ranch, but none of him from school. Maybe one at Bob's house? She wasn't sure.

Now she faced a thin man of about her age, with shaggy dark hair and eyes that held no warmth. Just as uneasiness began to prickle along her nerves, he spoke.

"My dad's dead."

"I'm sorry," she answered, taken aback. "Mine, too."

"Yeah, I heard. He helped Higgins steal my dad's retirement. Nothing left. Your whole family stinks!"

She took a step back, startled and suddenly afraid. Her dad's constant warnings about judgment came back to her, and she couldn't help retorting, "We lost everything, too, Larry. Everything."

"My dad always said your dad was the reason—"

Suddenly Tim was there, inserting himself between the two of them. "I think you ought to go, Larry."

"But her father—"

"She wasn't responsible for any of that. She was a kid, just seven. How old were you? Could you have stopped your dad from doing anything? Yelling at Vanessa won't do any good, but it'll sure as hell make me madder than a wet hornet. Now leave!"

Larry was clenching and unclenching his fists. He glared at Vanessa and Tim before turning and storming out.

As if from a great distance, Vanessa watched Tim close and lock the door. Tremors had begun to run through her, and her face felt like a frozen mask.

Her dad had warned her. For years he'd claimed this town would sit in judgment. She'd dropped her guard because of Julie and Ashley. Way too easily.

Slowly her hands came up, and she wrapped her arms around herself. "I've got to leave in the morning," she said shakily. "Do whatever the house needs. Drop a bomb on it. I don't care."

The urge to flee to privacy overwhelmed her, and she turned to go to the bedroom. Before she took a step, strong arms wrapped around her from behind and held her tightly.

"Easy," Tim murmured. "Easy. Just one jerk—"

"Saying what everyone thinks!"

"Saying what *he* thinks," Tim corrected firmly. "Sounds like his life was poisoned the same way yours was, by an angry father. That doesn't mean either man was right."

"I don't want to stay in this town," she argued, gradually regaining her strength. "I don't need any more of that."

He turned her, making her face him, enclosing her once more in his embrace. "It'll be okay. First of all, I'm damn near positive that you won't meet another soul like Larry. But even if you do, I'll be there. I promise. I'm not going to stand for that crap from anyone. How idiotic can you get? Like a seven-year-old girl could have anything to do with what happened? Most people have more brains than that."

"But I'm the only one they have left to yell at."

"Larry's a jackass. You're not responsible, and yelling at you for something other people did is downright stupid and cruel. It's a good thing he's on his way out of town in the morning, or I'd hunt him up and tell him a thing or two."

Surprise began to trickle through Vanessa as she listened to Tim. He was indignant for her. Angry on her behalf. Ready to protect her against the things she feared. And angry at Larry, while all she felt was awful pain. Shouldn't she be angry, too?

The feeling of being protected, however, warmed her somewhere deep inside. She'd never felt that way before, and however temporary it was, it came like a revelation. Someone could actually be concerned enough to take care of her.

"You're kind," she murmured, letting her head come to rest on his shoulder, letting tension seep out of her.

"I'm mad," he said. "There was no call for that. None at all. No one he should be angry with is in this house. Damn him."

"His father..."

"To hell with his father. To hell with yours, too, for that matter. Two grown men made big mistakes, and they're going to dump it on *your* head? I am completely out of patience."

A shiver passed through her, but this one wasn't uncomfortable. She leaned into the man, grateful for his strength. She had always thought herself strong, but she was beginning to see it differently. Not strong, but hiding. Now she'd been forced out of hiding, and she couldn't handle Larry's anger. Some strength.

Matt's voice came from upstairs. "Daddy?"

"What are you doing up?"

"I heard a man. Is Vannie okay?"

"She will be. Don't worry, son. You can give her a hug in the morning, if you want."

"Okay."

She faintly heard the sound of bare feet in the upstairs hall. "He's a good kid," she said, her voice thick. Only then did she feel that her eyes were burning with unshed tears. Tears for what? Was she having a breakdown of some kind? Maybe coming back here had been the worst thing she could possibly have done.

But with Tim's arms around her, she couldn't quite believe that.

"Come on," he said quietly. "Let's go sit in the living room. Maybe have a cookie, or I can reheat your cocoa. You must have had an adrenaline rush, and that burns calories fast."

Was that why she had started shaking? Maybe. She really didn't know. The attack had been unexpected, coming out of nowhere, it seemed, despite all her father's warnings. A man calling himself an old friend had suddenly turned into a threat.

"He wasn't a threat," she said slowly, mostly to herself, as Tim kept his arm around her shoulder and walked her into the living room.

"A threat to your peace of mind. I don't believe he'd have gotten violent."

"I don't think so." Not now. But had she? For a few moments there, she'd felt real fear. A gut certainty that Larry wanted to hit her. Probably a misreading of his body language, because he had certainly been angry. "He must be really seething that he didn't get to have his say."

Tim let go of her and motioned her to sit on the sofa. "Too bad. You will never be the person he needs to say it to. Now, do you want fresh cocoa or some cookies?"

Her stomach had knotted. Putting something in it had become necessary. "Milk and cookies?" she suggested. A childhood treat that had suddenly arisen in her mind, promising comfort. A different kind of comfort from what she had felt in Tim's arms. How could a man's hug have reached her so deeply, bringing warmth to the corners of her soul?

"Coming up."

Her thoughts drifted upward to Matthew, and she hoped he hadn't heard any of that ugly confrontation.

He'd obviously been worried, and that troubled her. Maybe she should move into the Higgins house until she could leave. She didn't want Matthew exposed to that kind of ugliness, not even briefly. He was such a bright and happy little guy. She hoped that never changed, although given the way life operated, it probably would, but she didn't want it to be soon, or because of her.

Tim returned with a tray bearing a plate of cookies, two glasses of milk and some paper napkins. "Dig in," he said cheerfully. "Dip if you like. Isn't that half the fun of cookies and milk?"

"Clearly you have a child."

He laughed. "Seems like. I'd quit dipping years ago because of drippy mess I always made, then he taught me that it didn't matter because it was so enjoyable. Makes me feel like a kid again, and you know, the mess isn't that hard to clean up."

She smiled and reached for a chocolate cookie and the glass of milk. Then, almost daringly, she dipped the cookie and quickly ate the soaked part.

"Yum," he said, then dipped a cookie for himself. "So, are you unwinding from our visitor?"

"Yeah, but I feel awful because Matthew might have heard some of that."

"I doubt it. He came because he heard something, but I'm pretty sure it was seeing me hugging you that made him wonder if something was wrong. If he *did* happen to hear anything Larry said, we'll talk about it tomorrow."

She swallowed another bite of cookie, washing it down with more milk. The whole thing with the cookies and milk was soothing. Tim made quick work of his cookie and set his glass on the coffee table.

"You and Matthew have a wonderful relationship."

"I'm lucky."

"No, I think you're good. A good father."

He turned his head toward her as he rested his arm along the back of the couch, and she was astonished to read something like sorrow on his face. "I'm sorry you missed that."

"Not in my early years," she said truthfully. "I don't have a lot of very clear memories from before, but I do remember feeling loved and secure. Bob Higgins blew that all up, so I can understand where Larry's coming from."

"That doesn't give him the right to dump it on you." Having said that as if it were indisputable, he fell silent, drumming his fingers on the back of the couch. "You're thinking about moving into the Higgins house, aren't you?"

His accuracy astonished her. She hadn't said a word about it. "What, do you read minds?"

"Faces, maybe." He looked at her. "Why? You'd be miserable and uncomfortable."

"Because I don't want Matthew to see anything like what just happened. I'd like to preserve his innocence as long as possible."

He smiled faintly. "Very kind of you. But innocence only lasts so long, and sometimes even at seven you have to deal with the way things are. You certainly ought to know that. Matthew's had his share of playground dustups and broken friendships. The innocence is bound to get chipped away. We just hope it's not in some awful, shattering way. But eventually it will be. That's life."

"But…"

He silenced her with a shake of his head. "I doubt he would have even understood what Larry was saying, beyond that he was angry with you. Matthew is perfectly able to understand people getting angry. He's even been known to do it himself sometimes."

His words seemed to release a pressure valve inside her, and she relaxed with a quiet laugh. "Point made."

"Yeah, he can become a little tempest sometimes. Not often. I'm blessed with a son who is usually happy. But once in a while, not so much. We've butted heads a few times."

"I find that hard to imagine."

"He has a mind of his own." Tim shrugged. "I don't want to stifle it, but occasionally I have to object. Depending on how determined he is, it can become quite something."

She could almost imagine Matthew standing stiffly, his face screwed up with anger, probably looking more adorable than frightening. "I feel sorry for Larry."

"Really?"

"He grew up with the same kind of stuff I did. I can imagine the bitterness his father must have felt and expressed countless times. Heck, I don't have to imagine it. I lived it. It has an effect."

"Of course. But do you go around taking it out on other people?"

"Maybe only because I don't have someone to take it out on. Bob was in prison. Now he's dead. Maybe I would have wanted to do exactly what Larry did."

He drummed his fingers again briefly. "I don't read you that way, but I could be wrong. I don't know you very well yet. Still, I don't see it. Larry's anger is misdirected. What have you done with yours?"

She put down her glass then leaned her head back against the couch and closed her eyes. "I think I buried it. I know as I got older I grew really angry with Bob, and with my dad, too, but for different reasons. I was mad because Bob hurt my parents, of course. But I was mad at my dad for his drinking and losing every job he had, which upset my mother until she looked ninety when she wasn't yet forty. I think Dad did that to her more than the loss of the ranch."

His fingers moved from the back of the sofa to rest on her shoulder, stroking gently. Pleasant shivers ran through her even as she thought about a past that was ugly and had sometimes been nearly unbearable. God, his touch was magical, tugging her out of the ditch of memory.

"And you?" he asked yet again. "I'm not asking about your parents. I'm asking how you dealt with all of it."

"I survived," she said flatly. "That's all I could do. I survived. I pulled inside myself until nothing could touch me anymore."

In that instant she realized a home truth about herself. She'd almost entirely squelched her emotional life to protect herself. She was barely more than half a person.

The recognition ripped something deep inside her, and the agony filled her. She'd not only hidden, she'd run, locking entire parts of herself away.

Jumping up, ignoring Tim when he called her name, she went back to the bedroom and closed the door. Leaning back against it, she stood shaking, horrified and agonized as she faced the real loss she had suffered.

Herself.

Chapter Six

Saturday morning came swiftly. The sale had been announced on the radio and in the local weekly, and despite the cold gray day, quite a number of people showed up to pick through the furnishings left behind by the Higgins family.

Vanessa had decided not to put prices on anything. She didn't care if she made a dime off this, so she sat in the kitchen and accepted whatever offers people made. Bit by bit the house began to empty itself of usable furnishings, and from her perspective the people who came were helping her out.

After Larry's visit, she was initially tense about this whole affair, but the people who came were friendly, and the majority didn't seem to have any idea who she was. Bob Higgins had faded into the background a long time ago for most, and the Welling name had vanished from the county twenty years ago. Older people who might have remembered simply smiled and welcomed her to town.

A very different reception from the one she had anticipated. A scandal that might have been on every tongue all those years ago had ceased to matter.

Maybe she ought to learn something from that, she thought. It was past. Long past. Now she needed to deal with the scars that had come after, and maybe place the blame where it really belonged: on her father, a man who had been unable to overcome his losses, and instead had lost himself and his family.

Look at Tim, she thought as he moved between rooms with Matthew nearby. He'd lost his wife yet had continued to make a good life for his son.

Her father clearly had a weakness of character, and after her realization the other night, she had to face the possibility that she might suffer from a similar weakness. Not as bad, obviously. She was maintaining a life and a job and had plenty of casual friends. But anything deeper than casual? She hid. Not in a bottle but inside herself.

Matthew eventually grew bored with wandering around the same rooms and watching people talk to his dad about furniture. He came to the kitchen to sit with Vanessa.

"How come you don't want this stuff?" he asked.

"Because I'm going to clean up the house and sell it. Furniture would get in the way."

He turned toward her, a frown creasing his young brow. "You're not going to live here?"

"That's not my plan," she said forthrightly.

He nodded slowly but didn't look exceptionally happy about it. "You have to go back to the museum."

"Yes, I do."

"But why can't you stay here?"

A million reasons. Many still to be sorted through. But there was one reason she thought he'd understand. "My job is too far away, kiddo. I'd have to fly back and forth, and I can't do that every day, or even every week."

He nodded again, gravely. "And we don't have a museum here."

"I'm afraid not."

"We can come visit you, though, right?"

Another bud of warmth blossomed in her heart. "You bet."

Another visitor approached, wanting to buy two end tables. Vanessa let them choose their own price, then suggested Matthew count the money and write it down on her list. That made the woman smile. "Cute boy," she said before walking away with her prizes.

Watching Matt carefully print the name of the item and the amount in the designated column, she felt a small shock of surprise. Were people paying more because she let them set their own price? Because the sum was mounting, and it was more than she had expected.

A little while later, Tim came into the kitchen to snag one of the sandwiches they'd brought with them and to give Matthew one, spread out on a napkin. Simple peanut butter.

"Tim? Do you think I made a mistake by not pricing anything?"

He pulled out the remaining chair and straddled it.

A table with only three chairs. That still struck her as strange. "Why do you ask?"

"Because people are paying far more than I expected."

The corners of Tim's eyes crinkled. "They're paying what they want to. If that makes them raise the price a little, I'm sure it's not by much. On the other hand, if you'd priced everything, no matter how low, they'd have felt obliged to haggle."

Maybe he had a point, she thought as Matthew asked what haggling was. Tuning out the explanation, noting only how patiently and clearly Tim explained, she wandered down a trail of thought triggered by Matthew.

He seemed to want her to stay. He professed understanding about why she couldn't, but had she detected a note of disappointment in his voice? Already he was planning to visit her? She wondered what Tim would think of that.

Of course, Matthew was only seven, and he could forget a lot before spring break or the summertime. He could get distracted.

Oddly enough, for someone who was an emotional recluse, she hoped he didn't forget. She genuinely liked the child. For that matter, she was growing fond of his father.

Dangerous territory for her, but she had a safety valve in her eventual departure. That date promised her security.

Apparently bargain hunters were early shoppers. The crowds died away until everyone was gone shortly after two. So was most of the furniture.

"One last truckload for donation or the dump," Tim

said. "Gee, that went well. I'm such a genius for thinking of it."

Matthew giggled.

"It was a brilliant idea," Vanessa said.

"And not too tough on you?"

She glanced at Matthew, wondering how much the
child had picked up and understood, then decided probably very little. "Not tough at all. Everyone was really
nice."

"And I helped," Matthew announced. "Does that
make me a genius, too?"

"Absolutely," said his father. "Define 'genius.'"

Matthew pursed his lips, then sighed. "I gotta use
the dictionary?"

"Always."

Matthew scowled. "That's like school."

"Precisely. Or homework, even. Okay, everyone,
jackets on. I want to air out this house one more time
before we go."

"You made it cold in here this morning," Matthew
said. "Do we have to do it again?"

"You won't care. We're leaving."

Matthew ran out into the yard to play in what was
left of the snow while Vanessa helped Tim open all the
windows.

"We're doing this why?"

"Because until the guy comes to test the air in here
on Monday, I have no idea what we might be breathing."

She nodded. "Still worried about lead?"

"Until I'm told otherwise, yes. Basically, since I first
aired it out, I doubt there's much bad in here. I was more
worried because the place had been shut up so long.

Now it's open a lot and it's probably safe. But if we find lead paint… I hate to tell you, Vannie, but that could get expensive, depending. I just hope the sagging paint is all latex, and the wallpaper isn't covering bad secrets."

"I never thought about all of this."

"No one ever does. We all live on assumptions."

An interesting statement, she thought as she finished opening the last upstairs windows. There was no mistaking that a strong, icy breeze was blowing through the house.

We all live on assumptions. She'd certainly brought a few of them along with her here. With the exception of Larry, she'd run into absolutely no judgment or hostility. The things her father had dreaded were mere boogeymen. At least so far.

Then it was time to close the windows, and once again she walked room to room with Tim.

"This will give us a great baseline reading on Monday," he said. "A house shut up for way too long—in this case almost two decades—can pick up a lot of bad things. Radon from the basement, for example. Most houses need a good airing from time to time, lead or no lead. So whatever the inspector reads on Monday should establish what someone living here would be exposed to. And what we might be exposed to as we strip it down."

"You suggested I stay here!" she said, pausing and staring at him.

He shrugged. "I didn't think you'd have a problem for a few days, not with me airing the place out again and again. And if you'd stayed here, I'd have kept on doing it. Come on, Vannie. You don't think I wanted to poison you!"

Horrified at what she had just suggested, wondering where that had come from, she leaned back against a papered wall and closed her eyes. Surely she didn't believe Tim would have exposed her to harm. So what had she been thinking? Or not thinking, was probably a better question. Was she acting on some gut instinct to make sure she didn't get involved? Because she was sure getting involved here, and her escape date suddenly didn't seem safe enough.

"Are you angry with me?" Tim asked when she didn't move or respond.

"No. Really, no. I don't know what I was thinking. I certainly don't believe you'd expose me to harm. And if I don't believe that about me, I definitely know you wouldn't bring Matthew here if you were concerned." She opened her eyes, shuddering a little as she tried to release tension. Really, she had to get over these hang-ups. Sometimes they made her act in stupid ways. Like this.

She and Tim resumed closing the windows. He looked thoughtful, however, and she was worried she'd offended him beyond repair. "I'm really sorry," she said as they closed the last of the windows.

Outside, Matthew had evidently found a couple of other children to play with him in the snow. Their piping, happy voices reached even through the closed windows.

"It's okay," he said.

She wasn't sure it was, but didn't know what else to

say. Trying to change subjects, she asked, "Does anyone call Matthew 'Matt'?"

"At school they do, I think. For me it's just an old habit. Claire and I did it when he was an infant. Big name for a little guy." He gave a brief laugh. "I don't think it's going to last much longer, though. He's going to decide what he prefers."

Back in the kitchen, Tim scooped the remaining cash into the bank envelope he'd brought for her to use, and passed it to her. She passed it right back.

"Down payment on everything you need to do here," she said. "Or at least a small start."

She summoned a smile then headed for the front door. A perfectly good day, and she'd made a mash of it. Well, that was certainly something she seemed to be good at. She ought to be locked up with her fossils.

Matthew was only slightly reluctant to head home. The kids he'd been playing with were friends from school, and they didn't live that far away. Tim had no problem promising there'd be more time to play with them while he was working on the house. That satisfied Matthew.

Vanessa wasn't such an easy puzzle. Her reaction, thinking that he might have let her stay in a house with poisonous air, had shocked him. Then he'd watched her expression alter and realized that it had shocked her, too.

The lady had some issues. He knew that, but now he'd gotten a taste of how deeply they ran. Far from simply fearing judgment over her father's past, she didn't seem to expect anyone to take care of her in any way. God, what a childhood she must have had. Vanessa

Welling against the world. Had her mother even filled in the gaps? He'd assumed so, but now he thought not. She must have practically raised herself in a lot of ways.

What a sorry couple of parents.

At home, he looked at his son's bright face and hoped he never failed that boy. Matthew deserved every unshadowed moment of childhood that life would allow. He deserved to feel safe and protected by his father. He deserved the magic and wonder of each new day.

But Tim wasn't a fool, and he knew he couldn't even guarantee that he'd always be there for Matthew. Claire had been stolen from them. Life happened to everyone.

But it battered some more than others, he supposed, although he was fond of saying that there was no way to tell what burdens another person carried. Nor could burdens be compared.

But he felt a deepening compassion for Vanessa. A lovely young woman who, the more he grew to know her, seemed to be very alone and locked up within herself. The only time she really loosened up was with Matthew.

He wished he could find a way to loosen the restraints life had locked her in, but he knew it wasn't his place and that it was also a dangerous pursuit. She'd built a life she felt mostly content with. Who was he to disturb the walls she'd built for survival?

Worse than that, he wasn't qualified to do so safely.

But that didn't keep him from feeling bad about it.

Let it rest, he told himself. She needed to resume her life in a week or two, and she wouldn't want to go home with her defenses full of holes. Who knew what she was dealing with back in Albuquerque?

Bones, yes. But he could also easily imagine some politics and possibly jockeying among the people working at the museum. Every workplace suffered from some of that.

Holding herself aloof might be the best protection she had. It must have been when she was a child.

So let her be. Ignore the impulse to dash in somehow like a white knight. And while he was at it, put away his desire for her.

Because that just kept nagging at him. He had some self-restraint, and while he occasionally caught a glimmer of interest in her smile or her eyes, he could easily be misreading her. And what if they had sex and it brought her walls down?

Even though he was a guy, he was aware that sex brought down some barriers. It had to. And Claire had once told him that women were especially susceptible to falling in love with a man when they'd had sex. He couldn't remember what the subject had been, but he clearly remembered her saying that. It kept his pants zipped most of the time.

He'd since gathered that not all women reacted that way. A couple of brief failed attempts at relationships had taught him that. Still…

Dang, he wished his parents were still around, especially his mother. He'd have loved to talk to her, to see what she thought of Vanessa and her barricades. Or even Claire's parents, who had utterly shocked him and probably half the town when they announced they were moving to New Zealand. Because of the *Lord of the Rings* movies.

Yeah, really. A couple of middle-aged Tolkien fans

on the adventure of a lifetime. When they called, they always promised Matthew that when he was old enough they were going to bring him to visit.

Which had resulted in the entire works of Tolkien being on his shelf. He'd read them start to finish to the boy and wondered if he'd be doing that again this winter.

Well, except they now had this Harry Potter thing going.

Tim sighed, looked at the time and realized that he hadn't even thought about dinner. Vanessa had gone to take a shower and said she needed to catch up on email. Matthew was settled in front of the TV playing a game that absolutely promised it contained no violence or graphic gore.

Taking a chance, he went down the hall to Vanessa's room, once his and Claire's room, and knocked.

After a few seconds, the door opened. Vanessa had turbaned a towel around her hair and was wearing a thick, fluffy green bathrobe.

"I was wondering," he said, his throat feeling suddenly tight and his voice sounding thick. "I need to run out and take care of dinner. Can you watch Matthew for maybe a half hour? He's in the living room playing a video game."

"Sure," she said with a smile. "Not a problem. Just let me get dressed."

As she closed the door, he walked away absolutely certain she hadn't been wearing a thing under that robe. His mouth turned as dry as the Gobi Desert.

Ah, hell.

It was cold enough on the run to Maude's diner to

chill his impulses and restore rational thought. *Man triumphs over hormones*, he thought with amusement as he walked inside and ordered dinner. He wasn't sure what Vanessa would like and had failed to ask her. Oversight. Duh.

But he ordered Matthew's favorite burger and fries with a side of veggies, then he ordered a grilled chicken sandwich for Vanessa and a steak sandwich for himself. He'd have no problem if she wanted to switch. Then, for safety's sake, a huge chef's salad.

"Feeding an army?" Maude asked.

"Screwup. I failed to ask what everyone wanted."

Maude harrumphed, her usual sour response to life. Thing was, her cooking made up for everything else. The diner was always busy, and everyone called it by her name, not its proper name, the City Diner.

Right now, except for a pizza place at the edge of town and the truck stop diner, she was the only game in town. Sometimes he wished they'd get some variety, but he doubted people around here had a lot to spend on eating out. Maude's was always cheap and always good. Who could compete?

By the time he got home, Vanessa was dressed in a tan chamois shirt and faded blue jeans, her damp hair caught in a narrow headband, and busy playing the game with Matthew. She sat cross-legged on the floor beside him, laughing at her own learning curve. Matthew was an expert, and it showed. Tim sometimes played the game with his son, and marveled at the boy's patience. It was as if he'd been born with a game controller in his hand.

"Hamburger?" Tim called from the entry. Matthew at once paused the game and jumped up.

"Let's eat, Vannie!"

She was still smiling broadly as she rose to her feet in one smooth movement without touching her hands to the floor. The woman must practice yoga, he thought as he continued into the kitchen. He was in pretty good shape, but he doubted he could have managed that.

Matthew knew the rules and didn't have to be reminded to eat his vegetables first. With plates on the table, Vanessa helped herself to a generous serving of the salad and only half of the chicken sandwich. Hardly surprising. Maude's portions were designed for hardworking men from the ranches. These days many carried home takeout containers. For lots of people around here, life had become more sedentary than in past times.

Matthew made conversation easily. "Do you ever dig up bones, Vannie?"

"I have a few times," she answered.

"Was it fun?"

"It was really exciting when I found something, but most of it…" She smiled. "It's hot, hard work most of the time, Matthew."

"Is that why you work in the museum?"

Tim almost laughed. Good question, though.

"Truthfully," Vanessa said, "I chose to work in the museum because I get to solve puzzles. For me that's more fun than finding the fossils."

Matthew swallowed some more of his hamburger before asking, "So it's boring to dig them up?"

"Not exactly." Vanessa paused. "It's hard to explain. I like the work. It's really exciting when you find something. But a lot of the time you're just brushing away dirt, and chipping at rock gently, hoping something will be there. You have to bring a lot of patience. What I do now? I'm excited most of the time."

"I still want to try finding some bones."

"Then you should. And when I get home, I'm going to send you some 3-D dinosaur puzzles."

"What are those?" His face lit with curiosity.

"You get a box full of thin wood cut in the shape of dinosaur bones, and a drawing of the dinosaur. You have to compare the puzzle pieces to a drawing of each kind of bone and then figure out where it belongs. When you get done, you'll have a dinosaur skeleton like in a museum."

Matthew beamed. "That sounds like fun."

"It definitely is. We have several different kits and I've tried them all. Cool stuff."

Tim thought he wouldn't mind trying one of them himself. The builder in him, he supposed. And a different kind of problem solving for Matthew.

After helping with cleanup, his son went back to his video game, leaving Vanessa and Tim in the kitchen with after-dinner coffee.

"I love that kid," she said unexpectedly.

"Easy to do." He smiled. "At least I think so."

"You wouldn't be wrong." Then, hoping he wasn't about to put his foot in it, he asked, "Your mother? You made her life sound very sad. Did you get lost in the shuffle?"

She lifted the teaspoon and stirred coffee that didn't need stirring. "She was overwhelmed. Sometimes she was working two jobs. Then with Dad's drinking problem, and him needing to move to find another job, she was always struggling herself. Finding a new job, making enough so she could squirrel some away for the next time he got fired. I told you how it aged her."

"I remember. But what about you?"

She shrugged one shoulder. "I got dressed, fed and sheltered. She made sure of that."

He noticed what was missing. "Did she care for you in other ways, too? Basic necessities are good, but not enough for the soul."

"The soul?" She repeated the words without looking up. "She took care of me the best she could."

But not emotionally, he suspected. She wouldn't have had much energy left over for that from the sound of it.

Then her head popped up. "Are you saying I'm emotionally crippled?"

At that point, he figured he should have kept his mouth shut. None of his business, no training to help him, and he might just have stirred up a hornet's nest. How could he respond to that? He hadn't exactly been suggesting that, but…but what? Getting too nosy for his own good? Then she surprised him.

"If so," she said, "you'd be right. I've been thinking about it lately. I've never really had a truly close relationship. I wouldn't know what to do with one. Maybe I was built this way, or maybe something inside me is frozen, but…" Again she hesitated. "I guess I always live in anticipation of having to move again. Leave everything behind. It's the way I've been ever since I can remember. I can't blame anyone for it, Tim. This is just how I am."

He decided he needed to let her off the hook he might

have put her on. "I'm sure lots of other people feel the same. It doesn't mean something is wrong with you."

"Maybe not. On the other hand..." She shook her head and once again studied the coffee she wasn't drinking. "I *do* wonder what it would have been like to grow up in one place, with lifelong friends. Would I have been different?"

She might well have been, he thought. But that was water over the dam now. The question was only if she was happy with herself and her life the way it was. He wasn't going to ask that question, because he didn't have the right.

He also had no comparison. He'd been firmly planted here his entire life. He knew damn near everyone, knew who could be trusted, who couldn't, whom he liked to spend time with and those he preferred to avoid. He knew almost every inch of his world intimately. Vanessa couldn't say that. In fact, from the sound of it, she avoided it.

"You know," she said after a bit, "I don't even date. Not really. Or maybe I should rephrase that. I've dated a few times, but not for long. Once things start to pass light friendship, I always bail. So am I crippled? I guess so. Other than your marriage, have you had other relationships?"

"Nothing enduring," he admitted. "I'd be the first to say that Claire's death made me reluctant to hang myself out there for another blow."

She nodded, her gaze meeting his at last. "That's how I feel most of the time. I think. I'm still trying to figure it out. I just know that I feel as if I'm standing back all the time. Staying on the outside. It's safe."

It would have been easy to answer with a flippant *whatever works for you*, but he didn't. Some instinct warned him that would be exactly the wrong thing to say, because right now something about her felt vulnerable to him. As if some of those walls had lowered just a bit. He didn't know if that was good or bad, but it was best left alone—by him, at least.

Damn, he couldn't remember ever feeling so uncertain in his dealings with another person.

He sat in perplexity, wondering why it even mattered to him. Nice enough lady. Too sexually attractive for his comfort. But she was leaving in a week or two for Albuquerque, and their contacts afterward would probably consist of email or phone calls discussing his progress in readying the house for sale.

Just treat her like any other customer, he warned himself. Because that's all she was. Any of her problems aside from the house were none of his business.

Tim wasn't the only troubled person at that table. This trip had awakened things in Vanessa, or maybe it had acted as a major revelation. Maybe she *was* closed off because of her childhood. She'd never really considered it before, because lots of people moved often when they were children. Much of this country had been on the move one way or another since the Second World War. Other people seemed fine, despite bouncing around.

But the definition of *fine* was what she was suddenly calling into question. Of course she was fine. She had a productive career that she loved. She had pursuits that she enjoyed. She just didn't let anyone get too close, and that didn't seem to bother most people.

Honestly, she didn't think most people wanted to know her too well. Or anyone else, for that matter. Skimming along the surface kept things from getting messy for everyone.

But maybe that wasn't working for her anymore. Why else was she questioning herself?

When Matthew went upstairs to get ready for bed, Tim went with him. She could hear the two of them laughing, water running in the tub. Normal sounds she hadn't heard in a very long time because she'd been an only child. Something about them made her ache.

Made her ache for things she'd told herself she never wanted and didn't need. Look at her parents. Who'd want to get married? Look at herself. She had no idea how to be a good parent. Tim might make it look easy, but she knew perfectly well how many mistakes could be made. And marrying someone meant letting them inside places she'd been guarding ever since she could remember, places where she could be wounded.

Why had she never taken a really hard look at this before? Why had she never begun to imagine that she might be warped by the way she had grown up? Just because nobody else seemed to notice anything was wrong?

Like tonight. She'd felt Tim pull back time and again as if he feared her response. He'd edged close to very personal things but had tried to be reassuring. Or had chosen silence.

Maybe he was just being respectful. Or maybe he sensed she wasn't quite right.

God, she needed to take a really hard look at herself and decide if she wanted to stay on her present path. Because the sound of Matthew's laughter upstairs really made her wonder.

Chapter Seven

"Tomorrow's a day off," Tim announced as he returned. "Shall we go into the living room? Bring your coffee if you want."

She left her coffee behind and went to sit on the couch with him. "Why tomorrow off?"

"Sunday. Today was long enough, and I happen to know for a fact that Matthew hasn't even started his homework. So I'll take him to the early church service tomorrow then bring him back to study. He always has more homework on weekends."

She nodded, trying to remember how much homework she'd had at that age. Not much, if she remembered correctly.

"Want to come to church with us?"

Everything inside her froze. See all those people? "No. Thanks," she added.

"I didn't think so. Anyway, Matthew likes the kids' service. And I don't mind catching up with people I only get to see on weekends. Surprising how many there are. The working life," he added on a chuckle. "I'll bring home something for breakfast. Then... Monday. Once we get the air in that house tested, we might be able to get to work. When you said gut it, how much do you want to gut?"

Vanessa, however, was still hung up at her reaction to going to church with him. She went to church nearly every Sunday at home, so her reaction had to do with this being Conard County. Her father's fears and hatreds riding her hard and strong.

She wished she had the courage to just go, but then couldn't see any reason. Face the demons she'd never have to face again? It seemed like a waste of energy.

"Gutting the house?" Tim prompted gently.

"Oh. Yeah. I don't know. I mean, I guess what I want to do is erase Bob. Paint, wallpaper. I don't think I was talking about tearing out walls or anything."

Still smiling, he nodded. "Got it. We can get the last of the furnishings out of there after the inspector comes. He said around ten o'clock."

"Okay." So much easier to talk about the house than going to church. Now wasn't that weird?

"I hope we get good news," Tim remarked. "The house isn't *that* old. There might not be any lead at all. Although I had to remodel a house that had asbestos in the joint compound used on the drywall. Safe as long as it was coated with paint, but the family didn't want it anyway. Removing it required hiring some skilled people who have all the protective gear. Just to be safe."

"Are you trying to scare me?" she asked, looking at him from the corner of her eye.

He laughed. "Absolutely not. I'm expecting to be pleasantly surprised on Monday."

"I hope you're right."

"I usually am." He winked. "I've remodeled a lot of houses around here. Very few problems, even on the older ones. It's been a long time since people became aware of the dangers of lead and so on. Many took care of it before I came along. And like I said, if it's sealed under paint, no real problem."

"But we have sagging paint," she reminded him.

"And we'll deal with it."

He seemed so sure of himself. The way she did in her lab at the museum, only he was confident in so many other ways. He knew his job, of course, but he also seemed comfortable in dealing with his son.

Today as she'd watched him work with all the people who traipsed through the house, showing them things, sometimes helping them carry out heavier items, he'd been so comfortable. Meanwhile, she'd sat at the kitchen table like a slightly nervous mouse.

Man, was that who she really was? A mouse? Timid?

But maybe it was just the situation. At home she didn't feel timid. She just didn't link up with other people a whole lot. An introvert. Nothing wrong with that.

Or maybe there was. She'd been completely thrown out of her comfort zone by coming to a place she'd been taught to think of as bad. Only it wasn't bad. Except for that crazy visit from Larry, everyone had been pleasant, and to judge by the people at the sale today, it seemed most had forgotten the past. Maybe she was being jarred by the difference between reality and expectation.

She spoke again. "I guess I need to reevaluate."

"What?"

"My opinion of Conard County."

"Maybe so. At this point Larry is the only person you met who lived down to your father's expectations."

She nodded. "It's true."

"But honestly, Vannie, I'm not sure the situation was as bad, as regards other people here, as your father thought. He got conned, too. I think most people around here were able to figure that out."

"Maybe. But I'm not going to take a poll. So far, with the exception of Larry, everyone's been nice."

"And don't forget that Ashley wants you to come talk to her class. You'll wind up being the famous dinosaur lady around here if you do."

"A much better way to be remembered," she agreed, smiling almost in spite of herself. "If I'm going to do that, I should call the museum on Monday and have them express me some materials to use. Graphics and models would be a whole lot more fun for kids than me just standing there talking and drawing on a chalkboard."

"Ah, we've evolved to whiteboards."

A small laugh escaped her. "But still. I should also get them to send some puzzles for Matthew. It's an awfully long time for him to wait for me to send them after I go home."

"So you're staying longer?"

Something in the way he asked it caused her breath to lock in her throat. Almost timidly, she looked at him.

"You're beautiful," he said, his voice just above a whisper. "So beautiful, Vannie. Do you even realize it?"

She shook her head once, stiffly, wishing she could draw a full breath.

He scooted down the couch until he sat right beside her. "I'm going to kiss you," he murmured. "You've got exactly one chance to say no."

She couldn't have said that word if her life had depended on it. It had been a long time since anyone had kissed her, and a full lifetime since she'd been as attracted to a man as she was to Tim. There could be no harm in this. Just a kiss.

"I shouldn't," he whispered just before his mouth settled on hers.

It was the gentlest of touches, as if he expected rejection and wanted to leave room for it. Light as butterfly wings, but the warmth it sent spiraling through her amazed her. Then his work-hardened hand cupped her cheek and he deepened the kiss, running his tongue along her lips until her head tipped back a little and she granted him entry.

As his tongue slipped into her mouth and swirled gently, she felt herself softening in every cell of her body, becoming pliable, hungering for more.

She was melting, an experience she'd never had before. How could feelings so strong make her feel so soft?

She wanted his arms around her, wanted to feel his strength, but just as she was lifting her own hand to encourage him, he drew back a little to sprinkle kisses on her eyelids and her cheeks.

"To be continued," he said huskily, then pulled away, placing distance between them.

To be continued? She didn't even want to open her

eyes, never wanted to lose the soft feeling that filled her, or the gentle but electric desire that had come with it.

Just one kiss…

In an instant, near panic filled her. What was she doing? If ever there was a way to get hurt, this was it. She wouldn't just be able to walk away and laugh it off. She knew how hard she could take things. Look at her whole life.

Jumping up, she uttered a smothered good-night and headed for the bedroom.

Some risks were too great. She needed to change a whole lot to be willing to take this one.

Yeah, she was emotionally crippled.

But she was also safe.

Tim didn't move. What had possessed him? Something in the way she looked at him, but whatever he thought he'd seen hadn't been there. So he'd kissed her, sent her into flight and made a total hash of something that had been perfectly fine until he acted like an idiot.

Closing his eyes, he reviewed what had happened. He'd been so sure she was reaching out to him. Asking for a taste, just a taste, of what it would be like if she crossed her barriers.

Just a little kiss, nothing more. Nothing that should have caused her to flee. While it had caused his blood to pound, she usually made that happen just by being around. He doubted she'd reacted as strongly with desire.

He'd felt, just briefly, the softening in her as if she wanted to yield, though. In the process he'd evidently pushed her past her defenses. Because he was damn sure he hadn't repelled her.

The expression on her face when he had backed away had been so soft, so blissful. He wished she could look that way all the time. Then something had hit her, and she'd jumped like a rabbit with a hawk after it.

Well, he'd done it. He'd sent her into protective flight, even though he'd pulled back quickly and said only, "To be continued." He hadn't forced himself on her, and he'd made it clear nothing more would happen between them right then.

But her flight had given him a measure of the scars she bore. The fears she tried to conceal but that buried her in isolation. Could moving around that much as a child really make someone so afraid of getting close, of potential loss? Or had there been more?

He of course had no idea. How could he? Worse, he'd upset her, and he didn't know how to fix it. Judging by the way she'd taken off, she'd probably start talking about moving to the motel.

He didn't like that idea. For her sake, mostly, but also for his.

All he'd wanted to do was help this woman get through what was plainly a rough time for her. Earl had told him maybe more than he should have, being her lawyer, about her reluctance to even come back here, and her distaste for that house.

But instead of helping Vanessa, he might have just made everything more difficult for her. Didn't that just take the cake?

In the bedroom, Vanessa sat in the padded Boston rocker that was tucked into a corner and calmed herself down. When the near panic ebbed enough that rational thought took control, she loathed herself.

How could she have reacted that way? It was over the top. So a man had kissed her then let her go. Just a freaking kiss. She hated to think how her reaction must have made him feel. She was afraid of rejection, but she'd just given Tim one of the worst types of rejections of all time.

She needed to apologize but didn't know how. What was more, she didn't think she should offer an apology before she got herself sorted out. She had to find a way to explain herself to him…and to herself.

The extremity of her reaction frightened her in and of itself. Was she truly that far gone? It was one thing to keep her emotions locked up and observe a safe but polite distance from others. Nobody seemed to have a problem with that. As she'd noticed before, nobody seemed to notice, either. While she knew people who'd pour their hearts out to her, she never reciprocated and they never seemed to detect the absence.

So her guardedness served her well enough most of the time. But not this time. This time Tim had expressed desire for her, and she'd fled as if he were a demon. That was awful.

In fact, she'd done the very thing to him that she was so afraid of. Despicable behavior. Shame filled her.

Of course, Tim might be able to handle it better than she could have, but that still didn't relieve her of responsibility to apologize for her flight.

Closing her eyes, she thought of the many nice and helpful things he'd done for her in her short time here, and knew she owed him some truly straight answers.

She'd already let him know that she didn't get close to people. She'd talked with him about something she never mentioned: her lousy childhood. But it was wrong to expect him to put it together and manufacture her excuses for her.

At last, rising, she marched out to the living room, hoping he hadn't gone upstairs. Whatever kind of mea culpa she could manage, he deserved it.

He was still sitting on the couch. He must have heard her coming, because he was looking toward the entryway.

"You okay?" he asked before she could speak a word.

"I'm fine." As fine as she knew how to be, except for scalding shame. "I'm so sorry that—"

He cut her off. "No apology needed. If you aren't scared to death of me now, come join me."

"Scared to death of you?" That's what she had made him think. Oh, God, she was an awful person. But she had run like a frightened deer. Not so much because she was scared of him, but because she was terrified of herself.

Somehow she needed to explain that. Sitting down gingerly on the couch, a foot away from him, she cleared her throat. Once again, before she could say anything, he spoke.

"I'm sorry I upset you, Vannie. That wasn't my intent."

No, she thought. That hadn't been his intent at all. He'd given her a gentle kiss, almost a testing, questing kiss, giving her ample opportunity to respond or pull away. Instead, she had run.

"I'm the one who is sorry," she said. "My reaction was out of all proportion."

He studied her, turning sideways on the couch, pulling up one bent leg and resting his arm along the back. "Wanna talk?"

She, who never talked about her real feelings, understood she would have to do it now. At least a little, because he deserved it. But it wasn't going to be easy, because it meant exposing parts of herself she didn't even like to review in the privacy of her own mind.

"I told you I was crippled. That was just a part of it that you saw. You got close to me, emotionally, and I reacted badly without thinking. For that I owe you an apology. You didn't demand anything of me. I could have just let the moment slip by. Instead, like a freak, I ran."

"You're no freak," he said quietly. "Look, you gave me only a sketch of what your childhood was like, but I'm not surprised from even that little you shared that you've got some pretty sturdy walls around yourself. Losing everything at an early age, a dropout alcoholic father who kept you moving all the time you were growing up… Just that makes it unsurprising that you don't want a close connection. I know what it feels like when somebody you really care about is ripped out of your life."

Yes, he certainly understood that. "But all you did was kiss me."

To her surprise, he smiled. "A kiss can be a gateway drug."

After a moment, in spite of herself, she had to smile back.

"Sometimes," he said. "Sometimes it's enough to

make folks take an instant cure. Either way, it's a big deal, and it was pulling you places you clearly don't want to go. I get it, and I don't blame you."

"You're awfully understanding."

"Maybe. I don't know. I've got my own hang-ups. I'm widowed. I've got a kid I've got to think about every time I make a decision. Losing Claire left a hole in me that will always be there, so I get that part. It took me a while to realize that I was just going to have to learn to live with it, because they don't make a patch to cover grief. And for a while I was sparing of my emotions. That wasn't good for Matthew. Even I could figure that one out. Thank God I did before I created permanent damage."

"All I see when I look at the two of you is that you're a good father." Then a snort escaped her. "As if I'm any judge of that."

He tilted his head a bit. "I think you'd be the best judge of a bad father."

She closed her eyes a moment, allowing tension to begin to seep away. He was making this so easy for her. He made her feel as if she could safely tell him anything.

But that was the real danger, wasn't it? Opening herself up, then getting kicked one way or another. There was certainly no point in opening up to Tim. She was leaving. She'd lose him, too.

But then an odd little notion prickled at her. It would be different, because she'd be leaving by choice. She wouldn't be dragged away against her will. So maybe he was safe to open up to because she was in control of the limits.

Then she felt shame again. She couldn't treat him that way. Invite him in, then toss him when she left. What if he developed feelings? Although why he should she couldn't imagine.

"Look," he said. "Let's just let it lie. No apology necessary. Your reaction was honest, and I understand it. No need for any soul baring on your part. Life leaves its marks on us all. We deal with them as best we can."

"But am I dealing?"

He placed his hand lightly on her shoulder. "As best you can."

He rose. "Come on, help me make some coffee cake. Matthew loves it when we have it on Sunday morning. Let's make him grin."

Making Matthew grin was always a worthy enterprise. Summoning a smile, she followed him.

Tim had several different recipes he used for coffee cake, but he chose one he could have prepared blindfolded because his mind was busy buzzing around the things Vanessa had said.

It had taken guts for her to come apologize for her behavior and to try to explain. For a woman who claimed she wanted no close connections, she nonetheless acted like one who actually cared about how others felt.

He measured cinnamon and brown sugar into a bowl with butter and asked if she'd mind crumbling it with the pastry cutter. "Matthew loves crumb toppings."

"Who wouldn't?" she responded.

The cake he was making wouldn't be very sweet, but it would be full of blueberries. His nod to being conscious of what his son ate. Ha.

With the oven preheating, he got to work making the cake.

"So this is a special occasion thing? The coffee cake?"

"Yeah. Easy enough to make, but they might take away my parenting license if I did it too often. And if I did it too often, it wouldn't be special anymore."

"Good point."

"Have you decided if you want to talk to Ashley's class?"

"I'm going to ask the museum to express materials to make it more interesting. Did I tell you that or just think it?"

"Darned if I know at this point." He laughed. "Sometimes my head gets crowded and some stuff slips out the holes in it."

She laughed. "Is that what you tell Matthew?"

"Often enough. Honestly, I get preoccupied and forget things. He's used to it. Sometimes he even works at being my memory, especially when it's about important matters. Important to him, anyway."

"I haven't noticed you having any memory problems."

"You haven't known me that long. I can get deeply absorbed in thinking about a project and I become absentminded. Trust me, Matthew never forgets a thing."

"I can just imagine. I bet it could be dangerous to make him a promise."

He winked at her over his shoulder, then went back to stirring the batter. "I never make promises. Too many things can happen. It frustrates him sometimes when I say only that I'll try. I get plenty of reminders, though."

After he oiled the square glass baking dish, he poured the batter into it. The crumb topping was ready, and he spread it over the top. "Everyone likes this," he remarked. "I hope you will, too."

"I'm sure I will. I'm with Matthew on crumb toppings."

But then the cake was in the oven and there seemed to be no more casual conversation. Forty minutes before the cake would be done, and here he was feeling awkward. It was a rare feeling for him, probably arising from the way he'd upset her earlier, and then the conversation between them that had threatened to become intense.

It had certainly been revealing, but he wasn't sure either of them wanted the intensity they'd been approaching. He doubted that, despite her self-questioning and self-criticism, Vanessa really wanted to let fly with her emotions. She was skimming her own problems in the way she seemed to want to skim most things. Touch on them, but don't really mine them.

He had to admit that might be the best thing unless she was talking to a shrink. She could recognize her scars without tearing them open. Name them, so he'd understand, but not root around in them.

What was wrong with that? But it reminded him to tread carefully. And that made him uncertain about what direction to take. He generally wasn't the type to resort to conversations about the weather unless some big event was on the way.

"The snowman is almost gone," she remarked. "He's looking sad. I guess the sun is doing that?"

"That would be my guess," he answered, relieved. "It sure hasn't gotten above freezing since the storm."

"I really enjoyed doing that." She smiled and finally looked at him with a relaxed smile, her eyes clear of shadows. "I'd given up hope." A little laugh escaped her. "I never thought I'd be part of building one that looks so classic."

"More hands to build it, maybe," he suggested. "It looks like it should be easy, but it's not, really." A click from the coffeepot reminded him it was still on. "Do you want more coffee or should I turn the pot off?"

"I'm done, thanks. There's a hope that I can sleep tonight."

That caught his attention. "Do you have problems sleeping?"

"Occasionally. Doesn't everyone?"

"I never do," he confessed. "Probably because I don't hold still very much. Always working or riding herd on a kid who operates at ninety miles an hour."

That drew a comfortable laugh from her. "He never slows down," she agreed. "He even plays video games at top speed. Boy, did he make me feel slow. He's clicking those buttons as easily as moving his fingers, and I'm fumbling around. You'd never guess the delicacy of some of my work." She shrugged. "Of course, I have no practice."

"That might be key," he remarked, at last pulling out a chair and sitting across the table from her. "He's been playing that game for several years."

"You don't have a problem with it?"

He shook his head. "Why would I? He's not living in the basement 24/7. He gets out to play, he's doing well in school. Now if that was *all* he did…"

"Yeah. I don't get why some people think it's a bad

influence. Kids can develop some real skills, and the latest studies show that even kids who play violent games become less violent than those who play none at all. Surprisingly enough. Of course, are these things really ever settled?"

"I wouldn't know, it's not my field." Relieved that she was talking, he let her run. "I just know that I don't let him play anything that isn't PG. I'm glad the boxes have ratings, because his last two birthdays and Christmas he wanted new games and I was able to check out their suitability without having to play them myself."

She nodded. "The one I played with him required a lot of problem solving. I was impressed."

"There you go."

"My dinosaurs are going to pale in comparison."

"I doubt it."

"I don't." Her smile widened. "Over the last few decades, we've had to put in a lot of interactive exhibits, moving exhibits. Kids aren't content to just walk through a museum and look through glass."

The last of the earlier tension was leaving him as well. He relaxed back into his chair, considering whether to get a beer, then deciding against it. She was so pretty when her face was unclouded, so happy-looking when she talked about her job. Just leave her be, he warned himself. No more kissing. No more giving in to the desire that kept riding him. He had no right to upset her balance, a balance he suspected had been hard to achieve.

"Do you think it's bad that you've had to put in all those interactive exhibits?" he asked.

"Absolutely not. When I escape my lab, I love watching the schoolkids come through. They get so excited and intrigued. I hope they carry that away with them."

"They're the important ones," he replied. "You know, when I was about twelve, my parents took me on a trip to DC. One of the most memorable stops for me was at the Smithsonian. But a funny story. My dad could get lost in artifacts for hours, but my mother was having none of it. She told him that while he might enjoy looking at brass buttons, I wouldn't, so we needed to go look at more exciting things. We went off to the Air and Space Museum, which was a blast, but somehow she squeezed in a look at the inaugural gowns of the first ladies."

Vanessa laughed. "I guess she wasn't interested in those buttons, either."

"That was my read." He grinned. "My dad was a contractor, too, but also a history buff. A man made for museums."

"I love museums," she said. "Everything about them. Some day I'd love to get to the antiquities museum in Cairo, and the Louvre in Paris. Just for starters. If I added any more to my list, I'd probably lose hope of doing any of it."

"The Smithsonian's easier to get to."

"Cheaper, for sure," she said. "I've been there a couple of times, and I'll go back. But right now we're working on making our museum one of the best places to go in Albuquerque. Of course, we're competing with the Museum of Natural History and Science. I think we have enough bridge topics to help us grow, though. And our research departments cooperate as much as possible, and we exchange temporary exhibits. You can't have too much science."

He enjoyed watching her climb on her hobby horse. It was a different side of her, a lively, assured and confident side, so different from most of what he'd seen of her. "So you're involved in building a new museum?"

"It's not new. We're just growing it. So far, so good."

"But the research is your thing."

"Very much so." She closed her eyes, still smiling. "I can get lost in my lab, forget the time, the day. Mysteries, puzzles—always something new to think about."

Well, she surely wouldn't find that here, he thought, wondering why the idea saddened him. From the start he'd known she was going home, that she had a career there. Why should that bother him now?

Maybe he needed to take a page from her book and avoid getting involved. He glanced at the clock. Still twenty minutes on the cake.

"I must be boring you," she said.

"Not at all." He really wasn't bored. Too many of his thoughts were selfish right now. Thoughts like he wished he had more time to get to know her, that she'd stay here longer than a week or two, that she wasn't so skittish, because for the first time since Claire he was ready to dive into a relationship, with Vanessa. She'd awakened a part of him he had begun to think was dead forever.

He wanted a woman again. He wanted to make her laugh, bring her a rose and do all that sappy stuff. Oh, man, he was headed for trouble, and he didn't know how to stop it. This train had left the station.

So he thought about Matthew. He needed to protect his son, and since Matthew seemed to really like

Vanessa, he needed to be careful that the boy didn't start hoping she'd be a permanent fixture.

He stifled a sigh, wondering how his mostly smooth life had suddenly become as roiled as a river during spring flooding. Unwanted thoughts and needs were messing everything up, and it was a losing situation. The only thing he stood to gain from this was creating another crater in his life. Not fair to Matthew.

Think with the big head, he told himself with some humor.

Then Vanessa proved she had more gumption than he thought. She shocked him by asking, "Could we try that kiss again sometime?"

His head spun. What the hell? She'd fled. But maybe knowing she had to go home made her feel safer. To hell with that, he thought, as a burst of anger hit him. "I'm not a science experiment," he said shortly.

"No, you're not. I didn't mean…" She trailed off, then eventually said, "I'm sorry, Tim. Good night."

He watched her leave, and for long moments didn't care that she was gone. Try it again? Why? So she could go home and not fear being kissed again? Screw that.

But as his anger ebbed, he sat alone in his kitchen, suddenly feeling lonely, and wondering if he'd misinterpreted her intention.

No, probably not, he reassured himself. After all, she *had* run away. If she was getting ready to try her wings, then she ought to try them with some man back home.

Not with him. God, why had he ever kissed her in the first place?

Glumly he regarded his own behavior and wondered about himself.

Chapter Eight

"How do we get this off?" Vanessa asked on Tuesday, her voice startling Tim.

Sunday had passed quietly. Vanessa and Tim seemed to have reached a silent agreement to maintain a mutual distance. Vanessa played video games with Matthew and joined him while he did his homework. Matthew's bubbling conversation was all that kept dinner from being utterly quiet.

Monday the inspector arrived and after a number of hours gave them good news. The air was fine, and if there was any lead in the house, he couldn't find it. There was some asbestos in the corners of rooms where drywall had been taped, so it was probably in all the drywall mud, but nothing to worry about as long as it was painted. They got the go-ahead for renovations, the only warning being to wear protective masks if they decided to pull down drywall.

Tim could live with that. But now Vanessa was staring at sagging paint in one of the bedrooms, and she'd been quiet for so long he'd almost forgotten she was in the house.

This version wasn't going well, either, he thought. Bad when they'd danced too close, possibly worse now that they were dancing away. Dang, he wished they could find a decent middle ground. He seemed to have ruined that by kissing her.

He came to stand beside her, eyeing the wall. "Latex paint can be cool."

"Meaning?"

"It's full of latex. A lot of that will come off in sheets." To show her, he pulled one edge, and the paint didn't resist. Down it came, all in one sheet, leaving little patches behind here and there. When it was done, it looked like he was holding a huge piece of Swiss cheese.

Vanessa surprised him by laughing. "I didn't know it could do that."

"Age and exposure to temperature changes helped us here. Don't try this at home." Her laugh pleased him, and he hoped she was loosening up a little.

But not every wall boasted sagging paint. He'd need to check it to make sure it was adhering well enough to paint over. Then there was the wallpaper. The paste had begun to dry into dust, pieces had left the wall, corners were falling down, but there was still a lot that would need heat to release it.

"I hate removing wallpaper," he remarked. "Tedious. But this stuff has to go, so we're going to do a lot of steaming and scraping. You'll be glad to know I have a couple of guys to help, so you won't be stuck with too much work."

She looked at him. "You never mentioned employees."

"Ah, but I have them. If this were my own place, I could take my sweet time. Customers wouldn't like that too much, so yes, I have help. The guys have been working on another job, but they're just about done, so we should see them soon. We'll make quick work of this for you."

"I don't mind helping."

"I didn't say you couldn't help," he reminded her. "Just that the two of us aren't going to try to complete this job before you have to leave. Plus, I'm sure you want to get this place off your back as quickly as possible." He returned to his examination of the wallpaper.

Well, that had certainly been her intention when she arrived here, Vanessa thought. Find the quickest way to dump this house and put this unwanted piece of the past completely behind her.

Oddly, now that she'd been in here so many times, and was now helping to change the entire space, she didn't feel the same hatred toward it. She was getting used to it.

So while it wasn't weighing on her the way it had been, and her desire to be done with it quickly was fading, she felt the wall growing slowly between her and Tim.

Worse, she knew whose fault that was: hers. She was

the builder of walls, and he was merely respecting what he sensed from her.

She left the room without saying anything, needing a few minutes by herself. She'd been afraid of coming back here, but apparently for all the wrong reasons. Except for Larry—and what was with him, anyway?— the people she'd met had been kind and friendly. They didn't hold her responsible for something that had happened when she was a child. Amazing that she had ever thought they would.

The fact that her father's fears had become so deeply embedded required her to look into her heart and mind and find the rest of the mistaken thinking she might have soaked up.

Her response to Tim was a great example. She was drawn to him as she'd never been drawn before. He awoke sexual feelings in her that she'd buried years ago out of fear. Why not let them blossom? Why was she shoving him away?

Regardless of the desire she felt, she had to admit he'd been a cheerful, friendly guy when she arrived, welcoming her into his home so she wouldn't have to sleep alone in the nightmare house or at the miserable motel. His son had already won a place in her heart.

So here she was giving that wonderful man a good look at her moat. That wasn't nice. At the very least, considering all that he was doing for her, she needed to be friendly. Not distant.

What's more, she wasn't only disturbed by her cool behavior to a man so helpful. She was disturbed that he seemed to want her to be gone quickly. Now she wasn't the one in a rush—he seemed to be. Of course, he attributed that to her own expressed desire, but she didn't quite believe that.

No, she had offended him. She'd just about hit him in the face with her weirdness. Why wouldn't he want her gone as quickly as possible? She was living in his house, making friends with his son and treating him coolly, if not rudely.

Man, she was messed up. And when she'd tried to reach past her barriers and suggest another kiss at some future date, of course he hadn't leaped at the chance. She could understand his behavior after her reaction, but what the heck was *she* thinking?

She'd gone from a self-contained professional into a dithering jerk in an instant. The path was clear. Avoid entanglement and go home. So why did she keep chasing that around in her head? Why couldn't she settle? One way or another, make up her mind about what she was doing here and what she wanted to do. Become again the person who had arrived here with very clear goals.

"I'm getting very tired of myself," she said aloud. She stood in the empty living room by herself, and faced the fact that everything inside her had somehow gotten very mixed-up in less than a week. But being unable to make decisions wasn't like her. Wandering around thinking the same thoughts over and over wasn't like her.

"There you are," she heard Tim say behind her. "I thought I heard you say something."

"Talking to myself." Slowly she faced him. Then she blurted something she shouldn't have. A thought that emerged only as it passed her lips. "You've messed up my head."

He froze, then put his hands on his narrow hips. "And just how the hell did I do that?"

Good question, she thought, horrified that she'd spoken such a thing. *He* wasn't responsible. She was. "Sorry. I'm responsible for my own mess."

He released a breath. "You know, it was never my intention to mess you up. But if you ask me, you were already messed up when you got here. A nicely organized mess, but still a mess. That's not blaming you, by the way. I heard enough from you to guess you were seriously hammered by your youth. We all live with the leftovers from that, and you have more bad than many. So what the hell is pushing you over the edge, Vanessa? You can pack up and go home right now if that'll make you feel better. I can finish out this job now that I know what you want. I just thought you might feel better by doing a little destruction on Bob's house. Maybe not. Your dinosaur bones are waiting."

He turned and took a step away before she called out his name. He stopped but kept his back to her.

"Tim... I'm sorry. I'm not blaming you, and I shouldn't have made it sound like I was. Coming here has rattled me. *You* rattle me. But that doesn't mean I should inflict the fallout on you. I need to get my head straight. I need to sort some things out. Just ignore me. It's my problem. Things I haven't realized, things I haven't faced—they all seem to be coming to a head. I need some counseling, but that's not your job."

"No, and I wouldn't know where to begin." He turned and looked at her again. "Let's just rip this place up. Take out your frustration and confusion on this house. God knows it could benefit from it."

Then he walked away, teaching her in an instant that she still knew how to feel lonely.

Yup, she was a mess.

Wednesday afternoon, the express package she'd requested arrived from the museum. Matthew watched eagerly as she opened it, but the first thing she noticed was the condition of her hands. Nicked, raw knuckles, three bandages…they hadn't looked this bad since she'd been digging up the fossils. The thought made her smile as she cut the tape with a box cutter Tim had given her to use. He, too, watched but from a greater distance. Matthew was practically on top of her.

After she removed the padding from the huge box, she began to remove items. "Posters," she said, reading the labels on three cardboard tubes. "Great, I can leave these for the classroom."

"Can you open them now?" Matthew asked.

"After I check the other stuff, okay?"

He settled back, watching.

An envelope contained stacks of several kinds of colorful pamphlets suitable to the age group. Then a bigger box that revealed three larger dinosaur models that someone must have cannibalized from individual boxes on sale in the gift shop. The kids could handle them and pass them around. Another box was clearly labeled—it contained a skeletal model of the T. rex, everyone's favorite. The students would absolutely love that.

And finally, at the bottom, were the two boxes she'd wanted for Matthew.

"These are for you," she told him. "One is a triceratops, and the other is a T. rex. They're wood puzzles so you can build the skeletons."

He took the boxes one after the other, studying the pictures on the front and repeatedly murmuring, "Thank you. Wow, oh, wow." Then he looked up at his dad. "Can I open them and start?"

"Homework?" Tim asked.

Matthew's face fell. He rose from the floor then hugged the boxes to his chest. They were almost too big for him to hold both at the same time. "After homework," he agreed.

"And don't rush it," Tim said. "I'm going to check it over. Then we can open your presents and see what's in there."

"He's amazing," Vanessa said, watching him walk toward the dining room. "Not many kids would have even asked." Not that she had all that much experience.

"We all have to learn about delayed gratification sooner or later," he answered. "Would I like to let him open them now? Of course. But then he'd never get to his homework. And I want to thank you, Vannie. Those are a really great gift."

"I hope he gets a kick out of them. And I guess I should call Ashley and ask her when she wants me to come in."

He leaned against the doorjamb, folding his arms and crossing his legs loosely at the ankle. "So you've decided to do that?"

She nodded as she began to replace items in the box. "Kids go nuts for this stuff. I've given talks like this before. Why deprive Ashley's class just because of where I am?"

"Still have bad feelings about this town?"

She gave a small shake of her head. "Not as much, but I have to admit I'm kind of looking out for Larry. Which is silly, I guess. He had his say. What more is there?"

"Well, if he tries to say any more, I'll be nearby. The guy has at least one small screw loose, to judge by that display. But I wouldn't worry about it, Vannie."

"I'm not, really. Just occasionally uneasy. I'm not used to people shouting in my face these days."

He paused then asked, "Did they used to?"

"My dad, of course. He was the last one."

"I hope the only one, although that's bad enough."

She shrugged one shoulder as she placed the poster tubes back in the box. "I didn't like it at all, but I'm still here." Then she tossed him a smile. "I have to admit I can hardly wait to see Matthew open those boxes. I hope he'll enjoy 3-D puzzles."

"He still plays with Legos, and he has a big bucket of them. Is this different?"

"It doesn't fit together as easily. It also includes a washable glue for putting the pieces permanently into place. But I recommend he put them together once before gluing."

Tim laughed. "Amen to that. Like, measure twice, cut once. A good practice with most things." He straightened. "I need to get that chicken ready for roasting. Oh, and Ashley's number is ASHLEY G."

"Seriously? How'd she do that?"

"Not on purpose. She laughed about it for years, but someone else pointed it out to her. She'd never noticed."

"I can see why. I hate having to dial letters."

"I run into trouble because the numbers are backward on the telephone from what they are on an adding machine or on my computer keypad. I still wonder why they did that."

"Because most people weren't using adding machines?"

He laughed. "Maybe so. Off to the kitchen."

Vanessa's first call was to Glenn at the museum to thank him for pulling together that wonderful box so fast.

"Hey, I'm all about education," he reminded her. Given that he was in charge of the museum's educational programs, there was no arguing with that.

Vanessa laughed. "True that. But I really appreciate it. I didn't think you could get it here so fast."

"Like I had to dig that stuff out of an ancient burial mound? Come on, you know we have stacks of it. It only took me a few minutes to pull together what you asked for. Still planning on going skiing?"

She hesitated. "No," she answered finally. "I'm working on the house with the contractor. It's kind of cathartic."

Glenn knew only snatches of her story, but he seemed understand her meaning. "Go for it. Sometimes I wish I had something to demolish."

After Glenn, she called Ashley, who sounded delighted to hear from her.

"You've been gone so long," Ashley said. "But you know, I think of you from time to time and I wondered where you'd gone. We used to be thick as thieves. So… any chance you could find time for lunch while you're here? I could ask Julie to join us if her husband can watch the baby."

Baby? For some reason the idea took Vanessa aback. Julie had a baby? Wow, some time had surely passed. Still, she hesitated. "I was just calling to tell you I got the materials to do a presentation for your class."

Ashley paused noticeably, and her tone changed slightly. "That's super. When do you want to do it? Just let me know."

Vanessa almost laughed. "You're the teacher with the lesson plan. I thought you'd tell me."

"Friday, then? In the afternoon, say, one? Because we'll be done with the necessary lessons and you'd be just what I need to settle them down a bit—they'll be getting antsy for the end of the day and the weekend."

"That's perfect," Vanessa agreed. "I'll be there."

Then Ashley said one more time, "Lunch on Saturday? I'd love to catch up."

Vanessa felt once again her own internal resistance to relationships, to this town, to all the bugaboos of her childhood. This time, however, her spine stiffened. "I'd enjoy that. What time and where?"

Oh, God, she thought as she hung up. A public diner. How many other Larrys might there be out there? Unless she could get ill before then, it appeared she was going to find out.

Tim proved to be as interested in the puzzles as Matthew. They opened them after dinner in the dining room, and Matthew went over the first sheet of directions carefully, asking for help when he didn't understand something. Tim did the answering. Vanessa would have gladly jumped in but restrained herself. She knew those models inside and out. Matthew—and Tim, apparently—was delighting in a journey of discovery.

Then came a large piece of flannel-backed oilcloth for Matthew to work on.

Tim showed Matthew how to match all the puzzle pieces to the list of parts, then sat back and let him make sure they were all there.

A builder instructing his son. Vanessa enjoyed the moment, enjoyed watching the interaction, thinking that Tim was a pretty good father. He showed an awful lot of patience as Matthew threw questions his way and started to hurry and needed to be slowed down.

"The thing is, son, you're not going to be able to finish this tonight, so put the brakes on. The box says six hours. You don't have six hours before bedtime."

Matthew scowled but listened.

Vanessa finally volunteered a word of caution. "Six hours is actually optimistic, I think."

"I suspected." Tim smiled. "But if he doesn't want to mess this up, he can't rush no matter how long it takes. Right?"

Matthew nodded, echoing, "Right," as his brow furrowed and his tongue stuck out between his lips. His concentration was intense. From time to time he looked at the picture on the front of the box as if to assure himself that these pieces would eventually look like the photo.

Tim brought coffee for himself and Vanessa and milk for Matthew. He looked over his son's shoulder at the directions and remarked, "This is going to go together in pieces."

Matthew looked up. "What's that mean?"

"You've seen me build things. Well, this works the same. You're going to put the legs together. Then the feet. You'll connect them. Then the spine and tail. Then the head. When you get all those pieces done, it'll be time to put them all together."

"Okay," Matthew answered and returned to his work.

Vanessa spoke. "We have summer camps for kids. They come to the museum and work on projects. Anyway, some of them get seriously frustrated that they can't see it all go together at once."

"I won't," Matthew announced. "I know what Dad means."

Vanessa smiled at him, but he was too busy to notice. She glanced at Tim and caught him staring at her. The heat in his gaze was obvious, causing a pleasurable shiver to run through her. Almost at once he returned his attention to his son, but she hadn't missed the message. He wanted her.

The hard part was facing up to the fact that she wanted him, too.

Matthew had painstakingly organized all the pieces on the dining table before Tim sent him up to bed. He seemed resigned to being unable to put any of it together until tomorrow, but he wasn't difficult about it.

"This is going to be so cool," was the last thing he said to his father as Tim switched off the light and left the room.

"So cool indeed," Tim responded as he shut the door.

Downstairs he found Vanessa still sitting at the table, looking at all the carefully laid out pieces. "He's going to be like you," she remarked. "I've rarely seen that much organization from a boy his age."

"Well, you gave him a really great present. He thinks it so very cool, according to him. So thank you, Vannie."

She smiled at him. "My pleasure. I never fail to get a kick seeing a child excited by science…even if it's a wooden puzzle."

"I know he can barely stand waiting to see it finished. Half the fun is getting there, though. I hope he's beginning to learn that."

"A lot of us never learn that." She leaned back in her chair and stretched a bit. "I need to move."

"Pace if you feel like it. Or we can move to another room. These dining chairs weren't exactly designed to sit on for a long time."

He hoped he wasn't imagining that she was relaxing with him again. The past few days had been uncomfortable while she tried to keep her distance and he tried to give it to her. They were together almost all the time. How much better if they could just relax.

She opted for the living room. He was sure after the days they'd spent scraping, peeling and carting, she probably felt physically tired. He was used to it, but he doubted she was. Her lab job must be largely sedentary.

"Why did you decide to leave excavating the fossils?" he asked. "I know you said it was hard work, and the lab is more exciting, but I think I'd be happier with the physical activity."

"Digging was hot and dusty, like I said. Discovery was as exciting as anything could be. But I realized after a few years that I was thinking more about the questions attached to each bone than about the work in progress. I'm fortunate, though. Our museum supports a number of digs, so if I wanted to take a turn at it again, I could."

"I think I'd like to try my hand at it. I'm sure Matthew would, although he might get bored fast."

"Maybe so. Every dig I was on started with a spectacular find of some kind, some bone jutting out of recently washed-away earth or recently revealed limestone. Still, after the first few exciting weeks, things would usually slow to a crawl while we hunted around for other finds. Finding a complete skeleton is extremely rare, because after the animal died, its remains were subjected to the elements and carrion eaters. So bones got washed away, rolled around, worn away, and only some of them would end up in a situation good enough to preserve them, if any of them did. While it may seem like we find loads of fossils, the truth is they're rare. Compared to the numbers of animals that must have roamed this planet, the fossils are few and far between."

"I guess so. But if they weren't we'd be tripping over them all the time."

She laughed, the sound pleasing him.

"What got you into this field?"

"Partly that when I was kid we lived for a while in upstate New York. Our driveway was gravel and the gravel was full of seashells. That rock came from a nearby quarry, so I asked about the shells in school and was told that long ago the whole area had been under the sea. That stuck with me enough that I got truly curious. When the school took us to the Museum of Natural History in New York City, the bones won the day. It was all I could think about doing when I got to college."

He wondered what things might strike Matthew that way, or if he'd even know until much later. Of course, nothing might strike him that way at all. If there was one thing he'd learned from his son, it was that interests could pass rapidly and be forgotten in the changing of the days and his age. Watching his son grow was the biggest adventure in his life.

"Anyway," she continued, "I was lucky, too. I went to college on a full scholarship. I discovered an aptitude for geology, which really helps in this field, and paleontology seemed to be in my own bones."

"A full scholarship?" he repeated. "How many brains have you got tucked in that head?"

She blushed faintly. "Enough."

"Well, I guess so. I knew you were smart, but wow."

He could tell he was making her uneasy, so he dropped it, but that didn't mean he wasn't impressed. He'd gotten to college the hard way: on loans and money from working for his father.

"I wouldn't have been able to go any other way," she said after a moment. "I worked, but that had to help out at home. So I was very, very lucky."

"I didn't finish college," he admitted. "Three years in, my dad was injured on the job, and he needed me to take over. And frankly, given that I had a company to take over, school seemed increasingly irrelevant. Dad wanted me to finish, but I didn't want him spending his savings on hiring someone to do what I could do. I'm glad I didn't. He and Mom were able to follow their dream and travel. I doubt they'd have been able to do that if I'd stayed in college. The way it turned out, they had enough savings to go, and I was able to send them a bit every month to keep them going."

She looked at him, her expression a mixture he couldn't quite read. "You did a remarkable thing."

He shrugged it off. "We do what we need to do. That was the right decision. Easy as rolling off a log, so I've got no complaints."

Except for Claire, he thought with the inevitable twinge of loss and sorrow. Since her passing, he'd been short on dreams. Very short. All he wanted was to see Matthew grown and ready to stand on his own two feet. Then…well, then maybe he'd find he could dream again. But once upon a time, all his dreams had been wrapped around Claire. More children. A houseful of grandchildren eventually. Big family holidays. Eventually retiring to sit on the porch of a summer evening holding his wife's hand as night fell. Simple dreams, gone now.

He'd never wanted a great adventure, had never wanted to leave his mark on the world in some fashion. That probably made him boring, but it also had made him content.

Now he was sharing a sofa with an extremely bright woman who probably had bigger dreams.

"Vanessa? Do you have dreams?"

"Dreams?" She looked perplexed.

"About where you want to be down the road. Ambitions. Director of something? Make a discovery that changes everything in your field?"

"Those big things are few and far between. Progress

comes in small increments most of the time. If I can add an increment or two, I'll be happy."

That sounded reasonable enough. Why that relieved him he couldn't have said.

"What about you?" she asked.

"I want to see Matt grow up. Then I'll consider other things. I don't seem to be very ambitious."

"I think you're plenty ambitious. You want to raise your son. Isn't that big enough?"

"I think so. Others may not agree."

She shook her head a little. "I wish my dad had been concerned about seeing me grow up. His money and his reputation were more important. Maybe I learned something from that. Maybe all the wrong things, but I learned. Money's not that important. As for reputation... well, you spend your whole life building that, and one mistake doesn't have to ruin you forever."

He felt his brows rise. "That's a strong criticism of him."

"He deserves it," she said, a note of anger creeping into her voice. "He might as well have ditched my mother and me. At least then we wouldn't have had to watch him drink himself to death. Anyway, I can get that it hurt like hell to lose the family ranch, but that didn't make him a failure. Drinking made him a failure."

Once again he felt his heart squeeze with pain for her. This woman was still suffering in quite a few ways. He waited for her to let the demons escape in any way she decided.

But then she changed tack. "Anyway," she said, "I think you've chosen a great path. Matthew's an amazing boy, and he seems totally secure. I can't imagine how wonderful that must feel, but I'm very glad he doesn't have to question it."

"And here I was feeling boring and unadventurous."

She smiled, the last anger vanishing from her expression. "Raising a child is the most important thing anyone can do in life. Doing it right is the best thing. You appear to be doing it right. Pat your back, Tim."

"I'm a long way from being able to do that," he said lightly. "Check back with me when he's thirty. But even then it won't be all my doing. Kids are born with their own personalities, and I have no doubt he'll do most of the hard work himself. All I can do is guide a bit."

Her expression shifted, and she looked away. Had he just put his foot in it again? Probably. He had no idea just how much she blamed her father for. How many scars he had left her with. "You've turned out pretty good," he said cautiously. "I think *you* get all the credit."

At that she smiled crookedly. "There were others along the way. Teachers and so on."

"I'm glad you had them."

"So am I. Anyway, I don't want to go over that all again. I've spent most of this week wrestling with myself, and I'm tired of it. I am who I am. I'm not going to be able to rearrange myself in one fell swoop."

"Why do you want to do that? Because coming back here stirred up old memories?" He felt his heart quicken as he waited for her answer. Why it should matter so much to him, he couldn't imagine. Especially since she was right. If she wanted to change, it was going to take a long time.

"I don't even know if it's possible for me to change,"

she answered slowly. "It's just that I've been thinking that living Rapunzel's life may be safe, but maybe it's not as interesting."

"Rumpelstiltskin could always show up."

At last she laughed. "But will he turn into Prince Charming?"

His heart hit full gallop, and he wondered if he was losing his mind. "Do you want a Prince Charming?"

"No," she said, unwittingly making his heart plummet. Then she picked it up again. "If I ever get close enough to someone, I'd just like him to be nice, reliable and good to be around. I don't want perfection, and I don't want some guy who spends hours in front of a mirror working out."

It was his turn to laugh. "I can understand that. But was Prince Charming that bad?"

"Think about his name," she said drily. "It tells the whole story right there. I know it's a fairy tale, but who would name their baby Charming?"

"Or their daughter Beauty."

They both started to laugh. "Yeah," she said on a giggle. "They couldn't have named her *Sleeping* Beauty unless they plotted against her from birth." Then she caught her breath. "Oh, I probably just offended a bunch of people."

"I'm the only one who heard you. Maybe some girls are named Beauty. It actually wouldn't be bad unless the poor child turns out homely. But Charming?"

"Don't bet against it. Unusual names seem popular now. Matthew will probably never know how lucky he is that you gave him such an ordinary, familiar name."

"No, he'll just grow up and go to court to change it."

That sent her into more laughter. When they calmed again, they were both a bit breathless. And then their eyes met.

In an instant Tim found it hard to breathe. The laughter had done to her what nothing else seemed able to do. She looked utterly relaxed, soft, open. Unguarded.

He wanted so badly to reach out to her, to kiss her, to just hold her. He was sure she wouldn't allow more than that, but he was almost as certain she wouldn't accept his embrace. He reminded himself how she had reacted to his kiss. And certainly her mention of repeating it had been a moment of impulse on her part.

Or maybe she was actually changing, just a tiny bit. Maybe in the midst of giving herself all that distance, she had been working away at something. She'd said, after all, that she was thinking about change.

Easy, boy. True change would take time. It wouldn't happen before she went home. At most he was seeing a few cracks in her armor, but he was glad to see them.

Then she reached out and touched his forearm. Rockets exploded in his head as he looked down at her hand. What was she about? She'd never touched him freely by herself. In fact, she had always seemed to avoid it.

He raised his gaze to hers and read an almost painful hope there, along with desire. "Vannie?"

"I guess I'm crazy, but I want to know…"

Her heart beat as rapidly as a sewing machine. Was she really doing this? Reaching out to a man for his touches, his kisses? Who knew where that would lead? Somewhere bad, she'd always told herself, but Tim seemed to be changing her irresistibly. He pulled her, drew her, touched her in long untouched places. Seeing him with his son had proved to her that he was none of the things she had feared.

Trying to steady her breath, she didn't complete her sentence. More avoidance. Talk about everything except a growing hunger that might consume her. "My dad threw himself away because he lost a ranch. You lost your wife but kept yourself together."

"For my son," he reminded her.

She shook her head as an ache blossomed in her heart. "Don't you see, Tim? My dad had me. He had my mother. He had a whole lot more reason to carry on, but he didn't."

He didn't answer. Not that she really expected him to respond to a statement like that. What could he say? But her heart continued to hammer rapidly, and she felt as if she stood at a cliff edge, ready to take a leap.

God, this could be such a huge mistake. She looked at her hand, tried to make herself pull it back, but she couldn't. She wanted more than that simple touch but scarcely knew how to ask for it.

He probably wouldn't really want to give her any more, anyway. After the way she'd been acting for a week? After the way she'd fled after he kissed her? She wasn't blinded by her scars, and she could read in his occasional glance that he wanted her. Or at least he was attracted.

But handling her must strike him as about as safe as handling nitroglycerin. Even sitting here filled with yearning, she couldn't guarantee to herself or him that she wouldn't suddenly panic and run.

"I'm such a mess," she murmured.

"Oh, Vannie, just shut up," he said.

Startled, she barely had time to register his words before he pulled her over so she sat across his lap and silenced her by covering her mouth with his.

Some corner of her mind registered that he was man-handling her, but the biggest part of her didn't care. In fact, the biggest part of her was thrilled that he'd taken the leap for her.

She let her head fall back against his arm and opened her mouth, giving him entry to a place no one had been allowed before. The few times she'd kissed, except for the other day, the experience had left her wondering what all the hoopla was about.

She knew now. As his tongue explored the delicate inside of her mouth, warmth began to pour through her, filling her like hot honey until she felt soft, safe and eager.

If that kiss had lasted for an eternity, she wouldn't have objected. Her arm crept up until her hand wrapped around the back of his neck, holding him close. *Don't stop. Oh, please, don't stop.*

He didn't seem ready to. His lips lifted as his free hand crept up toward her breast and cupped it with a gentle squeeze. She caught her breath as pinwheels of light exploded behind her eyes and warmth began to transmute into sizzling heat. Was that her saying his name breathlessly over and over?

Then his mouth returned to hers, and this time his tongue plundered her, striking a rhythm that caused her whole body to clench in response. His hand began brushing over her breast, over her hardening nipple, and she shivered with pleasure.

Why had she avoided this her entire life? The question blew away on the storm of passion he was unleashing in her, a storm that was rapidly turning her into putty in his hands. Her hand slipped from his neck to his shoulder, her fingers digging in as if she were afraid she might fall.

A tornado of pleasure whipped inside her, sensations beyond imagining, and she wanted more. So much more. A throbbing heaviness between her thighs seemed to be seeking an answer of some kind. She felt so empty and full at the same time.

Then the doorbell rang.

Chapter Nine

"Aw, hell," Tim said, after ripping his mouth from hers. He froze. Maybe they'd go away. Looking down at Vannie's sleepy face and slightly swollen mouth, he wished the visitor to the devil.

The bell rang again. Damn it. Then from upstairs he heard Matthew's sleepy voice.

"You okay, Daddy?"

His voice cracked as he said, "Fine. Go back to bed, buddy."

He looked down at Vanessa again and saw awareness brightening her eyes. Then saw them widen.

"Oh!" she said and squirmed quickly off his lap.

That only made him ache harder. "Damn," he said aloud.

"Matthew," she whispered as she tried to straighten

a shirt he hadn't been able to rumple enough yet to need it.

"Yeah. Best birth control in the world. A kid."

Astonishing him, a small giggle escaped her. "And someone who keeps ringing the doorbell."

As if in answer to her statement, it rang again.

"God, I'm going to have some words for whoever it is. It's after ten o'clock."

"Maybe something's wrong."

That possibility was the only reason he forced himself to stand and walk over to answer it. He had the awful feeling that an opportunity had just been lost forever.

When he opened the door, he was not pleased to see Larry standing there. "What's the matter?" he demanded. "You didn't attack Vanessa enough last time? You need to draw more blood?"

"No," Larry said. "I shouldn't have… I just wanted her to know I'm sorry." He looked past Tim, and by the way his eyes widened, Tim knew he saw Vanessa.

She spoke, surprising him. "Forget it, Larry. I've said plenty of bad things about my father."

"I'm not going to forget it. I was wrong. Like you had any more to do with all that than I did."

The wind was blowing in through the door, chilling the house rapidly. Much as he didn't feel like it, Tim stepped back. "Get in here. My heating bill can't take this."

Larry crossed the threshold, taking two steps so that Tim could close the door behind him. Then he grudgingly offered the guy some hot coffee. Maybe it would be good for Vanessa if Larry really *had* had a change of heart.

"Thanks," Larry said. "It's colder than…" He broke off, stifling the bawdy line. Then he asked, "Is it really that cold anymore? Look at the Arctic."

Tim let himself relax a bit. "It's cold *here* tonight," was his answer. "Come into the kitchen, if that's okay with you, Vanessa."

"It's fine. Maybe Larry and I could use a little talk."

Larry followed them into the kitchen while unzipping his jacket but not removing it. "I'd've come sooner, but I just got back in town a half hour ago." He settled into one of the kitchen chairs while Tim started the pot of coffee he'd set up for morning brewing.

Vanessa sat across from Larry, glad that would put Tim in the middle, the place usually enjoyed by Matt. She was willing to give this a shot, but old, familiar tensions were already settling into her bones. Larry had proved her every fear right, and she could feel her walls slamming into place, preparing for another verbal assault.

For the first time she regretted those walls. Just a few minutes ago, they had been crumbling before the gentle onslaught of Tim's sexual advances, and she'd been feeling so good. Now she was faced with the nightmare of the past again.

Nobody spoke while the coffeepot steamed and water dripped into the carafe below. Studying Larry, Vanessa realized he was as uncomfortable as she was.

At last Tim poured coffee for all of them and took

the remaining chair. "Are we just going to sit here?" he asked.

Vanessa looked at him, sensing his impatience. Well, she felt impatient, too, considering what Larry had interrupted, but she felt a strong need to finish this, and here was her opportunity.

"I guess I should start," Larry said. "My dad was angry about what happened, about what Bob did. And he blamed your father for drawing him into it. So when I heard you were in town, I blew up. I'm sorry."

"I'm not any happier with my father," Vanessa said. Might as well admit it. The man's conduct had shadowed most of her life.

Larry grimaced. "I told my mother what I'd done when I called her from the road. If she'd been close, she might have skinned me."

"Why?" Vanessa asked as anxiety began to rise in her. Her least favorite subject, yet one she hadn't been able to get out of her mind since facing the fact that she had to come here. "Everyone probably thought the same things your father did."

Larry shook his head. "Not according to my mother. First she ragged on me for attacking you. You were just a kid, she said, no older than me. You didn't have a thing to do with what happened."

"Very true," Tim remarked. Vanessa saw him relaxing, leaning back in his chair as he sipped coffee.

"Exactly. When she said that, well, I didn't need her to say anything else. I felt truly stupid. And bad. Then she told me something I didn't know because I'd never talked to her about it." He paused, lifting his mug of coffee and nearly draining it in on long draft.

"What was that?" Vanessa prompted.

Larry put down his mug and looked her straight in the eye. "She said nobody talked my dad into giving all that money to Bob. Nobody but Bob. She tried to talk him out of it again and again, warning him it was dangerous to put all his eggs in one basket. He was hell-bent on making money. She told me all his talk about it being your father's fault as much as Bob's was just because he felt like an idiot, he was furious and he wanted to blame someone. Bob got arrested, but your father left town. Apparently my dad thought yours got off scot-free. But as my mother reminded me, your dad lost his whole ranch. Not exactly scot-free."

"Not exactly," Vanessa agreed. Tension had filled her as it always did when this subject came up. She wished she could just release it, like air from a balloon. She wanted this to be over, but Larry had been strong enough and kind enough to come apologize for his outburst, and surely she owed him something. But what? "My dad was pretty messed up, too," she said finally. "He lost every job he ever had and drank himself to death."

Larry nodded. "I'm sorry. That's pretty bad. Then I show up like an idiot and yell at you. My mother was right. You were just a kid. I was just a kid. It's not up to either of us to pay for what they did, right or wrong. It's not like we could have stopped it."

Vanessa drew a breath and decided to share her part of the truth with him. "My dad believed everyone here hated him."

Larry shook his head. "Then I drop on you like that? I guess there aren't enough apologies for me to make.

As far as I know, my dad was the only guy who blamed your dad. I never heard a word of that from anyone else."

He paused, drummed his fingers on the table briefly, then pushed back and stood. "I guess both of us had messed-up fathers. And my mother is right. We shouldn't let them mess us up anymore."

"Wise woman," Vanessa said, wishing she could feel relief in her heart.

"Yeah, she usually is. Sorry for breaking up your evening, but the need to apologize was riding me. Maybe I'll see you around sometime."

Then he headed for the door. Tim went to show him out while Vanessa remained at the table.

When Tim returned, he brought a draft of cold air with him. "That might not have been an emergency, but I'm glad he stopped by anyway. You needed to hear that."

"Maybe so," she said, and a long sigh escaped her. "I put it all behind me, Tim. I really did. Until Earl called and told me about the house. Then it came rushing back like a runaway train. All the old feelings, the fears, the anger. As fresh as it had ever been."

"Then Larry."

"Then Larry," she agreed. "But even so, even as I've been running the maze inside my head trying to change myself, the thing is..."

"What?" he prompted eventually.

"I think scraping the walls in that house has been more therapeutic."

"Really?"

She smiled faintly. "Yeah. Really. Every time I pull

wallpaper down, it feels good. Like ripping up the past. So who knows? Maybe I *am* finally getting past it all. It might not change my personality, but maybe I can get rid of leftover anger and hurt."

"I hope so. And by the way, there's nothing wrong with your personality."

"I wish I believed that."

"You will when the anger's gone. Anyway, just ask Matthew what he thinks about your personality. I happen to know he likes you."

"The feeling is mutual." But that wasn't the thing topmost in her mind. Topmost was that an exquisite moment had passed. Larry had driven away the heated mist of desire that had overtaken her, that had lifted her so far out of herself that she felt like someone else. Deep inside, she knew she couldn't call it back. Not now.

Even from the grave her father had done it again.

"I think I'll go to bed," she said, rising. The turmoil and anger were back, not as bad, but bad enough to get in the way of anything else. "See you in the morning, Tim."

Tim listened to her walk down the hall. He was straddling two contradictory emotional states, and neither one was doing him a bit of good. He wanted to follow her down that hall and climb into bed with her and show her how good life could be. The other part of him felt that would now be a terrible intrusion.

Apology notwithstanding, Larry had reopened the very things that had been holding her apart from the start. She had been about to close the door on them, at least for a little while, when he'd arrived to shove it open once more.

Hell. Selfish as it was, he was still aflame with hunger for that woman, and no matter how much he told himself it was pointless and she didn't really want it, he couldn't smother it.

Not since Claire had he come as alive has he had been growing since Vanessa arrived. Why couldn't he have reacted this way to a woman who didn't have major problems to deal with? Why this woman?

It wasn't just that she was beautiful in a restrained way. Or that she was essentially kind, to judge by her treatment of Matthew and her willingness to talk to a classroom full of kids. Was it because he felt the same hollowness inside her that had afflicted him since Claire had died?

Well, that would be a royally stupid reason to get together. Damn, he knew perfectly well that no person on the planet could be expected to fill the empty holes in another. Nobody could replace Claire, and he didn't want it. Her place in his heart would always remain.

The emptiness in Vanessa…if she didn't figure out how to fill it on her own, he couldn't do it for her. Life just didn't work that way.

You made room in your heart for someone—you didn't patch it with them.

Maybe Larry's interruption had been a good thing. Maybe it had saved him and Vanessa from making a mistake.

If so, then why didn't he feel like it?

Cussing mildly under his breath, he dumped all the coffee and prepared the pot once again for morning.

She'd be gone in little over a week. Things would return to normal.

But he was going to miss her anyway.

The next two days passed in a haze of hard work. Nothing sexual reared its head, but maybe that was because they both worked harder than ever. They got the walls ready to paint. They debated whether to pull out the floor tiles that looked so dingy or if they could be saved by a thorough cleaning. They talked about new bathroom and kitchen fixtures.

Tim kept thinking of what he'd do if he owned this house. Maybe he ought to buy it, but he didn't suggest it to Vanessa. Somehow he didn't want to attach himself to her nightmare memories.

Vanessa announced she was speaking at the school on Monday, just after lunch, laughing as she said, "I guess it'll be my job to keep the kids awake."

Judging by Matthew's response to her stories, Tim figured that wasn't going to be a problem.

He swiped his spackle knife over the last patch on an upstairs wall and stood back. "Tomorrow morning," he said.

"What?" she asked.

He wondered if she had any idea how cute she looked with a bandanna over her hair, wearing a spackle-stained plaid shirt and jeans that were beginning to look as if they belonged to a serious construction worker.

"Saturday," he said, even though she knew. "A good day to go to the paint store and pick the colors you want to slap on these walls."

She chewed her lower lip. "Shouldn't we go with

plain white? Not that I'd want that, but any colors I pick might turn off a potential buyer."

He used the butt of the spackle knife to hammer the can closed. "If you talk to a real estate agent, you'll discover that one of the things we're going to do is make this house look like someone lives here. If you care how much you get for it, anyway. After all this work, you should."

She hesitated, looking around. "It doesn't feel like Bob's house any longer. It's as if working on it has made it *my* house."

He smiled. "Then choose your own colors, woman."

She laughed. "Okay."

They went downstairs. All the overhead lights were on along with a few work lights, and she leaned against the counter as he washed the spackle knife.

"What else would you do to this place if it were your own?"

"The kitchen," she said promptly. "New countertops, new appliances. And I might paint the cabinets, or just remove most of the doors."

He looked around. "I've got some used cabinets in a storage room that you might like. Much better condition than these."

She opened one of the doors. "You think the whole thing needs to be replaced?"

He came over to stand by her and point. "Water damage at the back of them. It doesn't look bad, but if we get into the cabinets, I might not like what we find behind them. If it's just the cabinets themselves, I can fix it with a little sanding and refinishing."

Inadvertently he brushed against her and heard her

quickly indrawn breath. Heat surged in him, and he backed away.

She remained staring into the cabinet, frozen. After a few second she spoke. "I wouldn't want to leave a mess for the new owner."

"If I pull one of these down, we're going to have to do it all. So come with me to storage tomorrow and see if you like the cabinets I have."

"Okay." She closed the door. "My list seems to be growing."

"Mainly because you've got a lot of sweat equity in this place. You'll get over it."

At that she laughed and helped him clean up, readying for the next workday there.

That afternoon, Matt came home from school announcing that he'd been invited to spend Saturday night with Jimmy Jackson. "Can I go? Can I take my dinosaur puzzle, too? He wants to see it."

Tim hesitated. "I'd hate for it to get broken."

"I can take the one I haven't started yet. We can sort the pieces."

Tim glanced at Vanessa. She'd gone to a lot of trouble to get his son those puzzles.

"I can always replace it," she said. "Don't worry about that."

Tim squatted until he was on eye level with Matthew. "Okay then. But be very careful and don't lose pieces. It was nice of Vannie to get them for you, and I'd really hate to ask her to do it again."

"I'll be careful," Matthew said stoutly. "So will Jimmy. He already promised."

"Okay then. When are you supposed to go over there?"

Matthew furrowed his brow. "Jimmy said you need to check with his mom."

"Ah. So the two of you outlaws plotted this today?"

Matthew grinned sheepishly. "Sort of."

Tim straightened. "I guess I need to check with Mrs. Jackson, then."

"Does this happen often?" Vanessa asked as Matthew trudged with his backpack into the dining room.

"Not that often, but much better than when he was five and brought Jimmy home from school with him and nobody had bothered to tell Jimmy's mom where he'd gone. We all learned from that escapade."

"I bet."

"Life with kids," Tim said easily. "You learn a lot. Listen, if you want to go shower, I'll just check on that roast I've been marinating."

That morning he'd put a pork roast in some balsamic vinaigrette, sealed it in a plastic bag and had let it soak all day. Usually he was left with enough after cooking the portion of tenderloin to make sandwiches for a day or two, but he suspected there'd be no leftovers this time. Everyone liked his roast made this way.

He glanced at the clock and decided he had an hour before he needed to pop it in the oven. Plenty of time to call Jimmy's mom and see what she thought of this overnighter. Or if she'd even heard of it yet. Then he'd hit the shower himself and get ready for a pleasant evening.

He always enjoyed evenings with his son and figured there'd be far fewer of them as time passed. Enjoy it while you had it was his motto. He picked up the phone. Not surprisingly, the Jacksons' number was on auto-dial. Jimmy and Matthew had been as thick as thieves forever.

"Hi, Mims," he said when she answered. "Tim Dawson. I wonder if you've heard the latest plans the boys have made."

She laughed. "I was just being informed. Sleepover here tomorrow night?"

"That's what I was told."

"It's fine with me. Bring Matthew over around two if you can. I'd like the two of them to wear themselves out so they're not up all night."

He chuckled. "Good plan. I hope it works."

"They're still young enough that no matter how hard they try not to, along about ten or so, as long as I have them in sleeping bags, they'll sleep in front of some movie. And I always pick a movie they know well so it won't keep them awake."

"I need to remember that. Okay then. I get the next round."

"Don't you always?"

He was smiling as he hung up. He liked Mims Jackson a whole lot and had ever since junior high when, for the first time, he'd noticed she was a girl. He'd been a lovesick puppy for all of three weeks, but then someone else had caught her eye, and he, oddly enough, had felt almost relieved to get back to his guy friends. He'd felt cut off during that brief, intense relationship.

It had been another three years before a girl had crossed his radar in a way that made him want to try again. That girl had been Claire.

He was looking through his freezer at vegetables, trying to decide which ones he wanted tonight, when he heard a sound and turned. Vanessa had made quick work of her shower. She was wearing a fresh green sweatshirt and fleece pants, her feet covered by black ballet slippers. A towel still wrapped her head.

"That felt *good*." She smiled. "Is the weather taking a turn? Back in the bedroom the wind sounded strong."

"I don't know," he admitted. "I suppose I should check. If Matthew's going to miss his sleepover, I don't want the news to hit him at the last minute. So do you have any preference for veggies tonight? I think I have just about every kind frozen."

"What does Matthew like?"

He looked at her over his shoulder and remarked drily, "I believe I asked for your preferences. He likes just about everything."

"Broccoli?" she asked, hoping Matthew didn't hate it.

"That's probably what he would have asked for. Okay, I've got plenty. Feel like peeling some potatoes? Matthew loved them mashed."

"Glad to help."

He set her up, then announced he was going to shower. The need to escape had been growing stronger since the scents of soap and shampoo had begun reaching him. From there it was a small step to imagining her skin, soft and still slightly moist from the shower. Then another small leap and he'd be in trouble.

The demons of desire were flogging him again, and he couldn't let them take charge. Since the other night when they'd come perilously close to going all the way, he'd felt like he'd gone too far. She was happy and relaxed when they were working, and ever so slightly nervous in the evening when Matt went to bed. Dang, did she think he was going to just pounce on her?

Well, maybe she had a right to worry, he thought as he climbed the stairs to go clean up. After all, he'd told her to shut up then dragged her into his lap like some kind of caveman. Finesse. He needed to find some finesse. He also needed to remember that this woman needed space, and he needed to stay clear as much for her sake as anything.

He should keep his attention on the job. It had been kind of fun, though, to watch her gradual change in attitude toward the house as she helped strip it down to bare walls. She seemed to have taken it away from Bob, at least emotionally, and made it somewhat her own.

Like that discussion of kitchen cabinets, and the changes she'd want to the kitchen if it was her place. When she'd arrived in town, she probably would have been unable to consider the house in that light, even to pretend. Now she was seeing the kitchen as it could be.

Larry, too, in the end had wound up being good for her. His apology and recognition that they'd both been too young to be responsible for anything their fathers had done had probably reinforced her slow healing from the past.

It still appalled him, though, that any father could have forgotten his responsibilities like that. Vanessa's father had been a weak man in the ways that counted.

But when Tim looked a Vanessa, he saw a remarkably strong woman. She might claim that her upbringing had turned her into an introvert, and maybe it had.

Certainly she seemed more comfortable with an emotional distance.

But a few times she'd let those barriers fall—mostly with Matthew, occasionally with him. Maybe the fear of loss and judgment that had been instilled in her for so many years was loosening its grasp.

He hoped so. She deserved a life full of people who cared about her and about whom she cared.

But his meanderings were pointless. He had a job to do for her, and they'd probably both be better off if he just paid attention to it. Rapunzel was entitled to her tower for as long as she felt she needed it, and he was no Rumpelstiltskin to steal his way in and demand something from her.

Thank goodness for the dinosaur puzzles. They'd been making the evenings much more relaxed than they might have been otherwise. Especially since he'd crossed the line the other night.

Oh, yeah, especially since then.

Matthew, ever the bundle of energy, was eager to join Tim and Vanessa in the morning on a trip to the storage room to look at the cabinets and to the paint store to look for swatches. The whole thing sounded like a great deal of fun to him.

Vanessa was glad he wanted to go. He made her feel comfortable, and with his chatter eased her past moments where she started to feel awkward for no reason than her own hang-ups.

The storage facility was behind a garage and car rental place not far from the train tracks. The building wasn't huge, but it was big enough that Tim had been able to rent a climate-controlled garage-size unit to stash the cabinets and other things he didn't want exposed to temperature and humidity changes.

She definitely liked the cabinets, as he'd promised. Much nicer than the ones already in place, and they looked new.

"Where did you get these?" she asked.

"Somebody ordered them and then didn't want them after all. So I picked them up for a song. I can modify them to fit easily enough."

"I like them," she said with certainty as she ran her hands over them. The wood might or might not have been the currently favored color, but she liked the warm mahogany look of them. "I love them," she said a minute later. "Just love them."

"Then I'll put them in. I just wish you'd be the one enjoying them." Vanessa, who had just started to wonder what he meant by that, was glad when he turned swiftly to point at some furniture. "Some near antiques we can put in the house if you want to make it look occupied. A loaner. My in-laws left the stuff behind when they jumped ship."

Matthew, who'd been looking into spaces behind things, announced, "They didn't jump ship. They went to New Zealand. They live with hobbits."

Tim arched a brow. "Is that what they told you?"

"They sent me a picture of a hobbit house under a hill."

Vanessa had to cover her mouth with her hand. Tim looked thunderstruck. "So...what exactly did they tell you?"

Matthew shrugged. "It was a postcard in a letter

they sent. They didn't say much, but the postcard said it was the Underhill hobbit house. So I looked up hobbits. They aren't much bigger than me."

"Oh, boy," Tim said under his breath, then asked, "You looked up hobbits?"

"Sure. They look funny, though, with all that hair on their feet."

"I see. Son, we're going to have to talk about this later, but right now I need to get Vannie over to look at paint."

"Sure."

Apparently, a photo was too real to just deny, Vanessa thought, amused, as they piled into Tim's truck to head to the other end of town and the lumberyard and home improvement store. The place was huge but was locally owned, to judge by the sign. Hadn't Tim said he'd read the books to his son? In was interesting to her to watch the way Matthew could weave fiction and reality so seamlessly. Sure, the books were just a story, but now he had a photo of a hobbit house, and he'd looked up hobbits to learn about them. She figured it might be hard to walk that one back.

"Maybe I'd better avoid Harry Potter," Tim muttered as they drove toward the store.

"No, I wanna read it," Matthew said.

"Just so long as you understand it's all *pretend*."

"Of course," Matthew said. "Magic isn't real. But dinosaurs are!"

"Were," said Tim.

"They're not all dead," Matthew announced. "I talked to my teacher about it. Crocodiles. Alligators. And some kind of fish I can't remember."

"I guess I'm going to have to go back to school," Tim said as he turned into the parking lot.

But Matthew was looking at Vannie. "What's that fish?"

"Coelacanth," she answered promptly. "For a long time we thought they were extinct, but then some fishermen found one. Then later we found out they were commonly being eaten as food in some fishing villages near India and Indonesia."

Matthew giggled. "Then maybe a T. rex will show up someday."

Vanessa shuddered playfully. "I certainly hope not."

"Remind me not to let this boy watch *Jurassic Park*," Tim said as he stopped the truck and turned it off. "Next thing you know he'll be doing his own cloning."

The home improvement section of the sprawling store fascinated Vanessa. She'd never visited one before because she'd always lived in apartments that came with maintenance. She realized as she walked around that she could spend hours here taking it all in.

But Tim guided her over to the banks of paint chips, and she was off on a new dream. So many pretty colors in varying hues and shades. How was she going to make up her mind?

"You don't have to decide right now," Tim said. "We can take home as many chip samples as you want."

Well, that was an invitation to plunder, Vanessa thought. By the time she had every chip that interested her even mildly, she had quite a stack in her hand.

Tim was smiling. "Any others?"

"I think I just overwhelmed myself."

Then Matthew approached with a strip of dark blue

paints that didn't get very light and passed it to his father. "I want these colors in my bedroom."

Tim surveyed them. "Really? It'll be awfully dark."

"I know, like night. Then we can put glow-in-the-dark stars on the ceiling."

"Oh." Tim was clearly trying to hide a grin. "We'll think about that," he said, his tone sober.

Matthew looked at Vanessa. "When he says we'll think about it, that means he doesn't really like it."

Vanessa laughed. "You never know."

"True," said Tim. "I didn't say no."

Matthew brought his strip of paint chips along as they left and headed for home.

The trees were tossing more edgily, and the sky had turned a dark gray.

"Autumn," Tim remarked. "Very changeable. I read once that the worst time to sail is in late autumn or early spring, because the weather is so variable and could get bad without much warning. That could be true, I guess. All I know is our weather seems to be bouncing around this week."

When they pulled up at the house, Vanessa eyed the snowman they'd built. While it had done a good job of lasting, right now it was little more than a heap of snow surrounded by yellowed grass.

Inside, they went to the kitchen, where Tim set about making peanut butter sandwiches for whoever wanted them. Vanessa wasn't feeling at all hungry yet, but Matthew was. He acted as if eating would bring him to two o'clock faster.

He pushed his color chips her way. "Can you keep that for me?" he asked.

"I certainly will, but I doubt anything would happen to it anyway."

"Oh, I don't know," Tim remarked jokingly. "We do have the invisible man running around who loses my car keys and makes small toys disappear."

Matthew giggled. "Yeah. Only you forgot where you put your keys."

"Probably so."

Matthew gave Vanessa a knowing look. "I'm too old for that now."

"I can see that."

The boy was so charming she had the worst urge to hug him until he squeaked. She guessed he wouldn't like that at all, however. He seemed to be sprouting a good deal of independence from what she had seen.

After Matthew had his sandwich, Tim turned on the radio to listen to the weather report. High winds all day and through the night, occasional gusts up to fifty. A front was passing to the north, and they might see a little snow but not much.

"That's not too bad," Tim said. The report continued for another few seconds, warning of dropping temperatures on Sunday night. "Winter's moving in, I guess."

"Halloween in two weeks," Matthew said. "I hope it's not too cold for trick-or-treating."

"Too early to know," said his father. "But you know we'll set it all up in the gym if it's too cold to be out. You won't miss a single cavity."

Matthew's spirits, which were already high, rose even higher. He practically bounced up the stairs with his father to pack for his overnighter. Fifteen minutes later, they returned downstairs, Matthew with a packed backpack and Tim with a sleeping bag. Matthew had not forgotten the dinosaur puzzle and hurried into the dining room to get it.

"Want to ride along?" Tim asked as he opened the door to let Matthew through. "Five minutes. Hardly worth pulling on your jacket again unless there's something you want."

"I'll stay here."

She watched them leave, but as they did she felt loneliness step into her heart. Dang, what was going on inside her? She'd decided to quit worrying about the sense that something was wrong with her, that she wasn't standoffish by choice. Once she'd made up her mind to just *shut up*, as Tim had told her the other night, she'd let go of a whole bunch of tension.

But now she was feeling *lonely*? That wasn't like her. She usually loved her alone time and filled it with activities she enjoyed, whether reading a book, cooking a sinful dessert to take in for the office or planning her next vacation. She *liked* being by herself. Quiet time, time to just flow without pressure.

Now loneliness was an almost alien feeling to her as an adult. Settling at last at the kitchen table because the light was marginally better in here, even with the grayness of the day, she spread out the paint chips she had brought back with her and tried to imagine what colors she would paint the house.

She'd never had to make such a decision before. Every place she had ever lived had white walls in one state or another. The idea of splashing color all over a room excited her, especially since seeing the bedroom she was sleeping in here. Clearly Tim and Claire hadn't been afraid of color, and the lavender walls in there truly appealed to her.

It had to be Claire's doing, she thought. The room seemed to boast a feminine touch, although what did she know about that? She supposed guys could like lavender and forget-me-nots. Why not?

But then, with all the colors spread before her, she felt the loneliness again and wondered if this was a hint of what Tim felt with his wife gone. Maybe so. He certainly hadn't erased Claire from the house. He'd simply moved upstairs.

She glanced at the clock on the microwave and saw that it was well past the five minutes Tim had promised. Of course it was. He was a friendly man, and it would never occur to him to drop his son off at the door and drive away without at least some conversation.

All the colors of the rainbow lay before her, the entire spectrum, some bold and some soft and pale, but they were all there. She realized impulse had caused her to select the brightest colors, because when she tried to imagine painting a room in such a powerful shade, she had the feeling all it would do would be to shrink the room.

Paler colors, she decided, pushing away the strongest. But then she saw Matthew's selection again, the deep-as-night blues he had brought home. Down at the bottom of the strip the colors were suggested as trim paint for rooms painted in other shades.

She could imagine Tim being reluctant to turn his son's room into a cave, but the idea of glow-in-the-dark stars was exactly the thing to tickle a boy Matthew's age. Maybe he'd do it if it wouldn't be too hard to paint over at a later date. Or maybe Matthew would forget about it by next week. Sad to admit she had almost no knowledge of seven-year-olds. She really liked Matthew, though. The house felt empty without him, and the evening was probably going to be emptier without his cheery voice, his fascination with his dinosaur puzzles and his running commentary on just about everything.

Then she giggled, remembering the expression on Tim's face when his son had announced that he had a picture of a hobbit house and had looked up hobbits. There would be some untangling of fact and fiction in the future.

She was still smiling at the memory when Tim returned and walked in the door. He smiled immediately upon seeing her. Sloughing his jacket, hanging it and his keys on pegs beside the door, he waved at all the paint chips. "Did you make a decision?"

"Seriously? Only that I decided against the really intense colors. I think they'd be overpowering. Beyond that I don't know yet."

"It takes a while. If you narrow it down by Monday, I can pick up some sample cans and we can paint small patches of wall so you can see them in the rooms."

"You can do that?" So much she didn't know.

"Sure." He smiled, poured some of the coffee that was left and joined her at the table.

"It seems a lot to do when I'll be going home late next week." Her heart stuttered as she said it. Then she admitted, "I'm going to miss Matthew so much."

"He's going to miss you, too. No question. But, if you want, you can always fly back here to visit. The door's always open."

"Thanks." But he hadn't said he was going to miss her.

"You also don't have to pick any colors at all."

She looked at him. "But you said…"

"I know what I said. But I didn't mean for you to struggle with it. I just thought some colors might appeal to you for some of the rooms." He gave a light laugh. "Instead you came home with nearly everything."

She had to smile at that, sore as her heart felt right then. "Unlike Matthew, who's full of certainty. I never had to think about painting a room before. I'm an apartment dweller."

"Ah." He shook his head a little. "You've missed one of life's great pleasures, transforming a room with a coat of paint. Or maybe you've missed one of life's greatest disappointments. The color your bedroom is now? It didn't start that way. Claire changed it four times before she was finally happy with her color scheme."

"That must have been annoying."

"Not really. But that's why I like the idea of splashing samples on a wall. Until you see a color with natural lighting in the room you want to paint, it's hard to be sure."

She could understand that. "So about what Matt wants…"

"I may just do it, if he doesn't change his mind in the next few weeks."

"Really? You'd do that for him?"

His gaze settled on her, warm and amused. "I'd do a lot more for him, or for anyone I care about. This is just paint and stickers. When he tires of it, I can cover it all up easily enough. Paint isn't permanent."

The way he said it made her grin, too. "We certainly peeled enough of it away."

"Exactly. But his room wouldn't need that. A good coat of primer and I can change it to the next color he wants. The only thing I ever worry about with him is that he can be so changeable. I'd hate to paint that room next weekend only to have him decide while I was in the middle of it that he really wants gray walls."

A laugh escaped her, easing the strange feelings that had been swamping her. Loneliness? Really? Missing Matt...okay, that was at least understandable. The boy was a charmer, like his father.

But feeling saddened because Tim hadn't said he'd miss her, too? She had no right to that. None at all. He'd been wonderful to her, and she'd done everything except totally freeze him out.

Except for the other night. Warm memories of their embrace, his kisses, his touching her intimately, so sadly interrupted by Larry's arrival.

She realized she wanted to pick that up where they had left off. She wanted the experience even though nothing would ever come of it. Just remembering it made her insides squeeze pleasurably.

"I'm going to buy your house," he said unexpectedly. "I told you I thought it was time to move on, remember? Well, that house has great bones, and it's a bit bigger. Enough bigger that my office wouldn't have to be the size of a janitor's closet."

She gave a small laugh. "You do have a point there."

"A couple extra bedrooms would come in handy."

Given that there was one here that was more of a shrine, maybe so. He could have turned that into his office, but he hadn't. She was kind of surprised that he'd even let her use it. Maybe he *was* moving on.

"So, okay, let me help you with the colors. Since I'm going to buy it anyway."

Impulsively, as he reached for the color chips, she laid her hand over his. "Are you sure you want to do that? This isn't just to take a load off me, is it?"

He met her gaze. "I'm sure," he said quietly. "It's time. So let's look at these colors together."

Chapter Ten

Later the weather became nearly savage. The wind gusted so strongly that the windows rattled from time to time. Tim turned on more lights and listened every now and then to the sounds, cocking his head as if locating them.

"There's going to be a lot of work around here this week," he remarked. "Roofing. Probably some trees blown down. Not good."

"Are you worried about it?"

"Only for my neighbors. This place is sound enough. Your house…well, it's been a long time since the roof was replaced. We may have to do some reshingling."

"Why do I think that may cost more than I can afford?"

He shook his head. "Earl said the house was insured

when I asked him about weather damage I might find. If this wind messes up your roof, you'll be covered. Don't worry about it unless you need to for some reason."

She was willing to do that. One way or another, it wasn't going to be her headache for long. But Tim buying it? She thought he'd been joking the first time he'd suggested it. Ready to move on? What did that mean?

She suspected she'd just have to keep wondering.

By evening, the wind had quieted somewhat. It was still blowing, but without the big gusts. Tim made them a dinner of red beans and rice. The warm dinner was perfect, because even though the temperature in the house was fine, the sound of the wind made her feel chilled. Or maybe there were some drafts.

Tim chatted easily about random things, but he didn't seem uncomfortable when silence fell. She wished she could be so comfortable, but even after all this time with him, silences still made her feel awkward.

She might not be good at conversing and making deep connections with people, but she loved to listen to them talk. And for some weird reason, she felt that she was failing to step up when a conversation quieted and she didn't have anything to say. Except with her colleagues. Odd.

She liked to drift on other people's conversations. How very entertaining she must be.

She looked at the dozen or so strips of color chips they'd separated out between the two of them as being the most pleasing. The question now, she supposed, was which colors wouldn't jar if they could be seen in juxtaposition.

"Oh, my," she said suddenly, a memory striking her.

"What?" he asked.

"I just remembered. When I was in college, a friend's family painted their house. She dragged me over there to see it."

"You had a friend," he interrupted quietly.

"Well…we weren't terribly close. I told you I have trouble getting really close. But I can fake."

His brows lifted. "Okay. So the house?"

"She thought her mother had gone nuts. I wound up wondering if the woman was color-blind. We walked in the front door into the living room and everything, *everything*, straight back through the dining room, was a deep crimson. Powerful. But that wasn't where it got curious. My friend led me to the back of the living room where we could see the hall. It was awful. The hall was also crimson, but one of the bedrooms off it was painted bright orange, and the next one was apple green. It was a shocker."

"Sounds like it." A smile hovered around his lips. "Maybe nobody had ever let her have her way with color before."

"Or something. We hurried out and my friend just doubled over, laughing so hard. I had to laugh, too. She swore I was the only person she'd ever invite to see it."

"And you had a friend."

She nearly glared at him. "What are you pushing at, Tim?"

"That you had a friend. You keep saying you don't get close, but you had a friend. How close does someone have to be? Living in your pocket? In your thoughts constantly?"

"No. But when I left college, I didn't even miss her. That says something. I leave people behind all the time and I don't miss them. There's a part of me that never gets touched. That's all I was saying."

He nodded but looked as if he were weighing her words. "You said you'd miss Matthew."

Her heart jumped nervously, wondering where he was going. "I believe I will. I miss him already. I guess he's the exception. Tim, I told you I'm a wanderer. I pack up and move without looking back. If I ever had strong feelings for anyone—and I don't remember them if I did—they were gone as soon as I moved on."

"Uprooted too many times. Maybe the lack of grief when you moved on was the real protection, and not what came before."

She nearly sighed. "Does it make a difference?"

"A helluva difference," he said. "And who's deciding to do the moving since you got your job at the museum? You? So at this point you wouldn't even know how many friends you've made there that you *would* miss if you left." He shook his head a little.

"I've been thinking about this ever since I came back here, and I'm not getting anywhere with it," she told him. "I'm tired of trying to figure it out, and I doubt I'm going to change. It was only coming back here that made me wonder about it in the first place. Seeing Ashley. Seeing Bob's house and dealing with all that again. Realizing how hurt I'd been by everything that followed his deception and wondering how it had affected me. You'd be surprised how easy it is to go through the motions of what is expected and never really feel anything."

He tilted his head, his lips tightening a bit, and closed his eyes. She waited, but he didn't speak for a long time. And she was through talking about this. It wasn't helping, and she couldn't make it clear that she lacked something inside.

"I believe," he said eventually, his eyes opening slowly, "that life taught you to be very careful about how you spend your emotions. People are just going to be ripped from you sooner or later. Basic truism of life. But you had way too much of that as a child, so you're extra cautious. Giving little away that it would hurt to lose. But what makes you think you aren't like millions of other people? Most of us don't commit really deep feelings in the majority of our relationships. Nobody has the time or energy for that. Anyway, all I'm saying is give yourself a break. You don't need to change yourself if you don't want to. Happens I like you just fine already."

Sweet words, and they warmed her heart. But she still needed to be clear. "I'm saying, Tim, that when my parents died, I felt nothing. When my dog died, I cried. That's weird. And if I walked away from my job tomorrow, I'd miss the job, but after a few days wouldn't even think much about the people I'd left behind. That's weird, too."

He nodded. "Okay. But why is it so important to you all of a sudden?"

"Because I don't think it's normal."

"Ah. I gathered that. But it's the way you are, for whatever reason, so just accept yourself. You're doing well, you're making the life you want. Nobody says you have to get close to anyone. If you're okay, why make a big deal of it?"

She looked down, realizing she was clenching her fingers so hard that they hurt. The problem was, she'd been okay until she got here. Until she'd walked into the bedroom he'd shared with his wife and had suddenly imagined what it might be like to have a truly intimate understanding with someone. To have a relationship worth grieving. Then, steadily, he'd been awakening desires in her for a closeness she'd always feared. And Matthew... God, to think she could miss having a child like him because of her walls. Somehow she didn't think she could fake a marriage the way she faked her friendships.

But he was saying something about that. About how not every relationship could be emotionally close. So maybe she wasn't faking all of it? Just because she didn't pour out her heart, or open it to everyone...

God, just let it go. The circle of her thoughts was closing around her like a noose, and she was really tired of it. He said she was fine. Apparently, she was going to continue being that way.

But there was another home truth, and hard though it was to speak it, she forced herself to do so.

"I would like, someday, to have a relationship like you have with your son. Like you probably had with your wife. And I'm not sure I'm capable of it."

"Now we're getting somewhere," he said gruffly.

Before she knew what he intended, he was scooping her off the chair and carrying her. Not upstairs, but back to the room he had shared with his wife. At least she thought he had.

He flipped on the light with his elbow and carried her to the bed, where he put her on the coverlet. Then he stood, hands on his narrow hips, looking down at her.

"This is the bedroom I shared with Claire. For a long time, I didn't want to change it, because when I walked in here I could almost feel her presence. Then I just closed the door on it, because it was as if I were holding both of us back."

"You and Matt?" she asked, her voice thick.

"Me and Claire. She's gone. She has a right to move on to her reward, not be held back by my grief. So, if I were holding her back, that wasn't good. Then I started thinking about Matthew and me, and how we needed to move on. There's just so long you can live in a mausoleum, Vanessa. This has been a lively one because of Matthew, but it's still a mausoleum."

She managed to swallow and absorb what he was saying. Moving on.

"Everyone has to move on sooner or later," he said. "Life doesn't let us hold still for long. I've been holding still in some ways. You've been moving on far too much. And worrying about it too much. So how about you and I see if we can meet somewhere in the middle?"

She cleared her throat. "I'm leaving..."

"I know you're leaving. And if you decide you never want to come back, I'll deal. Being geographically separated doesn't mean we can't connect emotionally. And I think the truth is, you're already connected to my son, and to me. Wanna deny it?"

She couldn't deny it. There was a lump growing in her throat, a very unusual sensation for her, as if tears wanted to roll. She almost never cried. Why did she feel like crying now?

She sat up, swinging her legs over the side of the bed, but she didn't leave. She looked up at him, wondering what was going on, because inside her she felt as if the earth were shaking and volcanoes were erupting. Strong feelings—the very kind of feelings she claimed not to have—were battering to be let out. All because of this man.

But what good would it do? "I don't understand you," she said.

"I'm saying that it's entirely possible to be close with someone who lives half a continent away. Distance can be either physical or emotional. It doesn't have to be both."

God, he looked almost iconic standing there with his hands on his hips, but then he moved, dropping to his knees in front of her. "Matthew likes you. He won't stop liking you because you go back to your job. If you send him a postcard from time to time, he won't forget you, either. I know my son."

The idea of sending postcards to Matthew didn't seem threatening at all. "I'd like to do that."

"So you can have a relationship with him. You could have one with me, too. Telephones, Skype and email all exist."

Despite the tightness in her throat, she felt like laughing, just a small bit. "And what kind of relationship would that be?"

"We'll just have to see. Right now I want to knock a few walls down by making love to you."

Her breath locked in her throat. Oh, man, she wanted that, too. Much as she'd been trying not to think about it, when he said it out loud, the desire to follow through overwhelmed her. Heat flowed through her veins, every nerve ending beginning to tingle in anticipation. Not even the memory of her one attempt at this, all the way back in college, could prevent the need from rising. Back then it had been awkward, inexperienced and ultimately unsatisfying, making her decide once was enough.

But it was different with Tim, for some reason. The longings she'd forced herself to bury until they hardly ever surfaced swept over her now, an irresistible tsunami of hunger.

Awash in powerful feelings, all her fears and objections were swept away. All she cared about was what this man was offering her right that moment. For once she didn't consciously or unconsciously count future costs. Past and future vanished in the incredible *now*.

She began to strip, wanting to get past this to what lay just ahead. She tugged her sweatshirt over her head and shimmied out of her fleece pants. When she straightened and cast aside her undergarments, she found flame burning in Tim's eyes.

"You're so beautiful," he murmured. But he didn't reach out to touch her. Instead, he pulled away his own clothes with impatience, tossing them without regard to where they fell.

Then they were locked in a primal space, both nude, anticipation so thick breathing became difficult. Vanessa's mouth went totally dry.

But it was a moment never to be repeated, and she knew it. She had free rein to look at him, to take in his broad shoulders, his narrow waist and flat belly, then…then…

She gasped with pleasure when she saw how ready he was for her. Reaching out like a child for candy, she closed her hand around his rigid member, feeling silky skin, a powerful pulse that caused him to move in her grip.

Tim closed his eyes, drawing several deep breaths, then opened them as he began to trace her with his fingertips.

The air almost seemed to pound with Vanessa's passion. Everything inside her quivered with longing and delight. His every light touch added flame to the heaviness of need that was overtaking her.

Her breasts became instruments on which he played a siren's song. His fingers slipped down to her middle, causing her to quiver.

She ran her free hand over him, too, testing muscle, feeling the nubs of his hardened nipples, reaching his hip and pulling because she wanted him even closer.

Then he slipped his hand between her legs and she crumpled, weakened by her hunger, weakened by his touch.

Tim felt her sag a little and caught her quickly, placing her supine on the bed. Her eyelids were heavy; her arms reached up for him.

He needed no further encouragement. He wanted this badly. Swinging himself onto the bed until he straddled her, he sought to learn her with his mouth, trailing his lips and tongue all over her.

She shivered as he licked her neck, but she bucked when he found the hardened berries of her nipples. His own passion throbbed so strongly that he didn't know how long he'd last. Nor was he worried about it. There were always second times in a night.

But the important thing was to make her feel everything he was feeling, to carry her into this powerful, almost painful but totally blissful experience with him.

As her body writhed beneath his touches, he knew she was with him, and his brain exploded with white-hot delight.

Thought was slipping away. Caution was slipping away. He searched out her every hill and hollow, and when his mouth found the cleft between her legs, she keened like a siren calling to him. Her nails digging into his shoulders told him all he needed to know.

One last moment of sense gripped him before it was too late. He leaned up and pulled open the drawer in a bedside table to get a condom.

Her eyes fluttered, and she saw it. Yanking it from his hand, she opened the package and pulled it out.

"Like this?" she whispered as she started to roll it on him.

"Yes..." Oh, man, it was too much, her delicate hands stroking him as she rolled it on, claiming him as much as he wanted to claim her.

"So sexy," she murmured, her voice cracking.

He tried to hold off a little longer, but he couldn't. He was locked in the grip of a hunger that now powered his world. Reaching down, he guided himself into her, feeling her warmth close snugly around him. He drew a sharp breath of pleasure, heard her mewl.

Then he reached up to hold her wrists and bent his head to kiss her breasts, sucking on them in rhythm to his movements.

Life took over, commanding, demanding. He couldn't have stopped for anything. This woman, this moment—nothing else mattered.

Vanessa saw pinwheels of color behind her eyelids, but she was hardly aware of them. She became ephemeral except for the feelings that tore her from earth and flung her to some other space with this man.

The heaviness between her legs, his weight there, seemed to fill an emptiness she hadn't been aware of until then. Everything left of thought, every part of her body, centered on the space between her legs, where a man now gave her the greatest gift and lifted her higher with every movement of his body.

Floating, struggling to a place she hardly knew, captive to the pain-pleasure that filled her. A pleasure so strong it almost hurt. More…more…

Then she reached the pinnacle and tumbled over into a gentler pleasure. But he didn't let her rest. He kept driving into her, and she began the climb again, hopeful, fearful she couldn't make it, then…

The entire universe exploded in a shower of stars. An instant later she heard Tim groan and shudder then collapse on her.

She lay limp, unable to even think. She had become experience, not thought, ruled by something beyond the mind.

Never had she been happier or more content.

The glow didn't last past morning. They'd made love again during the night, and Vanessa had begun to feel as if she never wanted to leave. To heck with everything else.

But she had a job, and Tim hadn't asked her to stay. Even as they were eating breakfast, the loss began to creep into her bones. She should have known better.

"Vanessa? Are you okay?"

She summoned a smile. "Never better. Last night was…incredible."

He smiled, but she suspected he didn't quite believe her. Her demons had returned.

She was saved, if she could call it that, but a phone call from work. It was the director of paleontology at the museum.

"I know you're on vacation, but can you finish it a little later? We need you back. On Friday we got a whole new shipment of bones—they seem to be from a very rare species, and they desperately need preservation and identification. Unfortunately, Carla was in an auto accident last night and won't be back for weeks or months, so we're down a hand, and we can't afford it. You're the best at identification anyway. Can you get back immediately? I'll make it up to you."

When she hung up, she looked at Tim and felt a crack begin to creep through her heart. "You'll never believe an emergency in a paleontology lab, but we've got one. One of my coworkers was in an accident, and they have a shipment of important bones that need preservation and identification. I've got to go back."

Tim grew very still. "When?"

"I need to arrange a flight today. I'll probably need to leave as soon as I pack." The crack in her heart grew

more painful. "I need to call Ashley, too. I'll tell her I'll
be back as soon as I can to talk to her class."

"It's that urgent?" His tone sounded tense.

"I'm sorry, but yes."

He nodded. "I'll get Matthew back here before you
leave so you can say goodbye."

"Thank you."

She rose, breakfast forgotten, and went to her room,
where she began to arrange a flight while she packed.
Impossible, she supposed, to explain to anyone why
this request from the director couldn't wait. The fossils had been waiting for millennia. Why couldn't they
wait for a few weeks?

Because they were already rotting from exposure
to the air and bacteria. Because time really *was* of the
essence. Because the museum had a grant to do this
kind of work, and failing to do it could cost them future grants. She got it. She doubted anyone else would.
And from the director's perspective, did it matter if she
took her vacation in a couple of months?

Of course not. And it shouldn't matter to her, either.

But it did.

Chapter Eleven

A little over two months later, with Thanksgiving in the rearview and Christmas just ahead, Tim and Matthew waited impatiently for Vanessa's return.

She'd been talking to them on Skype, and Matthew treasured the postcards she sent—all from the museum's gift shop, evidently. He'd kept asking when she'd come again, and now, at last, she was.

Finally her rental car pulled up in front of the house. It was a frigid night. Snow covered the ground. That didn't keep Matthew from running out—without a jacket, in his regular shoes—to greet her. She hardly got out of the car before he leaped at her. She surprised Tim by catching the boy and holding him as she walked toward the house.

Despite all their conversations, Tim moved more

slowly, unsure what to expect. He'd finished most of the major work on the house and was looking forward to showing her. He was also ready to argue again that she should sell it to him.

But mostly he was glad to have her back. To have her home. When they met on the sidewalk, he embraced her and his son as best he could and managed to drop a kiss on her lips.

"Welcome home," he said, not caring if it was a bad choice of words.

"I'm so happy to be back." Her face reflected her words, so different from when she'd first arrived and had looked ready for trouble. Now nothing but smiles.

Inside he had hot coffee, some sweet rolls from the bakery and a mug of chocolate for Matthew, who yammered a mile a minute and finally spoke a truth that resonated to Tim's core. "I missed you, Vannie," the boy said. "I wish you didn't ever have to go away again."

Tim's and Vanessa's eyes met over the boy's head. Uncertainty. He saw her uncertainty. What about?

"We've already had dinner," he said, feeling awkward. "But I can make you something."

She shook her head. "I ate earlier. I'm fine."

"Come see my dinosaurs," Matthew said, tugging her hand. "I want you to see them."

She'd already seen the completed models on Skype, but she still smiled and followed him to the dining room, where the models had pride of place on the big table.

"Wow, you did a perfect job! I guess I need to get you some more."

"They make more?" Matthew's face lit up. "I want to be a palee...palo..."

"Paleontologist," she supplied gently.

"Yeah, like you. Except I want to dig up the bones."

"You'll get a chance to try it out," she said. "I'm going to be leading a dig not far from here come spring."

Tim's heart nearly stopped. "I thought you liked the museum."

"I do. But the museum is funding this with donations, and I got tapped to lead. Some hiker from New Mexico found something really interesting, and he sent the photos to us. Permissions are still being worked out, and we'll be cooperating with local universities. But yeah, in the spring I'll be digging again, and Matthew's welcome to come try his hand. It looks like a spectacular find."

Tim was still wrestling with the idea of Vannie being so close from spring to fall and wondering why she had decided to return to work she'd left behind.

Questions he couldn't ask until Matthew was in bed. The hands on the clock seemed to be dragging.

As happy as Vanessa was to see Matthew again, she was even happier to see Tim. Except he seemed subdued, and she wondered if she'd done something wrong. When he came down from putting Matthew to bed, she had to ask.

"Did I make a mistake by coming?"

He looked surprised. "Hell, no. What makes you think that?"

"You're being too quiet." She felt her insides congealing. Had she made a mistake? Had she put herself in a position to be hurt yet again?

He drew her into the living room and sat beside her on the couch. "I'm thrilled to see you. As thrilled as

Matthew is. You said you don't like digging. Why are you going back to it?"

She bit her lip, tensing until she might snap, feeling as if she were about to open herself to the biggest pain possible. "Because… I want to be near you."

His eyes narrowed. "Seriously?"

"Seriously."

"Wow," he murmured. "I didn't dare… I couldn't hope…"

The next thing she knew, he'd lifted her onto his lap and kissed her so deeply she lost her breath. When he tore his mouth away, he asked, "Just how close do you want to be?"

She hesitated then admitted, "As close as you want me. As long as you want me."

She watched his face change. The last tension seeped out of it. He closed his eyes and said quietly, "I want you close, and forever might just about do it."

Her heart began to lift, the last of her fears scattered to the winds. "How close is close?"

"Like…married?"

"I'll only be here part of the year."

"I'll take whatever part I can get. I love you, Vannie. I'm ready to move on. Are you?"

She never hesitated. "Oh, yes. Yes, yes, yes. Forever."

He smiled and squeezed her until she squeaked.

All of a sudden Matthew's voice interrupted them. "So Vannie's going to be my new mom?" He sounded excited.

"Do you want me?" she asked.

He climbed right on her lap as she sat on his father's

lap. "Yup. I can go camping at the dig, right? And you'll be here in the summers, right? And I can dig up bones?"

Vanessa looked at Tim over his head, and they both started laughing.

"Yes, yes, yes," she said again. "To both of you."

It had been a strange courtship in some ways. She'd hardly been aware it was happening. But now she had a family again. A real, beautiful family.

Her heart soared, and she hugged the two men she loved most in the world.

She had never believed she would know this kind of happiness, yet now it showered her. She would hang on to it with all her might. Forever.

* * * * *

MILLS & BOON®

Cherish™

EXPERIENCE THE ULTIMATE RUSH OF FALLING IN LOVE

MILLS & BOON®

EXCLUSIVE EXTRACT

Beautiful, young widow Noelle Fryberg is determined to show her Christmas-hating boss, millionaire James Hammond, just how magical Christmas can be…Could she be the one to melt his heart?

Read on for a sneak preview of
CHRISTMAS WITH HER MILLIONAIRE BOSS
the first book in the magical **THE MEN WHO MAKE CHRISTMAS** *duet*

He'd lost his train of thought when she looked up at him, distracted by the sheen left by the snow on her dampened skin. Satiny smooth, it put tempting ideas in his head.

Like kissing her.

"Don't be silly," she replied. For a second, James thought she'd read his mind and meant the kiss, especially after she pulled her arm free from his. "It's a few inches of snow, not the frozen tundra. I think I can handle walking, crowd or no crowd. Now, I don't know about you, but I want my hot cocoa."

She marched toward the end of the aisle, the pom-pom on her hat bobbing in time with her steps. James stood and watched until the crowd threatened to swallow her up before following.

What the hell was wrong with him? Since when did he think about kissing the people he did business with? Worse, Noelle was an employee. Granted, a very attractive, enticing one, but there were a lot of beautiful women working in the Boston office and never once had he contemplated pulling one of them against him and kissing her senseless.

Then again, none of them ever challenged him either. Nor did they walk like the majorette in a fairy band.

It had to be the drone. He'd read that concussions could cause personality changes. Lord knows, he'd been acting out of character for days now starting with agreeing to stay for Thanksgiving.

It certainly explained why he was standing in the middle of this oversized flea market when he could—should—be working. Honestly, did the people in this town ever do anything at a normal scale? Everywhere he looked, someone was pushing Christmas. Holiday sweaters. Gingerbread cookies. One vendor was literally making hand-blown Christmas ornaments on the spot. Further proof he wasn't himself, James almost paused because there was one particularly incandescent blue ornament that was a similar shade to Noelle's eyes.

The lady herself had stopped. At a booth selling scented lotions and soaps wrapped in green and gold cellophane. "Smell this," she said, when he caught up with her. She held an open bottle of skin cream under his nose, and he caught the sweet smell of vanilla. "It's supposed to smell like a Christmas cookie," she said. "What do you think?"

"I like the way your skin smells better."

Don't miss
THE MEN WHO MAKE CHRISTMAS:

CHRISTMAS WITH HER MILLIONAIRE BOSS
by Barbara Wallace
Available November 2017

SNOWED IN WITH THE RELUCTANT TYCOON
by Nina Singh
Available December 2017

www.millsandboon.co.uk

MILLS & BOON®

Why shop at millsandboon.co.uk?

Each year, thousands of romance readers
find their perfect read at millsandboon.co.uk.
That's because we're passionate about
bringing you the very best romantic fiction.
Here are some of the advantages of
shopping at www.millsandboon.co.uk:

* **Get new books first**—you'll be able to buy
  your favourite books one month before they
  hit the shops

* **Get exclusive discounts**—you'll also be
  able to buy our specially created monthly
  collections, with up to 50% off the RRP

* **Find your favourite authors**—latest news,
  interviews and new releases for all your
  favourite authors and series on our website,
  plus ideas for what to try next

* **Join in**—once you've bought your favourite
  books, don't forget to register with us to rate,
  review and join in the discussions

Visit **www.millsandboon.co.uk**
for all this and more today!